M000204811

THE WASTES

a novel
by Alexey Osadchuk

To my Dear Reader, with gratitude,
Alexey Osadchuk.

UNDERDOG

BOOK TWO

Magic Dome Books

The Wastes
Underdog, Book #2
Published by Magic Dome Books, 2019
Copyright © A. Osadchuk 2019
Cover Art © Valeria Osadchuk 2019
Designer Vladimir Manyukhin
English Translation Copyright © Andrew Schmitt 2019
All Rights Reserved
ISBN: 978-80-7619-112-9

This book is entirely a work of fiction.
Any correlation with real people or events is
coincidental.

ALL BOOKS BY ALEXEY OSADCHUK:

Mirror World LitRPG series:

Project Daily Grind

The Citadel

The Way of the Outcast

The Twilight Obelisk

Underdog LitRPG series:

Dungeons of the Crooked Mountains

The Wastes

TABLE OF CONTENTS:

CHAPTER 1

"**W**E GOTTA GET out of here," I said after staring for a while at the broken shield. "It isn't safe."

Jay just nodded in silence. All this time she had been trying to keep no more than one step away from me, as if she was afraid I would just magically evaporate into thin air.

Taking a final look at the blaze, I breathed another heavy sigh. Black embers, smoking partially-collapsed hearths, ash mixed with mud... ugh, this was not at all how I imagined my return to the surface.

Gorgie ran back over to us, having been snooping around nearby.

"*Old tracks. Female. Younglings,*" he told me shortly.

"Curious..."

"Did he find something?" she asked with hope

in her voice.

"Looks like it," I answered. "Say, you know what's over that way?"

Jay looked where I pointed.

"The Yellow Bog."

"So it's a swamp..."

"A gods-forsaken place," Jay said with a shiver.

"Well, Gorgie says the women and children went that way a few days ago," I told her quizzically.

"Wait a second!" her pale face lit up with recognition. "I remember! Ah, of course! How didn't I think of this right away?!"

"What are you talking about?"

With a happy smile, she started to explain:

"The local hunters are frequent visitors to the bog. They know all the secret trails."

"Do you mean to say...?" I muttered. "When the men found out about the threat, they hid their families in the swamp, and went back to the village? But why?"

"How should I know?" she shrugged. "Obviously they weren't expecting to all get killed. They walked up behind their houses to catch a glimpse, then you see how it turned out... And it never used to be like this. The barons have always had their quarrels, but they never much committed atrocities."

"So something has changed..." I answered thoughtfully.

"We have to go to the swamp!" Jay said firmly and stopped in the middle of the road.

I turned.

"Why?"

"What do you mean why?" she asked in surprise. "There are people there. My aunt is there. We have to tell them what happened to their husbands and sons! We have to help them!"

Aw shucks... It's started again. And just like the time with the moss, it's too late to explain. I'll have to take the easy way out...

"I'm not going."

"And why not?!" Jay exclaimed.

"You told me yourself that the swamp is a gods-forsaken place. Or do you know the secret trails?"

"No," she answered, hurt.

"Then I would advise you to keep a healthy distance. Furthermore, I suspect the men left some nasty little surprises on their way back to town. I would have if I were in their place."

"But what about the women and children? They need help after all! We must..."

She wanted to keep speaking, but I interrupted her.

"You're wrong about that 'we.' What do I have to do with this? If memory serves, I owe these people nothing. Exactly the same as they owe me. You mentioned children... Well, look over here!"

As I said that, I spread my arms.

"What kind of person do I look like to you? I

am myself a child, you know. Somehow I don't remember your friends and acquaintances lining up to buy me out of peonage or rushing into the caverns to help me escape!"

Her cheeks went crimson. I meanwhile continued calmly:

"Furthermore, even if by some miracle we can avoid all the unpleasant surprises the hunters left and find their secret trail, what makes you so sure we'll be welcomed into their sanctuary with open arms? Do you think they want three more mouths to feed?"

Jay looked like a blazing fire. Her lips pursed tight. Eyes squinting. Her chest positively heaving.

"You..." she squeezed out between her teeth. "You... But you're a mage! The Great System has bestowed a true Gift upon you! You could use it to help these people! Fighting bad guys on their behalf!"

I flashed a crooked smile.

"I see that you don't understand a thing yet. But I'll still answer, even though I don't have to. You call it a Gift, but I had to work for it by the sweat of my brow, risking my life every step of the way. If anything — I earned it. Let me repeat! These people are no one to me! And I do not plan to fight for them, risking my life and Gorgie's. What's more, he is the only creature in this world I would be willing to lay down my life for."

"But you saved me!" she stated, raising her chin.

"Let's be fair — Gorgie did that," I clarified.

"Hrn..." the cat called out at once.

"Without him, I could never go toe to toe with a coldune. As a matter of fact, the only thing I ever did as a mage on my own is stun a fish."

"And yet I'm alive!"

"What were we supposed to do? Just sit there and watch you get eaten by a coldune?" I asked in surprise.

"You saw that the beast was about to get me, and you jumped in. Even though you didn't have to... What is the difference between me and those people in the swamp?"

"Nothing," I answered. "But this isn't about you."

"Then who is it about?" she asked in surprise.

"Our opponent," I answered calmly. "We were sure we'd win with you."

On Jay's face, I could read outrage, fury and seemingly offense.

"Do you mean to say that if a more dangerous creature had been after me, you wouldn't have helped?!" she asked, dumbfounded.

"Well, we aren't suicidal."

"And you can just say that so easily?"

"I am being honest with you," I shrugged my shoulders. "I don't want to offend you by lying. Should I have said something else?"

She shook her head.

"I don't know, Eric.... Your truth hurts just as bad."

"Listen, Jay..." I started, looking around. "I'm sorry I hurt you. But I have one very good justification — you're still alive. Do you want to die? Go ahead, it's your right. But don't demand that I do the same."

After listening carefully, she asked in a calmer voice:

"Then what do you intend to do?"

"What do you mean?" I asked in surprise. "My plans haven't changed — I'm going to Orchus. I'm going to rid myself of this oath and become a free man."

Jay thought for a moment. After that, clearly having made up her mind, she stated in a firm voice:

"Okay, Eric. Then this is where we part ways."

"But where are you gonna go?" I asked, perplexed.

"First to the swamp," she answered. "If I can't find the trail, I'll go home as I was planning from the very beginning."

"You don't wanna come to Orchus with me?"

"No," she shook her head. "I can sense that my family needs me."

"There's nothing I can do to change your mind?" I asked.

"What about you? Nothing I can do?" she answered with a smile.

"Heh... Gotcha."

She took a step forward, gave me jerky embrace and kissed me on the cheek. Then she smiled and walked over to Gorgie:

"Take care of him."

Once she was ten steps away, I shouted:

"Try not to do anything stupid!"

Jay smiled sadly and, waving a hand, ducked into a row of yellow bushes.

Gorgie and I were left alone again. To say I was puzzled would be to say nothing. For the last few days, she was afraid to stray more than a step from me, and today she was just up and going her own way. Although I do understand. Her beloved aunt is somewhere very close by and she's just supposed to walk past? No. I couldn't do that either.

I was also confused by how fast it all happened. In the depths of my soul, I was hoping Jay would come along with us. It was more fun the three of us. And I was used to her. Then just a quick goodbye and she disappears among the leaves.

Maybe I was too straight and to the point, too brusque? I just don't know any other way. Beyond that, I personally would always rather hear the truth no matter what it is.

"Hrn..." I felt the demanding touch of a wet nose against my hand.

"Yes, yes, buddy. We're leaving..."

* * *

In the middle of the day, we went up a small hill that gave us a good view of the plains.

I approximately knew which direction to find Orchus, and that was enough for the harn. He was leading me through the forest on old animal trails, keeping us well clear of large groups of people.

I should note that the young Baron Corwin was fulfilling his promise with zeal. These lands were just teeming with his mercenaries.

And the extreme cruelty of the scoundrels was striking. Many times, Gorgie warned me about yet another grisly mass slaughter near our path. I even took a peek at one of them an hour ago out of curiosity.

And I should have just walked past. It was two families inside. Based on the stoppers under the wheels of their carts, they were setting up camp in a forest clearing to spend the night. And that's where they were caught. Using our mental connection, Gorgie helped me interpret the tracks left by the raiders.

If I understood everything correctly, a few horsemen had also been visiting. All told, there were nine people.

They killed the men right away. Their breathless bodies were lying under a nearby tree. By all appearances, the women survived a bit longer, much to their misfortune. I found their corpses on in the farthest cart. Their torsos were cloven from groin to chest and their ears and noses had been cut off. Their eyes had been pulled out of their sockets, too... What made them treat these poor women this way?

I'll remember this bloody scene for a long time. And along with it the nauseatingly sweet scent of human flesh and the buzz-buzz-buzzing of the flies feasting upon it...

I didn't find the bodies of the children, although Gorgie assured me there had been three "younglings." The attackers must have taken them.

I left the meadow with an uncanny heaviness in my heart. It was exactly the same way I felt after I watched Crum and Happy die... And I had already thought a million times that perhaps I shouldn't have let Jay go it alone. Maybe I should have tried harder to convince her to come with me? Although, who am I to her? Not a father, not a brother. Just a fellow traveler. I sincerely hope she can find her aunt.

I stood on top of the hill and stared at the valley below in the evening light. Just off to the left, there's a river shimmering in the rays of the setting sun. Somewhere in the middle of the valley, the forest ends and an expansive field begins. To the right extends a craggy mountain ridge — the last bulwark of the Crooked Mountains. Not a cloud in the sky. A warm breeze ruffles my spectacularly grown-out mane. Watching over the idyll below you'd never think it, but blood is being spilled on those very lands this very instant. Lots and lots of blood...

I estimate Orchus is still another five days' walk. And that's if we don't get sidetracked. Somehow, I don't want to think about what I'd do if the capital of our barony is already under siege. I'd have to cut more sleep time, even though Gorgie and I are already not exactly spoiled in that regard. We usually get five or six hours a night as is.

Almost immediately I decided against spending the night on the hill — we'd be too exposed up there. We descended back into the forest.

A few hours later, night fell. When I was already thinking about where best to set up camp, the harn informed me of a strange scent coming from the east. And a few moments later, my nostrils also picked up on it. There was a fire burning not far away...

I gave Gorgie permission to go scout and, silent as a shadow, he slipped into the bushes.

"*Weak enemy. Prey. Female. Younglings,*" he reported a few minutes later.

"Is it the same bastards who were behind that slaughter in the clearing?" I asked in a whisper.

"Hrn..." Gorgie said negatively.

"New smell... I see..."

Based on the harn's sensations, the captives were still alive. Weighing all the pros and cons, I asked with a heavy sigh:

"You say the enemy is weak?"

"Hrn..."

"Weaker than a coldune?"

"Hrn..."

"Lots of food? You got my attention."

Food would be nice! Food would be awesome! We'll be out of fangbloom stems soon, and I don't want to use the valuable potions unless absolutely necessary. I also have no desire to go hungry again.

The harn had tried hunting, but wasn't successful. He said all the big wild animals had gone deep into the forest. And all the little creatures like squirrels and birds were high in the trees. Berry and mushroom seasons were already over. Despite the warm autumn days, the forest was gradually getting ready for winter. So hearing there was a large amount of food in possession of a "weak enemy" filled me with enthusiasm.

"I'm sold," I nod to Gorgie. "Let's go..."

We reached the unknown enemy's camp fairly quickly. Even if I had been alone in the woods, I probably still could have found it easily. The light of the fire was visible from a long way off through the dark trees.

We crawled up as close as possible. The darkness and wide trunk of a fallen tree made good cover.

I wonder which of these guys Gorgie considered weak? In the meadow there were three bearded fellows sitting around a fairly large bonfire. One of them is level nine and the other two are ten.

Not warriors, though they are armed. They look like cartmen. The three wagons on the other side of the clearing speak in favor of that theory. Every one of them is emblazoned with a black crow.

Based on their raucous mirthful voices, all three of them had been drinking quite a lot. Hm... Pretty easy-going. Or had I just grown used to always being on guard?

"Tim, what do you think — when will the boss come back?" one asked the red-bearded niner with a hiccup.

The bald man he called Tim gave a villainous smile and replied:

"I think tomorrow at the earliest. What, you got an idea?"

The broad chip-toothed mouth of the red-bearded man spread into a smile no less villainous than his partner's:

"Of course!"

"We're listening carefully, Vlas," came the third, largest of the group. By the looks of things, he was also the drunkest.

"Did you see that fine little chickee they brought in today?" the redhead asked. "Red as a cherry!"

"Hey, Vlas, if the boss hears you talking like that, he'll cut your balls off!" the big guy tried to cool his comrade's jets. "And ours too, just for knowing you..."

"Yeah, well who's ever gonna find out?" Vlas asked in surprise. "Did you hear what Tim said? Rath won't be back until tomorrow! Come on Piers, just admit it. You like her too! Hehe!"

"I'm not gonna lie," Piers nodded. "She's a looker. When I think of her, the blood in my veins starts running hot. But if we start acting up, Rath will definitely find out..."

"No he won't," the redhead smiled cleverly. "And we won't be acting up! She'll do everything herself! Of her own free will!"

"How are you gonna make that happen?" baldheaded Tim shot forward. Big old Piers did the same.

The redhead led a victorious gaze over his buddies and said:

"Because she wasn't brought alone. She had a kid. And for his sake, she'll do anything."

"The brains!" bald Tim exclaimed.

"Seems somehow inhumane..." the big guy knit his brow.

"But why?" Vlas objected. "She'll like it, too. I mean, we're not ugly guys. We're a couple of distinguished gentlemen."

"Yeah, and think back on when the Bear's retinue ran through our villages two years ago!" Tim snapped angrily. "She'll do it all herself. Nobody even has to raise a finger!"

"But what if she acts stubborn?" Piers asked with doubt in his voice.

"She won't," Vlas smiled. "Ladies will do

anything for their offspring. You'll see! Come on Tim, drag her over here!"

The bald guy gave a loud whinny, stumbled, and shuffled off toward the nearest wagon.

A few minutes later, he was back to the bonfire holding a terrified beautiful woman of thirty-five years by the elbow. All that time he was walking next to her, embracing her by the shoulders, and whispering something into the poor woman's ear. She was sobbing quietly and kept nodding very rapidly, agreeing to something. A thick red braid was sticking out of her gray shawl. There was an expression of hopelessness frozen in her big blue eyes, at the same time filled with valiant determination.

"Well, pretty lady, tell my friends here what you just told me!" the bald man announced, smiling vilely as he did. "Otherwise they won't believe me!"

"I'll do it!" the woman said firmly, and ran a heavy gaze over the scoundrels.

"Piers, you're in charge!" Vlas said. "You should go first!"

The big guy, shamed by her gaze, lowered his head.

"Pretty lady, go help our friend out," Tim said with strain in his voice, pushing the woman forward. "See, he's the most easily embarrassed of the bunch!"

Vlas gave a vile laugh.

The woman shuddered in fear and took a few

steps forward. Lowering a dainty white hand onto the big guy's arm, she timidly pulled him toward the wagons.

The unfortunate woman's blue eyes were tearing up. But she pursed her lips tightly and continued doing everything the scoundrels ordered for the sake of her flesh and blood.

Finally, Piers snapped to. He took a decisive look at the woman and, stumbling, climbed to his feet.

"Well, if you say so," he declared. "Then lead the way!"

What a nasty bastard! I figured at least one of them would be sympathetic to the poor woman!

Disappointed by the big guy, we waited for him and the woman to go behind the wagons. With him out of view, I figured we'd never find a better opportunity and got started.

I knew that I'd be taking part in the murder of a human in one second, but I wasn't experiencing any doubts. To be frank, these three and whoever they served ceased being people to me after what I saw and heard today.

With a gulper's ram, I slammed the two vilely snickering degenerates like a hurricane blowing a straw scarecrow off a cabbage patch. They didn't even have time to make a peep before Gorgie cracked their stupid skulls wide open. Truly — weak enemies...

Then Piers hopped out from behind the wagon to see what all the commotion was about, awkwardly holding up his pants. Before he could properly tell what was going on, he flew back a few steps like a broken doll. In two bounds, the harn was at the would-be rapist's side.

And a few moments later, the Great System informed me of another victory.

I took a look around. Silence hung over the cartmen's camp. It was only then that I noticed my body was shaking fitfully...

CHAPTER 2

I LISTENED TO MY FEELINGS. I wasn't experiencing even the slightest pity. Those bastards got what they had coming.

I looked over the loot. A standard set: Silvers and a corresponding number of esses. So that means these three are no different from the monsters of the caverns.

A muted woman's squeak distracted me from rummaging through the backpack. I raised my head. The harn perked up his ears and froze next to one of the wagons.

"It's over! Come on out!" I gave a muted call to the hidden woman. "Don't be shy! Nobody is gonna touch you!"

A few moments later, a familiar shock of red hair poked out from under the wheel of the cart. Her blue eyes open wide, her arms were shivering and her chest heaving rapidly.

The woman walked my way slowly, as if her legs were made of cotton. As she went, she looked over the cartmen's bodies with a shell-shocked gaze.

"What is your name? Where are you from?" I started asking questions when she stopped a step from me.

"V-veseya," the woman answered with a hiccup. "We're from Pinevale..."

"There are other people in the wagons. Are those your neighbors?"

The woman shuddered in fear and lowered her head.

"I know your child is in there. Don't worry, we aren't going to touch anybody. We only want food and, if possible, information. As soon as we get what we need, we'll be on our way."

"Did our Baron send you?" she asked, emboldened.

I shook my head silently. I don't think our Baron gives a great goddamn about any of us. But out loud I asked:

"How were you taken captive?"

"The Raven's mercenaries attacked our village. Killed all the men... And stuck the women and children in carts and wagons."

"Were there many wagons?"

"Yes," Veseya nodded. "More than ten."

"So where are the others?"

"I don't know. These three never mentioned them..."

The woman glanced scornfully at the corpses of the cartmen.

"I wish I knew what's making them commit all these atrocities." I said, floating an issue that had been bothering me.

"You can say that again," Veseya gave a heavy sigh. "It didn't used to be like this... I heard these guys say something like the young Corwin hired mercenaries, but can't keep them under control. And that's why they're marauding. They're acting very indecent... They also said the campaign is actually being conducted by Vestar the Black."

"The same Vestar who used to command for our Baron?"

"The very same!" the woman said, nodding fast. "Berence got rid of him many years ago. And he tortured his wife and child to death..."

"So that means our former commander got some forces together and has come back to get revenge," I said thoughtfully.

"That's about the size of it," Veseya sighed sorrowfully. "But what do we have to do with this?"

"Well, you can't make an omelet without breaking a few eggs..."

"Hrn..." Gorgie piped up.

I nodded and turned to the woman:

"You must know where these cartmen stashed their food."

"Yes, of course!" the smiling woman exclaimed eagerly. "I'll be back in a moment!"

After saying that, she quickly ran over to the

farthest wagon. The harn sensed he was about to get fed and followed after her.

I meanwhile decided to continue looking over our defeated enemies. I couldn't find any tablets or esses on them, but there was money. A few silver coins and a few copper on each. That was good. When I got back to civilization, I wouldn't have to show anyone my essences right away.

"Here I packed you up some food for the road," said the woman, passing me a bag with a smile.

Loosening the draw string, I glanced inside... I could tell immediately that she was trying to give me the best they had for my level.

"And I gave all our fish to your beast. From this morning's catch."

"Thanks," I said, and asked: "You going anywhere?"

"We'll make for an isolated farmstead that belongs to my relatives." Veseya nodded in the opposite direction of where I was going. "It's deep in the forest. But this filth won't be able to find us there. And you needn't worry about us. We come from hunting families. This forest is our home. We know every trail, tree and sapling in it. The soldiers will be back tomorrow, but there isn't a single decent tracker among them."

"But the tracks will still be here," I objected.

"That's true," the woman answered with a smile. "But we're gonna confuse them so much those blockheads will be searching until winter. We won't take the carts; we're going to set the horses loose. We're only gonna take what we really need. We'll cover everything here in the blood and guts of these scoundrels. Let them think a wild beast attacked while they slept. I mean, your cat left plenty of tracks around."

Okay then... This woman can handle herself. She reminds me in some way of Miri. You're never truly lost with someone like that.

"I think it's for the best if the others from your village don't find out I was here."

The woman nodded in understanding, then answered shortly:

"I swear no one will find out about you!"

The Great System didn't keep me waiting. Reading the confirmation with satisfaction, I said:

"Okay then, it's time for me to go."

"And may the gods go with you, good sir mage!"

✳ ✳ ✳

Last night we feasted! After so many days wandering the caverns and eating whatever we happened across, the simple grub from Veseya's bag was truly a royal repast!

In the cold light of day the next morning, honestly, I regretted eating so much the night before. My stomach felt uncomfortably tight. But it eased up in a few hours and we returned to our former pace.

Near midday, the forest ended. In its place came rolling fields.

"That's it," I muttered when we reached the forest edge. "Now we'll travel by night."

"Hrn," Gorgie said, and the scales on his neck scruff started vibrating.

I turned my head where he pointed. In the distance, at the right edge of the forest, there was now a column of dust. And it kept getting bigger and bigger, which meant someone was coming our way and fairly quickly at that. A few minutes later, a cavalcade of ten riders appeared on the country road.

"Ah, so there are the Raven's valiant little mercenaries," I whispered, cautiously peeking out between the dense yellow leaves of a large bush.

In the lead is, I believe, the commander. He's a big older guy with a mustache and aquiline nose. Level fourteen. Unlike his companions, he's decently equipped. I see chainmail, a beat-up steel helmet, a sword and shield with the emblem of Baron Corwin. A serious enemy.

The remaining soldiers are more reminiscent of the three from the clearing. For weaponry they had axes and short spears. I also see two bowmen. Levels nine to twelve.

They're riding right out in the open. Talking to one another loudly. They aren't looking around. They clearly already consider these lands their domain.

But before I was done looking over the first squad, a second appeared on the road behind it. And another an hour later. Then another...

All told, before sundown, five more horse patrols rode past us down the country road. Beyond that, there were two wagons and one large squadron of sixty infantrymen. Seemingly all of them were heading toward the capital of the barony, same as me.

After what I'd seen, it seemed too risky to go directly over the plains. Gorgie and I decided instead to take a detour through the forest along a rock ridge. Honestly, it was going to make our journey twice as long, but what could we do? We just felt more at ease with the trees as cover.

The first part of the night passed without incident. We were easily able to get around all the potentially dangerous places. But nearer sunup, the trail led us to a small lake with a lonesome farmstead perched on its shore. A high stockade fence, sturdy gates — it looked more like a small fortress in the woods.

The harn sent me a warning before we got too close. Something was happening there. I decided to take a look.

We went unhurriedly, trying to walk as quietly as possible. And the closer we came, the louder the booming men's voices sounded.

Stopping for a moment behind a large rotten log, thickly overgrown with years' worth of moss, I caught my breath. After that, I peeked out cautiously and saw what was out there.

The outlanders were four in number. They were sitting around the trunk of a wide tree on the edge of the forest. All men. Levels nine to eleven. One was holding a broad shield and axe; the rest were archers.

They were talking openly and constantly pointing their fingers at the stockade fence and gate.

At first glance, the farmstead looked abandoned. But there's no fooling Gorgie. There were two people hiding behind a wall inside. A man and a woman. Ready for an attack. Beyond that, the cat reported many children's tracks around. So there were at least two, maybe three children hidden in there as well.

Meanwhile, the outlanders finally reached some kind of agreement and started off. One, the very thinnest, walked around the clearing using the trees as cover.

The shield man waited for his partners to hide, stood up to his full height and walked toward the gates. The remaining two got their bows ready and took position behind the trees.

If I understood everything correctly, they weren't feeling bold enough for a head-on attack. Instead they were going to distract the farmstead defenders while the thin bowman tried to slip in between the stockade poles.

"Hail, good farmers!" the warrior shouted in a booming voice. "Prithee let a peaceful traveler spend the night?!"

Not waiting for a response, he asked loudly with a hint of mockery:

"Why so quiet?! Are the folk of these lands not a hospitable one?"

His raspy voice reminded me of the sound of two saplings rubbing together.

I heard one of the archers start quietly snickering.

Finally, a no less booming voice replied from the other side of the wall:

"By peaceful traveler, do you mean yourself, roaming scavenger?! One step closer and I'll treat you to an arrow right between the eyes! How do you like that for hospitality?!"

The bowmen started fidgeting and looking at one another. I could distinctly make out satisfied smiles on their faces. The fish had taken the bait.

The warrior shouted something back loudly, but I was no longer listening. I looked at the harn. The cat was ready to attack. One really shouldn't let such chances slip through their fingers.

For an instant, my eel lightning flickered in the darkness. I think only the farmers could have noticed. But even that isn't likely...

The archers, who had just been giving clever chuckles, slowly slumped to the ground. The harn slunk over to their bodies like a ravening ghost. I walked behind him, taking out Dragonfly as I went. Two short stabs into one neck... Then another... My conscience wasn't exactly eating at me. These rapscallions had come here to kill a family.

The harn finished things.

When the system messages arrived to inform me of the victory, Gorgie dissolved into the bushes on my signal, a silent shadow. A few long minutes later, another set of notifications came before my eyes, telling me the thin one had also died. I breathed a sigh of relief. The creep never even made it inside.

Done. The only one left was the big talker at the gates. And by the way, he was noticeably on edge. He was probably wondering why his partners hadn't gotten to work yet.

Finally, the farmsteaders moved from words to action. Arrows rained down on the loudmouth one after the other. And he, ducking behind his shield and spraying profanity, stumbled back right up against the forest edge.

Breathing heavily, the man ran into some shrubbery, which just so happened to put him in range of my Ram. A second later, Gorgie jumped out of the bushes with all his considerable heft and fell down hard on the big man's chest. Okay, he's done too.

Two or three arrows flew in our direction from beyond the stockade. One whizzed dangerously close to my cheek. With a gasp of fear, I fell onto my stomach. Whew... Just two fingers to the right and my eye would have gained a nasty little ornament.

When the farmstead defenders stopped

shooting, the harn slowly dragged the bodies of the downed men under the trees for cover. Unlike the cartmen, these three were carrying bags full of esses. No tablets though. They must have been using everything they earned on themselves right away. Beyond that, I found myself another couple dozen silver and copper coins richer. I didn't take the heavy weapons or any equipment — I'd never get far dragging all that stuff. Not with my characteristics.

I listened to my feelings again. As I rifled through the pockets of my downed enemies, I wasn't feeling the least bit squeamish. Happy was right. These items belonged to me by right now because I defeated these horrid men.

We quietly walked around the farmstead. Gorgie told me the defenders had split up. The woman was still at the gates, while the man had walked to the wall opposite. They must have been putting some diversion into action. Honestly, they'd have been too late. If we hadn't intervened when we did, the thin man would have already been stabbing them in the back.

An unfortunate raider's body was lying near the stockade. He was no more than three feet from his target when Gorgie caught him.

I breathed a heavy sigh. We'd have to leave that one. The farmer must have noticed the dead man and thus taken out his bow.

"That's all, buddy," I whispered. "Let's go. We have nothing else to do here."

* * *

— You have acquired Dry Gorse.

> *— Congratulations! You receive:*
> *— Experience essence (5).*
> *— Clay tablet "Herbalism."*
> *— Clay tablet of Agility.*
> *— Clay tablet of Observation.*
> *— Clay tablet "Knife Proficiency."*

I came upon the small unremarkable plant by complete coincidence while resting. Gorgie and I had been drawn to a small low-profile hill. It was densely overgrown with dry grass and bushes, and among the vegetation I discovered some dry gorse — a zero grass with extremely low value.

Unlike the gray moss, which grew in large sheets, I had to hunt for the gorse. After watching me eagerly crawl around on the ground for a bit, digging through dried grass, the harn himself got carried away hunting for more.

> *— You have acquired Dry Gorse.*

> *— Congratulations! You receive:*
> *— Experience essence (5).*
> *— Clay tablet "Herbalism."*
> *— Clay tablet of Agility.*
> *— Clay tablet of Observation.*

THE WASTES

— Clay tablet "Knife Proficiency."

"Found another," I muttered under my breath in a satisfied voice.

A mocking man's voice behind me made me shudder.

"How's the hunting?"

I feel a chill run down my spine. Slowly, not making any sudden moves, I turn.

Literally two steps from me there were three men standing stock still. I looked at their levels and went dismal. The lowest among them is twenty-two. The highest — twenty-seven. He looks to be in charge.

Tossing a quick gaze over their excellent equipment, I fell into a deeper state of gloom. The strangers are dressed like scouts. As for weaponry — short blades and compound bows. Each of them with ten or so amulets around their neck. Seemingly, I'd fallen into the hands of a group of forest rangers. To these warriors, I was no more than some farcical magician.

"Well, spill it," the twenty-seven turned calmly to me. The look in his ice-gray eyes pierced me straight through. On his sunburned bearded face, there's a crooked scar running from his left brow to the lobe of his right ear.

Meanwhile, the lowest-level of the three stepped forward and took the knapsack off my shoulder. Deftly undoing the draw strings, he dug into my belongings.

"Trash," he commented and flung the bag at my feet.

Despite the fear clenching my heart, I found the strength inside to mentally chuckle. You'll never get to the ephemeral backpack... Only over my dead body.

"You were asked a question, scamp," the third ranger furrowed his thick brow. Level twenty-four. Broken nose. Full lips. Big protruding ears. He looks somewhat like my old neighbor, who worked his whole life as a stevedore at the Orchus river port. They used to say he loved fist fighting for cash.

"W-what do you w-want to know?" I asked, hiccupping and screwing up my face into the most authentic expression of fear I could muster.

"Who are you? Where are you from? What are you doing here?" the head honcho interrogated in clipped phrases.

"Eric... Eric Bergman... A peon of Mister Bardan... I'm on my way to Orchus..."

I decided to speak the truth. I was sure these warriors had sky-high Lie Detection scores.

"He's telling the truth," came the big-eared one.

The head honcho nodded in silence as if to say he also thought so.

I looked at the men and tried to figure out who they served — Corwin or Berence?

Unexpectedly, the head honcho raised his right hand in a precautionary gesture.

"The beast is near," he said mutedly.

"Finally," the young one smiled in satisfaction.

I already knew what beast they were talking about. Gorgie was back from his hunt, and hadn't yet caught these hunters' scent. If I hadn't warned him, he'd have walked right into the line of fire of these rangers' arrows.

All the hair on my body stood on end when I started imagining what might happen to my friend.

"Strange," the head honcho frowned, pulling his bowstring taut. "The thing picked up our scent."

"How is that possible?" the big-eared one asked. "It'll be level seven or eight at most..."

It took me a lot of effort not to shudder at the highly accurate guess. A harn figurine appeared imperceptibly in my hand.

— Would you like to recall your pet?

Yes! Now! Then I set the amulet back in my backpack.

"It's gone," the head honcho said immediately, looking around perplexed.

This time I couldn't resist and breathed a sigh of relief.

"Oh abyss!" the big-eared one barked out angrily. "This is about to turn into another wild goose chase!"

The head honcho looked at me suspiciously.

"Well maybe it won't have to," he said and turned to me: "Get up! You're coming with us!"

If I had any remaining hope I'd been captured by rangers serving my Baron, they fell into oblivion as soon as we left the forest.

On a wide clearing at the foot of the rocky ridge, there was a military encampment. A few dozen tents of various sizes were surrounded by a wall of wagons, carts and carriages lined with armed sentries. And no matter where I looked, I saw the image of a black raven.

The neighing of horses, mooing of cows, bleating of sheep, barking of dogs, squealing of pigs, screaming of people — it all mixed together into one solid drone.

I walked through the camp with my jaw hanging down in surprise. Everywhere I looked — at bonfires and tents, under awnings and open sky — there were soldiers sitting, standing and just lying around. And they were all doing their own thing. Some were cleaning their weapons or mending clothes; some were playing dice or cards. And some were just snoring under the open sky.

There were also many women in revealing outfits with bright cosmetics on their face. Based on their wanton mannerisms, nobody was forcing these ladies to be there.

Walking past one such woman, the big-eared one immediately launched a greasy little joke in her direction. And much to my surprise the woman not only didn't get offended, she shot back a an equally indecent retort. And she accompanied her words with inappropriate gestures and shameless winking.

What I saw and heard made my face burn. I felt like I'd been dunked into boiling water...

Finally, we walked up to a large multi-colored hut with two sentries standing guard at the entrance. Both their levels are beyond twenty. They look like two solid steel boulders. Gorgie and I would barely be a mouthful to them.

"Is he in?" the head ranger asked calmly.

"He's waiting for you," one of the sentries boomed out in a deep bass.

The ranger nodded and, pushing me forward, threw out to his subordinates without turning:

"You've got one hour."

"Thank you, captain!" I heard the big-eared one say joyfully.

When we got inside the fairly cavernous yurt, I shuddered in fear. And there was good reason!

On a wide thick carpet running straight across the middle of the tent, there was a white viper curled up in a few rings! It was hard for me to hold back and not bash the snake with a Ram.

But the subterranean creep didn't react to our arrival in any way. Though I was certain that it was ready to attack at any moment.

Abyss! Where did I land myself?!

"Captain Morten! Finally! I've been waiting for you!"

When I heard the pleasant soothing baritone, I immediately turned my head to the right. The strong voice belonged to a middle-aged man. Tall with thick black hair, he had a short trimmed beard and a lithe figure concealed by expensive clothing and footwear. It was immediately apparent that this tent's occupant was very conscious of his appearance. A white-toothed smile played on his sophisticated pale face.

When I saw his narrow dark-blue eyes and level forty-five, my heart was ready to jump out of my chest. I'm really in trouble now...

"Greetings Master Chi!" the captain gave a short bow.

"Morten, have you captured the beast like I asked?" the man asked hurriedly, ignoring the greeting.

"Alas, sir, I have not," the captain shook his head. "We almost had the thing, but it suddenly caught our scent."

"How is that possible?" Master Chi asked in surprise. "You're wearing an amulet of stealth! I created it with my own two hands! Even a level-thirty creature wouldn't have been able to detect you!"

"That's true, sir," the captain answered. "But somehow this level-seven or -eight beast picked up our scent and disappeared without a trace."

"Curious..." the master muttered.

"And here's the really strange part," the commander of the forest rangers continued. "All that time this kid, who looks absolutely harmless on first glance, was right next to us."

After the captain said that, the mage started staring at me stubbornly.

"Furthermore, when we followed the beast's tracks a bit, we found a set of smaller footprints next to them."

Smiling, the master lowered his gaze to my threadbare boots.

"Curious... Let's quick check something then."

When he said that, the mage quickly turned and hurriedly headed toward a wide table covered with items and scrolls.

Lowering his hand into a round box, he pulled out a small square mirror. When he came back, he pointed it at me while staring at his own reflection for some reason.

A few seconds later, his brows climbed upward in surprise while his thin lips spread into a predatory smile.

"Captain," Master Chi said happily. "I can say with absolute certainty that your mission to capture the dangerous beast has been completed. You can leave the kid here."

"As you say," the ranger nodded.

"I consider your contract complete!" the mage declared. "Excellent work, it's been a pleasure doing business with you! You can go to my assistant for payment."

"Thank you, Master Chi!" a smile appeared on the captain's fearsome face for the first time.

With a bow, the man quickly left. And we were all alone.

"So then, you used a summoning amulet?" Chi chuckled understandingly.

A lump rose up my throat. How did he know?!

"At times, fate is not just," he said suddenly. "If not for my passion for unusual beasties, you probably would have made it past all of Vestar the dunderhead's sentries. But to your misfortune, I had my best trackers on your trail... And today my collection has gained two interesting new specimens."

CHAPTER 3

"

"**I** SEE YOU ARE bound by several oaths?" the mage asked, intrigued. "How'd you get those at your tender age?"

"Family debt," I answered shortly. My mouth went dry...

"I see," the man muttered. "And the others?"

"Oaths of silence."

"Well, those are no impediment to us, but the monetary ones may cause certain discomfort. Let's just get that sorted."

Master Chi gave a creepy chuckle and made a lightning-fast swipe.

— *Attention! You have been subjected to mental magic!*

I didn't even have time to make a peep before

I heard his commanding voice:

"Listen and do not move! From this moment forward, I am your master. You must obey all my orders. And here is your first and most important one — from now on, you may not do me any harm. That's all. Now get lost!"

I took a deep loud breath, filling my lungs with air. Using nothing but words, this creep had just rendered me motionless! I couldn't even breathe! Oh gods! Why is this happening to me again?!

"No need to worry about your obligations for now. My spell has temporarily suppressed them."

Temporarily? Does that mean I'll be free again if I kill this scumbag? That's how it worked with the vampire.

As if reading my thoughts, the mage chuckled and said:

"You're probably feeling sorry that you didn't try and attack Captain Morten and his underlings back in the forest, right? Let me assure you — you did everything right. I just read the description of your spells... Yes, yes... Stop staring at me like that. This Amulet of Reveal Essence allows me to see everything about you..."

After saying that, Master Chi gave the small mirror a shake.

"So, what was I talking about? Oh yeah! It never would have worked. The captain and his warriors are well equipped and protected by magical amulets. Although I must admit that lightning of yours is quite promising. It ignores all kinds of defense and immobilizes... Up against someone without high level resistance to all kinds of stunning and numbing effects, that spell would be truly amazing!"

At that moment, I was plagued by a few feelings. Hatred and disgust for the man intertwined with rage directed at myself. Worthless idiot! To be caught so easily!

But there was also another feeling... I was perplexed — the mage had simply and casually mentioned things he was never supposed to reveal.

"Alright," came Master Chi, still carried away with his discussion. "Let's say you activated your lightning and immobilized the captain and another person. And sure, let's not be petty — we can imagine all three of them ended up stunned. What next? Your beast would come and finish them off? Answer."

"Yes," I said, despite not wanting to speak.

"Well nuts to you! You and your beast!" the mage shouted joyously and gave me the middle finger. "Those fifteen seconds would not be enough for either you or your beast to get through the magical shields my amulets confer. You don't have deep enough supplies to fight opponents such as them. Ahem... I'm afraid to even imagine the rage in the rangers' attacks after a three ring circus like that."

The mage was speaking with such confidence in his voice that it was hard not to believe him.

"Okay," said Master Chi, rubbing his hands together. "Now that we've handled this one, let's get to the next question."

He came to his table and opened a small bright-raspberry colored chest. Then he turned and called me:

"Come here."

When I stopped a step from the table, the mage said:

"Take out all your belongings and place them right here."

His manicured hand pointed to a meticulously polished tabletop. Out of the corner of my eye, I notice he's wearing one signet ring on each of his fingers. His wide wrist is wrapped in a silver bracelet of exquisite handiwork. And it probably isn't just simple jewelry...

"If you try and act smart, I'll punish you," he warned, his thin brows furrowed. "I know that ratty knapsack is just a decoy."

With pain in my heart, I started taking out everything I'd so painstakingly accumulated.

"Well, well!" the mage exclaimed when he saw the mountain of esses. "This is three hundred gold in experience essences alone!"

When I set the Intellect tablets on the table as well, the master's thin lips spread into a satisfied but restrained smile. To be honest, I was expecting a stormier reaction.

But when I got to the items from the Stonetown arsenal, he shuddered.

"Where'd you get this stuff from?!" he shouted, his voice quaking. "Answer in detail!"

I winced. It was as if some invisible person was pulling the words out of me and assembling them into short, choppy phrases. The uncanny force made me tell the master everything that happened to me in the caverns.

My latest captor listened carefully. At times he winced and others he smiled, rubbing his pampered hands together. From time to time, he would ask leading questions. In the end, he managed to get everything he was after. Well, almost everything...

As soon as that thought crossed my mind, Master Chi said:

"Very intriguing. I have much to consider. But there's one thing you haven't yet told me..."

"What do you mean?" I asked quietly, my eyes pointed at the ground.

"Don't play stupid," he menaced with a finger. "I would like to know how you got your hands on the iridescent tablets! Hehe! Or did you think I'd believe you were just born this way? Stop. Wait a second... I almost forgot!"

The mage gently patted his forehead.

"The artifacts of the ancients you have on — where are they from?"

A cold sweat ran down my back.

"My parents gave them to me," I angrily spat out between my teeth.

Paying no attention to my tone, the mage

started thoughtfully stroking his chin and said:

"Alright, you can keep them. I would rather not have to carry you around after all!"

Then he boomed loudly:

"Haha! Just imagine the scene! And all the questions! Haha! So master Chi, who you carrying there? Oh! This is just my slave! Haha!"

After hearing the word "slave," a lump rose up my throat. I wanted to wail in impotence.

When he saw my gaze burning in indignation, the mage calmly said:

"It's good you're angry, slave. Very soon, we're going to need you mad. Shen!"

"Yes, milord!" I heard a vile hissing voice to the right.

Oh gods! That means we weren't alone this whole time! The shock made me jump back.

A short middle-aged man was standing perfectly still next to me. Gray hair. I'd even say pure white. The tips of his moustache slightly pointed. The gaze of his black squinting eyes turned me inside out. His pale face showed no emotion. All that created the impression that the entity standing before me felt absolutely nothing at all. Ghoulish, ravening and very dangerous. And for what it's worth, he was level thirty-six.

"How do you like our little hunter, Shen?" the mage chuckled. "He couldn't even sense you. And incidentally, his reputation with the order is over three thousand points."

When I heard him mention the order and

reputation, I tensed up.

"He won't be able to sense me anytime soon, lord," Shen answered dispassionately.

Master Chi snorted, nodded and said:

"Why don't you show him then. Let him know who he is dealing with."

"Yes, lord," the gray-haired man answered calmly and his face began to shift.

Oh, Great System! Just about every hair on my body stood on end! In the space of a few heartbeats, every trace of humanity fled Shen's face. As a matter of fact, it's hard to even call it a face now! His animalistic snout is a ghastly cross between the head of a bat and that of a snake. His wide mouth is packed with needle-sharp teeth. Triangular ears almost on his forehead. A broad flattened nose greedily pulling in the scent of prey. His black eyes harbor a desire to maim and kill.

Only then did I notice that my mouth was filled with bitter saliva.

"I have someone I'd like you to meet, slave!" the mage said, satisfied at my condition. "This is a blackblood! One of the most dangerous creatures of the Dark Continent!"

Savoring the look on my face for a bit, Master Chi said:

"Okay Shen, enough! We've had our fun. We have lots of work to do."

"Yes, sir," the blackblood answered dispassionately, having changed shape again.

"Tell the Baron I am returning home," the

mage started giving orders.

"Young Corwin won't like that," Shen stated coldly.

"That's his problem," the master waved it off, dumping all my belongings into the raspberry box. Seeing my heavy gaze, he gave a cheery wink.

"And how goes the military campaign?" the blackblood asked. I was getting the feeling the mage was trying to force Shen to dissent and question him by some method I was unaware of.

"Let him keep listening to Vestar the demented!" the master shot out in dismay. "They make a fine pair! A couple of idiots! They think the Bear ill and weak! Sure, Berence has grown old. But he's still the same clever little snoop as ever. He'll sit in his den and bide his time until guests show up. If only Valer the stupid pompous boy had ever once listened to my advice, he'd know now that one of Berence's little sons is engaged to a daughter of Count Boarg."

"Are the Boargs allied with the Berences?" Shen asked dispassionately.

"Imagine the surprise in store for our little upstart when the Bear and the Boar come from different directions to smash his army." Master Chi chuckled. "Now do you understand why Corwin's brigades are not encountering any resistance? It's nothing more than a clever trap. And I'll tell you one thing. This will not end with the upstart merely getting his feathers plucked."

"And you aren't warning him?"

"No, Shen. He made his bed, let him lie in it. I've had enough of that snot-nose. That ungrateful whelp made his choice in favor of a madman bent on revenge."

"I understand, sir," the blackblood answered coldly. "Any other orders?"

"Order a place made up for our newcomer. And treat him carefully. I have grand plans for the boy." After he said that, Master Chi turned to me with strain in his voice. "Walk with Shen. Do exactly as he says."

Obeying the order, I followed the blackblood out of the tent.

"By the way, I almost forgot!" the mage said as we were on our way out. "Shen, take care of Captain Morten and his rangers. I don't need any witnesses."

"Yes, milord." Finally I heard emotion in the blackblood's voice. "You have my gratitude!"

Out of the corner of my eye I saw the creature's thin pale lips spread into a bloodthirsty grin, revealing his sharp fangs.

Once upon a time, I was lucky enough to be able to visit the home of my school's natural sciences teacher. A quiet, lonesome man who dedicated his entire life to collecting butterflies.

He could be seen all kinds of different places,

sometimes quite unexpectedly. Be it a meadow, a forest clearing or the terrace of a fancy restaurant — in a word, he was everywhere his beloved insects might be found.

Always wearing a wide-brimmed straw hat, draped in all kinds of little boxes and holding a long butterfly net — the man had become something of a symbol of our city.

In the winter, when there was nothing to catch, the teacher locked himself in his house and spent ages studying his catch in great detail. But there were also days when he put on public showings of his collection, which had specimens numbering in the thousands.

One such day, I saw all his multicolored butterflies. Pinned to flat wooden boards in special glass cases and cabinets, they delighted the eye of his enamored visitors. Now, after seven days underway, I felt like just such an insect — an object of intensive study for Master Chi. Thankfully, we weren't quite to the pinning stage yet.

Every day he would summon me to his wagon and force me to tell him more of my story. Beginning with collecting the moss and ending with my exit from the caverns of the Crooked Mountains.

Sometimes I would have to repeat all the system messages about my heroic achievements several times. My tale about the monster hunter markers merited particular attention, and specifically the fact that the ancient magic reacted positively to my blood.

When I said that, Chi looked truly satisfied. His face gleamed like a freshly polished copper basin, a smile of joy plastered on.

"Shen!" he said to his dispassionate servant. "This boy is truly the crown jewel of my collection! Keep him safe. He's the apple of my eye!"

"Yes, lord," he answered melancholically.

"Just imagine! We have every reason to believe ancient blood courses through his veins! I think the Great System tried to kill him when he was born, but Bug intervened and something happened that was not supposed to."

"He's weak," objected the blackblood.

"True! But that is his advantage! Every time he gathers resources or fights, the Great System gives him the maximum possible reward! And iridescent tablets?! Given the right conditions, he'll be able to bring them to me like mushrooms after a rainstorm! His blood can give us access to our world's most ancient mysteries! Haha! If I told someone about this, they'd never believe me! Some pitiful zero is gonna make Master Chi Grand Magister! All the doors in the capital of the Kingdom will open for me! His Majesty will certainly want to get to know me!"

My heart skipping beats, I was soaking up all the information the mage could spout. And with every passing day, I grew gloomier. But still I refused to believe that I was doomed to spend the rest of my days in servitude to this ugly bastard.

Gorgie helped me not to break. My friend shared with me his confidence in the future, told me to keep my head down and, when the time came, to strike.

And so I did just that. Kept my head down...

At noon of the tenth day, our journey was nearing an end. The mage's train of five wagons accompanied by twenty well-armed soldiers reached its destination.

I must note that all the warriors and servants on the way behaved similarly to Shen, silently and implicitly carrying out every order whether from the mage or his top assistant. It was like they didn't notice me. Like I was just empty space to them.

The caged creatures the master caught before finding me were riding in closed wagons and not displaying any aggression. One of my travelling companions was a hexapod.

The highly dangerous cavern monster was sitting with its long appendages folded and looking like a lifeless clump of fuzz. For the whole duration of our trip, it stirred only once — when a sheep was brought in for it to eat.

The neighboring barony was no different from our own. The nature, architecture, people. If I didn't know I was in a foreign land, I'd have thought we were somewhere to the west of Orchus.

Based on the way the locals greeted our wagon train, Master Chi must have been a famed and influential figure here. Fear in the eyes of the city's elders and leaders followed by flagrant bootlicking spoke to the fact that Master Chi also enjoyed a kind of infamy.

When I saw the mage's estate, I was slightly surprised. The manor was a fairly large two-story building with lots of light. He also had a smithy, a farrier's, a manicured garden, an ovular fountain outside the front door, and plenty of white-sand paths both wide and narrow. Nearby and a bit to the right, I could see a pond with a white boathouse. To be honest, I was picturing the mage's home very differently. I mean, Bardan's manor looked grimmer with its window grates! But this... It's the normal house of a normal landowner...

His entire small staff came out to greet their master. They were just as silent and phlegmatic. Now that made my skin crawl. It felt like I'd just been brought to a puppet theater...

Hm... And there's the puppet master in the flesh. Smiling, he's beckoning me over with a manicured finger.

"Let's go!" he called. "We have lots more work to do!"

Slipping past the servants swarming around the wagons, I followed after the mage. I imagined slamming into him with a Ram and instantly felt more at ease.

The house greeted us with ideal cleanliness and freshness. Bright walls, elegant furniture, everywhere vases containing fresh flowers.

Following my gaze, Master Chi said in self-satisfaction:

"Everything you see around you — this home, its decor, my very own orangery, the furniture, the sheets, the glass vases — was made by my workers."

Taken aback, I looked at everything again with different eyes.

"Surprised?" the mage chuckled. "Let me tell you a secret. I was not born into wealth, but my father was a very practical man. Thanks to his thrift and stinginess, we never went hungry. Many considered him a miser. Fools! He was the very picture of good sense! It's been two hundred years or more since he died and still I thank him for what he taught me almost every day!" Seeing incomprehension in my eyes, he asked: "What level do you think a carpenter must reach before they can make something like this?"

The mage stopped next to a small carved chair and patted its lacquered back.

"You may answer."

"I'm not sure," I muttered and, frowning, gave a rough estimate: "Thirty? Forty?"

Chi folded his arms across his chest and told me victoriously:

"Not even close! Half that. And to be more accurate — eighteen."

I looked at the chair, perplexed. The warped carved legs, the dark burgundy lacquer, the neat upholstery, clean lines. This would have been quite expensive furniture. At the very least, my family home never had anything this nice.

"And now answer this question for me. What's better — to spend a huge amount of money on furnishings such as these or to make your own carpenter for no more than the cost of that sofa over there? Come now... Don't frown. It isn't my fault all these people ended up slaves. I bought them at the slave market. I gave them a roof over their heads, food, invested lots of tablets and essences into all of them!"

Well, and you also made them your puppets, may the abyss swallow you up!

"Alright," said Chi. "Let's go... Now it's your turn."

I wasn't totally sure what he was talking about but, obeying his order, I shuffled off after him, consumed by anger and hate.

We went up to the second floor. We came across a long corridor and stopped in front of a large exquisitely-carved door.

"Follow me," the master commanded and stepped into a fairly spacious room.

I looked around in a daze. No matter where I turned my head, I saw shelves laden with books and scrolls. At the far wall there was a huge table and large armchair covered in dark leather. There were also lots of unusual items around. From menacing skeletons of unknown beasts to little boxes and small chests.

And the mage was heading for one such chest.

"Shen is right," he said as he walked. "You're a weakling. A stiff breeze could blow you over. Before our endeavor may begin in earnest, I must attempt to improve your figures."

Taking the little chest under his arm, Chi walked over to the table. Plopping down in the seat, he threw back its embossed lid and started digging around inside.

"Where are you?" he muttered. "I'm certain I remember leaving it here. Aha! There you are!"

A small fiery-orange sphere the size of a chicken egg appeared in the mage's hands.

"Here!" he extended it to me. "Read the description but don't use it yet. I got it from an explorer fresh off a trip to the Dark Continent. You know, for the future. It cost me a pretty penny. It's an unbelievably rare item, there are no more of them on our continent... Hm... Although your tokens and Hunter reputation are indisputable evidence that these lands still harbor some mysteries."

He kept speaking, but I wasn't listening. My heart was just about to jump out of my chest.

My eyes refused to believe what they were seeing.

Sphere of Temporary Growth.

— *Type: Magical objects.*
— *Rarity: Epic.*
— *Effect:*
— *Increases level by 1.*
— *Effect duration: 30 minutes.*
— *Sphere disappears after use.*

"Well, how do you like it?" the mage chuckled. "Pretty nice, huh?"

Inadvertently forgetting where I was, I nodded joyfully.

"Hehe... Just don't get your hopes up. You're sure you gave me all your esses? Because you never know, you might go and ding on me for real. Then how are we gonna get iridescent tablets? So I ask you again, have you surrendered all your esses?"

"Yes, lord," I answered dejectedly in a rasping voice.

"Alright then," the mage nodded and pushed a small copper box in my direction. "Here. When I say the word, you start to use them."

I glanced inside. A few hundred clay tablets and another ten or so silvers.

"Too bad the sphere only gives plus one," the mage sighed, digging in yet another chest. "All you can do is unlock base characteristics. Skills, abilities and spells can only be activated from level three. And the ceiling is gonna be just ten... Mind will be stuck at two. But it doesn't matter. This way, if you lose your button and ring in battle you won't turn into a vegetable right away."

Master Chi finished sorting through the box, sat back in his chair and looked me stubbornly in the eyes.

"After you activate the sphere, don't you dare use any experience essences. Got it?"

"Yes, lord."

"Good. Then you may begin."

— Attention! Your level has been temporarily increased to 1.

— Remaining duration: 29:59 minutes.

"Now use the clays to bring your Mind, Strength, Agility and Endurance up to maximum. Alas, your Intellect and Health are already at the ceiling."

— Attention! You have used Clay tablet of Mind (20)!

— Present value:

— Mind: 5/2.

— Attention! You have used Clay tablet of Strength (100)!

— Present value:

— Strength: 13/10.

— Attention! You have used Clay tablet of Agility (100)!

— Present value:
— Agility: 12/10.

— Attention! You have used Clay tablet of Endurance (100)!
— Present value:
— Endurance: 10/10.

"Now," Master Chi continued in a calm voice. "Use the silver tablets to bring all your magic up to maximum."

Obediently, operating like a mechanical puppet, I used one hundred silvers, bringing all my abilities and spells up to one.

The mage was keeping a close watch over the process, holding a small mirror in his hands all the while.

"Eh-heh... You're still very weak... Take this too."

He extended me a small muddy-gray stone.

Small crystal of mana.
— Mana: 0/800.

"Hide it where no one will find it. You can slough off all your excess mana into it. You may begin right now. And you can level your beast on your own. Shen!"

"Yes, milord," the blackblood called back immediately, materializing out of nowhere. Unlike the first time, I was no longer shuddering at his unexpected appearances. Over the last few days, I'd gotten used to the constant invisible presence of the mage's assistant.

"Everything ready?" I asked Master Chi.

"Yes, lord," Shen nodded.

"Excellent!" the mage shouted and, smiling, turned to me: "Okay then, now we're gonna see you in action. Your first battle is in one day's time. Prepare yourself!"

CHAPTER 4

A S I LEFT THE MAGE'S STUDY, I felt a slight queasiness. At first I assigned it no meaning, but with every step I was feeling worse and worse. I glanced at my supplies and gasped! Energy was constantly flowing out of my body like a leaky wineskin.

When I reached the ladder that led to the cellar where my tiny room was located, I could barely see farther than an outstretched hand. I grabbed the rungs with the last of my strength and took my first step. A strong hand saved me from falling. Slowly turning my head, I saw Shen's pale face. In fact, that was the last thing I saw before I lost consciousness...

The first time I woke up for only a brief moment. Through the blur in my eyes, I could see that I was lying in a bed in a tiny little room. I was very hot. My clothing and the bedsheets were all soaked in sweat. A dull aching pain ensconced my entire body. Eerie vibrations were emanating from the crown of my head to the tips of my fingers and toes.

After that came a series of strange occurrences. Seemingly the half-sleep swallowed me whole. I finally came to my senses for good when my forehead touched something searingly cold.

Wincing, I opened my eyes.

"Gathered your wits?" came a familiar malicious voice.

Master Chi was standing next to my bed and carefully watching an elderly slave woman dab my face with something wet and cold.

"What's wrong with me?" I rasped.

"Can't figure it out on your own?" the mage asked mockingly. "What do they teach you in those schools?"

What is he talking about?

Seeing the lack of comprehension on my face, Chi rolled his eyes and lowered himself to answer:

"It's a side effect of activating a large number of tablets at once. Your body is changing and using a huge amount of energy. Hungry?"

"Yes," I nodded contentedly even though I'd most likely have eaten an entire cow that very second. So this is how Gorgie feels when he's famished. I'd have to give him more consideration when splitting up the food. Thankfully, with his energy supply, it never reached the point of fainting...

"But I've used tablets on myself before... And nothing like that ever happened."

"No comparison," the mage chuckled. "You were using iridescents, after all!" then he waved a hand and said unhappily: "I don't much care for delays, but the crossing over will have to wait. Fortunately for you, I have an old friend coming to visit me tomorrow. He comes bearing important news... Hehe, he's probably gonna try and spook me with those upstarts from the Order again..."

On his way out, he threw out to my nurse-maid:

"Get him fed and bring him a new set of clothes."

The woman complied and instantly leapt out of the small room, leaving me alone. Sitting up more comfortably, I decided to look at my figures.

— *Level: 0*
— *Mind: 5*
— *Strength: 13*
— *Agility: 12*
— *Endurance: 10*
— *Health: 10*
— *Intellect: 20*
— *Life supply: 110/110*
— *Energy supply: 65/110*
— *Mana supply: 210/210*

— *Skills and abilities:*

— *Gulper's Lair.*
— *Level: 1 (0/30).*

— *Muckwalker's Aquatic Regeneration.*
— *Level: 1 (0/30).*

— *Spells:*
— *Glitterspark Eel's Chain Lightning.*
— *Level: 1 (0/30).*

— *Gulper's Shattering Ram.*
— *Level: 1 (0/30).*

— *Muckwalker's Defensive Aura.*
— *Level: 1 (0/30).*

All the positive effects of my abilities and spells had noticeably improved. And my mana expenditure and cooldown times had gone down considerably. Master Chi said I was still very weak. Heh, he should have seen me two months ago.

After studying my characteristics, I listened to my feelings. I was contented. But this contentment was akin to that of a caged wild animal being thrown a hunk of meat. I got fed, but it only meant I would be ready for action when the time finally came.

* * *

"So then, let's repeat one more time," Master Chi says, sitting with a glass of wine and staring at the ceiling. For the umpteenth time, he is harping on about the rules for my conduct. "What do you do with loot?"

"I must surrender all loot to you, lord," I answer for the umpteenth time, reciting by rote.

"Correct," the mage nods and takes a sip. "And if someone wants to give you a gift?"

"I must not accept."

"And?"

"And I must inform you."

Master Chi wanted to ask another question, but a timid knock came at the door.

"Enter!" he commanded.

The door opened to reveal the head of a young servant.

"My lord, Master Ting's carriage will be arriving any minute."

"Excellent!" The mage exclaimed, slapping himself on the knees and jumping up nimbly.

"Order everyone to come down and meet our honored guest!" Turning to me, he said: "But you hide over there in the corner." And he added, menacing with a finger: "And make sure you keep your head down for me."

Submitting, I hid behind a heavy curtain. Through a narrow gap between the folds I had an excellent view of the entrance and dining table, which was set with all kinds of exquisite delicacies. And thirty minutes later, two mages came barging into the room. They were smiling gleefully and patting one another on the shoulder, hobnobbing.

Master Chi's very old friend was a plump middle-aged man. Luxuriant fire-red hair cascaded over his shoulders. His curly red beard was neatly trimmed, and the pomaded tips of his moustache twirled rakishly. Expensive clothing, flashy jewelry — in general, mages were defined by good grooming and fanciful mannerisms.

After them, a few servants hurried into the room carrying more dishes. As soon as Chi and his friend sat at the table, servers scurried up next to them.

"Wine?" asked Master Chi.

"Ragonian!" Master Ting answered in a deep bass.

"An excellent choice!" said Chi with a snap of the fingers. And the servant smoothly but at the same time nimbly poured bright pink nectar into two wine glasses.

For a few minutes, the mages savored the beverage in silence.

"Marvelous!" the redhead rendered a verdict.

"Incidentally, it's a year five!" Chi said with self-satisfaction. "And that, as you know, was the best year for grapes of this varietal!"

From there the men started in on the fine foods, which made my mouth involuntarily fill with saliva.

"What do you think of the young Corwin?" Ting asked first.

"A stubborn dunderhead," Chi answered flippantly with a wave of the hand. "His late father was marked by greater prudence."

"I must disagree with you on that account."

"I wonder if the Bear and the Boar have begun plucking his feathers yet."

"According to reports I've heard, Corwin has begun sieging Orchus," the redhead said.

"That means the trap will slam shut any day now. And what about the Order? Have they decided to support him?"

Master Ting shook his head.

"He's too restive."

"On whom then will they confer the baronial crown?" Master Chi asked, intrigued.

"A nephew of the elder Corwin — a very quiet and timid young man," the redhead answered profoundly.

"Ugh," Chi breathed a short sigh, shaking his head. "A little mind control could solve this issue."

The redhead took a heavy sigh.

"I do not agree. In fact, it would complicate things significantly. The courtiers would raise a stink, then it would be the events of two-hundred years ago all over again. We were driven to the brink of extinction as it was. And don't you forget that every little baron out there aspires to unlock the mana supply."

Chi just sighed in silence and took a deep swallow from his glass, which was immediately refilled by the lightning-fast swipe of a servant's hand.

The mages fell silent again, each thinking about something else. Master Chi started the discussion back up. Squinting, he turned to Ting:

"Well old bean, that can't be why you came to visit, right?"

"Indeed, my friend! You are absolutely right. I come bearing bad tidings for you."

Chi gave a careless chuckle.

"The old worm got another itch?"

"You'd do well not to speak that way!" Ting objected. "And your flippant manner frightens me! Beyond that, you are disrespecting the council of the Order of our barony. There were mages sympathetic to you before, but your Bug-may-care attitude has driven them all away. I believe I am the only friend you have left. I remember perfectly who saved my hide back in that tomb."

Chi gave a kind smile and patted the redhead on the shoulder.

"I know, my friend. That is why you are here drinking wine with me today. And as for our elders, here is what I have to say — that ditherer occupies a seat which does not belong to him. I was supposed to be head of our cell. You know that perfectly well!"

"Yes," nodded the redhead. "But he was appointed by the Five with the Grand Magister at their head! Their will is our law!"

Slamming his palm loudly on the tabletop, Chi hopped up nervously. His face went crimson, his lips screwed up into an evil grimace and his manicured hands balled up into fists so tight his knuckles turned chalky.

"Everyone knows Magister Shitang forced that dunderhead on us! That old snake was consolidating positions by placing his people in elderships throughout the Kingdom!"

Paying no mind to his friend's shouting, Ting responded calmly:

"That's just where your problem lies, old bean. You've grown so accustomed to creating soulless marionettes that you can no longer stand being subordinate to anyone. You are too proud to be an elder, too independent. And as a rule, with time, those who run afoul of our leaders become a dangerous hindrance. That's why I am here. To warn you. You've pressed on too many old sore spots. The council was saying so openly at their last meeting."

My heart aflutter, I was taking in all the information. If my father could hear what these people were saying, he'd be no less shocked than me. I had guessed this world was not as straightforward as I was led to believe. But not to this degree...

Meanwhile, their conversation was ongoing.

After the quick flare-up, Master Chi got himself together just as quickly and sat back down at the table. Smiling broadly and, raising a glass, he said:

"Let's drink, old bean. And to the abyss with all these scoundrels!"

The redhead chuckled sadly and raised a glass.

His goblet drained, Chi gave a sweep of the arm and every last servant left the room. When the door closed behind the last one, Chi walked right up to his fellow mage. Squinting conspiratorially, he began to speak:

"My friend, I no longer give a damn about becoming an elder of our back-woods Barony. My aim is to climb higher. I want to become Great Magister! And to do that, I will need trusted associates. I will need people like you, my friend!"

Ting frowned and glanced suspiciously at his friend. I could see perfectly well that the redheaded mage did not like what he was hearing.

"Chi, have you lost your mind?! Those words alone could get us turned to ash and scattered in the wind! You live among your puppets without a care in the world, but I have successors to think about!"

"Don't you worry about a thing, my friend," the master of the house answered in a calm voice. "I have a plan. And you know perfectly well that once I set myself a goal — I always get what I'm after. I have discovered a way to make many influential people dependent on me. You simply cannot imagine the kind of perspectives that have opened up before me! And if you follow me, you can share in my success!"

"Explain yourself," Ting asked, his right brow arched.

Master Chi stood easily from the table, rubbing his hands together and smiling intriguingly, then said:

"Why explain? Better to show you! Shen!"

"Yes, milord," came the blackblood, on the lookout as ever.

I must give the redheaded mage his due. He didn't even shudder when Shen appeared. And no surprise. He is level forty-three after all. Tricks such as these are no novelty to him.

"Is everything ready for the crossing over?" asked Chi.

"Yes, lord," Shen answered phlegmatically.

"Where are you planning to go?" Ting inquired.

Chi, still smiling happily, replied:

"Well, first of all, not me — we. And second, it's better to see a thing one time than hear about it seven."

Ting chuckled rakishly. Getting up from the table, he reached for a flagon.

"Well, in that case! I'm not going anywhere without wine!"

They laughed together and, embracing at the shoulder, headed to leave.

* * *

Thirty minutes later, we were on a small plaza in the manor's internal courtyard. Other than the two mages, Shen and myself, there were four warriors laden with bales, baskets and boxes of rations. The fourth and healthiest was carrying a bulging barrel on his right shoulder.

When Ting saw the food and wine, he smacked his lips in delight and took a swallow from his rather emptied flagon. Wiping his lips on a pure white kerchief, he finally saw me and frowned in surprise:

"Is that bag of bones coming with us, too?"

I was standing at a slight distance. On my back, a small pack of zero food. In my hands, a familiar raspberry-red little chest. Chi handed it to me with a smirk before leaving his study. May the abyss swallow him up!

The master gave a careless wave and, with a surreptitious wink to me, answered:

"Pay him no mind, Ting! The boy is carrying delicacies for us to eat."

The redhead shrugged his shoulders and got back to slurping at his flagon.

Meanwhile, Chi pulled a small scroll out of his pocket.

"A portal?" Ting asked with slight surprise. "Are we going far? I promised the missus I'd be back by dinner."

"Don't you worry, old bean. We'll have you back in fine form."

At that, Master Chi activated the scroll, which turned into thousands of glowing little sparks and dispersed, leaving behind a blurry arch the size of a normal door.

"Okay then, let's go!" the master proclaimed, walking first into the portal.

And the redheaded mage followed calmly behind him, as if taking a relaxed stroll. A moment later the rest followed. Meanwhile, Shen pushed me lightly on the back.

In the space of a second, we were transported to a stone platform on the tip of a huge rock. The wind was blowing from all directions and it was so cold and piercing I felt like the marrow in my bones was about to freeze solid. Ting's calm showed a crack.

"Where'd you drag us off to now?" he exclaimed, looking around in alarm.

"Old bean!" Embracing him by the shoulders, Chi was laughing uncontrollably, joyfully. "Don't you worry yourself so! We're merely in the Wastes! I put lots of effort into creating this place! And today, you are the first to look upon my creation! I call it the Hive. Down there is my entire collection. It took me a long time to gather all these specimens! Rare magical beasts from all corners of our world! And now, this location will provide me a level of power you cannot even dream of! This is where the first stage of my ascent to the summit will begin! And I am offering to let you share a portion of my future might!"

I turned my head, stunned and saw nothing but endless steppe in every direction. But what scared me most of all was whatever was resting there, in the bowels of the cliff. I finally realized what the nutty bastard had in store for me.

"This way!" Chi said, pointing to a wide opening in the cliffside.

But by the looks of things, Ting wasn't going anywhere. He shook his head and said contritely:

"They were right... You are losing your judgment and becoming dangerous! You spit on our laws and rules! And that cannot be! You make people into puppets and treat the nobility with arrogance. Your behavior is drawing too much attention to our Order!"

Chi opened his mouth in surprise and looked at his fellow mage.

"What are you saying my friend? My mind is clearer than ever before! It runs like clockwork!"

But the redheaded mage wasn't listening anymore. He breathed a heavy sigh and quietly said:

"Forgive me..."

A glowing object suddenly appeared in his hand. One sharp swipe and I found myself in a daze and watching another portal open. And gradually, figures enshrouded in black cloaks began to emerge from it.

There were seven of them. All over level sixty.

As soon as the portal disappeared, they surrounded Master Chi.

It all happened so fast I didn't even have time to blink an eye.

"Ting!" my master cried out in a voice not his own. "What have you done, you old fool?!"

The redhead was no longer looking at his associate, instead moving toward one of the dark figures.

"What took you so long, Ting?" one of the strangers asked calmly, throwing back his hood.

It was a tall bald man with sharp facial features. The powerful gaze of his black eyes stopped on Master Chi. In his turn, covering himself with a semitransparent dome, Chi shouted defiantly:

"You doddering old backstabber! You set this all up?! Why have you brought a pack of Executioners here?! Have you forgotten the law?! You cannot execute me extrajudicially!"

The bald man replied dispassionately:

"Hm... Didn't Ting tell you? The trial has already taken place, and a verdict has been rendered. You have been sentenced to death!"

What happened next felt like a nightmare.

As the old man said his last words, the dark figures lunged toward the reviled mage. With my characteristics, I couldn't quite make out what was happening. It was just too fast-paced.

Gradually conjuring a ball of lilac smoke around his fist with intricate hand movements, Chi gave a curt shout. Shen and the warriors immediately dashed out to meet the attackers.

Suddenly, the earth shook and I heard a loud roar from down below. That must have been the master summoning a specimen from his collection to his aid. But to his great misfortune, help never arrived.

The warriors died first. The Executioners dispatched them like little paper soldiers. Shen held out a bit longer. But he had no way of standing up to opponents almost two times higher level than him. Run through by several icy stakes, he fell at the bald mage's feet like a broken doll.

To be honest, I was surprised. Why hadn't my master ordered me to fight as well? Does he think he can win and is trying to keep me secret to the very end? Now there is a truly calculating bastard.

Master Chi's defensive dome cover was constantly flickering and blinking, but it was still holding out. I saw his amulets, rings and bracelets give a bright flash and fall to dust one after the next.

Finally, he finished casting the spell and tried to use it to strike his attackers. And that was the very moment the old bald man joined the fray. He extended a twig-thin hand toward the condemned mage. A coal-black arrow raced away from his long, dry fingers and, when Chi saw it, he squealed in a voice not his own. My mouth immediately filled with bitter saliva and a slight taste of rot.

Passing unimpeded through the defensive

dome, the arrow entered the mage's chest with a flourish of black. Chi choked on his own scream. His body started jerking in violent convulsions. A tar-black spot appeared where the spell made contact and expanded like an ulcer before my very eyes! A moment later, what was left of Master Chi fell to the ground like a formless sack. And I saw a message:

— Attention! The mental magic you were subjected to has been terminated!

At that very moment, I felt the ground beneath me shudder again. Tearing through the stone flesh of the platform, a gigantic level-thirty spider-like monster crawled out from below. While my former master's Executioners focused on the new opponent, I ran toward a small passage in the cliffside, not wasting any time.

A wail came from above mixed with the cracking of stones and hissing of spells, driving me farther and farther inside the cliff. I activated my amulet and Gorgie appeared, quickly got his bearings and led us forward into the darkness of Master Chi's Hive.

The farther we went down the tunnel, the louder the horrible din, howling, squealing and creaking from all sides became. The inhabitants of the Hive spun out of control after the death of their master.

The hallway quickly came to an end and we

jumped outside. It was a broad terrace. The harn tore off to the opposite edge of it without stopping. A narrow stone stairway started there and stretched to the foot of the mountain.

Meanwhile, the mountain continued to quake and everything was plunged into chaos. Shrieks of pain, snarling, roars of rage — it all mixed together into one deafening howl. I'm afraid to even imagine what was happening inside.

When we reached the middle of the stairway, something small and hairy jumped down on us from above. Not especially caring what it was, I rushed to activate Ram.

The beast flew back like a hairy blob, stunned by the spell. When the monster landed on the sharp outcroppings of rock below, the system immediately told me I had defeated a level-sixteen black biter.

I noted mechanically that it was not a magical creature. And that was a shame. It was an easy victory.

Finally the stairway ended and, not turning back, we ran onto the steppe. The distant roar and thundering of stones followed us for a long while.

With my elevated characteristics, I could run much faster than before. It was a glorious feeling! The cold wind beating right against my face, blowing away the hot tears of joy on my cheeks. We're free!

The harn was constantly telling me we were not alone. The beasts fleeing the Hive were small for the most part as, for the record, were we. Informed by self-preservation instinct, they were driven by a single-minded urge to get as far from their fearsome prison as possible. And twenty minutes later, when the harn sensed no other creatures, we decided to stop at a small ravine for a short breather.

Only then did I realize, when the initial fear had passed, that all that time I'd been carrying Master Chi's raspberry-colored chest.

"Bastard!" I shook a shivering fist menacingly in the direction of the mountain, just visible on the horizon. "Bet you never thought these things would come back to me!"

Spitting on the ground emphatically, I gave a nervous laugh. But it didn't reach the point of hysterics. Gorgie made me get myself together.

I calmed down a bit and opened the top of the box. Alas, to my disappointment it contained no more tablets or esses. But it did contain the monster hunter tokens, blots, potions of satiety and scrolls of fury. I don't know about the tokens, but clearly the mage was planning to give me everything else to help me fight his monsters. Well, at least I made away with something...

I quickly transferred the arsenal items into my ephemeral backpack. But the box was too heavy and bulky, so I threw it into some bushes. I also transferred all the quick-spoiling foods from my new bag into the freshness-preserving backpack.

After that I quickly had a bite to eat and sated my thirst, then we started for the west. If I'm not mistaken, that is the way that will take us to Orchus.

I walked at Gorgie's side, taking in deep breaths of the frosty air of the orcish steppe. I was immeasurably happy! I'm sure I'll remember this smell forever.

The smell of freedom!

CHAPTER 5

ONCE UPON A TIME, in natural science class, our teacher compared the Wastes to an endless sea. I remember guys from better-heeled families exchanging glances when he said that. Every summer they would go to the beaches of the Pearl Sea with their parents and come back overfed and sun-tanned. They looked down on everyone else for being poor. Father promised mom that we would go work on our tans one day, too. But it just was not fated to be. Now I understood that they were setting aside every extra copper coin to purchase artifacts of the Ancients.

At any rate, the only more or less large body of water I'd ever seen before was our Whitlake, which was fed by a wide navigable river called the Whitewater.

But this gave me an approximate idea of what a sea should look like. The wide-openness of the step made a big impression! To me, a person that grew up among houses, the distances were imposing.

But I must note that it was nowhere near endless. To the right, in the north, I could make out a mountain ridge capped with snowy peaks. It stretched along the horizon like the spine of a gigantic monster. To the south, based on the characteristic outlines, there was a forest. The large number of hills and hollows made the steppe look like a giant billowing grayish-yellow tablecloth.

And to think, my older brother Ivar died somewhere in these lands...

Incidentally, the orcish masters of the steppe were nowhere to be seen but, as father loved to say, "the night is young..."

Walking the dry packed ground, I thanked the gods for putting this year's rainy season on hold. Otherwise our journey would have been a true ordeal.

I wasn't cold either. My former master, out of concern for his slave, had picked me out some pretty good equipment for my level zero. And although I may have looked like a ragamuffin before, now it would have been easy to take me for just a normal traveler.

Comfortable pants made of thick fabric, a shirt, a crudely knit sweater, a vest of frayed leather. And an extra special thanks to the mage for the high boots of thick leather and the old hooded jacket of dark-gray sailcloth. But still — may the abyss swallow his soul.

By the middle of the next day, Gorgie led us to the banks of a steppe river. It looked like a gigantic snake curving around hills and stretching ever westward.

Short trees and bushes grew along its banks. We selected a stand of the low trees to set up camp for the night. The deciding factor in our choice of location was a small eddy nearby where the harn smelled fish.

Five minutes later, using the chain lightning, I stunned a large level-four pike. Sitting unmoving amongst the reeds, it was itself there watching for prey. But its hunt ended in misfortune. Today Gorgie will dine on fish.

The harn took a quick bound, dragged the greenish-gray fish on shore and snapped its spine. I also did my part, stabbing the whopper with Dragonfly.

— *You have killed Mottled Pike (4).*

— *Congratulations! You receive:*
— *Experience essence (800).*
— *Stone tablet of Agility.*
— *Stone tablet of Strength.*
— *Stone tablet of Endurance.*
— *Stone tablet of Wisdom.*
— *Stone tablet of Mind.*
— *Stone tablet of Accuracy.*

— Stone tablet of Speed.
— Stone tablet "Fisher."
— Stone tablet "Hunter."

Because I had a backpack full of food, the pike went to the harn. He scarfed it down in a matter of minutes, the glutton. Then he stood perfectly still on shore, watching for the next one.

On an old habit I'd picked up in the caverns, I didn't start a fire. There was no particular need for one, but it could certainly draw unwanted attention.

I activated Lair and looked at my now higher figures with satisfaction.

— Gulper's Lair.
— Level: 1 (0/30).
— Type: Active ability.
— Rarity: Common
— Description:
—A Gulper can create a temporary shelter in an appropriate location such as a secluded cave or hidden amongst large stones. Using magic, it weaves a web around itself which provides both defense and a kind of alarm system.
— Effect:
— Absorbs 500 units of damage.
— Creator is alerted to unauthorized entry.
— +5 life every 20 minutes (while inside)
— +5 mana every 20 minutes (while inside)
— +5 energy every 20 minutes (while inside)

— *Requirements:*
— *Intellect — 6.*
— *Expends 60 mana points.*
— *Note:*
— *Duration: 6 hours.*
— *Radius: 10 feet.*

Before I fell asleep, to Gorgie's enormous delight, we caught another three pikes. The last one was level five and noticeably larger than the rest. Closing my eyes, I smiled. If things kept up this way, we'd replenish our losses soon enough...

But alas, in the morning there were no fish.

"Hrn..." Gorgie commented, licking his lips sadly.

"Don't worry, brother," I reassured him. "You can have some of my chow for breakfast, and I'm sure we'll catch something else on the way."

We decided to walk along the river. Among the gray trees and bushes, we were harder to spot. Honestly, our biggest problem other than tracks could be the birds. Spooked by our approach, large flocks would all take off into the sky at once, revealing our location. All we could do was hope the local birdies' behavior wouldn't draw the attention of something more dangerous.

And speaking of danger, in the middle of the day, I bore witness to a nasty scene while hidden in some bushes with my heart fluttering. A gigantic level-thirty-five beast that looked like a centipede, was clacking its pointed feet very rapidly and flying down the opposite shore.

That big monster could hardly have been a steppe native. Obviously it was one of the specimens from Master Chi's fearsome collection. Fortunately, it didn't notice us. But a small group of gray antlered animals nibbling grass a hundred yards from the river weren't so lucky. The beast smelled fresh meat and tore off toward them like a lightning bolt.

Taking advantage of the opportunity and trying not to make too much noise, we ran far away from the bloody slaughter. The shrieks of pain from the animals the monster caught followed us for a long time.

Alas, no matter how we tried to avoid unpleasant encounters, the Great System had plans of its own. Nearer evening, the harn told me there was something fast and dangerous on our trail.

My now fairly decent figures allowed me to keep up an increased pace for a while, but still I couldn't compete with the speed and endurance of our clearly high-level pursuer.

We decided to stop and fight while my supplies still had something in them. We chose a small hill overgrown with dry shrubs for the purpose. I was hoping the elevation might give us an advantage.

I activated Lair and Muckwalker's Defensive Aura, then took a Blot out of my backpack, my hands shivering with anxiety. All told, my magical shields could absorb three thousand five hundred points of damage.

Okay, ready for battle!

I didn't notice the smoothly moving red silhouette right away. The dry steppe grass and bushes made excellent camouflage for the monster on our trail. I'm quite sure that if the harn weren't at my side, I wouldn't have known this predator was coming.

I looked closely. It was clearly a feline of some kind. Honestly, it was nearly double Gorgie's size. Thick fur on its chest, wide paws and long saber-like fangs on its upper jaws — it looked a lot like the southern tiger that lived in my hometown menagerie.

Another few longs jumps and I could see its level — twenty-eight!

Not beating around the bush, it rushed on the attack and was immediately sent flying back with a Ram. Despite the fact I used a scroll of fury, I was unable to do any damage. Seemingly, the orange tiger's thick fur gave it a bonus to defense.

— *You have attacked Firepaw (22)!*
— *You have dealt 0 damage!*

In a few jumps, Gorgie was on top of the beast. Based on the figures, the harn's blows were doing at most thirty percent of its total damage. But that was plenty.

Not drawing things out, I activated eel

lightning while the harn continued dealing his powerful blows. Gradually, the furry side of the immobilized beast turned into a smear of blood. I could easily make out the protruding white rib bones. And so of course I aimed my next few blows there.

Thanks to the mana crystal, which I'd filled to the brim, I could just activate ram after ram, not letting the firepaw so much as move.

— *You have killed Firepaw (22).*

— *Congratulations! You receive:*
— *Experience essence (4400).*
— *Gold tablet of Intellect.*
— *Silver tablet (10).*

— *Attention! The Higher Powers have taken note of your accomplishment! You have defeated 5 magical beings more than 10 levels higher than you!*
— *Congratulations! You receive:*
— *Experience essence (2000).*
— *Silver tablet (10).*

— *Attention! The Higher Powers smile upon you! You have replicated the feat of Err the Cold! You defeated a magical creature more than twenty levels higher than you, dealing minimal damage and not allowing your opponent to land a single blow!*
— *Congratulations! You receive:*

— Experience essence (2000).
— Iridescent Tablet "Firepaw" (1).

Raising both hands over my head, I jumped for joy. Another iridescent! Random the Just must have seen my suffering!

Hm... So why did it only count five victories? After all, I'd killed more magical creatures than that. Actually, I think I know what the problem is. Seemingly, the Great System doesn't count ghostly otherworldly creatures the same way...

Gorgie, eviscerating the orange tiger's carcass, ignored my "happy coldune" dance.

— Attention! Your pet has discovered:
— Pearl Firepaw Fang (2).

Reading the brief message, I grew intrigued and walked up to the dead animal's hefty noggin. So, what do we have here?

Pearl Firepaw Fang.
— Type: Universal ingredient.
— Rarity: Epic.
— Requirements:
— Butchery — 22.

With a heavy sigh, I gave the requirements another look. Level twenty-two butchery! Well, what can I do about that? This isn't exactly the red megabat eye with "common" rarity that Gorgie discovered before our battle with the thorntail. Here there were a whole two fangs labeled "epic!" These things could probably fetch a pretty penny!

Command Gorgie to snap them off? But that could ruin the valuable resource... Although, on the other hand, we were going to lose it regardless... Scratching the back of my head, I waved a hand and glanced into my ephemeral backpack. I have an iridescent tablet lying there unused, but I'm already thinking about these fangs...

— *Experience essence (15000).*
— *Iridescent Tablet "Firepaw" (1).*
— *Gold tablet of Intellect. (1)*
— *Monster Hunter Token (535).*
— *Hunter's Fury (13).*
— *Blot (10).*
— *Small Potion of Satiety (14).*
— *Ferocious Harn Summoning Amulet.*
— *Silver tablet (25).*
— *Stone tablet of Agility (4).*
— *Stone tablet of Strength (4).*
— *Stone tablet of Endurance (4).*
— *Stone tablet of Wisdom (4).*
— *Stone tablet of Accuracy (4).*
— *Stone tablet of Speed (4).*
— *Stone tablet "Fisher" (4).*
— *Stone tablet "Hunter" (4).*
— *Stone tablet of Mind (4).*

My heart aflutter, I activated the iridescent tablet. I open the "skills and abilities" section. Alas, none of them are magical. And every single one is "anatomically incompatible." What a shame... Oh well. There's still my favorite section — "spells."

— **Flaming Paw.**
— *Level: 0. (0/20)*
— *Type: Spell.*
— *Rarity: Epic*
— *Description:*
— *Devastating magical fire enshrouds the predator's paw.*
— *Effect:*
— *When the spell is active, damage dealt with the hands/paws is increased by 100 points.*
— *After successful attacks, a Weak Magical Burn is left on target's body.*
— **Weak Magical Burn**:
— *Removes 10 life points from target every 10 minutes.*
— *Duration: 30 minutes.*

— *Requirements:*
— *Intellect — 9.*
— *Expends 100 mana points.*

Rubbing my hands together in satisfaction, I close the description. One more epic spell for my arsenal!

Now I have to decide where to spend the ten

points...

I looked at all the firepaw's characteristics. Ugh! I want them all. Knowing I can't have them stings! But still I have to make a choice. First I'll go through my main ones.

Health... I'll bring that up — plus one hundred life into my supply... That brings the total to two hundred ten. No more than one hit for some level-eight giant rat. One hundred or two hundred — at this stage it doesn't make much difference. Yes, every point could be the deciding factor, but I also shouldn't forget that I have other defenses as well.

Intellect then? My mana supply has two hundred and some points. And with the crystal on top of that I'm well over a thousand. No. I'll leave that alone for now. But bringing up my mana regain speed would come in very handy. I make a mental note — Wisdom.

If I double my energy supply, I'll have more endurance, but not so much that I'll be able to keep up with high-level opponents. They'll still have much more energy than me. I could travel for longer. No doubt about that. But for fairness' sake I should note that the current state of affairs is working great for us. Neither Gorgie nor I are big fans of traveling long distances. Frequent breaks have always been more our speed.

Invest in Strength or Agility? Or maybe I should unlock Speed?

Or improve Mind? With the characteristics

from my button, I'd be up to fifteen points. I wonder what Master Chi's Mind score was. Or Ting's, for that matter.

The idea of improving that characteristic caught me hook line and sinker. The longer I considered it, the more confident I became. The Mind branch was always far out of reach to mere mortals. I now had the unique chance to take a peek beyond that fifteen-point "ceiling."

Weighing all the pros and cons one last time, I took a heavy sigh... If I don't try, I'll never find out.

— *Would you like to increase the Mind characteristic by 10 points?*

Yes.

— *Mind characteristic successfully improved.*
— *Present value including all item bonuses: 15.*

After reading that, I listened to my feelings. I wonder how much smarter I just became. I took a look around. For some reason I sniffed the air. I turned my head toward Gorgie, who was scarfing down meat. Hm... No changes... Looks like I should have unlocked Wisdom after all.

With a heavy sigh, I wanted to take a peek into my bag when suddenly, out of the corner of my eye, I noticed a flickering blue spot on the firepaw's fangs.

Intrigued by the strange occurrence, I walked

up closer and again opened the saber-like tooth's description.

> **Pearl Firepaw Fang.**
> — *Type: Universal ingredient.*
> — *Rarity: Epic.*
> — *Requirements:*
> — *Butchery — 22.*
> — *Additional information:*
> — *Being a creature that uses fire magic, the firepaw is highly sought-after by rare-ingredient hunters. Its fangs are of particular value, more specifically Black (legendary), Pearl (epic), White (rare) and Yellow (common).*
> — *Recommendations:*
> — *If you manage to find a firepaw fang, the first place you should take it is a knowledgeable alchemist — they're sure to give you a good price.*

Once finished reading, I gulped loudly. So then, that's what changed... Fifteen points had an interesting effect. But what if that's not all? I took a look around. I have to find a good place to hide the creature's head. What if I manage to find my way back here?

When I realized what I was considering, I chuckled. Return to the depths of the Wastes for the sake of two measly fangs? No thanks. I'd need something a bit more consequential to do something that crazy. But still, I might as well hide the monster's head just in case...

THE WASTES

✳ ✳ ✳

It's been two days since the battle with the firepaw. Over that time, we were fishing and hunting for local birds with quite some success. Gradually, my ephemeral backpack was filling up with essences and tablets.

We saw two monsters from the Hive. Their distant silhouettes were easily visible on the horizon. I was afraid to even imagine their levels. Neither Gorgie nor I had any sort of desire to actually meet one of those titans face to face. Even the chance of lucking our way into iridescent tablets was not tempting. Now that I was free, I was savoring every moment of life like never before. And Gorgie, by the way, was in complete solidarity.

We set up camp in a small glade. We purposely looked for a spot where we could do some morning fishing. But alas, I was just not able to get any sleep. Gorgie told me a few enemies were coming long before their arrival. We were slowly being surrounded on three sides.

"Weak. Sluggish. Two-legged. Not like you," the harn told me calmly.

Hm... Looks like the masters of the Wastes have come to pay us a visit.

There were five orcs. Two came from the right, two from the left and one up the center.

I asked Gorgie again whether anyone was coming up from the riverside, and was told no.

"Then let's give them a little surprise," I whispered into the cat's ear in a shaky voice. "Walk around them quietly from behind. I'll distract them."

With a satisfied snort, Gorgie dissolved in the bushes silent as a shadow. To be honest, I was shivering pretty hard. In Orchus, tales of fearsome orcs were used to frighten disobedient children. And now a small group of them had me surrounded on nearly all sides.

I could feel my knees trembling a bit. My heart was beating frantically like a wounded bird. When the harn let me know he was in position and ready to attack, it felt like a stone fell off my shoulders.

Filling my lungs with icy night air, I made a loud appeal to the darkness, trying to put on the most authentic imitation of fear I could muster. As an aside, I did a great job. Considering my state...

"W-who's there?! I beg you, please don't hurt me! I'm just a peaceful traveler!"

The shivering childlike voice of terror did the trick. Out of the darkness I heard snickering from several directions. It was at once gleeful and predatory.

Then gaunt slumping figures started to appear out of the bushes. Their stubby tusked faces were easy to make out in the light of the moon.

Levels ranging from nine to eleven. Their loincloths and vests were made of dark animal fur.

They were draped head to toe in bones, fangs and feathers. Two archers. The rest of them were brandishing curved scimitars.

Just when I wanted to start the attack, something happened that made me falter. The orcs started speaking in their crude barking language, and a curious message appeared before my eyes:

— *Attention! Your Mind score is high enough to activate the "Language of the Orcs!"*
— *Would you like to activate it?*

When I agreed, my vision went slightly dim... And a second later I could understand every word!

"... Doesn't much look like a runaway slave," the bald orc to the right barked.

The tallest and broadest-shouldered one replied. His veiny neck was adorned with the highest number of tusk-and-tooth necklaces.

"Who cares! Maybe he's not a slave. But he will be."

That was clearly meant to be a joke because they all started snickering shrilly. Their vile laughter sent a brigade of ants marching down my spine.

The lowest level of them, clearly the youngest, waved his scimitar rakishly and happily exclaimed:

"This is the easiest slave I've ever taken!"

"And the most worthless," one of the archers barked back. "Look at his level. Even a steppe gremlin would be more use!"

Cartoonishly radiating servility, I shuddered in fear. And again that laughter that chills to the bone...

"Okay Khat, drag him back to camp!" the big guy commanded and, losing all interest, turned his back to me. And all the others did so as well, except for the young one.

He twisted up his face into a fearsome countenance and started in my direction. He obviously wanted to scare me even more. No sense waiting for a better opportunity.

The young orc's scary expression stretched out in surprise when he saw the flickers of lilac on my right hand. It was a comical sight. A ram followed by an eel lightning laid all five of them low. Then Gorgie silently broke the orcs' spines and tore into their throats, starting from the oldest and biggest. I asked him not to kill the youngest and just keep him pinned down.

I quickly disarmed him and crouched at his side, waiting for the stun effect to expire.

"Do you speak my language?" I asked the orc, now terrified and staring at me. Where was that fearsome slaver now? A telltale smell struck my nose. By the looks of things, this steppe warrior had soiled himself in fear.

"Yes!" he said, nodding very quickly.

"Are there any more of your warriors nearby?" I asked while the harn slightly extended his claws, poking the tips into the orc's chest.

"N-no, there's nobody in the camp..."

"And which way is the camp?" I asked. But I didn't have to ask. Gorgie could find it in two shakes.

"O-over there," the orc said, motioning north with his eyes and sniffling with a broken nose, flattened by my Ram.

"Who are you?" I asked my next question.

"We're from the Clan of the Gray Mountain. This is our territory. Our main encampment is to the north, three days' journey from here."

"And what were you doing here?"

"We were sent to track down runaway slaves," the young orc answered and shuddered. When he mentioned the slaves, my facial expression must have changed.

"Is it far to human lands?" I asked, my heart skipping a beat.

"Thirty days' journey," the orc answered after a bit of thought.

When I heard that, I took a heavy sigh and asked a clarifying question:

"Do you mean the Western Baronies?"

"Yes," the orc nodded.

"Good," I said. "Now tell me something about your lands and neighbors."

The captive quickly brought me up to speed on local affairs. Of course, I wasn't going to believe everything. But I had no alternative, so I'd have to make do.

When the orc finished, I squinted and looked him in the eyes:

"And one final question. What were you planning to do to me?"

The tusked bastard's little eyes got all shifty and he quickly responded:

"We saw you and figured you were lost. We wanted to help. Let you sit by our fire. Give you some food. Then show you the way back to your people."

"I see," I nodded as I stood up.

The orc wanted to say something else, but Gorgie snapped his neck in a lightning-fast blow.

"Let's look through the loot and go pay their camp a little visit," I said to the harn. "I just know this valiant slaver was lying to us. I can feel it in my bones."

CHAPTER 6

E VERY ORC I KILLED netted me two silver tablets. Plus ten thousand esses for the whole battle. Beyond that, when looting their corpses, I found sixty-three copper and fourteen silver coins. The orcs were not carrying any esses or tablets.

As an aside, the money we found was not only from my homeland. The backs of a few of their silver coins depicted a different profile, which I recognized as the dreaded Steel King. His daughter was slated to marry our Prince Albert. There has been buzz about their long-awaited engagement for the whole last year. Even my father had a positive view of their union. He insisted that their marriage would significantly strengthen our kingdoms.

Hm... At any rate, I don't give a crap about the personal lives of the royals. Much the way none of them give a crap about me. The only thing connecting me to them is the fact that their faces are depicted on the coins in my pocket.

I bundled up the orcs' scythes, bows, knives, arrows and a few pieces of equipment and dragged over to the riverbank. We noticed the small abandoned den of some creature on its slope yesterday evening. That was where I stashed the bundle of captured weapons. On my way up the bank, a message appeared before my eyes:

— You have created a simple hiding spot.
— Congratulations! You receive:
— Experience essence (15).
— Clay tablet of Mind.
— Clay tablet "Hiding Spot Maker."
— Clay tablet of Observation.

I wondered why the Great System didn't react the same way when we hid the firepaw's head in the bushes. There were two epic fangs there, after all. Maybe it was because we didn't actually get the fangs out?

Hmm... There's no fooling the Great System. Back in the caverns, I tried several times to make false hidings spots with all my stuff but, alas, there was never a reaction. Clearly the primary deity of our world had a nuanced understanding of my intentions.

Walking behind the harn, I started thinking about the belongings of the cartmen or warriors who attacked the forest farmstead. I could have hidden them as well. Along with Master Chi's box, which I'd simply tossed into some bushes. It was probably worth something. That settles it! From now on, I will hide everything I can't carry.

A few hours later, Gorgie brought me to the orcish encampment. I could smell the acrid smoke before we came near, but I never saw any light from the fires. Only when I got up to an acceptable distance did I realize what the issue was. The steppe warriors were hunkered down in a shallow gully, which kept their small bonfire concealed.

So that asshole did lie to me. Gorgie had already caught the scent of two beings. The first was definitely an orc, while the second... Hm... Something very puny and very weak.

I carefully crawled to the edge of the gulley. Through the branches of a dry shrub, I had a good view of the whole thing.

A thin level-eight orc was sitting on a stone and greedily gnawing on a small bone. The disgustingly loud chomping made me wince.

Just a step away from him, shifting awkwardly from foot to foot, there was a small fluffy creature with big ears. Its tiny hands folded on its chest and a plaintive grimace on its face, it was watching the orc's every move. Based on the frequent gulping, the kid was very hungry.

A scrawny little body, level three, looks inoffensive. I don't think he's gonna give us any trouble.

The orc, still scarfing down food, gave a loud

dry retch. Just then, a small chunk of either meat or bone flew out of his mouth. The fluff-ball immediately tried to attack the fallen food, but he wasn't fast enough. The orc's crooked leg gave a sharp jerk and the little creature, its ears flapping comically, flew back several feet.

The orc immediately gave a vile chortle. I meanwhile winced again. Apparently they all laugh the same. The poor fluff-ball meanwhile slowly picked himself up and stumbled back over to the bonfire. Only then did I notice the loop of crude rope around his neck.

"Mee-ee..." the kid squeaked woefully.

— Attention! Your Mind score is high enough to activate the "Language of the Gremlins!"
— Would you like to activate it?

So that's what you are! Sure, let's activate it.

"You'll be fine!" the orc barked maliciously in reply. "I'm not happy with you. Today you go hungry."

The gremlin gave a sad sigh and lowered his little head in sorrow. His wide pointed ears drooped like two gray little leaves. Tears were welling up in the corners of his big eyes.

"Alright, brother," I whispered to the harn. "Let's take this babysitter down."

"Hrn," Gorgie agreed and smoothly bolted forward.

The orc, knocked over by a Ram, smacked

loudly against the gulley slope and stopped cold, his eyes staring fearfully at his approaching scaly demise.

— *You have killed Steppe Orc (8).*

— *Congratulations! You receive:*
— *Experience essence (1600).*
— *Silver tablet (2).*

The gremlin squeaked in fear and tried to run, but the harn blocked his path. The little one, shivering slightly, squeezed himself up into a ball and covered his little snout with his ears.

"Hey!" I called out quietly once I was down in the gulley. "Don't be afraid!"

The sound of my voice made the gremlin shudder and slowly raise his head. There was a look of mistrust and surprise in his light-gray eyes. He glanced at Gorgie, who was peacefully licking his lips, then back at me. His already large eyes grew even larger.

"Do you understand my language?" I asked, figuring it unwise to display my newly acquired knowledge of the gremlin tongue.

The fluffball nodded and quietly answered: "Yes..."

"Was that orc alone?" I asked.

The gremlin shook his head rapidly and answered:

"No. Five of our warriors went out onto the

steppe. They should be back soon."

"They won't be coming back," I grumbled. Actually, props to the kid — he was being honest with me. Seemingly he didn't like the orcs either.

"Hrn!" Gorgie called. He was standing next to a pile of garbage and sniffing loudly.

"Interesting," I muttered and headed in that direction, not letting the big-eared pipsqueak out of my sight. When I saw what the harn had found, I laughed with delight.

"Well, would you look at that? These guys run a pretty tight ship! They found our firepaw head and brought it to their camp!"

They must have been after us a long time.

"Hryrk is the one who found the monster head," the gremlin quietly informed me. "He's a great warrior!"

"Uh, I think you might be getting ahead of yourself calling him a great warrior," I snorted. "But that your Hryrk had a splendid nose for other peoples' stuff is indisputable."

"So, you killed the monster?" the gremlin guessed.

"Well, we did," I added some clarity.

"Hrn!" Gorgie confirmed.

The big-eared kid's eyes went amusingly wide and he looked admiringly from me to the harn and back.

"Listen," I decided to change topic. "You must be very hungry."

The gremlin nodded very quickly.

"Do they have any food left?" I asked.

"Yes," he answered.

"Then let's eat and, in the meantime, you can tell me about yourself and these warriors. Then I'll let you go. Deal?"

For the first time, the gremlin gave a timid smile.

We sat at the fire waiting for the poor thing to eat his fill, then I started to ask questions:

"So, what's your name?"

"Mee," the big-eared kid answered with a full mouth.

"Alright Mee. How did you learn my language?"

"The Clan of the Gray Mountain has many slaves from the west," Mee answered eagerly. "I have been hearing and speaking it for a long time."

"I see," I nodded. "Is the main encampment far from here?"

"Eight days' journey."

"And what were these six doing here?"

"They were sent to track down runaway slaves."

Good. The things I was hearing from the gremlin and young orc were lining up.

"Could the slaves really have made it this far?" I asked with mistrust in my voice.

"No," the gremlin shook his head. "We found their remains six days ago. Some beast tore them to shreds."

After saying that, the kid shuddered.

"Then why are you way out here, so far from your main encampment?"

"We were on our way back when Hryrk saw some human footprints on the riverbank. They were fresh, so the warriors decided to give chase."

I nodded thoughtfully. Seems like everything is coming together.

"Okay, enough about that. Now the next question... Who are you and why are you with them?"

"I am a slave of Hryrk, the leader of the squadron."

"You're not a slave anymore," I corrected. "Did you not get a message saying the mind control was broken?"

"No," the gremlin shook his head. "I was not bound mentally."

"So it was an oath?" I asked.

"No."

"If you were not bound by any oath or psychic magic, why didn't you run away?" I asked, struck.

The kid sighed.

"I was born a slave. I am very weak. I'd never make it on the steppe. I've seen others try to run away. They were stronger than me, but they were always brought back. And just so you know, the orcs actually celebrate when slaves run away. They send young warriors out to catch them. It's a kind of test of their mettle. But it happens very rarely. Gremlin-kind has been living in slavery for very many years. We no longer remember what it means to be free..."

I frowned. That was a new one on me. To live voluntarily in slavery? Nope. Not the life for me.

"And what do they make you do?" I asked, even though I already knew.

"Work, gather experience essences and tablets," the gremlin answered, shrugging his shoulders. "Then surrender all the loot to my master."

Hm... How familiar...

"Okay then," I said. "Now you are free and may do whatever you wish. But before you leave, swear an oath that you didn't see us."

Maybe it was just me, but I thought I saw a grimace of fear on the gremlin's little snout. He glanced toward the darkened steppe cautiously.

Hmm... A strange situation. I set him free, but the former slave wasn't especially happy about it.

I interrogated the gremlin a bit more about his former masters and decided I'd heard enough. Time to get out of here. The harn is acting impatient too. But first I need to look through all the loot. Although...

"Listen Mee, pick up all the most valuable items in this camp and bring them here."

The gremlin eagerly tore off and started digging through the orcs' bags. A little while later, a small mountain of stuff had grown up at my feet starting with a scimitar and ending with bone-and-tusk orcish necklaces.

There were also separate stacks of copper and

silver coins. Alas, there were no tablets or esses. Although Mee may have just hidden them for himself. After dumping all the coins into my backpack, I sifted through the bone pile disgustedly with my foot then asked with suspicion in my voice:

"Weren't there any esses or tablets?"

That made the gremlin shake his head and answer:

"No! I swear!"

Reading the system's confirmation, I nodded in satisfaction — another point for honesty.

"What are these tusks and bones you've brought me?"

"Every orcish warrior wears jewelry like this. It shows how many enemies an orc has killed. The more kills, the higher their respect in the clan," Mee quickly explained.

"I see," I said and waved a hand:

"You can keep them if you like."

The gremlin started turning his head in fear.

"What's the matter?" I asked, baffled.

"You defeated the orcs they belonged to. They're yours by right. Only you may take the honor and glory for defeating such great warriors. Beyond that, you will be challenged to duels by the families of the orcs you bested, because killing an orc makes you a blood enemy of their entire family."

"Well, in that case," I said carelessly. "I'll have to hide them."

I'm not exactly raring to go on a walk through the main encampment of the Clan of the Gray Mountain with these bone garlands around my neck. As a matter of fact, the farther I get from there the better.

But I have no idea what to do with this firepaw head. It seems to be following us. Although...

"Listen, Mee, you have the Butchery skill?"

"Sure," the gremlin nodded. "But it's just level two. Hryrk was taking this head to the main encampment so one of the hunters could help him get the valuable fangs out."

"What a pity," I said with a heavy sigh, standing to my full height and adding:

"Welp, I've gotta go. If you like, you can take some of these weapons. As for you, I suggest you get as far from this place as possible. There are many dangerous beasts on the steppe right now and they have excellent senses that can lead them to any source of smoke or blood."

The poor thing stood there not budging. His ears, big and wide like burdock leaves, were quivering slightly. A look of fear was plastered on his gray eyes. I felt truly sorry for the gremlin. Essentially, I was the reason for his unenviable position.

Yes, Mee was a slave, but it was relatively safer for him with the orcs. Although, on the other hand, was I just gonna kill him? So I left the temporary camp with contradictory feelings.

Taking him with me seemed unwise. Who's to say what this sweet looking creature had in his mind? Who could guarantee that my throat wouldn't be slit while I slept? What if all his fear was just for show?

When I was up the slope of the gulley, I heard a whining squeak behind me. I turned around. Mee was standing with his little hands pressed to his heart and crying.

"Mee-ee-ee!" he squeaked, and a strange system message appeared before my eyes.

— Attention! Mee the gray gremlin would like to become your familiar!

— Important! Once you agree, you will gain a family member who will be loyal to you for life! Remember! You must care for him and keep him safe!

When I read that message, I glanced at the gremlin in surprise. Oh gods! There was so much hope in his big gray eyes!

I turned to the harn and asked, though I already knew the answer:

"Well, brother, should we take the poor kid with us?"

"Hrn," Gorgie answered affirmatively.

"Alright then," I said and gave my assent.

As soon as I did, the fluffball gave a squeak of joy. Quickly windmilling his little legs, he ran over to me. Joyously embracing my leg, the gremlin breathed a sigh of relief. Bending over slightly, I stroked his fluffy head to reassure him. Okay then... Now we are three.

I hid all the orcs' most valuable things, got the standard hiding spot message and we started off west.

Mee was walking quite jauntily, keeping pace with Gorgie and me. After he became my familiar, I could see his characteristics.

— Steppe Gremlin.

— Name: Mee.

— Level: 3 (0/9000).

— Status: Loyalty to elder family member (permanent).

— Mind: 3/6

— Strength: 3/30

— Agility: 3/30

— Health: 3/30

— Endurance: 3/30

— Life supply: 50/50

— Energy supply: 50/50

— Skills and abilities:

— Butchery: 2/30

— Herbalism: 2/30

— Hunter: 2/30

— Fisher: 2/30

As far as I could tell from his quick retelling of his life's story, he got eleven silver tablets when he was born, which were immediately confiscated by his master. As were all those he earned for levelling up.

In return, they used clays to bring all his available characteristics up to three. And when he'd grown up a bit, he was sent off to work on the steppe. As far as I understood, that was common practice in orcish clans.

The gremlin had actually hit level three just recently, but in that time he'd already unlocked four skills. All the while, Mee was catching bugs, mice, frogs and little minnows. He was also gathering all the plants worth picking at his level. His master's senior slave always kept scrupulous track of everything he earned. Incidentally, he was human.

Everything Mee gathered had to be surrendered to the master's youngest wife at the end of the workday. When the gremlin told me that, my fists unwittingly clenched in rage and the veins in my temple bulged.

Oh well, it's no matter. A lot will be changing in little Mee's life now. And by the way, same goes for me and Gorgie. I imagine we'll have no problem extracting rare resources anymore.

But alas, our good luck is at an end. Based on the dark clouds gathering in the sky, it will downpour today. Seemingly, the rainy season is going to catch up to us nevertheless.

Mee confirmed that it was very dangerous to travel over the steppe at this time of day. Especially along to the Snakelet, which was what the locals called the nearby river.

"When lots of water starts coming down from the sky," the gremlin said. "The Snakelet goes beyond its banks and floods the whole steppe. Then the water cuts off the path west. We'll have to find shelter to wait out the rain."

"Do you know a good place?" I asked.

"Yes," Mee nodded and pointed to the northwest. "Do you see that dark spot?"

"I do."

"That's the Black Hills," he said. "There are lots of dry and spacious caves there."

"Then we should hurry," I declared, quickening my pace. "I think a drop already landed on my head."

It was a struggle, but we made it where he pointed just before the end of the day. The powerful downpour fell down from the sky like a ton of bricks. Add to that the damp icy wind, and we were really tuckered out. In a matter of hours, the rain transformed the steppe into a giant mud puddle.

Mee gave out first. With his little legs and low figures, this was a test he could not overcome. But despite the exhaustion, he was doing his best not to be a burden. And I understood him perfectly.

Strange as it may have been, Gorgie found a

solution. He picked up the gremlin by the nape of his neck like a kitten and, without particular strain, kept moving. Then a few steps later, I suggested an even better solution. I sat Mee on the harn's back and tied him down with a rope to make sure. In short, when our feet finally touched back down on hard stony soil, it was the greatest moment of the day!

The Black Hills greeted us with a strange howl and buzz.

"That's the wind howling," Mee said knowingly. "At first it's scary, but you get used to it..."

We went up and stopped at the entrance to the small cave, then Gorgie told me someone else was nearby. The rain must have been making his sense of smell a bit worse. But thank the gods they didn't catch us off guard.

"Hyenas!" Mee squeaked in a quavering voice when four furry silhouettes appeared from the cave's dark gaping maw.

The level-eight creatures, growling and laughing a vile laugh, came trotting in our direction. They were each about as big as Gorgie. Based on their wet fur, they'd also been caught in the rain and most likely got hunkered down in this cave not long before we arrived.

The gremlin's squeaking only put them on their mettle. After a bit of thinking, they ran forward. It was a lightning-fast attack. All I could do was activate a Ram.

We got lucky — the passage was so narrow all four of the fell beasts got hit. Gorgie slammed into the immobilized beasts' chests and started dealing out powerful blows left and right.

Seeing the cat wouldn't make it in time, I used another Ram and just in case got lightning ready to go. But we didn't need it. A few minutes later, it was all over.

Breathing heavily, we were standing inside the cave over our defeated enemies, not fully understanding the battle was already won. Mee was particularly impressed by the speed of our victory.

"Now I get it!" he shouted in admiration. "You're a Great Shaman!"

I just chuckled, but didn't have the time to respond. At that very moment, the scales on the back of the harn's neck stood on end. I meanwhile tasted rot in my mouth.

A gigantic silhouette eclipsed the cave entrance.

CHAPTER 7

HEAVILY THUMPING its thick legs, into the cave stumbled a creature I was dimly familiar with. Gorgie and I even exchanged astonished glances. Before us was a descendant of an otherworldly monster — a level-thirty Ice Golem. But this one was ten or so levels higher than the ghostly version I tangled with in the caverns. It stood perfectly still, leading its half-blind gaze over the interior of the dark cave and loudly breathing in the scent of the dead hyenas' blood.

Already knowing the ways of this sluggish but very dangerous magical monster, I held the gremlin's mouth shut and commanded a retreat. The optimal decision for the time being was to get as far from this dimwitted but very tough creature as possible.

Slowly, trying not to make any abrupt movements, we stumbled deeper into the cave. The eviscerated hyena carcasses would distract the predator for a time.

The golem's long arms came down almost to the ground. Its broad sloping shoulders, hefty chest and short legs made it somehow reminiscent of an enormous ape.

Its thick ice-gray hide sparkled slightly. A long sharp horn that looked like an icicle stuck out of its narrow forehead. With every powerful exhalation, the area around the creature was enshrouded in a slate-gray cloud of icy vapor. Gorgie and I never figured out the effect of that clearly magical ability before. But my intuition may as well have been screaming that it was better to stay out of that fog.

Apparently we got lucky. The creature didn't notice us. All its attention was wrapped up in tearing the hyena carcasses to shreds.

When made it fifteen steps away from the bloodbath, Gorgie told me there was another way out of the cave. The loud chomping and crunching of bones signaled that the golem was still busy.

A few minutes later, we hopped out of the cave on the other side of the mountain. Exhaling with relief, we exchanged glances. Unlike the harn and I, already accustomed to monsters after the last month, poor Mee was beside himself. A look of horror was frozen in his wide gray eyes. His gaunt chest was heaving. I thought I could even hear his little heart beating.

"Hrn," Gorgie turned his head, motioning to

the right. I looked that direction. Beyond the ledge, I could see the rounded features of the entrance to a different cave. Obeying my request, the harn nimbly scrambled upward and disappeared from view. Not even a minute later, his satisfied snout appeared from behind the stone.

"All clear," I said to Mee, who was clinging to my leg. "We can go up."

Based on the old small bones and dried excrement, a small predator once lived in this cave. Inside it was dry and relatively safe. At the very least, the Ice Golem couldn't reach us for now. As long as it didn't decide to expand the entrance to the small cave.

Alas, there was no wood around, so we couldn't start a fire. And it was a shame. The warmth of a fire couldn't have hurt. After activating lair and removing my wet clothes, I suggested we all eat some food and get some rest.

The next morning greeted us with the same overcast sky and downpour that wouldn't let up even for a minute. I stood on the cliff ledge and took in my fill of the depressing gray steppe, then went back into the depths of our temporary shelter. Hmm, apparently the rainy season was going to be extending out our already long journey by quite a bit.

I sat down next to the sleeping Gorgie. I wanted to doze off as well, but Mee distracted me.

"Here, master," he extended me something, smiling timidly.

Before I looked at what he'd dragged over, I frowned and answered sternly:

"Alright, Mee. Listen up and listen good. I am not your master. And you are not my slave. We are family, you and me. Does that make any sense to you?"

"Yes," the gremlin nodded in fear.

"And don't be afraid of me," I smiled and patted him on the head. "I promise I will never hurt you. Do you understand?"

"Yes, older brother," Mee sighed in relief.

"There we go!" I raised my pointer finger. "That's better. And if you drop the 'older' and just call me 'brother,' or even just 'Eric,' it will be even better!"

"Gotcha, Eric," the boy answered.

"Now there's a good boy!" I gave his shoulder a light pat. "And now, brother, show me what you've got there."

"Here," the gremlin eagerly extended me something again.

I saw three clay tablets and a few experience essences in his little hands. The two clays were standard Strength and Agility. But the third caught my attention.

— *Clay tablet "Rider."*

— *Level: 1.*

— *Category: Skills.*

— *Effect: + 0.1 to current progress in Rider skill.*

— *Weight: None. Takes no space.*

"Where'd you get that from?" I asked.

"I was got it while riding your beast," Mee answered.

"Great!" I smiled.

"I'm glad I could make you happy!" said the gremlin. "Take them!"

Rolling my eyes, I gave my head a terse shake. Several generations of slavery were no laughing matter. Ridding him of all these habits was going to be a prolonged endeavor.

"Have I upset you again?" Mee asked in fear.

"Yes," I nodded. But then, seeing the gremlin's eyes go wide, I hurried to add: "But it isn't your fault, brother. This is the fault of the bastards who held your entire race in slavery for centuries."

"I don't get it," the gremlin shrugged his little shoulders, perplexed.

"With time I'm sure you'll figure it all out," I promised and patiently started explaining:

"Commit this to memory: all the tablets and esses you earn belong to you. But still showing them to me was the right thing to do. It means I can monitor your development and give you advice about the best way to use your loot."

The gremlin considered it briefly, then asked:

"What if I really want to give them to you? If it is my earnest wish? Will you accept them?"

"Of course," I answered. "But I'll give them right back to you. And I'll add some more from my reserves. You see, I am very invested in you becoming strong, agile and stout. And I don't want anyone to be able to kill you."

The boy fell silent, but his happy gaze was more eloquent than any words.

"So you can use those tablets on yourself right now," I said and added. "And hold onto the esses for now. Well, you already know that."

Mee just nodded in silence and got to activating the tablets.

— Attention! Your familiar has unlocked a new skill — "Rider!"
— Present value: 0.1/30

"Congratulations!" I said, giving him a light pat on the back. "You're a rider now! The hard part is over, now we just have to come up with a saddle you can use!"

✳ ✳ ✳

"Hrn," Gorgie commented with dismay on some noise coming from the neighboring cave.

It's morning of the second day. We've been cooped up in this cave the whole time, afraid to stick our noses out. I got my hopes up for nothing — the meat of the hyenas we killed only distracted the golem temporarily. The insatiable beast simply devoured all the unclaimed fare, then sniffed us out and yesterday tried to follow our tracks out of the cave.

But luckily the exit was too big for the horned monstrosity. The rest of yesterday evening and the whole night we sat anxiously listening to the monster trying to break its way out. Our only escape, meanwhile, was to go back down to the ledge and sneak across the cave where the ice giant had set up camp. We couldn't consider going directly down to the foot of the hill. One false move and one of us risked a fearsome death on the sharp stones below.

This morning, fearsome pounding was added to the frustrated roars, shaking the walls. The ice golem was not giving up. In fact, it had moved on to more extreme measures. It was clearly trying to widen the cave exit. Based on the rain of stones and flying dust, it would succeed soon enough. And you don't exactly need to have a mind like a steel trap to realize what that would mean for us.

Once on the ledge, the monster would be able to smell our location. And from there it would only be a few seconds. Our cave was not large, and the golem's arms were long enough to reach us and scarf us down one by one.

"Are we gonna die?!" Mee squeaked with horror in his voice.

"Only if we sit here twiddling our thumbs," I answered.

"But what can we do against such a giant beast?!" the gremlin exclaimed.

"Oh, brother, you can't even imagine how many ways you can find to escape a situation that appears to have no way out on first glance!" I chuckled and Gorgie and I exchanged a meaningful glance.

"I don't think the golem will be leaving empty handed," I continued. "That means the only way to get rid of the monster is to drop it down onto the rocks."

"And how are we gonna do that?!" Mee asked, not comprehending.

"We're gonna make it mad," I said.

"Hmm, are you sure that's a good idea?" the boy asked in fear.

"Yes, brother. It's the right move," I answered. "Once we get it mad, it won't be thinking straight. It will stop being cautious. Beyond that, boring through the narrow passage should sap its energy supply a good amount."

"And then?"

"Then he'll run into this thing," I answered, taking one of the dark brownish spheres out of my backpack.

After the kid read the Blot's description, he gulped loudly.

"But first," I muttered, hiding the sphere. "We have to find out how the golem will react to my offensive spells. I used Ram and Lightning on a copy of a distant relative of his before and, as far as I can remember, it worked perfectly. To tell the truth, though, it only ever sent its icy carcass flying back three feet at most. So we're gonna have to really jam to take this titan down."

Based on the baffled expression on the gremlin's little snout, he wasn't understanding much of what I was saying.

"Okay," I waved a hand and, with a nervous chuckle, added:

"The sooner we get started, the sooner it'll be over."

I gave Gorgie a command to stay put and started off. He wanted to attack the golem himself, but I said no. The harn would have to get close to the beast to hit it. Beyond that, I had my doubts he'd be able to do even minimal damage. The monster's hide just looked too imposing.

And another thing. I shouldn't forget that the monster could cast ice arrows. The cat's scales would hardly be enough to save him from the high-level monster's gigantic icicles. And that ice breath, too... Nope. If anyone was going to be playing on the golem's nerves, it was going to be me.

Trying not to make any noise, I carefully crawled out of our shelter and went down onto the narrow ledge. I slowly crept up to the entrance, which our pursuer had been trying to enlarge for almost an entire day. And by the way, it had stopped making noise. Its energy supply must have been down quite a lot. The golem was taking a breather.

In no rush, I peeked out from behind a stone. Exactly. The monster, breathing heavily, was standing still at the wall. Its small closely-set eyes were smoldering with malice. There were wisps of dark gray fog emanating from its mouth, blanketing nearby stones with frost.

Like I said! There's more to this breath than meets the eye!

Well, what now? A good opportunity to run a test.

I feel my heart beating out of my chest. I raise a shivering hand. Lilac smoke immediately enshrouds my palm. Let's get started.

— You have attacked Ice Golem (30)!
— You have dealt 0 damage!

Entirely as expected, the Ram didn't do any damage. It was also not able to knock the creature off its feet. The ice giant just teetered slightly and took a clumsy step backward. But the fifteen-second stun worked exactly right!

Sticking to the plan, I activated lightning before the monster could come to its senses. Great! The behemoth was stuck again!

Okay, that was it for me. Based on the way its eyes were circling in rage, the cave was about to take another pummeling. But before going into our shelter, I left a whole five Blots on the narrow ledge.

The monster's first powerful blow after coming to its senses came when I was midway up. It took me some effort to keep hold and not fall. With a sigh of relief, I kept scrambling up but, at that very moment, the golem landed its final blow.

The rocky mass shook hard. My right leg lost support and slipped. I painfully hit my forehead on stone then grabbed on and hung by my arms.

Breathing heavily and trying not to look down, I started probing the wet stones with my feet for a good ledge or crack. Just when I thought a fall was unavoidable, an unseen someone grabbed me like a kitten by the scruff of my neck and pulled me upward. A second later, panting, I was lying on the stone floor of our cave. Turning onto my back, I saw a fearful look on the gremlin's face and Gorgie's scaled snout looking at me with reproach. And he was partially right to do that.

The sound and snapping of falling stones forced us to quickly look outside. Next to me, just a few yards away, I saw an icy gray body in the smashed passage.

Finally having broken out of the cave, the golem found itself right in the Blots I just set. The five spheres must have all hit at once, completely draining its energy supplies. The monster lost the ability to move and slowly started falling to the ground below. Gorgie, seeing our enemy's state, quickly went down and landed a few blows. But alas, as expected, he wasn't doing any damage.

Their levels were just too mismatched.

Not wasting any time, I kept the harn safe by lashing the golem with an eel lightning. The spell gave us twenty seconds. Gorgie realized he wouldn't be able to get through the beast's defenses and switched to tactics I thought might be more effective. After a short acceleration, his scaled body rammed the icy side of the incapacitated giant. Great! The golem stirred a bit.

When the harn started a second loop, I began feverishly trying to come up with ways I could actually damage this ice chunk. And suddenly it dawned on me! After a moment's thought, I started activating.

— *Would you like to summon Snow Ghoul Spirit?*

"Yes! Now!"

As soon as I assented, five hundred points were drained from my mana crystal. For a moment, I felt a slight burning in the place where the otherworldly creature's spirit once bit me.

The familiar pale silhouette seemed to appear from out of nowhere and stood to my right. Somewhat confused and not knowing what to do, I froze. But as soon as I thought about attacking the golem, the Snow Ghoul Spirit tore off and slammed into our enemy at full speed.

The Great System immediately told me I'd just taken thirty-five percent of the ice beast's life and it abruptly gave a loud disgruntled roar.

In a single burst, Gorgie and I landed a double blow, making the monster start to slowly topple over. Teetering, the golem started falling toward the chasm like a big chunk of chopped ice. A second later, its body was reeling down toward the sharp stones that jutted out at the foot of the cliff.

A fearsome thundering, squealing and scraping of stones informed us that our enemy had landed. We watched it try to tumble over and escape for a few minutes but, in the end, it fell silent. Too many wounds. Plus an empty energy supply. Its regeneration was simply not up to the task.

— You have killed Ice Golem (30).

— Congratulations! You receive:
— Experience essence (6000).
— Gold tablet of Intellect.
— Silver tablet (10).
— Monster Hunter Token (55).

— Attention! The Higher Powers smile upon you! You have replicated the legendary feat of Dalia the Magnificent! You defeated a creature more than 30 levels higher than you using a magic spirit!
— Congratulations! You receive:
— Experience essence (3000).
— Iridescent Tablet "Ice Golem" (1).

While I came to my senses, breathing heavily, Gorgie dove down the passage the golem had created. And a few minutes later, the gremlin and I watched him carefully studying the lifeless body of our vanquished foe.

— *Attention! Your pet has discovered:*
— *Sapphire Ice Golem Horn (1).*
— *Gray Ice Golem Claws (10).*

Whew, so much loot going to waste. Although... I glanced at the gremlin, who was pressing himself up against my arm. If the horn and claws were epic rarity or higher, it was worth thinking about levelling the kid's Butchery.

Alright, let's see what the ice golem has to offer. I'll start with "Spells."

— ***Ice Arrow.***
— *Level: 0. (0/20)*
— *Type: Spell.*
— *Rarity: Epic*
— *Description:*
— *Using magic, the ice golem can cast an ice arrow at a target.*
— *Effect:*
— *Deals 150 damage.*
— *Weak Magical Frostbite is left in the damaged area.*
— ***Weak Magical Frostbite.***
— *Removes 15 life points from target every 5*

seconds.

    — Duration: 30 minutes.

    — Requirements:
    — Intellect — 9.
    — Expends 100 mana points.
    — Note:
    — Range: 40 ft.

Smiling wearily, I opened the ice golem's "Skills and Abilities." And wouldn't you know it, I was right! I had good reason to be suspicious of that breath!

    *— **Ice Golem's Breath.***
    — Level: 0. (0/20)
    — Type: Magical ability.
    — Rarity: Rare.
    — Description:
    — Using magic, the Ice Golem exhales a cloud of ice that slows down enemies and takes their mana.
    — Effect:
    — Reduces enemy speed by 50%.
    — Takes 15 mana points every 5 seconds.

    — Requirements:
    — Intellect — 7.
    — Expends 80 mana points.
    — Note:
    — Duration: 30 minutes.

— *Radius: 13 feet.*

And I'd made up my mind on characteristics before.

— *Attention! You have unlocked the Wisdom characteristic!*
— *Present value: 10.*

"Well?" I turned to Mee, who had been transfixed on the iridescent tablet in my hands that whole time. "Should we go down and look at the loot Gorgie found?"

Once down, not paying any attention to the rain, we looked over the ice giant, dumbfounded. Perfectly still just an outstretched hand away from the monster, it looked like Mee wasn't breathing. Compared with the gray carcass, the gremlin boy looked like a bug.

"You are a Great Shaman!" he whispered yet again.

"That may be," I winced and rubbed the Snow Ghoul's mark. "But the truth is we just got very lucky. To be honest, brother, Gorgie and I walk a razor's edge just about every day."

Having stared long enough at the vanquished beast, I decided to start looking through the loot.

Sapphire Ice Golem Horn.
— *Type: Universal ingredient.*
— *Rarity: Legendary.*

— *Requirements:*

— *Butchery — 30.*

— *Additional information:*

— *Being a creature that uses ice magic, the golem is highly sought-after by rare-ingredient hunters. Its horns are of particular value, more specifically Sapphire (legendary), Gray (epic), Snow (rare) and Ice (normal).*

— *Recommendations:*

— *If you manage to find an ice golem horn, the first place you should take it is a knowledgeable jeweler — they're sure to give you a good price.*

Gray Ice Golem Claw

— *Type: Universal ingredient.*

— *Rarity: Epic.*

— *Requirements:*

— *Butchery — 30.*

— *Additional information:*

— *Being a creature that uses ice magic, the golem is highly sought-after by rare-ingredient hunters. Its claws are of particular value, more specifically Sapphire (legendary), Gray (epic), Snow (rare) and Ice (normal).*

— *Recommendations:*

— *If you manage to find an ice golem claw, the first place you should take it is a knowledgeable alchemist — they're sure to give you a good price.*

Opening my backpack, I checked how many silver tablets I had and took a heavy sigh. I have to raise the gremlin's Butchery. Something is telling me this loot is worth much more than twenty-eight silver tablets. Well, or so I'd like to think.

CHAPTER 8

REASONABLY FIGURING that it would be better to divvy up tablets in a dry cave than under the pouring rain, we went back up. The golem's body was probably not going to attract any creatures looking for a meal. Between the cloudy whitish slime that seeped out of its wounds instead of blood and its rock hard flesh — this monster was definitely not edible. And if someone came by and wanted to make off with our loot, we'd have a bird's eye view.

I found a comfortable spot to sit at the far wall of the cave, then turned to the gremlin sitting next to me:

"While I sort through all the tablets, you better eat up. After improving characteristics, your body will need lots of nourishment and energy."

"Alright," Mee answered, undoing the drawstrings of his small knapsack.

And meanwhile, I opened my ephemeral backpack.

— *Experience essence (51430).*
— *Gold tablet of Intellect (2).*
— *Monster Hunter Token (590).*
— *Hunter's Fury (13).*
— *Blot (5).*
— *Small Potion of Satiety (14).*
— *Ferocious Harn Summoning Amulet.*
— *Silver tablet (55).*
— *Stone tablet of Agility (14).*
— *Stone tablet of Strength (14).*
— *Stone tablet of Endurance (14).*
— *Stone tablet of Wisdom (14).*
— *Stone tablet of Accuracy (14).*
— *Stone tablet of Speed (14).*
— *Stone tablet "Fisher" (14).*
— *Stone tablet "Hunter" (14).*
— *Stone tablet of Mind (14).*
— *Clay tablet "Hiding Spot Maker" (2).*
— *Clay tablet of Observation (2).*
— *Clay tablet of Mind (2).*

Bringing the gremlin's Butchery to the ceiling would take twenty-eight silvers, but that wouldn't be the end of it. It was hard to imagine him taking out the horns and claws of a golem with just three points of Strength and Agility. Considering the Stones we had for those, it was going to take another ten Silvers. Beyond that, I couldn't forget about Endurance and Health. Starting tablet activation without deepening his supplies would be a huge risk to Mee's life.

I glanced dubiously at Gorgie's stats. Fifty-five points would significantly improve our tank.

— *Ferocious Harn.*
— *Name: Gorgie.*
— *Level: 7 (25300/36000).*
— *Status: Loyalty to master (permanent).*
— *Mind: 1/1*
— *Strength: 69.5/105*
— *Agility: 70.4/105*
— *Accuracy: 5.8/105*
— *Intuition: 7/7*
— *Wisdom: 14/14*
— *Animal instinct: 14/14*
— *Speed: 68.5/105*
— *Flexibility: 46/105*
— *Intellect: 38/70*
— *Mana supply: 430/430*
— *Health: 70/70*
— *Endurance: 60/70*
— *Life supply: 750/750*
— *Energy supply: 650/650*
— *Scale armor: 35/35*
— *Defense: 350/350*
— *Damage: +191.5...+605.1*
— *Bite: 35/35*
— *Paw swipe: 35/35*
— *Pounce: 7/7*

— *Animal regeneration: 14/14*
— *Hunter: 27/35*
— *Fisher: 15/35*
— *Resistance to Hexapod poison: 7/35*

Wait a second! I'm lost here. Where did he get so much experience? After the battle with the hyenas, he was at just over twenty thousand five hundred. Checking it all over yet again, I scratched the back of my head pensively. Hm, he also got another few points to main characteristics. What is going on? But then it finally hit me! I quickly opened the system message tab. I found the messages about the battle with the golem and smiled in satisfaction. In the end, the harn was able to land crits and deal a bit of damage! And he received his reward for doing so.

After a bit more thought, I make up my mind. I'm going to stick to the plan. If I don't, I'll be sorry I didn't try.

"Okay," Mee announced, wiping his lips on his sleeve. "I can't cram any more in."

"Alright," I nodded, activating lair. "Let's start with Mind."

Over the next few minutes, I fed the gremlin all my clays and almost all my stones.

There's no way to activate Wisdom without Intellect. I could have sacrificed one of my gold tablets, but the gremlin didn't have any need for a mana supply without having magical abilities or spells.

I had my doubts about who best to give the Hunter and Fisher tablets to — Gorgie or Mee. I had enough of those for almost three points per ability. But in the end, I decided to improve those skills for the harn. He was mostly the one finding legendary horns and hooves for us anyway. So he got preference.

When it came time for the silvers, I took a heavy sigh. I looked at the gremlin's enamored little snout and just kept handing him tablets. I advised him to invest five into Agility and Strength, then pull Butcher up to the ceiling. After all that, I had seventeen more silver tablets left over.

I took another close look at Mee's characteristics and came to the conclusion that a hundred per supply would be enough for his body to take activating the tablets just fine.

"Here," I said to the gremlin, extending him seven silvers. "Five into life and two into energy."

He nodded silently and the glimmering sheets in his hands dissolved into thin air.

So then, let's see where that got us.

— *Steppe Gremlin.*
— *Name: Mee.*
— *Level: 3 (0/9000).*
— *Status: Loyalty to elder family member (permanent).*
— *Mind: 6/6*
— *Strength: 10.9/30*

— *Agility: 10.9/30*
— *Health: 8/30*
— *Accuracy: 2.8/30*
— *Speed: 2.8/30*
— *Observation: 0.2/30*
— *Endurance: 7.8/30*
— *Life supply: 100/100*
— *Energy supply: 98/98*
— *Skills and abilities:*
— *Butchery: 30/30*
— *Herbalism: 2/30*
— *Hunter: 2/30*
— *Fisher: 2/30*
— *Rider: 0.1/30*
— *Hiding spot maker: 0.2/30*

His energy supply was exactly two points short of where I wanted it, but it wasn't critical. As we'd seen, Endurance tablets dropped fairly often. It was a matter of two clays or one stone tablet.

In total, I had ten silvers left and I decided to hold onto them just in case.

"Thanks!" the kid squeaked happily and pressed his whole body up against me.

"No problem," I smiled and stroked his head. Gorgie joined in too, licking the little guy's face a few times in approval.

Then a few instants later, Mee lost consciousness. And his body started to change.

* * *

It's been four days since we used the tablets. The kid spent two of them unconscious. All that time I was sitting next to him and, when necessary, feeding him a potion of satiety. Gorgie was keeping an eye on the surrounding area and reported there were no creatures nearby. So he had to go out onto the steppe to find prey. Yesterday he even dragged in a dead steppe antelope.

On day three, the kid came to his senses and immediately threw himself on what was left of the meat. After that, he rested until he got hungry again, filled his belly another time and, on the morning of the fourth day, woke up totally refreshed and sprightly.

Because the downpour had shifted to a very fine drizzle, we decided to go down to the golem carcass and test out Mee's new ability.

As expected, nothing had disturbed the ice giant's body. Despite the rain, there was a nauseating smell of rot emanating our way from the foot of the cliff. We had to wrap rags around our faces just so we could stand being near the creature's corpse.

We decided to start with the claws. They weren't all that big or as valuable as the horns. Gorgie and I crouched next to him and hunkered down to watch.

Mee opened his little knapsack in

concentration and began taking all kinds of butchery implements out of it. To be honest, there weren't that many things. A thin piece of twine, a scraper, a narrow little knife and a bigger knife, which Mee picked up back at the orc camp.

After that, he spent a few minutes walking around the carcass and examining it. Utterly silent, we were watching his every move. First he hunched over one of the golem's paws and felt one of the claws. Then he turned around and started looking for something on the ground. A moment later, he picked up a small stone and returned to the creature's paw. Within an hour, we heard the crunch of breaking bones, and the banging and huffing of our little laborer. At the end of all the careful manipulations, he delicately extracted a Gray Ice Golem Claw. The kid extended it to me victoriously, himself crouching wearily on a stone. I glanced at his supplies. His energy was down thirty points.

"Tired?" I asked compassionately.

"A bit," Mee nodded. "I'm gonna take a rest now before I start on the next one."

"No rush, rest up," I reassured him. "And it'd be nice if you also had a good tool instead of these rusty hunks of scrap."

"I'm not high enough level for a good tool yet," the gremlin objected.

"Well, experience is no problem," I answered with a wave of the hand. "What matters is squeezing every level for all it's worth."

"Speaking of that," Mee said, taking a handful of esses and tablets out of his bag. "Here's what I got for extracting the claw."

— *Experience essence (1000).*
— *Bronze tablet of Strength.*
— *Bronze tablet of Agility.*
— *Bronze tablet of Endurance.*
— *Bronze tablet "Knife Proficiency."*

"Great!" I exclaimed. "Because of the level difference, the system rewarded you handsomely!"

"I think so," Mee said. "But I shouldn't use them yet."

I thought for an instant and answered:

"You know something? You're right. I don't know how it'll go with the horn, but you can handle the other claws as is. And I hope that Random will bless you with even more loot!"

After the gremlin took a rest and got started in on the next claw, I decided to ask him a question:

"I've heard the orc chieftain is amassing a horde. Is that true?"

"Yes," Mee answered. "The orcs have long been discussing a raid on the western lands of the humans. It will be a Grand Campaign!"

"And is it also true that it will start after the rainy season?"

"Yes," the gremlin nodded. "The shamans say

this winter will be a long one. That is the best time for a campaign."

"Hey, speaking of shamans. How many are there?"

"That all depends on clan," Mee answered. "The Elder Clans have more shamans."

"What about the Clan of the Gray Mountain?"

"It used to be one of the strongest clans on the steppe, but many of its warriors died in a war with its neighbors."

"Okay, perhaps the war weakened their chieftain, but you still haven't said how many shaman's they have."

"The Clan of the Gray Mountain has one shaman and his five apprentices."

"What level is the main shaman?"

"Thirty-seven," the gremlin answered.

"Ahem... We'd better keep our distance from an enemy like that. And what level are his apprentices?"

"The lowest level is twenty-three."

When I heard that, I scratched the back of my head, mystified.

"Then we definitely have to avoid an encounter with the local warlocks," I muttered.

When the gremlin heard that, he added:

"As a rule, humans shouldn't let orcs see them at all. Especially in orcish territory. As a matter of fact, the orcs look on all other races as potential slaves. So any orc that sees us on the steppe will be honor-bound to take us captive."

"All the worse for them," I chuckled. "By the way, how many clans are there on the steppe in total?"

"I don't know an exact number," the gremlin responded. "But there are a lot."

"Okay then, we need to somehow get in front of the horde."

"True. The strong rains will be over in a week's time. Then the cold will set in. And as soon as the earth is firm, the horde will march west."

"So that means we have a little over a week after the rains end to get moving," I voiced my conclusion.

Getting out the golem's horn and remaining claws took the gremlin almost two days. Beyond the important ingredients, he also ended up with a few thousand esses and more than twenty bronze tablets. And removing the legendary horn was enough for the Great System to reward him with a generous five silvers!

To say Mee was happy would be to say nothing at all! Until very recently, he could only dream of loot like this! And I could understand. I myself am sometimes taken aback by the generosity of the gods.

All this time, Gorgie had been patrolling the area around the Black Hills, providing us with food. Once I tried to accompany him but the downpour and mud made me slow as a turtle. In the end, as not to be a burden to the harn, I had no choice but to turn back.

But I didn't waste time sitting idle, so I gathered some zero grass the gremlin pointed out to me.

When Mee finished up with the Ice Golem, he walked up to me with a question:

"Rick, what do you say to me heading out on scout duty with Gorgie?"

I squinted and asked:

"What scheme have you cooked up now? Tell me."

Smiling, Mee lowered his eyes then took a fleeting glance at the harn, who was lying down near the wall.

"You see, Rick, when I think about the fact that there are two firepaw fangs somewhere out there, my heartbeat just takes off!"

I chuckled glumly.

"Something the matter?" Mee asked, noticing my state.

"No," I shook my head. "Everything is fine. You just reminded me of an old friend."

So he wouldn't ask any questions, I quickly turned the conversation back to his idea.

"Well, you understand that the hiding spot we put it in is a bit farther away than Gorgie is going, right?"

"Yes, it's approximately two days away from

the Hills. But Gorgie could make it faster than that. Even with me on his back. Beyond that, I wouldn't mind rummaging around in the orcs' stuff a bit. I think there could be something else I need."

I considered it for a time. Hm, the Epic firepaw fangs would not hurt. Heh... Plus I just can't seem to get rid of them. And the kid could use some more good loot. I have to admit — Mee is right. The harn could make it much faster.

With a heavy sigh, I looked at my friends. Two crafty pairs of eyes were staring at me with hope.

"I see you two have already made up your minds about this, eh?"

"Hrn," Gorgie answered affirmatively.

"Don't worry about us, Rick," Mee said reassuringly. "We'll be back before you can even blink an eye."

"Ugh! If it's what you want, go ahead."

The gremlin gave a delighted squeak and ran over to Gorgie, taking out some intricately woven rope construction as he went. Nimbly tying it around the harn's neck and chest, he jumped up onto his scaled back. I scratched the back of my head. Looks like we're gonna need a proper saddle soon.

The kid wasn't sitting too confidently, so I suggested he invest a couple of tablets into the Rider skill. Beyond that, I gave him a few Potions of Satiety and a couple Blots just in case.

After those couple tablets, Mee was gripping his improvised saddle fairly capably. When all the preparations were finished, they said their goodbyes and got underway. And I was left on my own.

For the next twenty-four hours I was on tenterhooks and constantly cursing myself for agreeing to the risky venture. Honestly, around ten hours after Mee and Gorgie took off, I did get a message saying the hiding spot had been dug up. That served as a brief update and slight reassurance. I hope Mee won't take too long with the fangs and they'll be back soon.

Trying to somehow distract myself, I concentrated on searching for zero resources. I combed through all accessible caves and scoured every corner. That was exactly what I was doing when my friends came back the next day and caught me off guard.

I must admit, I couldn't remember the last time I was that happy! I went out to greet the travelers. They were also happy, but also badly shaken up.

"There's a group of people coming toward the hills from the north!" Mee told me right away.

"*Blood. Tired,*" Gorgie added shortly.

CHAPTER 9

"**A**RE THEY FAR?" I quickly asked.

"No..." Mee turned his head. "I think they're at the foothills already."

"How many are they?"

"I saw three, but I didn't see their levels."

"Gorgie says they're tired and he smells blood," I said. "Do you think it could be the runaways your former master was tracking?"

"No," Mee answered. "I definitely remember a tracker saying some an unknown beast had torn the runaway slaves to shreds. And that most likely it came from the direction of Dread Cliff."

"Dread Cliff?" I asked.

"Yes, it's off to the east. Where the monsters live."

Hm... That means Master Chi's Hive has been christened Dread Cliff by the natives.

"Curious," I said thoughtfully. "Then who are

they?"

"Captives often flee," Mee answered with a shrug.

"Sure," I said. "Let's not panic. There are plenty of caves here. Let's just hope they don't come into ours. We'll just hunker down quietly and then decide what to do next."

I understood that the people were above all potential allies, but who could say what they had in mind? In any case, we have to prepare for an encounter. But we also aren't going to stick our noses out of this cave. First let's just take a closer look. Maybe we won't have to even meet them. We'll just sit them out, they'll go their way and we'll go ours.

But my hopes were dashed. An hour later, when we'd started thinking they weren't going to notice us, the harn told me one of the three strangers was hiding near the entrance to the big cave. Then an instant later, we heard a firm male voice.

"Hey, there in the cave! How about we do this with no bloodshed? What do you say?"

Our silence didn't give the man even a second's pause. Calmly, he continued:

"A boy and a gremlin make strange company for a walk in the heart of the Wastes! Something is telling me that you fled orcish captivity just like us! Am I right?!"

The stranger spent a bit of time in silence and continued:

"By the way, I noticed fresh tracks from some predator! I think it'll be safer for you to join up with us! Together we'll have an easier time taking down the beast! I, Randelph Larsen, do solemnly swear that if you are kindly travelers we will do you no harm!"

After receiving confirmation from the Great System, the gremlin and I exchanged glances.

"Looks like they aren't just gonna leave us alone," I whispered with only my lips.

Mee took a heavy sigh, quickly dug in his knapsack and started taking out all his tablets and esses.

"Here," he whispered. "Hide these in your magic pocket."

I nodded and immediately transferred his stuff into my ephemeral backpack. That way, we'd have nothing but junk in our knapsacks.

"I'm coming in!" the redheaded middle-aged man cautiously stepped into the cave without waiting for a reply. He was level seventeen, which put me on guard.

Veiny, medium height. His movements smooth like an animal's. A few scars on his face. He could easily read our tracks, probably a scout or ranger. But despite his martial appearance, he had an open and likeable face. Although that may have been high Charisma. I'd seen that before.

The stranger's clothes were badly tattered, but he was carrying an orcish bow and the handle of a scimitar peeked out over his shoulder. They clearly were not able to escape without a fight.

"Where are you?" he asked. "Or was my oath not enough for you?"

We had to come out, otherwise this doubtlessly dangerous warrior might have taken our silence the wrong way. Using my amulet, I recalled the harn. Mee's eyes looked like saucers when I did, seeing the summoning amulet in action for the first time.

Slowly walking out from behind the stone, I raised my hands and as plaintively as I could said:

"Please sir, don't kill us!"

Mee was standing behind me, embracing my leg with both arms.

An open smile of relief dawned on the redhead's previously tense face.

"So you are a boy," he smiled. "I'm glad we were able to reach an understanding."

He quickly walked around the cave and peeked out the other side. He spent a bit of time standing on the narrow stone ledge looking down. After that he snorted and stroked his beard pensively.

"Not a bad cave, but we found a better one. Ours has a whole three exits, but here there's basically just one. Come with me, I'll get you warmed up by the fire. You must be chilled to the bone."

In point of fact, we had tried to start a bonfire once before but, after the harn's daily patrol, he told us the smoke smell made us too easy to track down. So we decided not to keep risking it. Over the preceding month, I'd gotten used to living without fire so it was no big deal.

Randelph led us to a small cave one level lower, where his companions were sitting around a fire. The damp shrub branches were throwing up an incredible amount of smoke. The gremlin and I winced in unison. An excellent way to attract all the beasts in the area!

The redhead, noticing my facial expression, gave another thoughtful snort.

"Bruni!" he gave a muted shout to a buff man with dark blonde hair fussing around near the fire pit. "Have you lost your mind?! Why'd you throw so many wet branches on the fire?! Set them next to it so they can dry off first."

The brute furrowed his narrow brow, looked at Randelph then turned his gaze to us. I could read surprise in his big blue eyes. Broad shoulders, hands like shovels — by all appearances, this Bruni could never have been a ranger.

A bit farther away was a third person, lying down. Gray hair, a narrow wrinkled face, gaunt constitution, a dirty rag stretched tight over his right side — that must have been the blood Gorgie was smelling. By all appearances, he was not just asleep, but unconscious. If not dead already.

"Randy, who'd you drag in this time?" Bruni buzzed.

Entirely ignoring Larsen's admonishment

about the fire, he stood up to his whole enormous height. The levels of the two men, sixteen for the younger one and twenty for the gray-hair, led me to believe fate had brought us together with a group of warriors.

"These are our friends in misfortune," Randy said, taking the wet branches off the fire. "I swore we wouldn't hurt them. So be gentle."

Bruni just snorted indistinctly and took a few steps in our direction. Walking a circle around us, he gave another snort and walked toward the fire.

"Alright," he grumbled. "I'll do my best."

"Guys, come sit by the fire," Randelph invited us, himself taking a seat. "Let's warm up."

"So Randy, shot anything yet?" the big guy muttered sadly. "My belly's about to start getting restless."

"No," the redhead shook his head. "It's like everything around here died."

And it's no surprise. Two days of the golem rampaging plus Gorgie's patrols — if there still was anything alive in these caves, it must have hidden itself very well. But I decided to make the first move, hoping to establish amicable relations.

Pretending to rummage in my knapsack, I took a few chunks of steppe antelope meat out of my ephemeral backpack, which the harn had hunted before leaving to get the firepaw fangs.

"Here you go," I said. "My treat!"

"Well, well!" Bruni lit up. "Where'd you drum up this small fortune?"

"We found a dead antelope on the riverbank," I lied without a blink.

Bruni took one of the meat chunks and sniffed it.

"This'll do!" he rendered his verdict. "We've had worse."

An hour later we were eating the big fellow's poorly-cooked, tough meat. And by the way, he was eating most of all.

In that time, I was able to get a decent look at all three. They had lots of old scars on their faces and hands. The looks, movements and chopped phrases — I was right — these were warriors. But it remained to be seen who they served. They weren't from our barony. That was for sure. The accent wasn't right. Most likely northerners. Hm, might they be from the retinue of the Steel King? That was probably it.

The gray-hair hadn't come to his senses yet. I suspect it's already too late for him. The dirty rag covering his wound was soaked through with blood. I think even if I activated Lair right now, it wouldn't do much good, just prolong his agony.

Following my gaze, Randy said:

"An orc stuck a spear into his side."

"Tusked degenerate!" Bruni barked.

"Were you taken captive?" I asked cautiously.

"Yes," nodded the redhead. "By the Black Wolves. What about you?"

"Clan of the Gray Mountain," Mee squeaked. "Our master's family was having a celebration. He and his warriors were inhaling the smoke of the dope grass."

"And you ran away under cover of all the noise?" Randy chuckled.

The gremlin and I made honest eyes and nodded simultaneously.

"Hehe, I guess those lowlifes noticed you were gone too late!" Bruni chuckled. "If they ever even noticed."

"So what do you plan to do next?" the redhead asked. "Where are you gonna go?"

"We were going west, sir," I answered. "To human lands."

"You got family there?"

"No," I shook my head and pointed to the gremlin: "Mee is the only family I have."

The big guy took a heavy sigh and Randy stroked his chin pensively, then said:

"I'm sorry to disappoint you, kid, but you'll end up under the same kind of slavery in human lands. The laws of our Kingdoms protect only the rich and powerful."

Heh, you're telling me.

"You can say that again," Bruni confirmed. "They'll put you with the tramps and send you off to work for some fatcat. And I won't even mentioned what they'll do to the gremlin."

After that, Mee shuddered and squeezed up against me in fear.

"But that isn't the worst part," Randy said. "The way west is impassable."

"Yeah," I nodded. "We wanted to wait for the water level to go down."

"No," the redhead interrupted. "When I said the way west is impassable, I was talking about something else."

"Orcs," the big guy muttered wickedly.

"A few clans sent warriors before the rainy season to patrol the steppe on the border with our lands," Randy explained.

"The area is teeming with wolf riders," the dark-blonde giant muttered, clenching his fists.

"They're the elite of the orcish warband," Randy added fuel to the fire. "It wouldn't just be hard for a person to get past them, a mouse could hardly make it. But what am I saying? You already know that perfectly well."

They fell silent, staring pensively at the fire. I meanwhile was thinking deeply. If there's no way to go west, where should we go? The strong rains will end very soon. This is the best time to get underway.

As if reading my thoughts, the redhead started to speak.

"The western tract is not the only way out of the Wastes. There is also Drake's Ridge."

"True," Bruni nodded. "But honestly, winter is already on the horizon. We'd run the risk of getting stranded in the Pass of the Seven Winds."

"Those parts are best avoided this time of year," the redhead agreed.

"Is there really no other way?" I asked, putting

a naive look on my face.

The men both frowned and exchanged glances.

"There is one," Randy nodded. "But it's no good for kids at your level. Even me and Bruni would have a hard time."

I mentally noted that the redhead had not mentioned their third companion. I took that to mean neither of them believed he'd be getting up either.

"You'd be better off sitting in some secluded spot and hoping nobody notices you," Bruni said, but I could hear notes of doubt in his voice.

No, big fellow. That is not the way for us. Sooner or later, we'd be caught. Slavery again? No thanks.

Apparently, the plan Mee and I cooked up was not going to work. The orcish chieftain was no fool. He was afraid of information leaking. The wolf rider squads had the border sealed tight. And they were on the hunt for human trespassers. If they were elite warriors as Randy said, we'd surely be found.

Drake's Ridge is also no good. In the winter, the mountains are not exactly the best place for a stroll. All we have left is to figure out what these two have in mind.

They clearly have a plan. But based on their intonation and facial expressions, they don't much like it themselves.

"Randy, check on the captain," Bruni said calmly. "I don't think he's breathing."

The redhead nodded and placed his right hand on the gray-hair's neck. I closed my eyes for a moment.

"You're right," he said quietly. "His suffering is at an end. Let's drag him deeper into the cave, then tomorrow we can lay his mortal remains to rest."

Bruni nodded and stood to his full height.

A few minutes later, the men went back to the fire.

The big guy sighed heavily and muttered:

"Litz was of course a real scoundrel, but he fought valiantly."

"But what good was his valor?" Randy objected maliciously, getting a more comfortable seat and extending his hands toward the warmth of the fire. "All of our brothers at arms died thanks to that idiot. It was just because he wanted to prove himself to the Duke and dragged us all into a trap!"

"And the sergeant warned him," Bruni nodded glumly.

"Here, here!" Randy supported him. "Seima, my sister's husband, was torn to shreds by wargs before my very eyes! I mean, we grew up together. What am I supposed to tell her now? And that's if we can actually get out of this asshole of the earth."

They both spent a bit of time in silence. Only a furious wheeze spoke to their extremely agitated state.

"Understandable," Randy continued once he'd calmed down a bit. "In my time, when I signed up for the retinue, I knew that sooner or later I'd have to lay down my life in battle. But I didn't think my comrades and I would be dying for no reason. And I didn't think some captain's vanity would get all our boys killed in an utterly dumb and senseless battle. Bruni, why on earth did that idiot have to put us in such a dangerous position?"

"You know why," the big guy snorted. "So that if we won, the captain could ride his white steed up to the Duke's pampered ass and give it a big, wet smooch."

"May the abyss take him!" Randy cursed through his teeth.

As I listened, I realized that despite the downpour, mud and most importantly their distaste for the foolish commander, these men had dragged his near lifeless body all this way. If you ask me, something like that merits respect. To be honest, I was starting to like these guys.

"By the way, you still haven't told me your names," Bruni suddenly said.

"Hehe, you know something? That's right!" Randelph chuckled openly. "You already know too much about us!"

I smiled in response and, placing my hand on the gremlin's shoulder, said:

"This is Mee, and my name is Eric."

"Eric... Eric what?" Bruni asked.

"Bergman," I answered. "Eric Bergman."

"Bergman. Bergman..." Randy said thoughtfully, stroking his red beard. "Feels very familiar. Where are you from?"

"Orchus. But my parents were born in the west."

"Where exactly?" Bruni inquired. "My family is from that area."

"Achena," I answered.

The men's faces instantly went gloomy. And it's understandable. Who doesn't know the tale of the epidemic and the torched city?

Suddenly Randy raised his head and looked at me closely. I could tell from his face that he had probably remembered something.

"Listen, Eric," he began. "Any chance your dad was a miner?"

I felt a brigade of ants start marching down my spine.

"He was," I answered excitedly. "Did you know my father? Aren Bergman?"

"No," Randy shook his head.

I exhaled sadly.

"But I think I knew his son," Randy answered. "Ivar Bergman. In those days, he was in the Orchus retinue. It feels like a lifetime ago. Hehe, fifteen, no, sixteen years back."

I listened to the redheaded warrior in silence, but my heart was about to jump out of my chest!

"I can see you recognize that name." Randy said, fired up.

"Yes," I nodded quickly. "Ivar was my

164

brother."

"What do you mean was?"

"Sixteen years ago, my parents were informed that he was killed here in the Wastes."

"Hm, well that's right around the time I last saw him," Randy said dubiously. "Are you sure we're talking about the same person?"

"I don't know," I shrugged. "But we're the only Bergmans in Orchus."

"Then I'm totally lost," Randy said, confused. "If we're talking about the same person, the Ivar I knew simply could not have died in the Wastes at that time."

I felt my heart, already pounding out a fervent rhythm, start beating even faster.

"W-why not?" I whispered my stupid question, hiccupping.

"Because the Ivar I knew never went to the Wastes. As a matter of fact, sixteen years ago, when I last ran into him, we were in the port area of the capital city. The Yellow Crab tavern. The same place we first met. And as you know, that's pretty far from the Wastes."

"You can say that again," Bruni tossed his two cents in and added dreamily: "What I wouldn't give for an hour in the Yellow Crab right now... A couple mugs of dark beer couldn't do me any harm."

Listening to Randy, I couldn't believe my ears!

"How is that possible?" I asked, dumbfounded. "I mean, my parents got a death certificate and everything!"

"The paper-pushers must have gotten something mixed up again," Bruni snorted scornfully, distracted by his dreams of dark beer.

"But father went to the chancery..."

"Bruni's right," Randy nodded, interrupting me. "Those pencil-pushers are always burying our brothers before they've gone."

"But sixteen years..." I said, looking around perplexed.

"Now that is a valid point," agreed the bearded redhead, the big fellow also nodding. "Your brother should have turned up by now."

"Did your father ever speak with his commander or brothers in arms?"

"No one from his company ever returned," I shook my head.

"What a mess," Bruni said in surprise.

"This all sounds very strange," Randy frowned.

"Would you happen to remember anything else?" I asked with hope. "Maybe my brother said where he was planning to go?"

"No," the redhead answered, furrowing his brow. "I only remember that his unit was accompanying the Baron. That's it. But there was no talk of the Wastes."

"What a tangled web," Bruni again gave his estimation.

"Well, I have to unravel it!" I said, clenching my fists. "What was it you said? The Yellow Crab tavern?"

Randelph gave a sad nod. Bruni chuckled and said:

"You're getting ahead of yourself! First you get to our borders, then..."

"Speaking of that," I interrupted him. "As far as I understand, you have a plan? You think we could maybe join forces?"

The men exchanged glances and looked at us with pity.

"Yes," Randy answered. "We know one way. But believe you me, you're probably not gonna like it."

Got it. He doesn't want to say. He's afraid we might say something if we get captured.

"Speak. I swear I'll take your secret to the grave!"

"I also swear!" Mee squeaked.

The men again exchanged glances. Bruni shrugged his shoulders and said to Randy:

"Okay then, tell them. Hehe. When we see the looks on their faces..."

The redhead chuckled.

"We intend to try our luck to the south," he said briefly.

I stared at the laughing men in incomprehension. Then I turned my gaze to Mee, who looked shaken-up.

"There's only one way to the south — the Stone Forest," he whispered nervously. "Even the orcs are afraid of that place."

"I'll be direct," Bruni answered. "You'll be a burden to us."

"Alas, Eric," Randy shrugged. "Your levels..."

"Yes, I've heard. But what if we have something to offer you?"

Bruni slapped his knee and laughed:

"Bug take me! You know, I like this kid!"

"Okay then," Randelph shrugged. "Surprise us."

"Very well," I nodded calmly. "Just no sudden moves."

As I said that, I activated Lair and summoned Gorgie.

CHAPTER 10

"**Y**OU'RE A MAGE!" Bruni exclaimed, dumbfounded.

"You know, I could tell something was off about you!" Randy said, smiling nervously. And all the while, he was staring at the harn, who was nestled up at my feet.

I must note that the men displayed admirable restraint. They reached for their weapons, but didn't attack.

"That's Gorgie," I said, ignoring Randy. "He's the reason I'm still alive."

"Is he the thing that left tracks everywhere?" Randy inquired, showily stashing his sword back in its sheath. I could tell he was shaken up but trying not to show it.

"Yeah," I nodded.

"I'm sure you knew we were coming for a few hours then," the redheaded ranger laughed.

I smiled and nodded.

"So why didn't you order it to attack me?" Randy asked, still watching the harn out of the corner of his eye. "After all, if I understand correctly, the beast whose corpse is currently rotting at the foot of the cliff is your doing?"

"What beast now?!" Bruni exclaimed. His kind-hearted simpleton's face stretched out in surprise.

"The ice golem," I calmly answered in Randelph's place. "The level-thirty magical monster. And the reason I didn't order you attacked was because you were behaving yourselves."

In a different situation, I'd have kept quiet, but this was not the time. We needed allies.

After I said that, I could read several emotions on the men's faces. Surprise, disquiet and seemingly glee.

"Just to be fair, there is another thing," I decided to add. "We got lucky with the golem — we provoked the thing. It fell for our trick and basically dug its own grave. If we faced off on an even playing field, it is not likely we'd be speaking right now."

The men, smiling, exchanged glances.

"Okay, now we have a chance!" Bruni said cheerily.

"I must admit, Eric," Randy chuckled. "You managed to surprise us!"

"So, am I correct in my understanding that

you would not be opposed to us keeping you company?" I asked.

"You are correct," Randy nodded, smiling. "But I have a few questions."

"I'm listening."

"A mage boy, and nulled on top of it, journeying through the Wastes accompanied by a gremlin and domesticated harn — that is more than strange." said the redhead, squinting. "Don't you think?"

"Couldn't have said it better myself!" Bruni nodded.

"Well, you see all kinds of stuff in the Wastes..." I answered with a snort. "An odd mage boy. Odd soldiers from the retinue of the Steel King."

When I mentioned the fearsome northern ruler, the warriors shuddered and frowned. Gorgie could sense their tension and yawned wide, revealing his long sharp fangs.

"Honorable rangers," I calmly turned to the men and immediately mentally noted that the clumsy Bruni was, to put it lightly, not exactly cut out for the title. "I don't want any trouble, and I would like to tell you what we're doing here. But first I suggest we come to a mutually beneficial agreement and seal it with an oath. At this time, neither of our causes will be helped by you knowing how we got here. But for your peace of mind, let me assure you that we did not come to the Wastes of our own accord and bear no ill intent toward your lord. I swear that to you right now!"

After receiving confirmation from the Great System, the warriors noticeably calmed down. Seeing the state of my potential allies, I decided to keep going:

"I understand you have just lost your commander but, if we are to continue together, I'd like to know which of you will take over his position."

"Randy," Bruni immediately answered, patting his comrade on the shoulder. "I'd be hopeless as a commander."

"What do you say?" Randy asked, staring me in the eyes searchingly. "Are you willing to obey my orders?"

"I am," I answered calmly. "But on one condition."

"What is it then?"

"If you act like your old captain," I nodded toward where they'd dragged the gray-hair. "You can forget about obedience."

"Fair," Randy nodded and added sternly:

"But if any of you do not carry out an order of mine, we are no longer together. Agreed?"

After that, he extended his hand for a handshake.

I considered it for a moment. The redhead had basically agreed, but at the same time he gave me a clear indication he would not tolerate disobedience. Oh well though. He's right. I'd leave a stupid commander all on my own, but the orders of a smart one must be obeyed.

"Agreed," I answered and extended my hand.

"Me too," Mee squeaked.

"Hrn!" Gorgie came as well, which shocked the men.

"He's intelligent?!" Bruni asked, dumbfounded.

"You might say that," I smiled, stroking the harn's armored head. "Smarter than many humans."

The warriors liked that. They looked at my pet again with new eyes, this time containing much more admiration.

For around an hour, we discussed our temporary agreement and oath. When all the formalities were smoothed over, and the Great system had confirmed the purity of our intentions, I asked a question that had been troubling me:

"So, the Stone Forest — what kind of place is that?"

Mee shuddered and pushed hard up against my arm.

"I see your little companion has some idea," Bruni nodded gloomily in the gremlin's direction.

"I'm curious what he has to say," said Randy.

"Will you tell us?" I turned to Mee.

First of all he glanced at me, then took a heavy sigh and answered;

"The orcs believe that, at the dawn of time, before the epoch of the Departed, two titans faced off in a grand battle — Taikho the Light and Rho the Dark. They grappled with one another for five days and five nights until, finally, Rho was defeated. Darkness had been vanquished, but it managed to do some damage on its way out. The lands where the ancient monster's black blood was spilled grew up into the Stone Forest." The kid fell silent for a moment, then continued: "They also say the descendants of Rho the Dark live there to this day — the forest trolls."

"Vile and stupid brutes," Bruni barked maliciously.

"You've come up against them before?" I asked.

The men nodded at once.

"Bloodthirsty monsters," said Randy. "Once a troll has your scent, they'll track you to the very end."

"So how do you fight them?" I asked.

"Ideally, you don't," Randy said. "Strong. Good defenses. But very slow moving. And that, by the way, is our main advantage."

"If you ask me, the surest way to survive an encounter with a troll is to hoof it," Bruni told me. "Thankfully, the thick-skinned dunderheads can't run too fast."

"Yes," Randy agreed. "Speed will save us."

"I'm not gonna lie," I chuckled. "That method is right up my alley."

"Our man!" Bruni chuckled.

"But that's not all," Mee said quietly. "Trolls are not the scariest thing we might run into."

"Are you talking about the Dark Ones?" Randy asked morosely.

"Yes," the gremlin nodded.

"The orcs believe there are dark beasts there?" Bruni asked. "I always thought it was just fairy tales."

"No sir-ee!" Mee answered seriously. "Where do you think the shamans get their power from?"

The warriors exchanged sullen glances.

"Do you mean to say the shamans have sold themselves out to Darkness?" Randy asked with strain. "Look, I'm not asking just because. It's very important information. Especially in light of what's about to happen."

"What are you talking about?" I asked.

"Oh, come on!" Randy exclaimed. "Do you really not understand? You're a mage!"

"Well..." I hesitated. "The thing is, I'm not exactly the most learned member of magical, hm, society."

I was actually just pretending — it was clear to me what the ranger was driving at. Honestly, if I hadn't been to Master Chi's manor, it would have been hard for me to speculate.

"Randy, to be honest, I don't totally understand what you're referring to either," Bruni admitted.

"If it becomes known that the orcs are flirting with Darkness, the shamans will have hell to pay," Randy answered shortly and added: "The Order will send the Executioners."

"So that's what you're talking about," the big guy snorted and said respectfully:

"The Executioners are no laughing matter."

"If they thin the shamans' ranks, the horde is not likely to go west," Randy said.

With a heavy sigh, he glanced at me.

"Eric, no offense, but mages are scum of the highest order. Think how much good they could do for the common people, how many wars they could prevent. But no! They only intervene when they stand to benefit or when they perceive a threat to their interests!"

After saying that, the ranger sighed heavily and fell silent.

I just chuckled back. You're telling me! You're talking about the Order's Executioners here. I have seen them using dark magic with my own two eyes. They have zero compunction about that, and yet they're supposed to come punish the shamans for using dark magic?

"I don't think they've sold themselves out to Darkness," Mee interrupted.

"What do you mean?" Randy asked in surprise. "Well, you just said..."

"That isn't what I meant," the gremlin hurried to explain. "Every year, the great kurultai of the shamans selects an apprentice to be sent into the Stone Forest to try and tame one of the dark spirits."

After he said that, the gremlin took a fleeting glance at me. Surprisingly, that gaze made a chill run down my spine. A hunch fell into place like a tiny little puzzle piece. Mee had seen me summon the Snow Ghoul Spirit, which was why he sometimes referred to me as a shaman.

Darkness. Taming spirits. What does it all mean? Is there a portal to the other world in the Stone Forest?! That little sneak! Why didn't he tell me? Although, Mee isn't at fault here. I wasn't asking the right questions.

"And how are the candidates selected?" Randy inquired.

"They fight among themselves to the death for the right to enter the Stone Forest," Mee answered.

"So am I understanding correctly that they don't all succeed in capturing a spirit?" I clarified.

"Yes," the gremlin responded.

"And sometimes they don't all come back?" I asked again.

The kid nodded and said:

"When a shaman dies in the Stone Forest, a fearsome ghoul is unleashed on the steppe."

Overall, I get the picture. The orcs know about a portal that triggers once a year. They send their strongest apprentice there for the chance to kill an otherworldly wraith. Why an apprentice though? I have only one answer — they'd have the highest chance of receiving the coveted spirit vial.

Beyond that, if they're absorbing spirits there must be a shrine and altar somewhere nearby, probably next to the portal. And in its turn, it might be part of something bigger.

All those thoughts made my heart start to beat faster.

"What kind of ghoul?" Bruni asked, agitated.

Mee shrugged.

"Different kinds. The orcs say it's the spirit the shaman failed to pacify obtaining a body and entering our world to get their revenge."

There was one final aspect to figure out.

"Mee," I asked. "When do they hold the kurultai?"

"Two months before the rainy season." I heard his answer and breathed a sigh of relief. Most likely, the portal had already opened.

"But the top candidate comes for the spirit at the beginning of the first month of winter," Mee added quietly. "In other words, right about now."

One hour later, the conversation fizzled out. The time had come to rest.

Despite my warning about the Lair's alarm and the harn's animal senses, Randy was sleeping with one eye open.

But Bruni, probably in view of his simple nature, was less concerned. Still, it could all be for show. I'm not the only one who sees an advantage in being underestimated.

To tell the truth, the way our allies were acting didn't concern me much. I didn't want to think about the otherworldly portal either. All my thoughts were revolving around the news about my brother.

I was very stirred up by the news that he'd never been to the Wastes. That means the Bear's clerks were lying to my father. Although it's not likely they'd have gone and done that without their lord's knowledge. Ahem, definitely something of a shady story.

That meant a whole unit had disappeared in an unknown location along with its captain. Hard to believe the old Bear didn't know. Something must have happened. Something the retinue soldiers' families weren't supposed to find out about. It was simpler to send a death certificate.

I imagined the way my parents would have reacted if they discovered the truth! Thinking back on my father and mother, I took a heavy sigh. A lump rose up my throat all on its own.

They never told me much about Ivar. I never figured out why. All I could do was guess. But from the brief conversations they did let me hear, I had formed a definite picture of my older brother. Brave, daring and willful. Strong and agile beyond his years. The favorite of his whole school. But despite being pampered by tons of attention, my father said he was a good kid.

Father tried to make excuses for him, saying his son was always drawn to the warrior's path. And that the Baron's scouts only added fuel to the fire. After they found the up and coming kid, they blew smoke up his ass with bogus tales of grand campaigns, battles and glory in combat. In the end, all their tall tales made Ivar's head spin. Of course, I also shouldn't discount the fact that the Bear's recruiters probably had high Charisma. And that was how the young boy ended up ensnared in their web. Heh, I of all people should know about that.

My thoughts about Ivar were contradictory. And it wasn't like there was a sudden flood of brotherly love filling my soul. As a matter of fact, I had never considered him a good kid, since he abandoned my parents. I'd like to believe he was pressured by somebody but, even at my level, I was able to shake off Frodi's charms eventually.

Yes, Ivar was my brother by blood, but I didn't even know what he looked like, the tiny portrait in mother's curio cabinet excepted. That was how he looked at age nine, very much like father. Now, if he even was alive, he would be thirty-two years of age, an adult man. I'd be curious to look him in the eyes. To see whether he felt any remorse about what happened. To tell him about mom and father's tears. About their sorrow when they heard he was dead.

Already drifting off, I promised myself that I'd do everything in my power to uncover his fate. First and foremost, in memory of my parents.

But I wasn't able to sleep for too long. In the middle of the night, I was awoken by something wet touching my cheek. A second later, I realized it was Gorgie's nose. Cracking open my right eye, I saw the outlines of his lithe scaly body. My right hand mechanically landed on the cat's wet nose.

"Hrn!" Gorgie said agitatedly.

"What?" I immediately heard Randy's tense voice from the darkness.

"There's a band of orcs approaching the hills," I told him, quickly getting up off the ground. "They'll be here soon!"

CHAPTER 11

"**R**IDERS?" a frowning Bruni asked Randy, who'd just appeared at the cave's threshold.

The redhead went off with the harn an hour before to do some scouting, and they had just returned.

"No," he shook his head. "Normal hunters. Seven of them. The highest level is thirteen."

The big guy breathed a sigh of relief and asked:

"What are they doing?"

"They set up camp on the northern side of the hill," Randy started explaining. "They dragged over an antelope."

"We gonna wait 'em out?" I asked.

"That won't be possible," the ranger answered. "Two orcs already went out to scout. They'll see our tracks soon enough. Your beast is keeping an eye on them now."

"That's good," I told the big guy matter-of-factly, flexing my wrists. "And we'll be able to eat some fresh meat."

"First we need to disarm the scouts carefully and preferably without making any noise," Randy said thoughtfully.

"Well, I can help with that," I smiled.

A few minutes later we saw two orcs cautiously moving between the stones and attentively studying their surroundings. Middling height, they cut a veiny figure. Tusked countenances. Levels ten and eleven. Armed with bows and short spears.

Randy asked me to tell him in detail about a few of my spells and was pleasantly surprised. He quickly put together a simple plan of action. Honestly, it was obvious that the ranger wanted to know a lot more about my capabilities. But he was behaving like a reasonable person, so he didn't pressure me. He'd probably never had to command a mage before today, even one as weak as me.

The orc scouts were slowly but inexorably moving right into our trap. Based on their periodic exchanges of short phrases, they were not aware of our ambush.

According to the plan we'd worked out, I was supposed to immobilize the orcs with lightning. Then Randy and Bruni would tie them up in a couple seconds and drag them into our cave for a brief but exhaustive conversation.

Overall, it was all going according to plan so far. Right up until one of the orcs suddenly stopped and looked sharply in the direction of where I was hiding. An instant later, I heard him give a loud guttural cry. At that very moment, one of Randy's black arrows sunk into his eye, flying in from the right.

I hadn't used my lightning yet — they were too far away.

The second orc reacted instantly. Nimbly blocking his dead comrade's body from the flying arrows and loudly screaming for help, he ran ahead.

From the right, I heard muted cursing from Bruni behind his stone. The situation had spun out of control. The dead orc's well-leveled senses and observation played against us.

The orc that shouted for the whole surrounding area was not able to run far. The harn's scaly body flickered like dark lightning out from behind a stone and slammed down on the runaway's back. A moment later, he choked on his own scream. But alas, it was too late — the rest of the orcs were probably already running our way.

Randy jumped out from behind the stone on the left and started quickly gathering his loosed arrows.

"Order the harn to drag the orc's body this way!" he shouted to me. "And have him stay in view! We want the orcs to think their comrades were attacked by a beast!"

Gorgie instantly carried out the order and unhurriedly dragged the corpse in our direction.

Just when I thought the five other orcs hadn't heard their comrade's cries, they finally appeared. The orcs ran in silence. With spears and bows at the ready. They looked somewhat unhurried as well. I think they realized that there was no one left to help because the screams had stopped.

Strange as it may have been, Randy's improvisation worked out. As soon as the orcs saw Gorgie hunched over the bodies of the scouts, their caution disappeared without a trace. Loudly, howling and screaming curses at the predator, they dashed forward with spears pointed forward. They must have been hoping one of their comrades was still alive.

The harn easily dodged several arrows and jumped behind a broad stone. His loud mocking growl seemingly roused the attackers even further which I did not fail to take advantage of.

— *You have attacked Steppe Orc (13).*
— *You have dealt 29 damage!*

— *You have attacked Steppe Orc (11).*
— *You have dealt 63 damage!*

— *You have attacked Steppe Orc (11).*
— *You have dealt 52 damage!*

— *You have attacked Steppe Orc (12).*

— You have dealt 41 damage!

— You have attacked Steppe Orc (10).
— You have dealt 72 damage!

Pushing Mee forward, I said:

"Hurry up, you don't have much time. Gorgie will help you."

The gremlin nodded decisively and, getting a powerful grip on his thin knife, ran in the direction of the frozen orcs. Bruni, Randy and Gorgie were already there.

A few seconds later, I saw four victory notifications. Randy tied up the fifth orc tight and dragged him over to the stones. And there he quickly interrogated him.

"We have to get out of here," he said somberly after the interrogation. "These are hunters from the Clan of the Red Wolves. Their temporary camp is two days' travel from here. Soon they will take notice and send some more serious warriors."

✳ ✳ ✳

I would characterize the road south in a few words: mud, cold and inhuman exhaustion. Our two days underway felt like a never-ending nightmare. Even the higher-level Randy and Bruni were having a hard time.

It was as if the ranger had a premonition of

disaster and was pulling us forward with a singular obsession. And despite our exhaustion and the unwelcoming steppe, today we finally reached our destination.

"The Bridge of Bones!" Mee said with awe in his voice when we saw the massive skeleton of some monster lying across the bed of a troubled river.

By the way, the gremlin had traveled all that time on the harn's back, and was the most rested of our group.

"They say that hill over there was formed from the skull of this beast," Randy shared some knowledge, breathing heavily.

I should note that the ranger proved not to be the most talkative guy. Of course, he did speak, but it was always more about things that he himself was interested in.

He especially enjoyed asking me all kinds of questions. For example, about my magic, how I got here, or the harn. I naturally kept mum and just handed out the odd crumb of information, which always made Randy furrow his brow and scratch his head unhappily. And yet, he was in no rush to answer my questions either. In fact, I was getting the impression that the redheaded scout must have been weighed down by so many oaths he'd have looked a holiday tree if I could see them.

And as for Bruni well, to put it lightly, the big guy knew only very particular pieces of information. And fairly surface level ones at that.

For example, he knew little about mages, the value of esses and tablets, or the political situation in the kingdom. But he had a brilliant understanding of the capital's finest gastronomic routes, or which tavern served the tastiest blood sausages and brewed the best beer. He was familiar with every innkeeper of good repute and remembered the names of all their pretty waitresses. I'm sure that if I were to find myself in the capital with Bruni right now, I would have a nice place to sleep and tasty food to eat.

But alas, the men were still not saying a word about their unit or the reasons that drove their commander to set out for the Wastes. The story of the careerist captain was troubling me more and more.

"We have to hurry," Randy said, looking from side to side in alarm. "I've got a bad feeling about this."

I also looked around. A wet gray steppe. A raging river. The ghastly ancient bridge, the Stone Forest forming a wall of trees and darkening the horizon. I wonder what exactly is bothering our commander.

I took a glance at Gorgie. The cat was calm.

The closer we came to the bridge, the more on edge Randy became. His anxiety transferred onto all of us. As we walked, we were looking from side to side, constantly keeping an eye on our surroundings and where we were placing our feet.

When we made it twenty steps from the

bridge, Gorgie said he felt a strange premonition, but couldn't quite tell what it was.

Once next to the titanic skeleton, I opened my mouth dumbfounded and stood perfectly still. Over the centuries, the bones had been transformed into gray stone. The gigantic ribs were playing the part of supports. In the spinal column, meanwhile, where the creature's spinal cord had once been, the orcs had laid down a floor of wide wooden boards to make it easier for their shamans to pass. In comparison with the bridge, the raging river seemed like nothing more than an irritated stream.

"Onward! Let's go!" Randy spurred us on.

"Hrn!" Gorgie repeated, his scales constantly vibrating.

Yet we never made it inside the bridge. One hundred yards away, three riders crested a hill.

"Wargs!" Bruni barked.

"Prepare for a skirmish!" Randy shouted and, turning to me, said:

"We're going to need all your skill here! That is a shaman and his retinue!"

Seeing that we were not going to flee, the two riders dug their heels into the wide sides of their wolves and dashed forward. A lupine howl rolled over the steppe, turning the blood cold in my veins. The wolves were level eighteen and the orcs twenty, which put our chances of victory into serious doubt.

"Hide!" I shouted to the gremlin, activating muckwalker's aura.

Randy and Bruni's first arrows flew at the riders. The shaman's defensive amulets, which by all appearances his bodyguards were draped in, worked flawlessly. The black arrows fell to dust without doing a single point of damage.

I hadn't attacked yet because the distance was still too great.

Bruni's quiver was quickly emptied. Throwing the bow aside and pulling out a scimitar, the big fellow gave a roar of fury and ran out to meet his enemies.

Sixty-five feet. I can already make out the grinning tusked faces of the orcs. Strong, broad-shouldered — they are noticeably different from the other orcs. Pointedly not using bows. They clearly want to take us captive.

Fifty feet. The wargs look somehow like wolves, but also like bears. Big massive bodies. Broad necks and thick paws. But despite their high level, they are noticeably slower than the harn.

"Get ready!" I shouted and activated a spell.

The lilac cloud of a gulper's ram broke away from my hand and shot off into the riders. Several different-colored flames sparked up around the orcs' bodies. Alas, I was not able to stun them or send them flying back. But still their wolves did get knocked off track. It was an amusing sight when the orcs realized they were up against a mage.

Bruni, no longer moving slow, brought his sword down full bore onto the nearest warg's head.

And surprisingly the blow landed!

"You broke through their defenses!" the ranger exclaimed gleefully. His bowstring started thrumming again with renewed force. Black arrows rained down on the orcs like a swarm of angry wild bees. They were blown away by this new turn of events. The shrieks of pain and angry growling, the ring of steel and war cries of the retinue men all came together into one solid din.

My Ram's fifteen-second cooldown felt like fifteen hours. And Lightning wasn't active yet — I was still six feet short.

Randy's bow stopped thrumming. Out of arrows.

"Stay here and save your mana!" he shouted, running out to help Bruni. "Don't forget about the shaman!"

I had three seconds to recharge.

The warg that struck Bruni is already lying on the ground twitching in predeath convulsions. Its master, run through with a few arrows, is lying in the distance and not showing any signs of life.

A second before the spell reloads. Bruni turns onto his side. The long tip of an orcish spear is sticking out of his back.

My teeth clenched in anger, I activate the spell.

My Ram has already thrown the second rider to the ground. Gorgie, distracting the warg from Bruni all that time, got up next to the wounded enemies in a few long jumps and began sowing death. Randy's scimitar gave a few slashes, separating the orc's head from its body.

At that very moment, the shaman entered the game. A powerful wave of burning air knocked the harn and ranger off their feet.

And though Gorgie had gotten up already despite his limping, Randy was lying motionless like a steaming broken doll.

To my surprise, the orcish warlock was in no particular hurry. His wolf, expressing no emotion, was slowly ambling toward the skirmish.

Gorgie, stumbling and shaking his head in rage like a fist-fighter that just took a nasty punch to the ear, gave a start forward. But I stopped him with a shout:

"Back!"

The scales on his right side went slightly dark but, based on his figures, the cat was doing fine. He must have reacted to the attack at the last moment and the shaman's spell only grazed him.

"That was the right decision, slave!" shouted the grinning shaman.

I finally caught a glimpse of his level — eighteen.

I quickly ran a gaze over the battlefield. The orcs, wargs and my companions had died in a matter of seconds.

"Surrender if you know what's good for you!" shouted the shaman. "Today is a special occasion for me. I'm going to let you live."

I looked at my mana supply — and once again

praised myself for my Wisdom. If my opponent is feeling chatty, I need to take advantage of that.

"So, you get lucky?" I shouted, smiling. "Did an otherworldly creature grant you a vial?!"

The shaman's smiling face slowly stretched out in astonishment.

"How do you know the mysteries of orc-kind?!"

His fearsome cry was supported by an angry growl from the wolf. Gorgie didn't let that go unanswered and growled back provocatively.

"You're wrong about that, shaman!" I shouted. "This mystery does not belong to the orcs!"

The orc's evil sloping eyes looked like tea saucers.

I chuckled and added:

"Like scavengers, you use that which you have no right to!"

Well, I was hoping to send the warlock over the edge and I had done just that. Why did I want that? Easy. He had been temporarily weakened by his fight with an otherworldly creature and subsequently absorbing its spirit. He must have spent a good deal on elixirs and potions. That was why he was holding back.

Obeying the shaman's will, his wolf ran on the attack. I allowed the gray beast racing in my direction to come near. Then I activated ram, sending it flying back several yards. And at that very moment, the shaman sent a dark cloud of small sharp spines our way, heading off Gorgie's attack. The spell only slightly hit Gorgie, the main force landed on me.

With a loud wail, the harn flew back and fell silent. I also took a nasty hit. I was lying on my back in the mud. My eyes were going dark, and I could taste a briny flavor in my mouth. I probably bit my tongue in the fall. I got lucky. The muckwalker aura absorbed all the damage. But I was left defenseless.

— *Would you like to summon Longtailed Ysh Spirit?*

Giving my assent, I immediately lost six hundred mana points. Seeing the semitransparent giant snake appear out of thin air and wrap itself around my body put the shaman into a state of shock. His lower jaw started quivering.

I noticed Gorgie start to stir out of the corner of my eye, trying not to draw attention. He was mad at the warlock. Very mad. But the warg was just about to wake up. Something to keep the harn busy.

Getting up off the ground, I felt a sharp pain in my side and gasped. I glanced at my life supply, which was slowly bleeding points. Apparently I hadn't merely bitten my tongue.

"Surrender if you know what's good for you!" the shaman wailed, pointing both of his dark-yellow-smoke-enshrouded hands in my direction.

"I'll be a good master!"

Only then did I notice that the orc was still quite young. We might have even been the same age.

"Your supplies and storage crystals empty after battling the entity?" I clarified mockingly. "Is that right?"

The shaman sent a weary scowl at the Ysh's powerful body. The snake's triangular head was staring unflinchingly at my opponent. M-hm, this thing has quite the stare. I should know.

Trying to keep the orc distracted, I took a few short steps in his direction. Around ten more feet and lightning will be active.

Instead of answering, the shaman launched an amber ball at me. The Ysh reacted immediately and coiled up into a series of tight, scaly rings. The system told me that my shield had absorbed six hundred damage. Woah! I wonder what level that spell is!

I took another few steps forward.

The ram's effect wore off and the warg, obeying an order from its master, ran in my direction again. But Gorgie was on the alert. Activating Thorntail's Jump, he got behind the wolf and dealt his most powerful and crushing blow yet. A loud squeal of pain informed me the warg had bigger things to worry about than me.

"Say goodbye to your mutt," I told him, chuckling. Swallowing a clot of blood, I took one more step.

Three more feet and I can attack. For a few moments we just stood opposite one another like two stone statues. The moment of truth. I can see a lack of confidence in the orc's eyes. We're like two gamblers trying to guess what cards our opponent might have up his sleeve.

We attacked at the same time. The shaman lashed me with a ghostly thorny branch. I meanwhile took a long jump to get in range then launched an eel lightning.

The orc's eyes bulged in fear and he froze like a statue. Two ice arrows like thin sharp icicles, reinforced with scrolls of fury, and the shaman's defenses were blown to smithereens.

I saw the bone amulets and talismans around his neck falling to dust after every blow. In his eyes, I saw anticipation that every spell I cast might be the last for him.

Then a third arrow penetrated the orc's heart and brought our stand-off to a close.

I wanted to run and help Gorgie, but the Great System informed me the fight was over.

Running a sullen gaze over the bloody battlefield, I slowly slumped down to the ground. My eyes went dark. The last thing I saw before losing consciousness was Mee's frightened little face.

CHAPTER 12

I CAME TO all at once. I shot up on an elbow and looked around half blind. I think I'm in a tent. Although based on the dimensions, this might be more of a yurt. I was lying on the floor covered by an animal fur one step away from a small fire pit hastily assembled out of large river stones.

Captured again? Impossible!

Shivering in panic, I opened the message tab and, after a brief read-through, exhaled with relief. No mind control or other nasty things of that nature. Better already.

After that I looked over my body. I didn't see a single bruise, scratch or scrape. But I remembered for certain that I had plenty of them at the end of the battle.

I quickly ran back through the last few minutes of my fight with the shaman. I hurriedly patted down my stomach, chest and ribs. I raised my hand to my mouth. Surprising. There was no blood. Hm, but what about the blood I was spitting up after the shaman's attack? What is going on?

The canopy of the tent suddenly started to move and made me get ready to deflect an attack. But fortunately no one was coming to hurt me. A satisfied scaly face stuck in through the flap.

"Hrn!" Gorgie growled, overjoyed, and slipped inside.

I was immediately licked head to toe and pressed down by his massive armored carcass.

"I'm very glad to see you too, my brother!" I said tenderly, stroking the harn behind the ear. He fell onto his back and, rolling his eyes in pleasure, gave a loud groan.

After examining my pet carefully for damage and not finding anything, I breathed a sigh of relief. Then I finally realized what was bothering me.

"Big buddy! You hit level eight on me!"

"Hrn!" the harn replied in satisfaction, continuing to lie on his back.

And meanwhile, I opened his characteristics.

— *Ferocious Harn.*
— *Name: Gorgie.*
— *Level: 8 (2100/44000).*
— *Status: Loyalty to master (permanent).*
— *Mind: 1/1*
— *Strength: 78/120*
— *Agility: 79/120*

— *Accuracy: 5.8/120*
— *Intuition: 7/8*
— *Wisdom: 14/16*
— *Animal instinct: 14/16*
— *Speed: 77/120*
— *Flexibility: 52/120*
— *Intellect: 44/80*
— *Mana supply: 490/490*
— *Health: 70/80*
— *Endurance: 67/80*
— *Life supply: 750/750*
— *Energy supply: 720/720*
— *Scale armor: 35/40*
— *Defense: 350/400*
— *Damage: +201.1...+637.2*

— *Bite: 35/40*
— *Paw swipe: 35/40*
— *Pounce: 7/8*
— *Animal regeneration: 14/16*
— *Hunter: 36/40*
— *Fisher: 17.8/40*
— *Resistance to Hexapod poison: 7/40*

"Congratulations!" I said, patting him on his armored side. Then I asked:

"And where's Mee?"

"Here," came a quiet voice behind me.

The gremlin's big eared face stuck out from behind the cloth flap. There's a happy smile on his tired little face.

"Wounded?" I asked, concerned.

"No," the boy nodded.

"Thank heavens!" I sighed with relief. "Randy? Bruni?"

The gremlin shook his head as he got comfortable next to the fire.

"Too bad," I sighed heavily. "They fought valiantly."

We spent a moment in silence, each thinking about our own thing.

"You were also a hair from death after the battle," the gremlin told me. "If not for your magic, you might have been a goner."

"What are you talking about?" I asked in surprise.

"Don't you remember?" Mee looked at me with wide-open eyes.

"What am I supposed to remember?" I answered with a question of my own.

"For example when you ordered me to bring you down into the water."

"Water?!" I asked, dumbfounded.

Mee looked at Gorgie in incomprehension, then at me.

"What's the last thing you remember?"

"The fight with the shaman," I started, squinting. "Then his death. Then a severe pain in my chest. Blood in my mouth. Lots of blood. That's all. What happened next?"

"After the shaman died, you briefly lost consciousness. Then you woke up and started saying to put you in water. At first I thought you were talking nonsense. It was so strange it almost hurt. But you said it was for some kind of spell."

And then it finally hit me! Ah, of course! Muckwalker's Aquatic Regeneration!

"Now do you remember?" Mee asked, seeing my reaction to his words.

"Only the fact that I have such a spell," I shook my head.

"I see," the gremlin nodded. "Anyway, as soon as we dragged you into a water-filled ditch, you activated it and dark-green slime covered your body."

"And then?" I asked, intrigued.

"While you were in the water, I found this tent among the shaman's possessions and set it up on the edge of the forest. And when the slime went away a bit later, taking all your scratches and scrapes with it, we brought you here."

"How long have we been here?"

"Two days by now," Mee answered and added: "Don't worry. The area is quiet for now."

"What about the orcs?"

Mee shook his head.

"Only a shaman may cross the bridge and only in service of a ritual. Other orcs are not allowed to come here. Such is their law."

I nodded understandingly. Looks like the warlocks of the orcs guarded their secrets jealously. But in any case, it would be dangerous to stay in one place for long.

"Sorry, Rick," Mee said quietly. "We had to throw the bodies of your fellow humans into the river. Along with those of the orcs and wargs. To get rid of the evidence."

I sighed heavily and placed a hand on the gremlin's little shoulder.

"Don't apologize. I think Randy and Bruni would have done the same in your place."

Mee silently undid the drawstring of his knapsack and started placing some items on the fur. I took a look. Esses, a bronze ring, a steel bracelet, a bone amulet, a small stone knife a few differently colored flasks and a gray crystal.

Sorting it all into two piles, the gremlin pointed at the larger one:

"This is all the most valuable stuff the orcs had on them. Well, with the exception of tents, weaponry, furs and other baubles."

"And this?" I pointed at the smaller pile.

"That's Randy and Bruni's stuff," Mee answered quietly.

I breathed a heavy sigh.

"I see."

"It isn't much," the gremlin said. "A few thousand essences and ten tablets. This must be what dropped for them in their final battle."

I looked closely.

— *Experience essence (7940).*
— *Silver tablet (10).*
— *Messenger Amulet.*

"Hey, what's this?" I asked, intrigued and picking up a small round bronze medallion.

Messenger Amulet.
— *Type: Single-use artifact.*
— *Rarity: Epic.*
— *Effect:*
— *Conveys a message.*
— *Note:*
— *Activates only in the hands of the recipient.*
— *Recipient: Captain Isamu Takeda.*
— *Sender: Sergeant Randelph Larsen.*
— *Disappears after use.*
— *Weight: None. Takes no space.*

I looked at the gremlin in surprise.

"Do you see this item's characteristics?"

"Only that it's a messenger amulet," the gremlin responded. "Can you see more information?"

"Yeah," I nodded. That must have been my fifteen Mind points.

"What's in it?" Mee inquired.

"I can't read the message itself," I answered. "But one thing is clear — Randy was no common soldier. I think this is a message for his commander. And based on the fact it's epic class, it must be an important one."

"And you intend to find its recipient?"

I considered it, then nodded:

"If we survive and get out of here — yes. At the very least, we should do it to honor the memory of Randy and Bruni."

After picking up the esses and tablets of the retinue men, I started looking through the orcs' things.

— *Experience essence (25370).*
— *Ring of agility (1).*
— *Amulet of strength (1).*
— *Bracelet of agility (1).*
— *Stone knife (1).*
— *Potion of endurance (2)*
— *Elixir of speed (3).*
— *Small crystal of mana (1).*

Rubbing my hands together in satisfaction, I smiled — one more mana crystal! Alright then, let's take a look.

Small crystal of mana.
— *Mana: 0/500.*

Hm, five hundred points. That means these crystals don't have a standard capacity. But nevertheless, this is just amazing! This trophy alone is enough to make the battle with the shaman worth it.

And I still haven't even looked through my personal loot.

Let's keep going.

Ring of Agility.
— *Level: 8.*
— *Category: Simple.*
— *Agility +9.*
— *Durability — 43.*

Amulet of strength.
— *Level: 10.*
— *Category: Simple.*
— *Strength +12.*
— *Durability — 82.*

Bracelet of agility.
— *Level: 9.*
— *Category: Simple.*
— *Agility +7.*
— *Durability — 52.*

Stone knife.
— *Level: 12.*
— *Category: Rare.*
— *Strength +10.*
— *Damage +25.*
— *Durability — 149.*

Potion of Endurance.
— *Level: 7*
— *Type: Energy potion.*
— *Rarity: Rare.*
— *Effect:*
— *Restores 30% energy.*

— *Quantity:1 dose.*
— *Note:*
— *Not to be taken more than 1 time per day.*
— *Weight: None. Takes no space.*

Elixir of Speed.
— *Level: 8*
— *Type: Speed elixirs.*
— *Rarity: Rare.*
— *Effect:*
— *Increases speed by 25%.*
— *Quantity:1 dose.*
— *Duration: 10 minutes.*
— *Note:*
— *Not to be taken more than 1 time per day.*
— *Weight: None. Takes no space.*

"Ahem," I turned to the gremlin after carefully studying all the items' characteristics. "All these bonuses would be nice but, as they say, the hat doesn't fit. Who was wearing these rings and amulets?"

"The shaman had the knife and bracelet, his fighters had the other stuff," Mee answered.

"I see," I said, stashing it all in my backpack. "We'll set it aside for brighter days. At the very least until you grow up a bit."

Only then did I notice that there was a small cauldron hanging over the fire on a stubby tripod. Mee started stirring it intently. And whatever it was it smelled delicious.

"Hungry?" he asked when he saw me drooling.

My stomach groaned loudly in response.

Mee laughed. "Patience! We'll eat soon."

I looked at Gorgie. The gremlin followed my eyes and said:

"Don't you worry about him. I have plenty of warg meat stashed away."

I nodded silently and thought distantly that Mee was a godsend for our little crew. A very practical kid. Heh, he and Crum would definitely have been able to find a common tongue.

Okay. While he cooks the food, I've got time to look through the loot I got for defeating the shaman and his guard. I opened the notification tab.

— *You have killed Orc Rider (20).*

— *Congratulations! You receive:*
— *Experience essence (4000).*
— *Silver tablet (10).*

— *You have killed Steppe Warg (18).*

— *Congratulations! You receive:*
— *Experience essence (3600).*
— *Silver tablet (10).*

— *You have killed Orc Shaman (18).*

— *Congratulations! You receive:*

— *Experience essence (3600).*

— *Gold tablet of Intellect.*

— *Silver tablet (10).*

— **You have killed Steppe Warg (18).**

— *Congratulations! You receive:*

— *Experience essence (3600).*

— *Silver tablet (10).*

— *Attention! The Higher Powers have taken note of your accomplishment! You're a team fighter! While part of a team, you managed to defeat 5 creatures more than 10 levels higher than you!*

— *Congratulations! You receive:*

— *Experience essence (2000).*

— *Silver tablet (10).*

— *Attention! The Higher Powers have taken note of your accomplishment! You're a team fighter! While part of a team, you managed to defeat 5 creatures more than 15 levels higher than you!*

— *Congratulations! You receive:*

— *Experience essence (3000).*

— *Silver tablet (15).*

— *Attention! The Higher Powers smile upon you! You have replicated the legendary feat of Roland Stoneheart! You defeated a mage more than 15 levels higher than you!*

— *Congratulations! You receive:*

— *Experience essence (3000).*
— *Iridescent Tablet "Orc Shaman" (1).*

I wiped the sweat off my brow with a shaky hand. Sixty-five silver tablets for one battle, plus an iridescent. It must have been the first time I got that much loot at once. My heart aflutter, I open the description of the iridescent.

— *Iridescent Tablet "Orc Shaman."*
— *Effect:*
— *Unlocks 1 characteristic of your choice from Orc Shaman.*
— *Unlocks 1 ability of your choice from Orc Shaman.*
— *Unlocks 1 spell of your choice from Orc Shaman.*
— *Unlocks 1 profession of your choice from Orc Shaman.*
— *+10 to any characteristic/skill/profession/spell.*
— *Weight: None. Takes no space.*

Great! Unlike the monster iridescents, this one also allowed me to unlock a Profession!

Okay. Let me get right to spells. Woah! The shaman has more than ten! So then, let's take a look. Five defensive, six offensive. Hm, so what do we have here?

— ***Wave of Healing.***

— *Level: 0 (0/20).*
— *Type: Spell.*
— *Rarity: Epic.*
— *Description:*
— *Using magic, the orc shaman creates an invisible healing wave, which is capable of healing wounds and repairing damage.*
— *Effect:*
— *+10 regeneration.*
— *Restores 20% life.*

— *Requirements:*
— *Intellect — 10.*
— *Expends 120 mana points.*
— *Note:*
— *Regeneration effect duration: 30 min.*

I could feel my heartbeat speeding up. I was holding one of the most useful spells in existence both for war and peacetime! Healing mages are highly respected and cherished members of their communities. And as a rule, they are very well-off. Finding this spell was a true gift from the gods! So my rival wasn't as simple as he appeared.

It took some effort to get myself together and continue studying the tablet.

Because I'd already made up my mind about the spell, I moved on to Skills and Abilities.

The shaman had more than ten. Beginning with Riding, and ending with Night Vision. I was a bit perplexed at first. There were so many options it was hard to know where to look first! But in the end, I decided on what I deemed to be the most useful. Beyond that, I had already seen it in action.

— **_Dome of invisibility._**
— _Level: 0 (0/ 20)._
— _Type: Magical ability._
— _Rarity: Epic._
— _Description:_
— _The orc shaman uses magic to cover himself in a dome of invisibility._
— _Effect:_
— _Creates a dome of invisibility._

— _Requirements:_
— _Intellect — 10._
— _Expends 120 mana points._
— _Note:_
— _Effect duration: 10 min._
— _Radius: 10 feet._
— _Effect dissipates after caster enters combat._

That ability must have been what was keeping the wolf riders and shaman concealed before. Beyond a doubt, this skill would benefit all of us.

Okay then, I think I've made up my mind on the spell and ability. All that's left is to solve the profession issue.

That was all fairly standard and expected — herbalist, fisher, hunter and stuff like that. Right up until my gaze landed on the final one.

— **Potion Making.**

— *Level: 0 (0/20).*

— *Type: Magical profession.*

— *Rarity: Epic.*

— *Description:*

— *Using magic, special materials and corresponding recipes, the orc shaman is able to create magical potions.*

— *Effect:*

— *Create magical potions.*

— *Number of available recipes: 0.*

After closing the description, I scratched the back of my head quizzically. So that means it is possible to have a profession you can't use. I'd need recipes first.

I reread the descriptions of the spells, abilities and professions again, then looked at Mee. At that moment, the kid was blowing on a spoonful of stew. Hey, what if?

"Brother," I addressed the gremlin. "I just got an idea. I think I should give you a gift."

After saying that, I showed the gremlin the iridescent tablet. Mee happened to be tasting his cooking just then and I made him shudder.

"But what about you?" He asked, coughing. "These tablets are the only way for you to get stronger."

"I know," I nodded. "But here's the thing. This tablet contains a very useful and valuable spell, which can be used to heal. Something is telling me it will save our lives a couple times at least."

"So what's all the fuss about?" Mee asked. "You take it so you can heal us."

"No," I shook my head. "We have to think rationally."

"What are you talking about?" the gremlin asked in surprise.

"I'm saying that if you have this spell, we'll be able to improve it much faster. Twenty silvers and say hello to level one! And thirty will get us up to two! Do you understand what that would mean?"

The gremlin considered it briefly, then nodded:

"I see what you're saying. Five iridescent tablets versus fifty silvers — now I understand what you mean by 'think rationally.'"

"Heh," I took a heavy sigh. "Too bad I wasn't thinking this rationally when I used the firepaw tablet on myself. It would have been a better fit for Gorgie. Oh well. Anyway. It's no use swinging fists after the dust is settled."

After I said that, I extended the glimmering sheet to the gremlin. He accepted it reverentially with quavering hands and squeaked out excitedly:

"Thanks!"

I just waved it off with a smile. I listened to my feelings. Not a drop of regret. I'm doing the right thing.

CHAPTER 13

"WHERE DO I START?" Mee asked, his voice quavering in worry.

"First you have to unlock Intellect and bring it up to ten," I answered. "That way you'll meet the Great System's minimum requirements to activate the spell and ability."

"I see," the gremlin nodded.

— Attention! Your familiar has unlocked a new characteristic — Intellect!
— Present value: 10/30.

— Attention! Your familiar has unlocked the mana supply!
— Present value: 120/120.

I looked at Mee and smiled. His little eyes were open wide. The short fur on his body was all standing on end, which made him look like a little nubbin of pure fluff.

Poor kid. I knew where he was coming from. I felt the same way not long ago. He and I weren't so different, in essence. Heh, if someone told me two months ago that I'd become a mage, make it through the caverns of the Crooked Mountains, domesticate a cave harn, then defeat an orc shaman in the heart of the Wastes, I'd never have believed them.

"Keep going, as we discussed," I encouraged him.

— Attention! Your familiar has unlocked a new spell — Wave of Healing!

— Attention! Your familiar has unlocked a new ability — Dome of Invisibility!

— Attention! Your familiar has unlocked a new magical profession — Potion Making!

"Congratulations, brother!" I said, smiling. "You're a mage now!"

Mee gave a timid smile. There were tears welling up in the corners of his eyes.

"Kid, what's the matter?" I asked in surprise.

"Well, you see, Rick," Mee answered, hurriedly wiping away tears. "It just occurred to me that I am the first gremlin to become a mage. In the last one hundred years at least. As a matter of fact, I don't know if there has ever been a mage of my kind before."

"Not even in gremlin fairy tales?" I smiled.

"I don't know," the boy shrugged. "We don't have any fairy tales, legends or songs."

"Why might that be?" I asked, perplexed.

"Long ago, at a kurultai of the orcs it was decided that gremlins have no reason to tell one another old wives' tales."

"The utter brutes!" I barked angrily through my teeth. "They aren't satisfied just to have you as slaves! They also had to rob gremlin-kind of its soul!"

"The soul of gremlin-kind," Mee muttered thoughtfully. He seemed to like the phrase.

"Yes, precisely," I nodded. "Your songs, belief, tales, legends. All that is your history. Your soul. By the way, do you know why the orcs did that?"

"I've never thought about it," the gremlin shrugged. "Why?"

"I think they're afraid of you," I answered.

"How could that be?" Mee asked in incomprehension. "You saw them in battle! They're great warriors! Their shamans are very powerful!"

"And nevertheless they are not immortal!" I smiled back. "You've seen that with your own two eyes!"

The gremlin wanted to object, but got stuck midword. I saw an expression of understanding suddenly dawn on his little face.

"The chieftains and shamans of the orcs are no fools," I continued. "They understand that, if you band together, you could become a problem.

That's why year after year you're robbed of the things that could unite your race."

"Can fairy tales and legends really bring people together?" Mee asked untrustingly.

I chuckled.

"You better believe it! How would you feel if I told you that your ancestors fought the orcs and won? Or that the gremlins once had great warriors, chieftains and mages of their own? And after all, they probably did. There's no way they didn't! And they must have composed legends and songs to commemorate their deeds! After all, the orcs must have taken these memories from you for some reason."

Mee stared at a fixed point, his eyes open wide. I smiled. The little guy was overwhelmed. He-he, I should build on that.

"So you just told me you've never ever heard of a gremlin mage before. Right?"

Mee nodded mechanically.

"That means you have just become a figure of gremlin lore!"

The kid gulped loudly.

"Mee, the Great Vanquisher of Orcs!" I acclaimed with a broad smile. "How do you like that?"

The gremlin gulped again, and his gaze looked both uncomfortable and seemingly afraid. I took a heavy sigh. Welp, I scared the poor guy. I have to distract him.

"Alright," I said calmly. "Calm yourself,

brother. That's enough for today. Better we eat your grub. It's probably ready by now. The smell from the pot is driving me crazy! By the way, you have to eat up. You're going to be activating a lot of tablets soon."

After saying that, I glanced into my backpack.

— *Experience essence (105405).*
— *Gold tablet of Intellect. (2)*
— *Monster Hunter Token (590).*
— *Hunter's Fury (13).*
— *Blot (5).*
— *Small Potion of Satiety (13).*
— *Ferocious Harn Summoning Amulet.*
— *Messenger Amulet.*
— *Stone tablet of Wisdom (14).*
— *Silver tablet (105).*
— *Pearl Firepaw Fang (2).*
— *Gray Ice Golem Claws (10)*
— *Sapphire Ice Golem Horn (1)*
— *Clay tablet "Herbalism" (75).*
— *Clay tablet of Agility (75).*
— *Clay tablet of Observation (75).*
— *Clay tablet "Knife Proficiency" (75).*
— *Bronze tablet of Strength (11).*
— *Bronze tablet of Agility (8).*
— *Bronze tablet of Endurance (11).*
— *Bronze tablet "Knife Proficiency" (8).*

Sure, all that bronze was given to me by Mee for safekeeping. And beyond that, there were ten silvers and almost nineteen and a half thousand esses that also belonged to him. We had saved up a good amount. And now we were going to eat up and start using our savings to better our healer.

It's been two days since I woke up after the fight with the shaman. Mee is still unconscious after taking his "dose" of tablets. But I think he'll come to by evening.

In comparison with the first time, the gremlin's tablet assimilation process was going okay. I didn't notice any sharp spikes or drops in Mee's supplies, and there was no way not to be happy about that.

While splitting up the loot, we mutually agreed to improve our newly minted mage's figures as much as possible.

We started with Wave of Healing. The first level-up went smooth as butter, but the second gave us some trouble. According to a system notification, Mee had to reach level five first.

After a brief discussion, we came to the conclusion that urgently levelling up twice for better healing wouldn't be such a crime. Thankfully we had plenty of esses. And the six tablets from levelling up couldn't hurt.

Mee used his thirty silvers and raised his first spell to two, then we read its description and all our doubts fell away on their own. We'd made the right choice.

— **Wave of Healing.**

— *Level: 2. (0/40)*

— *Type: Spell.*

— *Rarity: Epic*

— *Description:*

— *Using magic, the orc shaman creates an invisible healing wave, which is capable of healing wounds and repairing damage.*

— *Effect:*

— *A mage may simultaneously heal themselves and 2 allies.*

+20 regeneration

— *Restores 40% life.*

— *Requirements:*

— *Intellect — 10.*

— *Expends 100 mana points.*

— *Note:*

— *Regeneration effect duration: 50 min.*

The regeneration effect lasted another whole minute, twice as long. Its life supply regeneration was twice as fast, too. Meanwhile, it used twenty points less mana. And most important — it had a new effect! Now Mee could heal all of us at the same time!

Yes, the spell cost us fifty silver tablets and just over twenty thousand esses, but it was worth it! As a matter of fact, if we could have brought it up to three right then and there, we'd have done so without hesitation. But alas, for that, Mee would have to be level ten.

We decided not to touch Dome of Invisibility for the time being. The effect's ten minute duration was more than enough. Beyond that, we also had the harn with his keen senses, which helped us avoid all kinds of nasty encounters.

There was also no sense in investing tablets into Potion Making without any recipes. We'd definitely be able to figure out that profession someday, but now was not the time.

When Mee's level increased, the ceiling of all his characteristics and abilities went up as well. And when it came time to invest tablets, the first thing the gremlin asked was to bring his Mind up to maximum. And I could only be happy about that.

Then partially with Stone and partially with Silver, we unlocked and raised his Wisdom as well. We were one stone tablet short of its ceiling. But that was no big deal. We'd be able to hit it later. Now the gremlin's mana restore speed was on the level with mine.

We decided not to waste any tablets on Intellect just yet. The five-hundred-point mana crystal I got from the shaman plus his one-hundred-twenty supply was enough for Mee to use his heal spell six times!

From there, the Clays and Bronzes allowed us

to significantly increase his Strength, Agility, Observation, Endurance and Knife Proficiency.

We also decided to wait with Herbalism. Mee could level that skill on his own just fine.

I glanced at his characteristics again. I needed to check. Maybe I was missing something.

— *Steppe Gremlin.*
— *Name: Mee.*
— *Level: 5 (0/20000).*
— *Status: Loyalty to elder family member (permanent).*
— *Mind: 10/10*
— *Wisdom: 9.8/10*
— *Strength:17/50*
— *Agility:23/50*
— *Health: 8/50*
— *Accuracy: 2.8/50.*
— *Speed: 2.8/50.*
— *Intellect: 10/50*
— *Observation: 7.7/50.*
— *Endurance:13.3/50*
— *Life supply:100/100*
— *Energy supply:153/153*
— *Mana supply:120/120*

— **Skills and abilities:**
— *Butchery:30/50*
— *Knife proficiency: 11.5/50*
— *Herbalism:2/50*
— *Hunter:2/50*

— *Fisher: 2/50*
— *Rider: 5.1/50*
— *Hiding spot maker: 0.3/50*
— ***Wave of healing.***
— *Level: 2 (0/40).*
— ***Dome of invisibility.***
— *Level: 0 (0/20).*
— ***Potion Making.***
— *Level: 0 (0/20).*

We left the gold tablets of Intellect untouched. We were only going to use them if absolutely necessary. They were our future financial independence.

With just over fifty Silvers left, Mee categorically refused to take them before losing consciousness. His argument was that we also needed to beef up Gorgie — our main fighter and defender. I checked on the calmly sniffling kid and, covering him up tighter, glanced at the harn lying next to him.

After the level-up, his armor had become even darker. New scales had grown in as well, broader and thicker. And he had grown significantly larger. Yep, Gorgie had really changed since our first meeting.

I glanced at the beast's changed characteristics.

— *Ferocious Harn.*

— *Name: Gorgie.*
— *Level: 8 (2 100/ 44 000).*
— *Status: Loyalty to master (permanent).*
— *Mind: 1/ 1*
— *Strength: 83/ 120*
— *Agility: 84/ 120*
— *Accuracy: 5.8/ 120*
— *Intuition: 8/ 8*
— *Wisdom: 16/ 16*
— *Animal instinct: 16/ 16*
— *Speed: 85/ 120*
— *Flexibility: 52/ 120*
— *Intellect: 45/ 80*
— *Mana supply: 500/ 500*
— *Health: 80/ 80*
— *Endurance: 73/ 80*
— *Life supply: 850/ 850*
— *Energy supply: 780/ 780*
— *Scale armor: 40/ 40*
— *Defense: 400/ 400*
— *Damage: +234.2...+746.6*

— *Bite: 40/ 40*
— *Paw swipe: 40/ 40*
— *Pounce: 8/ 8*
— *Animal regeneration: 16/ 16*
— *Hunter: 36/ 40*
— *Fisher: 17.8/ 40*
— *Resistance to Hexapod poison: 7/ 40*
— ***Thorntail's Jump.***
— *Level: 1 (0/ 40).*

When I used tablets on Gorgie, he was participating actively. And that wasn't the least bit unusual. My top concern was his defense and life level. He insisted on defense. Thanks to my fifty-five silvers, plus three more the harn got for levelling up, we had almost enough for everything.

At first I raised Armor, Health and Regeneration to the ceiling. After that, I did the very same with his offensive abilities.

Thorntail's Jump, alas, had to be left unchanged. It would have taken forty tablet to improve, and I decided to invest them in other characteristics.

Intellect only got one point. That happened to be enough to use the spell nine times.

From there, I raised his Intuition and Wisdom to the maximum while the rest were evenly distributed between his main stats.

While looking back over the harn's characteristics, a thought came to mind. Quickly closing the window, I dug into my backpack and took out a bronze orcish ring.

— *Ring of agility.*
— *Level: 8*
— *Category: Simple.*
— *Agility +9.*
— *Durability — 43.*

"Why don't we try putting this on you, brother," I muttered, hunched over Gorgie's right paw.

The Great System reacted instantly:

— Attention! Your pet cannot use item Ring of Agility!

"What a pity," I muttered, disappointed and scratching the back of my head. "What about this one?"

I took the steel ring off my finger and tried to put it on one of the sleeping harn's claws.

— Attention! Your pet cannot use item Steel Ring!

And much to my dismay, it had the same reaction to my button. Without no explanation, the Great System was giving me a clear indication that it was no use trying to trick it. And that was a shame. Nine extra Agility points would definitely not hurt Gorgie.

With a heavy sigh, I got up and left the tent.

A frosty evening breeze slithered right under my collar. I took a look around. Silence. Nothing but the wide-branching black trees that dominated this forest. Due to their hardness, they were known as stonetrees. They were also the ultimate origin of the forest's name.

The rains stopped three days ago. The temperature has dropped noticeably. The earth is gradually freezing over and turning to stone.

THE WASTES

Winter is beginning.

I sighed glumly. I could see my breath. I guess the orcish horde will start west any day now.

Oh well. We're going south. Gorgie found a trail leading into the depths of the Stone Forest. Based on smell, he said the orc shaman had used it as well. Most likely, the portal to the other world and monster hunter altar were this way.

Hm. And where there is an altar, I might also find other structures built by my ancient order. At any rate, we won't know until we go see.

CHAPTER 14

TWO DAYS AGO, we packed up our little camp and headed into the depths of the Stone Forest. By the way, it was stone in name only. To my eye, it was basically a normal forest, just the trees were a bit taller and wider-branching.

The trolls, offspring of an ancient monster that died here at the dawn of time, hadn't given us any trouble yet. As a matter of fact, nothing had given us any trouble at all. We had just been walking calmly down a path the orc shamans had trammeled over many years of journeying. And all the while, the harn was studying the surroundings, periodically telling me something was happening out ahead.

Yes, I can't deny it. The forest had quite a dark feel. And the ghastly orcish "art" lining the trail only added to the creepiness. The whole way, we were occasionally stumbling across fearsome sculptures made of old skeletons of humans, gremlins and another few kinds of creatures. All we could do was guess why the inhabitants of the forest hadn't pulled that mess down. But based on the grave-like silence, and the harn's calm demeanor it didn't seem like these areas were particularly popular with the local fauna. I had my guesses, but it was still too early to make any assertions with hundred-percent certainty.

Finally, nearer midday on the third day, the orcish trail brought us to the otherworldly portal. And for the record, I could sense it long before I saw it. The familiar sensations of slight fatigue and weakness wouldn't let me go for even an instant. Something was off about this place. It wasn't like the portal in the underground city. This one was behaving strangely. Like a fire that had been put out but was still smoldering...

The closer I got, the nastier it felt.

"Rick, did something happen?" Mee asked, disconcerted when I stopped a hundred yards from the portal.

He was sitting atop Gorgie on a rejiggered saddle he'd taken off the back of a warg. As a matter of fact, that landed him a couple stone tablets of "Leatherworker." But that wasn't all. In one of the orcs' travelling bags he found an old sling, and the whole time we were underway he'd been practicing using it to launch stones, periodically getting various tablets for his trouble. Yesterday he even unlocked his very first combat ability — "Sling." The level wasn't too impressive yet, but we were still happy. The groundwork had been laid.

Beyond that, the gremlin was starting to handle his knife with more flair. For our whole journey he'd also been practicing knife throwing. He hadn't gained any combat abilities from that yet, but I figured the Great System would give him his due soon enough.

"Rick?!" Mee shouted out again.

I took a deep sniff of a wolf pelt I found among the shaman's things and answered:

"See that ugly tree over there?"

Mee turned his head where I pointed.

A big huge, wide-branching and freakish tree, it was split down the middle by otherworldly magic and had black slime stuck to its entire surface. It would have been hard to miss.

"Is that what I think it is?" Mee asked.

"Yes," I nodded, wincing. "That is the otherworldly portal I told you about."

"Is it having any effect on you?" the gremlin asked anxiously. "I can't feel anything."

"Slight weakness and dizziness," I responded. "I feel like I'm standing on the edge of a latrine pit."

"I see," the gremlin nodded and added:

"I just got the impression something might have been bothering you."

I must note that ever since Mee's Mind went up, he had changed noticeably. He was more thoughtful and judicious. And most importantly, he was slowly but surely starting to rid himself of his slave moods and fears. The Mind, magic and new abilities were making him more self-confident.

"I'm definitely a bit ill at ease, yes," I admitted. "The thing is the portal seems to be behaving strangely. Not like the one in the underground city."

"What's so weird about it?"

I stroked the back of my head pensively.

"Hm... I'm trying to get to the bottom of that right now. There, underground, it was very straightforward. I don't know if it's an appropriate comparison or not, but down there it was like clockwork. This portal feels more like a pustule that's just about to burst."

"But you said the shaman caught himself a spirit," the gremlin frowned. "That means the portal won't open again until next year."

"True," I shrugged. "But my feelings say otherwise. Something is clearly afoot here. Although I might be wrong. It could be like this here all the time."

"Maybe that's why there are no living creatures around," the gremlin forwarded a theory.

"It's not like the orcs would have attempted to close the portal," I said. "And maybe that made it snowball."

"So how do we get it shut?" Mee inquired.

"With ghostly crystals, which sometimes drop after defeating an otherworldly beast."

The gremlin started thinking.

"What?" I asked. "As far as you've seen, have the orcs ever had ghostly crystals?"

"No," he shook his head.

"What about these?" I showed him a hunter token.

"Nope," the gremlin shook his head. "To be honest, I never saw all that many shamans. And I saw even less rare loot."

"Makes sense," I nodded and winced again.

Seeing my state, the gremlin asked:

"Maybe we shouldn't go close to the portal?"

I shook my head and answered:

"We're already here, so we have to get a good look. If you don't want to come, you can stay here."

The gremlin shook his head very rapidly.

"No! I'm coming with you!"

"Hrn!" Gorgie emphasized decisively, supporting our healer

"Then let's go!" I declared and took the first step toward the portal.

The closer I got, the nastier I felt. Fortunately, I didn't taste any bitterness or rot in my mouth. It was hard not to be happy about that.

Sixty-five feet away from the ugly giant, my companions had seemingly also started to feel something. The scales on the back of the harn's neck were standing on end. And he was occasionally baring his teeth and growling frighteningly. Mee, his head tucked between his shoulders in fear, was fitfully clutching the cat's armored neck.

"What do you feel?" I asked him. "Nausea, dizziness?"

"No," the gremlin squeaked.

"Then what?"

"Worry in my heart," Mee answered unconfidently. "Like something's about to happen. Something scary..."

"Hrn," Gorgie agreed.

With every step, the invisible pressure was growing stronger. Other than that, the land around the giant black tree was strewn with bones, which didn't exactly add to our shared sense of optimism.

Finally, I reached the edge of the greasy black puddle the disfigured tree towered in the center of. The ultimate source of the otherworldly magic was rooted inside the split of the tree trunk like a voracious parasite nourishing itself on the innards of a powerful giant. Greasy smoking ooze was seeping out of the bark and falling from the branches onto the ground with a hissing sound.

I looked around. Yep. The orcs were clearly not too concerned with closing this portal. They clearly don't fully understand what this thing is. And these bones around... This must be the shamans' doing.

"I'm done!" I announced, turning to my friends. "Let's go! We also need to find the altar."

"Hrn!" Gorgie told me, his snout pointed to the southwest.

"You sure that's where it is?" I asked. And that just made the cat snort patronizingly and trot off that way.

We hadn't quite reached the altar yet. With less than an hour left before sundown, Gorgie let me know that there was something alive beyond the dense wall of trees. Hurriedly liberated from the saddle and travelling bags, the harn dashed out to scout around.

"What's out there?" I whispered when my pet came back an hour later.

"*Smell of death. Youngling. Blood. Dying,*" he told me shortly.

With two sets of alarmed eyes staring at me, I got up off the ground. For fairness' sake, I should mention that neither I nor my companions were feeling any fear. It was more like pre-battle jitters.

"Okay then," I whispered, my voice quavering in worry. "Let's see what's going on over there."

The gremlin nodded in silence and started undoing the drawstrings of the leather pouch hanging off his belt. That was where he kept the stones for his sling, which he had been dutifully collecting all the way here. Out of the corner of my eye, I saw a mana crystal appear in one of his hands and the sling in the other. For the record, I'd filled all the crystals to the brim a few days earlier.

"Lead the way," I said to Gorgie when all our preparations were complete.

I didn't have to ask the harn twice. His black scaly body disappeared among the trees.

Twenty minutes later, we walked up to the fairly wide clearing. In the center of it, there was a big huge rock of a familiar shape. An altar.

Glancing out from behind a broad tree trunk, I took a look around. The cloudless night and full moon gave me a great view of the whole glade. Just like around the portal, the ground was strewn with bones. Looks like the orcs have been taken by a kind of lunacy. They just couldn't get enough of sacrificing living souls. But that was not the end of it... They also had to dismantle the corpses, then scatter the body parts. As if that would have any impact on the process.

I spat angrily. What bloodthirsty scum!

A light touch to my shoulder made me shudder slightly. I turned my head and saw Mee's anxious little face.

"Look," he whispered, pointing at a dark stone lying on the opposite end of the clearing.

"Are you talking about the stone?" I asked in surprise.

Mee nodded.

"What's wrong with it?"

"It's breathing," the gremlin answered shortly.

I frowned quizzically. How could that be? I stuck my neck out as far as possible, trying to catch a glimpse of the uncanny breathing stone. At that very moment, Gorgie appeared from the darkness and told me there was not a single living soul nearby.

I nodded toward the unusual stone.

"What's that?"

"*Youngling*," Gorgie snorted in reply and took the first step into the clearing.

We hurriedly crossed the meadow and stopped next to an unknown creature which the Great System identified a few seconds later as a level-two forest troll youth.

As an aside, if not for the system information, I'd hardly have called this creature a youth. It was at least as large as Bruni, who died back at the Bridge of Bones. A large heavy torso, rough gray skin, thick appendages, a bald slightly flat head — so, that's what a forest troll looks like. Beyond that, the "tyke's" broad maw was packed full of sharp triangular teeth, while his wide fingers ended in twisted claws — I could only imagine what his daddy looked like.

"By the way," I turned to the gremlin. "Your little theory that trolls have dark origins doesn't hold water."

"Why?" Mee asked.

"This, hm, kid is not at all like an otherworldly beast. All these orcish legends are just empty rumors and hokum."

The gremlin sighed sadly and said:

"I feel bad for him. I wonder what happened to the poor guy?"

"Based on the tear wounds on his back, some animal must have attacked him," I posited.

The harn got right up to the troll and cautiously sniffed the wound. A moment later, he told us the kid had been attacked by a warg. The harn also said the youngster crawled here from the south.

"I might be wrong, but it seems to me that the shaman's bodyguards must have done this to entertain themselves while the shaman did his thing. Honestly, there is one important question bothering me though. If this is a child, where is his mother? Still, to be frank, I am not exactly burning with desire to meet this little bruiser's family."

"I want to heal him," Mee suddenly spat out.

"Have you lost your mind?!" I asked, astounded. "Look at this monster! One swipe of his big old mitt and you're a dead gremlin."

"Yeah, but what if he doesn't attack?" the gremlin glanced at me with hope. "After all, Gorgie didn't kill you. He was half-dead when you found him, too. You told me yourself..."

I shook my head.

"No comparison. That was a coincidence. Beyond that, if the amulet hadn't worked, the harn would have devoured me."

Gorgie stayed out of our conversation. He was walking around the meadow and sniffing lazily.

I glanced doubtfully at the troll's big old carcass, then at the gremlin.

"Are you sure you want to do this?"

"Yes," Mee nodded decisively. "He's scary and his size is frightening, but he's just a child. I'll never forgive myself if I don't try to help him."

I took a heavy sigh and scratched the back of my head. Well, we were looking for a helper. What happened to the easily scared gremlin from before? It must have been more influence of his improved Mind.

"Gorgie!" I called the harn. "Come over here. Little Mee is about to do something stupid. If his patient suddenly attacks, you know what to do."

After that, I prepared to hit the big creature with Lightning. Let him wake up. If it doesn't work, we can at least earn a couple tablets and esses.

"Go ahead," I nodded and took a couple steps back.

Mee slowly extended both hands forward and activated the spell. A bright green wave broke free from his hands and gushed toward the wounded troll. The healing progress had begun. If the gremlin ended up with a pet, this would be quite the trick...

"Well, how's it going?" I asked a few minutes later.

"His supply was almost down to zero," Mee answered, pointing at the wound:

"The regeneration process has begun..."

I looked where he pointed.

Truly. The tattered edges of his wound were changing color right before my eyes. The shivering dark spots on his flesh started oozing a cloudy yellow fluid. A horrid smell of rot struck my nose.

While watching the Regeneration in action, I

swore that I'd get myself a characteristic like that I ever got the chance. The muckwalker ability was nice of course, but there wasn't always water nearby.

A few minutes later, when all the pus had come out, his flayed flesh started slowly growing back together. And eventually, all that was left of his once fearsome wounds was some crude scoring.

Mee turned his head in my direction and smiled happily. At that very moment, the troll opened his eyes. And the first thing he did when he saw us was give a protracted howl.

I even winced it was so loud. Meanwhile, the gremlin stumbled backwards in my direction. Finally, the troll shut his mouth and tried to raise himself up on an elbow.

— *Attention! Your Mind score is high enough to activate the "Language of the Forest Trolls!"*
— *Would you like to activate it?*

Acquiescing, I turned to Mee:

"Do you have any idea what you've just done?"

The frightened gremlin shook his head.

"He just called his mommy for help!"

Then, to back that up, several voices howled back from deep in the forest.

CHAPTER 15

"DID YOU GET an amulet of domestication?" I asked Mee, who was shivering in panic.

"No," he replied.

"That means it didn't work," I muttered, looking at the troll who was slowly coming to his senses.

"Hrn!" Gorgie was alarmed and telling me that our patient's relatives were already nearby.

Seemingly, they had us surrounded.

"Let's get out of here!" I announced.

"What about the youngster?" Mee asked.

"Will he survive?"

"Yes," our healer nodded.

"But we won't if we don't get out of here."

After an hour of aimless wandering through the forest, we realized we would never get away. Slowly but surely, we were being driven into a trap like wild animals. Even the harn's animal senses were no help.

Our pursuers knew this area like the backs of their hands, and functioned like a single organism. The harn was seemingly probing for a new way to go when the trap suddenly slammed shut. If Gorgie were on his own, he'd probably have been able to escape the tight constricting ring but, alas, my Speed left something to be desired. What am I even saying?! I was anything but fast.

"Stop!" I leaned against a tree, breathing heavily and looked at my friends. "We've really... Done some running... I bet they could have attacked a while ago. It looks like they're trying to drain our energy supplies... To make it a sure thing."

"Hrn," Gorgie agreed.

"Then what should we do?" Mee asked.

"Let's do something they aren't expecting. We'll pick a good spot and hunker down for a fight."

Alas, a few minutes later, we realized we wouldn't find one. We'd have to make do with what we had. To be more precise, it was a small hill overgrown with young trees and with little ravines on two sides. It was a middling place for defense, but still better than meeting the troll family out in the open.

By the way, speaking of them... Based on the frequent barks and howls they were exchanging, they must have realized we'd stopped moving. It all seemed very strange to me. Our legends and fairy tales always portrayed the trolls as these stupid, dumb creatures that were easy to trick and not hard to run from. I'd like to look into the eyes of the clever bastard that came up with those old wives' tales. Or better yet stick him in the Stone Forest to have him run away from the "stupid, dumb creatures" himself. Here we were clearly up against a well-organized opponent that made rational use of their advantages.

Not an hour later, the ring closed around us and started gradually contracting. The trolls were no longer roaring and howling. They were coming our way fairly quickly, as the frequent snapping of tree and bush branches attested.

Based on the stream of information coming from Gorgie, I concluded that there were at least twelve trolls.

My hands quivering, I'm squeezing my Blots. I only have five of them left. I look at the gremlin. He's all quivering anxiously just like me. I notice a guilty look on his face. Uh, nope. That's not gonna fly.

I placed a hand on Mee's little shoulder and as calmly as possible, said:

"Brother, look at me."

Mee raised an eye timidly.

"Stop blaming yourself."

"But..." he tried to object.

"You haven't done anything wrong," I interrupted as softly as I could. "As a matter of fact, all you did was help a suffering child in need.

Yes, he didn't behave the way we were hoping. But who could have known they had everything down so pat? The most I was expecting was for your patient to attack us, not for him to summon his whole family. Actually, I'm sure they'd have sniffed us out sooner or later anyway. That means healing the young troll didn't really change anything. Do you understand?"

"Yes," Mee nodded.

"That's great," I smiled. "Better get ready for battle. They'll be here any minute now."

Giving the gremlin an approving shoulder pat, I nodded at the harn. He by the way, was absolutely calm. A bit of the willies excepted. That's normal before a battle. Our main fighter's general sense of ease calmed us down significantly.

When I told Mee the trolls were well-organized, I was distantly thinking over how the shaman and his bodyguards were able to just wander these woods unpunished. And how they ever got their hands on the young troll in the first place...

But I wasn't able to finish the thought. Big huge silhouettes started to appear beyond the trees around our little hill.

One... Two... Three... I counted up to a total of sixteen. Levels ranging from eleven to seventeen. And as I expected, the troll child was just a smaller version of his adult counterparts. None of them were less than ten feet tall. Sloping shoulders, broad ribcages. All of them were armed with long knotty wooden clubs. Their sharp claws and fangs looked pretty scary as well.

I felt all the hair on my body stand on end. Seemingly, the goddess Fortuna was not on our side this time. We weren't likely to be emerging victorious from this one.

I traded glances with Gorgie.

"When I give the command, you grab Mee and run as far from here as you can," I told him mentally.

The cat tilted his head in surprise and gave a dismayed growl.

"I hope you don't go wild after my death and eat him," I joked.

The harn just snorted back and turned away showily, as if to say, "it's still too early to bury each other."

Heh, I wish I had your confidence...

Meanwhile, the trolls started coming out from behind the trees. I took a look around. The giants looked like huge boulders come to life. One troll stopped directly opposite the narrow rise we took to the top of the hill. He looked especially boulder-like. Level seventeen. A head taller than the rest of his tribe. The largest and seemingly most dangerous. Beyond that, based on the way the other trolls treated him, the big guy was in charge.

His small closely-set little eyes were glimmering in rage from beneath his protruding brow. It was like I could feel his hatred in my skin. The harn and I exchanged glances.

"Let's kill that one first," I muttered.

Gorgie growled back, agreeing.

Why haven't they attacked yet? The answer to my question came a moment later.

Another figure stepped out from behind the broad backs of the big fanged brutes. Short and gaunt. On the backdrop of the boulder-like giants, he looked out of place. I might have even called him a different species.

But on closer inspection, I concluded he was also a troll. Based on the light wrinkly skin and gray fur on his back, shoulders and chest, this was an old man. Clearly a local elder of some kind and perhaps, which would be worse for us, a shaman as well. He was wearing a few bone pendants on his neck. And the long crooked staff in his powerful mitts was topped with what appeared to be the skull of a monster. That did not add to my optimism.

The hunched old man took one more step and I was able to see his level — twenty.

Bad. Very bad...

Looks like we just stepped in some shit. A level-twenty possible mage supported by sixteen powerful warriors? No. We can't win here.

What happened next made me rethink my opinion about what Mee did.

"Why are you here, Farhas?!" the largest troll suddenly barked gutturally at the old man. It was clear the big guy was not a fan of the elder's meddling.

The harn, gremlin and I exchanged glances of incomprehension. Either I was missing something, or we just found an unexpected ally.

"I want to look on the kind souls who healed my grandson, Erg," the old troll answered calmly. And the whole time his eyes were fixed on us, watching to see what we'd do.

The giant troll snorted like a bull and answered wrathfully:

"You're only guessing that!"

The old troll snorted mockingly.

"No, Erg. I know. Or do you doubt my abilities all of a sudden?"

A moment later, we watched the hefty boulder-like troll lower his head in shame under the gaze of the hunch-backed old man.

"But they defiled the Tree of Spirits and the Altar!" one of the trolls shouted. The rest started stirring and grumbling, supporting the shouter.

I can't say what came over me, but I could not keep quiet.

"We didn't defile anything!" I shouted as loud as possible.

For the record, the language of the trolls was even harder on my throat than that of the orcs.

To say the forest giants were stunned would be to say nothing. The way they were staring. Their mouths agape.

"As a matter of fact, that isn't all!" I continued with strain. "I don't know who had the bright idea of making blood sacrifices to an otherworldly portal, but you should all give that blockhead a good pummeling! And the altar of the hunters where we found your dying boy has also been badly desecrated!"

For a second, the trolls looked like stone statues. Then the old man, his head tilted to the side, took a few steps forward.

"Erg," the old man's voice was calm, but for some reason a chill ran down my spine. "I need these outsiders alive. At the very least, until I can figure out what this boy is talking about."

"Who are you and how did you get here?" Farhas asked, intrigued. We were standing a few paces away from one another, separated only by a narrow rise in the very center.

The elder was the one who initiated negotiations. He was just painfully interested in what I had to say.

We agreed to a ceasefire for the length of our discussion. Honestly, it was just a verbal understanding, no official oaths. So I was ready to summon the Ysh spirit and hit the old man with lightning at any time.

"We are peaceful travelers," I answered. "We make for the west."

"Why are you going through our forest?"

"The steppe is teeming with orcs right now."

"And you figured you could make it this way?" the old man chuckled.

"Yes, that was the plan," I nodded. "Our chances of avoiding an encounter with wolf riders on the steppe were exactly zero. But here..."

"Your chances were no better here," the gray-haired troll interrupted. "I trust you've come to realize that?"

"Well, if your grandson hadn't started shouting after we healed him..."

"Oh!" he smiled. "You can't even imagine how greatly your encounter with my grandson increased your chances of survival."

I can't say exactly what was written on my face, I can only say the way I felt. It was something akin to disarray and internal contradiction. I was talking to an entity with, to put it lightly, a repugnant and — why hide it? — frightening appearance. In other words, a monster that was used to scare badly behaved human children at night. But at the same time, this entity was expressing himself no less eloquently than an Orchusian clerk. There could be only one explanation on that account — a high Mind score. Based on the look in Farhas' eyes, the expression on my face was more than telling.

"It's hard not to be happy to hear that," I answered and nodded behind him: "But it looks like not all your tribesmen share that perspective."

The old troll waved it off carelessly.

"Don't you worry about Erg. He's still young

and hot-blooded, but he knows his place. And he's not your biggest problem."

I just nodded in silence. What could I possibly say? Even a fool could tell who gave orders around here.

"I'm glad we were able to reach an understanding," said the elder. Then he asked with strain:

"So, I trust we'll be able to have a conversation?"

"That all depends on what we'll be talking about," I answered evasively. "And what is on the table."

The mouth of the gray-haired troll stretched out into a satisfied smirk, revealing all his powerful fangs.

"So, you'll negotiate? Good. I love making deals. But don't you think you're perhaps not in the most advantageous position?"

"Simply put, I don't have a choice?" I asked. Then I nodded toward the trolls, who were waiting patiently for their leader:

"Agreed. The advantage is on your side. If we don't come to an agreement, my companions and I will most likely die. However, there is one 'but.'"

"And what might that be?"

"Many of your tribesmen would also die."

After that, I prepared for an attack. Who's to say how this strange old troll might react? But he pleasantly surprised me again.

"Fair," he said after a brief pause. "And I also

know that you brought divine judgement on my daughter's murderers. Yes, yes. Don't be surprised. I can smell the belongings of the young shaman and his warriors on you. I'm sure they didn't give them to you of their own free will."

"Two of our group died in that battle," I said morosely. "I'd prefer not to lose anyone else, and I imagine you feel the same. All we want is to reach the western border of the steppe. Did we really not prove the purity of our intentions when we healed your grandson?"

The old troll looked thoughtfully at me. The skin on his face reminded me of the bark of an ancient maple tree. Just as dry, cracked and grooved with a plethora of deep wrinkles. His dark almost black eyes studied me closely from under his heavy brow.

"You're right!" he finally squeezed out. At that, the old troll started speaking fairly loudly, obviously so all the trolls would hear him. "The lives of my tribesmen are important to me, just as important as that of my grandson! But it isn't all so simple... After all, my warriors are right — you desecrated the Tree of Spirits and the Altar with your presence!"

Hm, curious. Either it's the fruit of a vivid imagination, or the elder is purposely giving me the chance to make my case. And our fate is going to depend on what I say and how I say it. This situation reminds me of walking through a swamp. One false move and you're waist deep in muck.

Alright. I'll try to cross this treacherous terrain.

"I repeat!" I had to also raise my voice, which the elder reacted to with a barely perceptible smile. "We are peaceful travelers! We make for the west! A group of orcs fell upon us at the Stone Bridge! We defeated them, but lost two of our companions! We rested and healed our wounds for a few days, then went deeper into the forest! Then we came across the wounded child! He was dying! We couldn't simply walk past and stopped to heal him! I swear that we bore no ill intent in our thoughts or actions! We sincerely regret if we did anything wrong! And may the gods be my witnesses!"

Based on the way the giants started stirring, my words were having a positive effect.

I intentionally didn't say a word about the portal or the altar. The elder's approving gaze was a clear indication I was doing and saying all the right things. And that we would talk in greater detail later, without the others around to hear.

"Hoager! Dago!" the old man barked authoritatively, turning to his warriors. After his shout, two sizable figures stepped forward. "Stay here with me!"

The trolls nodded in silence.

"Erg!" Farhas continued giving orders. "Take the others to the Black Fang! We'll be there soon to join you."

To my surprise, the giant turned around with no further questions and walked toward the forest.

The other trolls followed.

Hmm, either this old man was underestimating us, or more likely was absolutely confident he would win, given he decided to weaken his positions. I was having a hard time believing he suddenly started trusting us. A moment later I realized that I was right. Gorgie told me most of the troll soldiers were hiding among the trees. We were still encircled.

Now we'd have to try not to let the old man know I was aware of his trick.

The gray-haired troll looked around and sat on a large mound that was overgrown with moss and nodded opposite indicating where I should sit. After I sat down, he asked:

"So what's this about an otherworldly portal?"

Despite his calm tone, I could feel tension in his voice.

"To the northeast. Over there," I nodded to the place we'd come from. "The old tree with the split trunk. That's it."

"The Tree of Spirits?" the gray-haired troll furrowed his brow. "You mean to say that it is actually a door into other worlds?"

"Exactly," I answered. "And based off the creatures that come through the door, these other worlds are not exactly looking to make friends, to put it lightly."

"You're saying the spirits only come in order to kill?" the elder asked with mistrust in his voice.

"Yes."

"But why?"

"They don't have any other choice," I shrugged.

"What is that supposed to mean?"

"The otherworldly beast or as you put it, spirit, is only alive while the portal is open. As soon as the passage closes, the monster will disappear. But there is an exception. A beast may remain in this world if it can kill and subsume a living creature from our world."

The old troll frowned, perplexed, and rubbed his hard chin. It was hard to guess what was going on in his head.

"What about the good spirits that serve the shamans?" he finally asked.

It took some effort not to laugh. The last thing I needed now was to accidentally disrespect this elder. But it gave me an approximate idea of the nonsense the orc shamans were filling the gullible trolls' heads with.

"There's no such thing as good spirits," I answered calmly. "There are bloodthirsty monsters driven by a singular desire — to survive at all costs. But you're right in one sense. Sometimes whoever kills the otherworldly beast is rewarded with a blessing by the god Random. That lucky individual can then absorb the spirit of the monster they killed."

"Yes," Farhas nodded. "The blood-letting at the Altar."

I winced in disgust.

"There's no need for a sacrifice. That's not how the hunters' altar works."

The elder frowned.

"You're saying surprising things which contradict our ancient knowledge! Hunters, portal, otherworldly beasts... Why should I trust some boy newcomer?"

Based on the way the trolls sitting in the distance tensed up, they could hear our conversation perfectly.

Looks like this old man's cold blood is starting to heat up. And I can't blame him. These orcish tales must have been around for generations.

Not saying another word or making any sudden movements, I started to remove my outer garments.

"What are you doing?" the elder asked, perplexed.

I threw my jacket on the ground and said:

"My father always said it's better to see something once than to hear about it a hundred times."

Undoing the buttons on my shirt, I continued:

"You have your doubts. And I get that. What am I even saying?! As a matter of fact, I'm impressed by your patience! And that's why I'm offering to let you see with your own eyes. Look!"

I threw my shirt onto my jacket and spread my arms.

The gray-haired troll's heavy jaw slowly sunk down. His sloped forehead seemed to grow even more wrinkles. I could read disbelief in his wide-open black eyes.

"Based on the way you're looking, may I be so bold as to suggest that you have seen marks like this before?" I asked, picking up my shirt while straining not to shiver in the cold.

Out of the corner of my eye, I noticed Farhas' underlings looking stunned.

"Have you overpowered two spirits?" the elder finally spoke. His voice was quavering slightly, giving away his true feelings. "You are a shaman!"

"No. I am a Hunter of otherworldly monsters!"

I mentally chuckled as I said that. I was laying it on pretty thick, giving the kind of sappy speech you'd expect to hear from a sentimental town mayor. I imagined the foxman's mischievous face if he could have heard me then.

Farhas regained his composure with striking speed, unlike the other trolls.

"Does that mean you came here on purpose then?" the old man asked with a clever squint.

"Oh!" I shook my head. "Believe you me, you couldn't be farther from the truth. More than anything else, we want to keep as far from any portal as possible. Especially that one."

"Why?" the troll's ears perked up.

I breathed a heavy sigh.

"Something is off about it... As if it truly has been desecrated, but very long ago. I've seen another portal before. It opened precisely every twenty-four hours. In a sense, it was more dangerous than your Tree. But then why does every passing hour I spend next to this one fill my heart with dread? It's as if something is about to happen. Something horrible and irreversible. Why did the orc shamans make sacrifices next to the portal?"

"Spilling blood next to the Tree is thought to attract more powerful spirits," Farhas answered gloomily. "You think that could have something to do with its apparent instability?"

"I don't know," I shrugged. "It seems very likely. I can't see any other explanation. Otherworldly visitors have a heightened sense for living creatures of our world."

"And death and blood make the best bait," the old troll said pensively.

I had many more questions for the troll. For example, why were the orcs allowed to traipse freely through their woods? Or what was the elder's daughter doing next to the altar with her son? And how did it happen that the trolls were unable to protect her given their high level of coordination?

But I didn't ask them. After all, it wasn't really any of my business. But still I had one question I just had to know the answer to.

Leaning forward, I started tracing a familiar symbol on the ground with my pointer finger. Once finished, I wiped my finger on my pants and looked at the old man.

"This is the symbol of the monster hunters.

Have you ever seen it before?"

Farhas looked perplexedly over my design, which looked vaguely like two interlaced fishhooks.

Hm, no need to answer, old troll. I can tell by your eyes that you've seen it.

Finally, Farhas raised his head and looked at me. There was nothing menacing in his gaze. In fact, it burned with a fire of curiosity and understanding.

"Let's go, hunter!" he said, quickly standing to his full height. "I know where we can find your symbol!"

CHAPTER 16

WALKING NEXT TO FARHAS in silence, I was feverishly thinking over what to do next. Even an idiot could tell we were being led to the ruins of structures that once belonged to the monster hunters. And we weren't likely to encounter another ghost holding down the fort with its magic either.

We are now being led to a fragment of wall which supposedly has the fishhooks etched into it. But what next? After all, the old man is agitated. He needs answers. I'd built this up into such a thing. I needed to make it seem justified.

I don't know what horizons my thoughts might have disappeared beyond if our path hadn't been blocked by a big old pile of tree trunks, rocks and dirt. Here and there, dead animal skulls adorned the tips of especially prominent branches, staring at me from their empty eye sockets.

The old troll turned and looked me in the eyes searchingly.

"Here are your symbols," he finally spat out and pointed toward a wide black pillar towering beyond the wall.

The light of the moon, the skulls, the grisly heap looking like a giant hedgehog... I felt a shiver run down my spine.

I turned my head where he pointed and said: "A grim place."

"Agreed," the old man nodded. For a brief moment, I saw fear in his eyes.

"So, where did all this come from?" I led a hand over the formless heap.

"The Boundary was erected by our ancestors. Trolls are forbidden from crossing it. We just make sure it stays in good shape."

"A sacred place?"

"No," the elder answered darkly. "Cursed. It's protected by mysterious and cruel charms. Many of my tribesmen have paid with their lives for the few crumbs of information we have."

Hm... I think I get the picture.

"So, the wall is not to protect this place, correct?" I asked quietly.

Farhas looked me in the eyes and answered darkly:

"We don't want to lose any more of our warriors." He spent a bit of time in silence and continued: "For the first time in many years, I am hearing answers to questions that have long troubled troll-kind. I hope I will also receive an answer to this one."

As he said the last sentence, he was nodding toward a pillar that towered over the predacious enclosure.

"Alright then... Let's not waste time," I answered and wanted to take a step forward, but the old man stopped me.

Squinting and slightly tilting his head to the side, he said:

"I trust you understand we don't want any surprises."

I frowned.

"Were my oaths really not enough for you?"

"In any case, I'll be going with you," the old man announced, ignoring my question.

I saw a cold determination in his eyes.

"What about the curse?" I couldn't hold back a smirk.

The old man was not embarrassed by my tone. He smiled back.

"Today you demolished all my preconceived notions of the lands where we dwell. And I have every reason to believe this isn't over."

Gorgie was first to the top of the pile. He stopped for a few moments, listening and sniffing, then gave a short growl and lunged forward.

"All clear," I commented on the harn's conduct and stepped first into the enclosure.

Farhas took a heavy sigh as if he was about to dunk his head underwater and followed. Only the Great System could say what this old man had in his heart at that moment. I looked over at his warriors. They were going to stay back and await their leader. Based on the anxious looks on their faces, watching their elder scramble up the heap was out of the ordinary, to put it lightly.

An hour later, we were standing opposite the gigantic pillar, which was covered with a thick layer of black moss.

"So, this is the Black Fang?" I asked.

"The very same," the elder responded and nodded toward some dark bushes. "I do not know what's beyond it. No one has ever returned."

"And where is the symbol?"

"Just a second," said the old man, and he started looking around on the ground. A bit later, he lifted a flat stone off the ground and started clearing some of the growth off a small section of the pillar.

The more the black pieces of moss came away, the more I could see familiar shapes on the cleared surface.

Out of the corner of my eye, I saw Mee giving a scrutinizing gaze. He was watching the expression on my face with hope.

When Farhas finished and tossed the stone aside, I chuckled:

"To be honest, I was hoping I'd never see one of these symbols again."

"Unpleasant memories?" the troll inquired, looking over his handiwork.

"That's putting it lightly..." I muttered back.

"What next?" the old man asked.

"Wait," I answered shortly and walked up to the pillar.

The first thing that jumped out at me when I got a closer look at the hunters' mark was its quality. This was a true work of art. Ornate imagery. Runic script. Milky white marble. The tips of the hooks still had some of their gilding. The symbols I'd found in the caverns of the Crooked Mountains were executed somewhat more simply.

Looking over the fanciful designs, I had no choice but to click my tongue in admiration.

"What?" Farhas called back just then. It was like I could feel his whole body starting forward with my back.

"It's highly skilled work," I answered. "This craftsman really put in effort."

"I hear surprise in your voice," said the old man. "Is something the matter?"

"We-ell," I drew out pensively. "I have a strong feeling that this place isn't quite as ancient as the one where I first encountered this symbol."

And for the record, I couldn't help but be pleased about that. After all, if there was an armory here, its contents would be better preserved.

THE WASTES

I took a fleeting glance at the troll. Based on the careless look in his black eyes, his race was probably ignorant of the complex arts of stone carving or gilding for that matter.

I finished looking and extended my right hand to the familiar groove. As they say, the moment of truth. I hope it works!

— *Attention! Blood analysis: Positive.*

— *Mark activated. Would you like to continue route to next mark?*

— *Cost of service: 50 mana points.*

"It worked!" I exclaimed, unable to hold back and showing my companions the droplet of blood where my index finger had been pricked. And meanwhile, a familiar arrow appeared in front of me.

Farhas stared at my finger in incomprehension. I could read doubt in his eyes. And I understood. He didn't see the message. The gray-haired troll was looking at me exactly the way he should have. Like a boy enthusiastically showing off a tiny cut on his finger.

As not to give rise to more doubts in the trusting old troll's heart, I pointed at the dark bushes and said:

"Come, this way!"

* * *

While making my way through the dense dry brush, I was glancing occasionally at Farhas. His face looked bleaker with every step. It looked like the old troll was no longer thrilled he agreed to this mad undertaking. I tried to explain that the symbol was showing me the way and that I could see an arrow, but he seemingly did not believe me.

Gorgie, sensing my worry, was constantly at my side. Ready to deflect the somber troll's attack at any time. Mee, sitting on the harn's back, was concealing a stone for his sling in his little hand.

Overall, tension was mounting, and that had me pretty nervous. The troll's muted grumbling and heavy breathing, the thorny bushes, the ghastly silence of the forest... A conflict could flare up at any second.

Just when the old man's grumbling turned especially displeased, we reached the next marker. And more accurately, we reached another pillar, twin brother of the one the trolls called the Black Fang.

And the way Farhas' jaw dropped... Where'd all his skepticism go?

The symbol we uncovered beneath a layer of moss took its drop of my blood and fifty mana points, then pointed us to the southeast.

For the next half hour, thankfully, we walked down a fairly wide path that curved around all the rougher patches of undergrowth, which was latched dead together, all interwoven. Despite the thick top layer of soil and leaves, I sometimes saw pieces of paving stone beneath my feet. That meant this was not some mere animal trail, it was an unkept road.

I was also delighted at Farhas' change in mood. His angry sniffling and grumbling had disappeared. And the looks he shot at me no longer contained the same mistrust.

A little while later, he broke the silence:

"I don't understand..."

"What?" I asked.

"We've been on cursed ground for over an hour, yet we still have not been damned by fell magic," Farhas explained, looking around with fear.

"I have two ideas about that," I answered calmly. "And they both could be true."

For fairness' sake, I should note that my calm was for show. The farther we went, the more I started thinking about the mysterious sorcery purported to kill all outsiders who trod upon this land. But I wanted to look confident and in control of the situation in front of the troll elder.

"Would you care to share them?" Farhas asked, intrigued.

"The monster hunters were quite shrewd," I started. "In their day, I'm sure they'd have taken care to provide plenty of 'entertainment' for the beasts on their way to their fortifications from the portal."

"What fortifications now?"

"A fortress, city, castle..."

"You mean to say there's a city in front of us?" the troll's eyes turned fully circular.

"It is a possibility," I answered seriously. "And the whole area around is most likely jammed full of magical traps."

The old troll froze and started looking around warily.

"Don't worry. None of them got us yet, so their supplies must be empty. And there certainly isn't anyone to refill their mana."

"You said you had two ideas."

"Yeah," I nodded. "I think if there is any dangerous hocus-pocus around here, it would perceive me as a friend."

After that, the old man took an unwitting step forward, closer to me.

We walked the rest of the way to the next marker in silence. As we trudged down the trail, from time to time, we noticed yellow animal skulls and bones among the trees. Many of them were of quite impressive dimensions, and several were obviously "fresh" because the moss had yet to swallow them up. If the traps were responsible, it would follow that there must have been some mana left in their supplies.

Farhas peered into the darkness of the forest with sorrow. I couldn't say whether it was fear or a desire to see the remains of a family member.

Although, if his words were to be believed, no trolls had visited this side of the Boundary for several decades at least. Their bones would have already long been buried beneath a layer of moss and soil. Then again, maybe not? Could I really believe the old troll? What if they sent scouts out here from time to time and hadn't ever stopped trying to investigate? While I mulled that over, I came to the conclusion that I'd have done just that in the trolls' place.

Nearer sunup, the path led us out of the trees onto a wide clearing with a big old potbellied tower in the middle of it. Encircled by a tall stone fence, it looked like a small castle.

"A watchtower," Farhas said, breathing wearily.

Catching a puzzled gaze from me, he asked mockingly:

"What? Surprised at my familiarity with your architecture?"

"To be frank — yes," I said, not wheedling.

"When I was young, I was taken captive by a western baron," the elder explained. "I still have dreams about the mines where I was forced to work."

"So you escaped?" I asked.

"Yes," he answered shortly. "Orcs helped

me..."

Hm... So there's the end of a thread I could pull on to maybe find the reason the trolls and orcish shamans get along. Though if I may be so bold, there could be several such threads.

"Rick, look!" Mee shouted, pointing at the massive gates where the path ended.

"I see," I answered.

By the looks of things, the craftsman who made that marker did not suffer from excessive modesty. I was reminded that the symbol that opened the door to Stonetown was the size of a small keyhole. But this anonymous craftsman was clearly on a hot streak. Two sizable fishhooks adorned the most prominent part of the middle of the two gate doors, their golden barbs glimmering in the rays of the predawn sun. Anyhow, neither the thorny bush branches nor the omnipresent black moss touched the local fortress or, as Farhas called it, watchtower. There must have still been mana in the supplies.

"I'll go first," I turned to my companions. "Just in case, try to follow in my footsteps."

Mee and Farhas nodded in unison, and Gorgie snorted in agreement.

Once next to the gates, I froze, looking closely at the gigantic symbol. Finally finding the groove that visually linked the two tips, I placed my palm on the bronze surface.

A light prick followed, then a familiar block of text came before my eyes. At that very moment, the gates gave a shudder and slid aside surprisingly silently.

I turned. Mee and Farhas were standing still as stone statues. They had identical expressions of surprise and admiration on their faces.

"Let's see what's inside," I said and headed forward. Based on the rushed footsteps behind me, my companions were trying to stay as close to me as possible.

The inner courtyard of the watchtower greeted us with silence and desertion. Also, in the middle of the small square was a towering bronze statue of a broad-shouldered warrior, clad head to toe in armor.

The inscription on the pedestal said we had the honor of gazing upon Gunnar the Destroyer himself, Vanquisher of the Horror of the Depths, Killer of the Black Fear and so on, and so on, and so on...

The appearance of the bronze giant amused me.

"What are you laughing at?!" Farhas exclaimed. "This Gunnar guy doesn't exactly look like a jester!"

He and Mee were looking at the statue with reverence and took my mirth with incomprehension, to put it lightly.

"Oh!" I said, drying tears. "He's certainly not a jester, but I am still quite sure this statue would amuse him as well."

"Who is he?" the old man asked, frowning.

"The founder of the order of monster hunters. And by the way, everything written about him here is the pure truth."

"Then what are you laughing at?"

"Because I saw another statue depicting Gunnar the way he really was — as a common unprepossessing fisherman. Believe you me, this hunk of metal is pretty far removed from the original. But I'm laughing because I was reminded of a sly foxman and what I thought when I first saw a statue of the founder of the order. I thought then that a person with such fearsome sobriquets should look just like this."

When I finished, I nodded at the bronze idol.

"So he was a common fisherman?" Farhas asked, perplexed.

"Yes," I answered. "Take a closer look at the symbol. It's two fishhooks. You've probably seen ones like them in the west."

"Oh yeah, you're right!" the old man said, scratching the back of his head. "How didn't I guess right away?"

Once we'd gotten our fill of the statue, we started looking around at the internal courtyard. A small stable, a cowshed, a barn, a smithy and another few practical structures — I had to admit that the hunters had built themselves some pretty fine digs.

There was a fairly wide platform running along the wall and narrow arrowslits that allowed archers to fire on attackers. Other than that, every three feet I saw ovular indentations on the inner side but I honestly couldn't tell what they were for.

"Let's see what's in there," I said to my companions, pushing open the tower door.

Like the main gates, it opened without a sound. We crossed the threshold with trepidation, came inside and stopped, turning our heads in all directions.

I'd never in my life been inside a tower of any kind but, for some reason, this was exactly how I'd always imagined them. In the middle of the wide round room was a rectangular hatch. Clearly the entrance to an underground tunnel that would lead somewhere deep in the forest. There was also a stairway going up, clinging to the wall like a stone snake. Along it, approximately every five paces, there was an arrowslit.

"You wanna go check?" I asked the harn, nodding at the stairs.

Gorgie snorted in agreement.

"Be careful," I warned him. Honestly, there was no need. The cat understood perfectly where he was and how to conduct himself.

His bendy black shadow glided up the steps fairly quickly but at the same time exactingly. And a few minutes later, I already knew the stairs were safe and the upper platform contained nothing of interest.

"Well?" I turned to my companions and tapped my right foot a few times. "All we have left is to check what's down below..."

All that Time, Mee and Farhas hadn't breathed a word. But now they nodded in near perfect syncopation.

The hatch was quite heavy, so we had to get the troll to help, but it didn't seem to be much trouble for him.

Gorgie dived down the hole first and, a few seconds later, gave a quiet growl to let us know everything was fine.

While going down the stairs, I was expecting my nose to be struck with a smell of damp, but there was nothing of the kind. In fact, it was dry and even warm. And by the way, the passage was quite high. Farhas didn't have to triple over to fit. He just stooped his head a bit.

Mee had discovered a torch in the wall and was already hurriedly striking a flint. A moment later, its timid flame lit up the insides of a cellar.

"What is this?!" the troll asked, puzzled and batting his eyes at the well-organized rows of shelving.

I gave a happy laugh and answered:

"Welcome to the armory of the monster hunters!"

CHAPTER 17

IN COMPARISON with the Stonetown armory, this one couldn't exactly boast of grand dimensions. The small room was seven paces in length and five wide. But if you ask me, the value of an armory isn't in its size, but its contents. I walked slowly along the shelves with a happy smile. Almost everything on the shelves was in decent condition. And lots of it looked familiar...

Those three short long chests over there are full of Potions of Satiety. And those trays there on the third shelf are laden with Blots. I also saw some Fury scrolls in cases.

"Now this is something I haven't seen before," I whispered, glancing with interest at a box with rounded edges.

As I cautiously lifted the lid, I was expecting it to crumble to dust at any second, but it didn't. Apparently I guessed right — this place was "younger" than Stonetown by several centuries at the very least.

The inside of the box was split up into twenty identical slots by narrow dividers, each of them containing a steel sphere the size of a quail egg.

Picking up one of them, I delved into the description.

Tick Sphere.
— *Type: Munition.*
— *Rarity: Rare.*
— *Effect:*
— *Once stuck on a target's body, a Tick will reduce their mana supply by 30%.*
— *Note:*
— *Must have reputation 300 with the Monster Hunters to purchase.*
— *Price: 6 tokens.*
— *Sphere disappears after activation.*
— *Weight: None. Takes no space.*

"Great," I whispered, carefully closing the lid of the box. "New ammunition for our slinger."

But there was also some disappointment. The lower section of one of the shelves was completely full of boxes approximately two and a half times the length of a forearm. I opened one of them and found it empty. The same happened with the other six boxes.

I didn't want to guess what used to be there. What would be the point? Obviously their contents were needed by the former occupants of this tower, just like the contents of most of the other boxes.

Running a sad gaze over the armory, I breathed a heavy sigh. I set my sights too high... In the end my fellow hunters only left me a tenth of the treasure that was once stored here. If not less...

I was about to go back to my companions, who were standing at the stairs, but my attention was drawn by a small niche in the stone wall behind the last shelf. Curious that I didn't notice it before.

I took a few hurried steps and found myself exactly opposite a precise indentation. Inside it was a thin scroll that reflected back a familiar pale blue magical glow.

"And here is the map," I whispered with just my lips and extended my right hand.

Hold up! Hey, what do we have here?

Next to the scroll was a small barely noticeable box. In fact, if not for the magical glow emanating from the map, it's not likely I'd have been able to see the box. And I'd probably have taken it for a fallen piece of stone facing if I did.

Despite its resemblance to stone, the box was almost weightless. It opened like a matchbox with some clever mechanism, which I spent a good ten minutes figuring out. The longer I held it in my hands, the more worried I felt. It just didn't look like the kind of thing made to hold meaningless baubles. Accessing the niche itself required more than a thousand points of reputation with the order.

When I finally got the box open, I stared at its contents with acute fascination. The rectangular cavity was divided into twenty narrow slots shaped like elongated honeycombs. Alas, only three of them had anything inside. Three crystals. And they looked dissimilar to one another in shape and color.

The first, bright and fiery, looked like a red-hot piece of iron. Seemingly, if I touched it there would be no avoiding a burn. The second crystal was the polar opposite of the first. Frost gray and sharp-tipped like a chunk of ice. I got the impression frost might cover it at any second.

The third crystal looked the most, ahem, safe. In fact, calling it a crystal felt like a stretch. If not for the characteristic shine, I'd have taken it for a common brown stone.

"I'll start with you," I muttered, carefully pulling the little brown rock from its slot.

A description of the item immediately came before my eyes.

Elemental Crystal "Earth Tremor."
— *Type: Magic confinement crystal.*
— *Rarity: Epic.*
— *Effect:*
— *Contains the spell Earth Tremor.*
— ***Earth Tremor.***
— *Description:*

THE WASTES

— One of the most powerful earth magic spells, created by Master Terrence the Wise.
— Type: Offensive/ Area of Effect.
— Rarity: Epic.
— Magic School: Earth.
— Effect:
— Caster chooses a section of land and starts an earthquake there.

After reading the first part of the description, I gulped loudly. The "toys" these hunters had to play with were no joke. Now I could see what the foxman was talking about when he spoke of the order's former grandeur. Scratching the back of my head, I continued reading.

— Requirements:
— Intellect — 15.
— Expends 5000 mana points.
— Radius of effect: 165 feet.
— Duration: 5 minutes.
— Note:
— Must have reputation 2000 with the Monster Hunters to purchase.
— Price: 500 tokens.
— Crystal disappears after activation.
— Weight: None. Takes no space.

It didn't say a word about damage. But I knew firsthand what it was like for the earth to shake and tremble, and what consequences that could have. There was an earthquake six years ago in Orchus. The Gray Quarter was almost entirely destroyed. Father surprised me on that day. He said it was a fairly weak one in comparison with the kind that sometimes happened in the mountains. But still it killed a lot of people, and left even more without a home...

Setting the crystal carefully back in place, I got to the other two. Hm, both offensive and affecting an area instead of just one target. The same extortionate requirements for mana, reputation and tokens.

And though my reputation with the Order was no issue, the mana requirements made me grate my teeth. But that wasn't the main problem... Even if I could miraculously rustle up a few more mana crystals or, engaging in a bit of fantasy, if my intellect went up five hundred points, I still wouldn't be able to get all three. I simply didn't have the tokens. Even considering my steep discount, I could only take two spells. And I'd be left with ninety tokens after that. And after all, I still wanted to fill out my reserves of Satiety Potions, Blots and Ticks. I'd already compromised on the Fury scrolls and decided I could do without them.

With a heavy sigh, I read the description of the two remaining stones again.

Elemental Crystal "Heaven's Wrath."
— Type: Magic confinement crystal.

— *Rarity: Epic.*

— *Effect:*

— *Contains the spell Heaven's Wrath.*

— **Heaven's Wrath**

— *Description:*

— *One of the most powerful fire magic spells, created by Magister Pyrus.*

— *Type: Offensive/Area of Effect.*

— *Rarity: Epic.*

— *Magic School: Fire.*

— *Effect:*

— *Caster indicates a point and calls down a rain of lava upon it.*

— *Requirements:*

— *Intellect — 15.*

— *Expends 5000 mana points.*

— *Radius of effect: 165 feet.*

— *Duration: 3 minutes.*

— *Note:*

— *Must have reputation 2000 with the Monster Hunters to purchase.*

— *Price: 500 tokens.*

— *Crystal disappears after activation.*

— *Weight: None. Takes no space.*

Elemental Crystal "Ice Storm."

— *Type: Magic confinement crystal.*

— *Rarity: Epic.*

— *Effect:*

— *Contains the spell Ice Storm.*

— **Ice Storm.**

— *Description:*

— *One of the most powerful ice magic spells, created by Ava the Great.*

— *Type: Offensive/Area of Effect.*

— *Rarity: Epic.*

Magic School: Ice.

— *Effect:*

— *Caster specifies a point and activates an ice storm over it.*

— *Requirements:*

— *Intellect — 15.*

— *Expends 5000 mana points.*

— *Radius of effect: 165 feet.*

— *Duration: 4 minutes.*

— *Note:*

— *Must have reputation 2000 with the Monster Hunters to purchase.*

— *Price: 500 tokens.*

— *Crystal disappears after activation.*

— *Weight: None. Takes no space.*

Despite the fact that I didn't know whether I'd ever be able to activate any of these spells, it was clear to me that I needed to take the crystals. Even if I didn't have the tokens to buy everything, it didn't matter. Something was telling me it would be a long time before I'd find something like this again. All that remained was to decide which crystals to buy.

In the end, I was deciding between Earth and Ice. I took an immediate liking to the earthquake. It lasted longer than the others. Beyond that, I was planning to go back to Stonetown one day. And I knew perfectly well what a localized earthquake could do in the caverns. My first iridescent tablet could attest to that.

As for the choice between Ice and Fire... It was hard for me to know which would be more effective, so I factored in the spells' durations. Ice Storm lasted a minute longer than the rain of fire. I still couldn't be sure. Maybe I was making a mistake. But even so... In any case time would tell.

— *Congratulations!*
— *You have acquired:*
— *Elemental Crystal "Ice Storm" (1).*
— *Elemental Crystal "Earth Tremor" (1).*
— *Removed with discount (50%):*
— *Monster Hunter Token (500).*

I dismissed the system message and closed the box with the one remaining crystal then set it back on the shelf with pity. Oh abyss! Bug take these stupid tokens!

I didn't want to think about whether I'd ever be back here. It was better to cast all the gloomy thoughts out of mind and concentrate on the armory's other items. Said and done. I turned sharply and walked toward the shelves of Blots.

My sour face set my companions slightly on edge. All that time, they were standing patiently at the arsenal entrance as if held there by some spell and carefully watching my every move. Their lack of reputation meant they were not even allowed to enter.

Gorgie was not down with them. The harn was out scouting the surroundings. Well, and why hide it, he was also "marking" them.

Farhas was leaning his right shoulder against a wall and lightly embracing his knotty staff. It was like I could feel his scrutinizing gaze with my skin. My heart was telling me he was going to make more trouble for us yet.

Mee looked like a curious little gopher. Stretching out like a string bean, he was trying to see everything inside. A wide-open mouth, ears splayed out like burdock leaves — it took some effort not to laugh.

I had ninety tokens left in my pocket. Where to start? Hold up! I slapped my forehead and went back to the niche. I was so upset about the fire crystal I'd totally forgotten about the map. With my discount, it cost just one token.

I didn't activate the map just yet. First I was going to finish up my purchases. Placing the glowing scroll into my ephemeral backpack, I headed toward the shelves.

I decided to take an equal number of Blots and Ticks. The former had already saved our lives a few times, while the latter had yet to prove themselves. But I had every reason to think the little spheres would be awfully useful in battle.

With my remaining tokens, I was going to buy

some satiety potions — an indispensable item. I was glad to have the chance to fill my reserves of this elixir. I'd already grown accustomed to thinking I always had a substance on hand that could sate my thirst and hunger. They were also a foolproof solution to the problems caused by assimilating tablets.

When I started opening boxes and chests, there was a surprise waiting for me. More than one! Looking captivatedly over the dark bulbs of potion and brown spheres of Blot, I couldn't believe my luck. They were all more advanced than before!

Medium Potion of Satiety
— *Type: Edible.*
— *Rarity: Rare.*
— *Effect:*
— *Sates thirst and hunger. Restores 70% of life force.*
— *Quantity:7 doses.*
— *Note:*
— *Must have reputation 500 with the Monster Hunters to purchase.*
— *Not to be taken more than 3 time per day.*
— *Price: 2 tokens.*
— *Weight: None. Takes no space.*

Reading the potion description closely, I decided to run down the plusses and minuses of this improved version. I'll start with the price. The new one is twice the cost of the old one. That means it makes sense to compare one Medium Potion to two Small ones. The first thing that jumps out at me is that you get one less dose. But in some measure that is compensated by the fact you can take it more times per day. It also restores twenty percent more lifeforce per sip of elixir. That means this kind can restore two hundred and ten percent of your health every day instead of one hundred.

Hm... Not a clear-cut case. But I could only take what was there.

I closed the full box of potions with pity and got to the trap shelf. I took a dark brown sphere the size of an apple out of the box.

Fortified Blot.

— *Type: Trap.*

— *Rarity: Rare.*

— *Effect:*

— *A creature caught in a Blot will lose 35% total energy.*

— *Note:*

— *Must have reputation 300 with the Monster Hunters to purchase.*

— *Price: 6 tokens.*

— *Disappears after triggered.*

— *Weight: None. Takes no space.*

This one was more straightforward. If I took the battle with the ice golem as an example, I'd only have needed three of these versus five of the old ones. And price-wise I'd still be coming out ahead.

Okay. Enough ogling. Time to fill out my reserves.

— Congratulations!
— You have acquired:
— Medium Potion of Satiety (5).
— Fortified Blot (14).
— Tick Sphere (14).
— Removed with discount (50%):
— Monster Hunter Token (89).

Welp, that's about it... Running a sad gaze over the remaining riches, I walked toward the exit.

Farhas unstuck himself from the wall. I could see on his face that the old troll had a ton of questions.

I was only a few steps away when my eyes suddenly started to go dark. I felt such a pressure in my temples that I thought my head was about to burst like a rotten tomato. I lost my breath for a moment... The unexpectedness even made me get down on my right knee. Surprisingly, I was able to remain conscious! That hadn't happened before...

The sudden spell gradually retreated. Still kneeling, I raised my head. I saw the surprised and alarmed faces of my companions. Gorgie was already at my side. He must have been able to sense my nasty feelings.

Getting out ahead of all their questions, I

turned to the old man:

"How many warriors did you leave at the Boundary and how many did you send back to your settlement?"

Farhas frowned.

"Why are you asking? And what is happening to you?"

I sighed impatiently. We're wasting time.

"It's a reaction to the portal. It's about to open. I've never reacted this badly before. Something truly ghastly must be trying to climb through into our world. And as for your warriors... Otherworldly beasts have heightened senses after crossing over. Whose trail do you think they're gonna pick up when they emerge from the portal?"

CHAPTER 18

TO MY SURPRISE, the old man took my words seriously.

"As soon as we found my grandson, I sent him to our settlement with one of the warriors," he quickly answered. "The others are waiting for me at the Boundary."

"Then your family still has a chance to avoid death," I said, getting up off my knees. "In fact, your death may be what saves them."

My head was still spinning a bit, but I was able to maintain balance. It felt like a hard punch to the gut. And we were quite far from the portal after all... Something strange was happening there. Something I wanted to keep a healthy distance from.

"The way you're talking it's like we're already dead," said the old troll with a frown. "I have sixteen of my clan's strongest warriors. Do you really think we cannot handle one lone spirit? The apprentices of the orcish shamans take them on all alone."

"Everything is different this time," I answered, heading for the stairs.

"Different how?" the old man asked, accompanying me with his gaze.

I stopped and, turning, started to speak:

"The portal closed just a few days ago. It was only supposed to open again next year. That on its own speaks to the fact that everything is different this time. But I'll go on. There was once a stretch of many days in a row when I felt an otherworldly portal opening near me every day. To put it lightly, it made me feel vile. But that was puppies and rainbows in comparison with what I'm feeling now. And let me remind you that we are currently several hours' journey from the portal."

I could see in the old man's eyes that I'd gotten through to him.

"Do you think the spirit trying to escape into our world is going to be stronger than the ones that came before?" he asked.

"The man who taught me everything I know about otherworldly portals once mentioned something he called 'higher creatures.' I think we're about to meet one."

The old man's right brow crept upward.

"This is the first I've heard you say 'we.' I figured this wasn't your battle and you'd want to leave."

I scratched the back of my head.

"I won't insult you with self-serving lies about how, as a monster hunter, I am obliged to defend the world from otherworldly filth of all kinds."

The old man chuckled and nodded. I meanwhile continued:

"I'll be direct. After crossing over, the beast will immediately pick up our trail. As I already said, thanks to the magic of the portal, it'll have staggeringly powerful senses and we won't have much time. But we have an advantage. The farther it gets from the Tree, the weaker it will become."

"You said that once the portal closes, the beasts disappear."

Mee joined the conversation.

"Alas, buddy, I'm afraid I have to disappoint you," I said, placing my hand on his little shoulder. "Something's telling me it won't be quite that easy this time."

"You still haven't told me the real reason you decided to stay," the considerate old troll said.

"That one's easy," I answered. "On the steppe, I chanced across a few descendants of the higher creatures. Believe you me — you and your warriors stand no chance on your own if it's something like that. And that means it would acquire a body. And after it scarfs all you down..."

"...It will follow your tracks," the troll finished my sentence, understanding.

"Exactly," I nodded and raised a pointer finger: "I'm sure this tower still has some surprises for us."

Then, taking a glimmering scroll out of my backpack, I added:

"And this will help me figure out what they are."

* * *

— *Attention! Would you like to use item: Map of Fort Stout fortifications?*

"Hm... So that's what you're called," I muttered, agreeing.

— *Tab created: Map of Fort Stout fortifications.*

I'll be honest, I was secretly holding out hope as I opened the tab. First and foremost, I was hoping greatly for the hunters' defensive systems — the upcoming battle promised to be a hot one. And second, who knew? What if the fort's arsenal wasn't the only place I could find useful doodads?

A map of the tower and its surroundings unfolded before my eyes.

"My predecessors dug this place up pretty good back in their day," I muttered, looking over the map.

"What does the map show?" Mee asked, not straying a step away from me.

We were standing on the watchtower's

overlook platform, the very highest point, and waiting for a reinforcement of sixteen troops, which Farhas went out to get an hour before.

In that time, the portal made itself known one more time, but was still in no hurry to open. Every minute, my connection to it became more and more palpable. Remembering the nasty bout of nausea from earlier, I winced involuntarily. It would be hard to explain what exactly was happening at that portal. The closest comparison would be a very old pustule just about to pop...

"Another attack?" Mee asked with sympathy.

"No, little buddy," I hurried to reassure him. "I just remembered something..."

I lowered my eyes and met his inquisitive gaze. Oh yeah! He was asking about the map!

"My predecessors worked very hard to provide for this fort's defense," I started describing what I'd seen on the diagram. "The marked pillar the trolls call the Black Fang is part of an alarm circle. There are, by the way, a few more of them and they are interconnected by an invisible line."

"Magic?"

"Exactly," I answered. "Something akin to my Lair. Warns you when someone crosses it. And by all appearances, the circle used to activate a trap if an outsider crossed the line."

"Now I see what Farhas was talking about," Mee nodded and immediately asked: "But you said, 'used to?'"

"Yes," I answered with a sad sigh. "Almost all

the traps are deactivated."

"Almost?" Mee asked with hope in his voice.

"The tower's supply still has a bit of mana left in it. I'm trying to figure out a way we can make this otherworldly monster's life just a little bit harder."

I didn't tell the gremlin the mana situation was catastrophic. I didn't want to scare him before the battle. It's easier to fight with hope in your heart. Especially given a few "green" spots were actually still around. When the trolls got here, I'd have to send Gorgie out. Have him leave some tracks around the traps. Maybe the beast would buy it.

Beyond that, there was still a final surviving spot of magic inside the tower. The map showed it as a dimly flickering light blue dot. Based on its pale shade, its supply was almost devoid of mana, but still it was active. I figured Mee should know about it. Maybe it'd stop him shivering. And I understood where he was coming from. Any minute now the portal would be opening and some ghastly otherworldly beast would be running this way. And for the record, the trolls still hadn't arrived.

"By the way," I said, distracting the gremlin from his clearly unhappy thoughts. "The big armored fellow down at the bottom is not just a statue."

"What do you mean?" Mee asked in surprise.

"Let me tell you," I said and triumphantly

declared:

"It's a combat golem!"

That only seemed to make the gremlin shiver even harder.

"Don't you be afraid!" I patted the little guy on the shoulder. "That thing still has a little mana left in it. I still don't know how exactly, but I think I can make it fight on our side."

While the elder was away, I figured out how to use the statue of the order's founder. As it turned out, the map was not simply an indicator of location. I could also use it to partially control the tower's defensive systems. For example, I could transfer mana from the fort's supply to any magic trap and back.

When I realized the usefulness of the tool in my hands, I actually forgot how to breathe! Just the perspectives it unveiled!

My ardor was cooled by the supply's figures. It had just over three percent of its total mana. And half a percent of that was going to maintaining the alarm line and markers.

Thanks to the simplicity of the control mechanism, I quickly got the hang of moving mana from one spot to another. Unfortunately, only those with over two thousand reputation with the Order and at least twelve Mind could actually use it though, so it was all on me. And the first thing I did was deactivate the markers and alarm system. In light of upcoming events, they wouldn't be much use to us now. I would be able to sense the portal opening without any alarm. Meanwhile, our tracks would point the way for the beasts better than any markers.

That brought the overall supply up to almost three and a half percent mana, then I tried to feed one of the magical traps outside the wall. The names like Fire Wave or Acid Mud inspired confidence. But alas, I was not fated to see them in action. Too little mana. All the gray dots on the map required at least fifteen percent. In the end, I dumped all available mana from the tower into the golem. His supply turned out not to be quite so demanding.

As much as I was trying to conserve energy, I had to run a little test. I needed to know what I was dealing with.

The golem control tab contained a list of simple commands. For example, "Attack" or "Stop." When I selected "Move," I was told to choose a point on the map, while for "Attack" I had to set an opponent.

Mentally wishing myself luck, I ordered the golem to move a few steps to the right. And an instant later, my heart aflutter, I watched the bronze titan fairly easily jump down from his pedestal and move to the point I'd selected.

When Mee saw the statue start walking, he

gave a muted squeak and grabbed me by the arm.

"Ah, I wish we had one of these in Stonetown!" I admired.

"Hrn!" Gorgie agreed right away.

"So, what else can he do?" Mee asked, emboldened.

"We're about to find out..." I answered, excited by my new toy. Then I gave it an order to "Defend" the tower entrance.

Quite hastily, the Bronze Gunnar went up to the door and blocked it with his wide triangular shield. He was squeezing a hefty club in his right hand, the top of which was reminiscent of a half-open flower with a sharp spike in the middle. If memory serves, it was called a flanged mace.

All the golem's movements were accompanied by a metallic clang, adding even more ghastliness to the overall picture.

"Does that take a lot of mana?" Mee pulled me out of contemplation.

I quickly checked the supply.

"A tiny amount, but it is still noticeable," I answered. "But he only made a couple moves."

"That means he won't last long in battle," the gremlin contested.

"Then we'll save him for when the going gets really tough."

* * *

About an hour later, Farhas' figure appeared on the edge of the forest. Behind him loomed the silhouettes of the other trolls.

The gremlins and I welcomed our allies with a simultaneous sigh of relief. To be honest, I was already feeling little pangs of doubt in my heart of hearts. What if the warriors ignored the voice of reason and refused to follow their elder? Who could say what these huge creatures might have had in mind? Based on Mee's reaction, I was not alone in my fears.

When Farhas saw the statue in front of the tower door, the look on his face was a sight to behold.

"Don't be surprised!" I shouted from above and waved my hand in greeting.

The old troll just slightly shrugged his shoulders and commanded his warriors to go into the courtyard. The trolls turned their heads in incomprehension and, their mouths agape, looked all around apprehensively. I understood them. For ages, this place was thought to be cursed. Most likely, when they were kids, they heard quite a few scary stories from their grandparents about the Black Fang and the dark charms that killed all those who dared enter these lands.

As soon as the last troll came inside, Gorgie went out to leave tracks around the "green" traps.

"More wizardry?" Farhas asked, nodding at the golem standing in the doorway when I came downstairs.

"Yes," I answered. "But he won't be able to fight long. We'll only use him when things really get rough."

"I see," the old man nodded and said:

"On the way here, we were picking up rocks to drop on the enemy's head from the walls. I hope the walkways will be able to support all my warriors."

I glanced at the bulging bags each troll was carrying. Based on the outlines, the stones they contained were as big as my head. If a bunch of big rocks like that suddenly rained down on the beast's head, it probably would not be too happy.

I turned my gaze to the massive stone stairs leading to the wall and, smiling, said:

"I'm sure these fortifications have seen worse."

"Well, we're about to test that," the elder chuckled and barked:

"Erg! Position your warriors!"

The level-seventeen giant gave a somber nod and started issuing commands.

We spent a bit of time watching Farhas' men climb up onto the walls. To be frank, I wasn't worried for the ancient structure — it was built for the express purpose of defending against monsters.

After we made sure the wall wouldn't collapse under the weight of his soldiers, the elder turned to me:

"We'll wait for your cat and close the gates. Then we'll go up onto the tower's overlook platform. That's the best position for the mages."

"We might as well close the gates right now," I waved it off. "That wall is no obstacle to a harn."

The gray-haired troll gave a respectful chuckle and looked back at the wall out of the corner of his eye. He was clearly impressed by Gorgie's abilities again.

The old man said something else, but I wasn't listening. A rotten and bitter flavor appeared in my mouth and made me wince hard. Beyond that, my eyes went dark for a second and a wave of nasty shivering ran over my body.

"Has it begun?" Mee and Farhas asked at almost the exact same time.

Continuing to wince, I spat bitter saliva a few times, then answered:

"Get ready. The portal has opened."

CHAPTER 19

AN HOUR LATER, Gorgie was back. The beast was noticeably shaken up. The scales on the back of his head were standing on end and constantly vibrating. He easily overcame the wall, slunk across the inner courtyard and, a few instants later, was sitting at my side.

"Hrn!" he growled angrily, shaking his scaly head.

"There's something big and quite fast coming this way," I said, putting the cat's information into words. "The creature is near."

Farhas barked something sternly to his warriors and they answered him with a joint war cry. The sound launched a brigade of ants marching down my spine. A strong wall, sixteen giants armed with heavy cudgels, a combat golem and our spells — could it be that we did in fact stand a chance of emerging victorious?

The sun was about to go beyond the horizon when the sound of cracking wood reached us from the dark looming forest in the distance. The otherworldly creature came barreling our way over hill and dale. It was not hard to tell which way it was moving from the shaking treetops. Having ignored all the green traps, it was strictly following the trolls' tracks. Curious. I wonder why. Maybe it's to do with their numbers? A lone target wasn't as attractive? Either that or Gorgie hadn't left enough tracks.

A few seconds later, a section of the wall of young trees on the forest's edge was blasted to smithereens and a coal black blob the size of a fully-grown bull spilled out into the clearing. It was hard to tell from a distance what exactly we were dealing with. It looked like a ghastly mixture of spider, crab and cockroach. Based on its abrupt and jerky movements, this monster must have had fairly high Speed and Agility.

The monster stopped short. Its long whiskers, looking like shoots of cane, seemed to be doing their own thing. The creature determined our location fairly quickly and burst off with an unpleasant bony chirr.

When the otherworldly cockroach was just a few yards from the wall, clacking its narrow pincers, I finally managed to get a good look.

"Level twelve?" Farhas asked, perplexed.

To be frank, I was also baffled. I took a glance at the harn. But he wasn't reacting to us at all. He was still running his gaze over the clearing. And meanwhile, his scales were standing on end while his powerful sides quivered in tension.

All the while, the monster was coming closer to the wall. The first stones rained down on its head. I couldn't see what was happening at the base of the wall but based on the characteristic sound of chitin crunching and the joyful cries of the trolls it was not hard to guess — the otherworldly insect was not doing so hot. A few seconds later, the trolls shouted victoriously. It's over — we won.

Farhas looked at me, raising his chin proudly. His entire appearance seemed to say I had been sowing panic over nothing.

In my turn, I didn't give a damn about the trolls' condescending gazes. I was sincerely delighted that my fears were unfounded. I still remembered the millipede on the steppe. Its dimensions, level and speed. If a big monster like that showed up here, I'd like to have seen Farhas' ugly mug then. If they wanted to celebrate the victory, I would join them with a clear conscience. The only thing I had to regret at that time was the fact that I didn't get any tokens. Ugh... And there were so many useful doodads left in the arsenal...

Once down in the internal courtyard, we wanted to open the gates, but Gorgie gave a loud roar of warning down from the overlook platform. I froze in place. And an instant later we all heard a fearsome sound from the direction of the forest.

The trolls on the walls also started growling, pointing their hefty fingers into the distance.

Not wasting any time, I ran over to the stairs leading up the wall. Mee wanted to follow me, but I ordered him to go up the tower. He'd be safer there with Gorgie.

Once on top, I froze like a statue. And I had every reason.

It looked like the forest had come to life. The treetops were all in a flurry. The cracking and rasping were so loud I found myself wanting to cover my ears involuntarily.

"I was wrong," I whisper through dried out lips.

Despite the increasing volume, the old man still heard me.

"About what?" he asked with a loud gulp.

Heh... Where's that haughty tone now?

"I was expecting a higher creature, but the portal surprised us. This is an outbreak!"

"What does that mean?"

"Nothing good. The beasts are just gonna keep coming."

I could see on the old man's face that he had a good deal of questions, but he didn't have the time to ask them. The first five beasts had entered the clearing. Unlike the frontrunner, they didn't stop. They just came racing directly in our direction.

The trolls got ready to throw stones.

"Let them come closer!" I shouted, extending a

hand.

There was a high chance the giants would ignore me but, much to my surprise, they listened. Seeing my hand enshrouded in dark lilac smoke probably did the trick.

The cockroaches were in wedge formation, their flat bodies pressed down to the ground and nimbly scurrying their crooked appendages. A few were clacking their pincers impatiently.

Thirty feet away from the wall. The middle one raced out in front, driving the others on.

Ten feet. I finally was able to see the otherworldly monsters up close. Sharp claws, mandibles dripping with some vile liquid and tipped with sharp hooks. The feet — a chill ran down my spine. It took effort to maintain self-control.

"Attack!" I shouted, casting a Fury-reinforced Ram at the insects.

— You have attacked Black Armorbug (12)!
— Critical hit. You have dealt 123 damage!

— You have attacked Black Armorbug (12)!
— Critical hit. You have dealt 119 damage!

— You have attacked Black Armorbug (12)!
— Critical hit. You have dealt 115 damage!

— You have attacked Black Armorbug (12)!
— Critical hit. You have dealt 121 damage!

— You have attacked Black Armorbug (12)!
— Critical hit. You have dealt 113 damage!

The invisible wave toppled all the running creatures and sent them sliding them a few yards back. Stones immediately hailed down on their motionless bodies. A muted cracking of chitin then squelching of innards and the first message appeared before my eyes.

— You have killed Black Armorbug (12)!
— Congratulations! You receive:
— Monster Hunter Token (20).
— Large ghostly crystal (2).

Then a few seconds later, almost at the same time, I received another ninety tokens and ten crystals of various sizes.

Before the monsters' bodies even disappeared, the next wave of cockroaches appeared from the forest.

I checked my supplies. Wisdom was doing a great job bringing my mana back up.

Meanwhile, Farhas didn't any waste time. With clipped orders, he again deployed his warriors to their positions.

"Step to!" he roared. "The beasts are already near! Mage in the center! Attack only on his command! Sure shots only! Flanks intercept any that don't get hit by the spell!"

I still had yet to figure out what abilities the

old troll had, but I could say one thing for sure — he knew how to command. And most importantly — his orders were carried out without question.

Meanwhile, Farhas continued:

"Hoager! Dago! When the bugs die, be ready to go down and pick up the rocks! Our reserves are not infinite!"

There were seven cockroaches in the next wave. They quickly overcame the distance to the wall, and were immediately greeted with a Ram from me.

I was yet again amazed at the elder's foresight when my spell hit only six of the bugs. The seventh, running a bit to the left, avoided that deplorable fate and jumped full bore onto the wall then, quickly flitting its legs, rushed upward. Stones immediately flew at it along with an ice arrow from me. I could be stingy with mana some other time. With such powerful support, it would be a shame to not get the tokens.

I had a fleeting thought that I should call the gremlin down to the wall with his sling, but I decided against it when I saw the seventh bug skitter over the parapet and attack two of the trolls. It didn't survive long. The giants' heavy clubs turned its head into a messy pulp in the space of a few instants. Honestly though, the creature managed to land a couple fairly deep wounds on our defenders.

"Mee!" I shouted. "We need your help!"

Then turning to the wounded trolls, I said:

"Come down and get healed up."

The next morning greeted us with frost but, for the most part, we didn't notice. There simply wasn't time. The creatures were giving us too much action to care about the cold. Bugs just kept rolling in and breaking on the walls of the fort like the black waves of the Dead Ocean. And each wave was bigger than the last.

The trolls ran out of rocks in the middle of the night. But they were no longer feeling bold enough to go beyond the walls — the attacks were too frequent. So the warriors had to switch to clubs. Naturally, that resulted in almost all of the defenders getting wounded. A few of them several times. Farhas would then send them into the interior courtyard to heal.

The potions of satiety were a big help, and I was sharing them generously. But the biggest impact, without a doubt, was made by little Mee. I'm sure that, if not for his Waves of Healing, we'd never have been able to hold the fort down. The trolls looked on him as our savior and, in point of fact, that's what he was.

I by the way, just about got taken down. An especially nimble cockroach dodged a club blow and tried to slice a chunk off me with its pincers. The Muckwalker Aura absorbed all the damage and saved me. Gorgie, not having strayed even a step from me before then, distracted the creature while the trolls finished it off.

For the whole night, the harn was my "eyes," giving me clear, unerring and most importantly timely instructions on where to direct my spells.

Today was the first time I used the Golem Breath. As it turned out, it was quite a useful spell. It created a whitish fog in a twelve-foot radius around me that halved the speed of all creatures caught in it and lasted for half an hour.

Farhas also finally proved his mettle and used two attack spells at once. The first time was in the middle of the night when my Ram covered more than a dozen individuals and the warriors had just run out of stones. The gray-haired troll sent a series of six-foot stone spires flying up out of the ground with lightning speed that impaled the paralyzed bugs straight through.

It was striking to watch and got results so impressive they made me shiver. The spell must have been level four or five. I yet again found myself thanking the heavens that we managed to reach a peaceful agreement with the trolls...

The second spell from Farhas' arsenal was not quite as showy as the first, but no less deadly. And by the way, I had seen it before. The orc shaman had attacked me with the same spell. A ghostly thorny branch.

Honestly, though, the troll elder's sorcery was much more powerful than the young orc's. The semi-transparent lash, studded with sharp spines, easily tore through the bugs' chitin armor. Level-four at the very least. By the way, I think I figured out the old man's secret. It's his gnarled staff. I'd bet my hand it was not some mere creepy-looking stick, but a true magical artifact. Seemingly, it was also making all of Farhas' spells stronger. The old man hadn't let it out of his hands for the whole last day.

When the final attack was thwarted, and there seemed to be no more coming, we all fell wearily where we'd been standing. Except Mee. The gremlin was still tirelessly taking care of the wounded. Over the night, he'd changed noticeably and grown bolder. Where was that timid little gremlin now? The one I met at night cowering next to an orcish bonfire? It was amusing to watch the fearsome giant trolls making way for the little healer. There was nothing but respect and veneration in their eyes.

I was sitting next to the troll elder and watching the last fell beast we killed disappear into thin air.

"Did you see that?" I asked, nodding toward the disappearing beast.

"You mean their levels?" Farhas wearily answered with a question.

"Yes. If I'm not mistaken, the twelves stopped coming two hours before sunup."

"That's right," the old man agreed. "The last wave was level-fifteen bugs. Their armor was stronger and they moved faster. What do you think?"

"The portal's still open..." I shrugged.

"That means we can't let our guards down," said the old man, standing heavily.

I nodded and also got to my feet. I was going to go down into the arsenal and fill out my reserves. As my mother used to say: "there's always a silver lining." I didn't always understand what she meant by that, but today I think I finally grasped the true meaning.

I opened my backpack and counted the loot. Two thousand six hundred sixty-five tokens and two hundred sixty large crystals! Looks like I'll be able to buy that last crystal after all! Beyond that, Random generously granted me sixteen small vials containing the imprisoned spirits of black armorbugs. At first I couldn't even believe my eyes. Heh... As always, mom was right! There's always a silver lining...

At the tower entrance, I crossed paths with the golem, still stuck in a defensive pose and went down into the basement.

When I opened the box containing the crystal, my hands were noticeably shaking either from exhaustion or worry. Although I suspect it was a bit of both.

I admired the bright fiery specks of the crystal for a bit then made my payment.

— *Congratulations!*

— *You have acquired:*
— *Elemental Crystal "Heaven's Wrath" (1).*
— *Removed with discount (50%):*
— *Monster Hunter Token (250).*

"Great," I whispered, smiling. "Now let's get the rest."

Tossing a smoldering glance over the shelves and estimating how much it would cost to buy all their riches, I rubbed my hands together in satisfaction. I had more than enough tokens.

— *Congratulations!*
— *You have acquired:*
— *Medium Potion of Satiety (45).*
— *Fortified Blot (61).*
— *Tick Sphere (41).*
— *Hunter's Fury (35).*

— *Removed with discount (50%):*
— *Monster Hunter Token (526).*

I peeked into my backpack. There were almost one thousand nine hundred tokens left. I patted down all the shelves one final time with pity but, alas, didn't find anything else.

Ugh, too bad. I was just getting a taste for it.

I walked from corner to corner one last time, patting down all the walls hoping to find some secret niche I might have missed, then left the basement. And just in the nick of time. My mouth was filling with familiar bitter saliva.

Hopping out of the tower, I wanted to shout at Farhas about the new threat, but there was no need — every last one of the trolls was already in position on the wall. They were perfectly still like stone statues and staring into the forest.

Farhas turned, and our gazes met.

"Come up here!" she shouted darkly. "We've got guests!"

Judging on his expression, he really did not like what was happening beyond the wall.

Once up, I peered out past the parapet. Just looking at the thing that had my allies so worried made me lose my breath.

The forest fringe and trees beyond it had ceased to exist over the last night. The otherworldly bugs had turned the once narrow little path we took to the tower into a wide swath of denuded land.

And now there were three big huge bugs slowly moving their thick crooked legs over the cleared land in our direction. They were the size of a Conestoga wagon. Their wide flat armor was covered with saber-like spikes. The heavy considerable pincers were pressed to their chests. Their two black eyes and two pairs of long whiskers seemed to be doing their own thing.

"Thirty," Farhas darkly commented on the creatures' levels. "It will be quite an endeavor to get through their armor..."

"But there are upsides," I said, looking closely at the approaching monsters. "If that's all the faster they can go, we have every chance to defeat them."

"Do you think your ram is gonna work against these giants?"

"I'm not sure," I answered. "But I have a couple more surprises up my sleeve."

"I really hope so," Farhas whispered barely audibly, but I heard him.

Well old troll, this wouldn't be the first time Gorgie and I had to put a big nasty creature in its place in order to survive...

I wanted to suggest an approximate plan of action but then our otherworldly guests surprised us all. When the first had traversed half the no-man's-land between the tower and former forest, the shield-like shell on its back suddenly split in two, revealing two pairs of transparent wings. Then, a moment later, the monster shot upward in a cloud of frosty dust.

For a few seconds I looked on baffled as its gigantic carcass descended upon us from the sky. Gorgie gave a fearsome roar, tearing me from my stupor. I'm sure that's what saved me.

After a moment's thought, I summoned the spirit of the Ysh and jumped down from the wall into the interior courtyard. The semitransparent giant snake instantly wrapped itself around my body, taking all the damage from the fall. I still took a good shake though. My eyes went dark for a moment. I even went deaf for a second.

Meanwhile the creature careening down from the sky sprayed a cloud of coal-black dust, covering a few of the trolls. A thunder of falling stones, roaring and shrieks of pain came down from the wall. Through the black fog it was hard to see what exactly was happening up there.

Ignoring the pain in my right side I stumbled, coughed and stood to my feet.

— *Attention! Spell "Wave of Healing" has been applied to you!*

"Rick! Over here!" I heard the gremlin squeak to my right.

While I figured things out, the harn's flexible shadow appeared next to me. An insistent jab to my back showed me the way to run. The black dust was not going to settle any time soon. It was all around. In a daze, I walked forward cautiously with my left hand on the harn's scaled back all the time. Seemingly, the otherworldly beetle was using some sort of masking spell.

"Rick!" I heard Mee's voice crystal clear.

All that time I could hear the battle raging somewhere above me. Stones scraping, lots of trolls roaring, chitin crunching — it all mixed together into a solid ghastly din.

The first thing I saw appear from the black fog in front of me was a bronze shield and behind it the whole golem. A familiar pair of wide ears were poking out behind its legs.

"Rick!" Mee shouted with glee and ran out to meet me.

After a brief embrace, we hurried to the tower's overlook platform — the trolls needed our help urgently.

I overcame all the steps with difficulty and finally made my way to the top. Just in the nick of time! The two other beetles were already in the air. Just a bit and they'd also be falling where the wall was a few minutes earlier and where our allies were still fighting in black fog.

To my surprise, Ram worked properly. The two nose-diving crushers, and that was what these otherworldly beetles were named, were sent flying a few yards back by the wave of lilac. It must have worked because the monsters were in midair.

The crushers, paralyzed by the spell, slammed to the ground. They tumbled a few times, breaking appendages and splaying their wings, then stopped perfectly still. Gorgie wanted to run at their downed carcasses, but I stopped him. The monsters would come to their senses long before the harn would be able to get through their armor.

Meanwhile, the black dust was gradually settling and I could see what was happening down below. The first crusher was still alive, which could not be said of several of the trolls, whose bodies were lying among the stones like broken dolls.

Among the heaps of rubble, I saw other fighters as well, but thank the gods they were merely wounded. Among them was Erg the big fellow. He was lying under a stone slab, unconscious but still alive. The black bug just happened to be dashing toward him and five trolls with Farhas at their head were trying to hold back the onslaught. It's not hard to guess why the otherworldly creature wants so desperately to get through to Erg. It needs to acquire a body.

"Not today," I whispered angrily and lashed the crusher with lightning.

When the bug fell to the ground motionless, the trolls slightly stumbled back in surprise.

"You don't have much time!" I shouted. "It's gonna wake up soon!"

I didn't have to tell the warriors twice. Roaring ferociously, they flung themselves on it. They rained down many fast blows on its chitin armor with their heavy clubs. In a matter of seconds, the bug lost half its legs and one pair of wings but, alas, it wasn't all that easy to kill.

Understanding that time was ticking inexorably, before the trolls broke through the monster's armor, I decided to put our trump card into play.

Opening the fort map tab, I chose the nearest red spot and selected the command "Attack."

The golem reacted at once. Tearing off, he made for the creature, which was just coming to its senses. And he was fairly nimble for a big hunk of metal.

I must give the crusher its due. It was not

going to give up so easily. Even without half its appendages, the beetle had no problem flinging the tenacious trolls in all directions. And they flew back like ragdolls.

And that was the very moment the golem joined the party. Its bronze flanged mace whistled into the creature's chitin side. Its black armor crunched like an eggshell and green slime sprayed from the wound.

The beetle shuddered. Forgetting the trolls, it turned to its new opponent and tried to grab him with a huge pincer. The golem easily deflected the flying appendage with its shield and landed another crushing blow. This time the flanged mace made a dent in the monster's right eye, turning its eye socket into a gaping hole that oozed green slime. After a second's thought, I sunk an ice arrow into the hole.

The otherworldly bug started staggering like a street brawler that just took a powerful box to the ear. And the golem, in his turn, was not thinking about stopping. The flanged mace was flickering constantly, turning the beast's head into a slop of black chitin and green slime. And a few seconds later, we watched the defeated monster's body disappear into thin air.

I didn't read the victory message, because two more of the bugs appeared in the gap in the wall.

I glanced at the fort's magic supply. There was still half of what we started with. The golem had used a huge amount of mana, but it was worth it and then some! With help like him, our group could probably take down even scarier monsters!

I raise a shivering hand. The lightning is still on cooldown. I'll have to use a Ram. Let's see how it works on the ground.

Lilac smoke enshrouds my hand.

— You have attacked Crusher (30)!
— You have dealt 0 damage!

— You have attacked Crusher (30)!
— You have dealt 0 damage!

Alas, no damage got through. The bugs were still on their feet. They gave a slight teeter, but that was it. The stun didn't work the way I was expecting either. I was only able to immobilize one of them. The second, blocking its broodmate's body, was still moving.

I impatiently checked the lightning — less than a minute before I could use it again. And Ram — fifteen seconds.

On my command, the golem dashes forward, blocking a powerful pincer blow with his shield. The trolls, their clubs thrown away, reach for the stones. Large rocks fly at the bug. Thankfully, with the wall collapsed, we have plenty of ammunition.

The beetle, clacking its mandibles furiously, got distracted by the trolls, which the golem took immediate advantage of. The flanged mace, shredding its chitin armor, slammed into the monster's side. The first blow was followed by a second, then a third, and a fourth...

With its dying breath, the monster tried to reach its opponent with its left pincer, but my ice arrow brought the standoff to a close.

Quickly dismissing the victory notification, I directed the golem at our final enemy.

The crusher came to its senses and hit us with a surprise. Releasing a cloud of black fog, it sharply shot upward and flew a crooked path over the dilapidated wall and the golem running its way. It was hard to say whether this maneuver was deliberate or random but, one way another, the beetle was now outside the range of my spells. And worst of all, while Farhas and his soldiers tried to escape the fog, the creature managed to land right on one of the wounded trolls, who was lying unconscious among the stones.

Grabbing its prey with two feet, the crusher again took off into the air and flew toward the swath of downed trees. All I could do was clench my teeth and fists and watch this creature carry one of our warriors away.

The beetle didn't fly very far. It landed sixty-five feet from the wall and I watched an otherworldly beast acquiring a new body for the first time.

If I didn't know exactly what was happening, I'd have called it a captivating spectacle. The body of the troll and the crusher simultaneously flickered with a bright blue flame. Then the absorption began, culminating with the otherworldly newcomer acquiring a body from this world. The whole process took one or two minutes at most.

The monster's level and name remained the same but its torn-out appendages and rumpled wings looked like new.

It was also moving somewhat more lethargically, which I took to mean this newly-minted inhabitant of my world was disoriented by the absorption.

We had to take advantage of that!

I wanted to order the golem to attack the monster, but I was stopped by Gorgie giving a warning growl. I cast a gaze where the harn was pointing and my heart went cold. Over the treeless terrain, quickly clacking their many segmented legs, two level-fifty millipedes were racing our way.

"Ah, some higher creatures have come to pay us a visit after all," I whispered in a quavering voice.

CHAPTER 20

COMPARED WITH the armored crusher, "armed" with fearsome pincers, the millipedes frankly looked a bit weak. But their speed and levels spoke for themselves. I'll never forget watching a similar creature catch up to a herd of steppe elk and tear half of them to bits. And that one was only level thirty-five.

The crusher's reaction to the newcomers baffled me at first. But then, when I realized what was happening, my mouth spread into a happy smile.

When the giant bug saw the millipedes, it gave a sharp shudder and took a step back. Its shield-shaped shell split apart, liberating the wings.

Well of course! That's all logical and expected. They aren't allies anymore! From the moment the crusher obtained a body of our world, it turned into prey to the otherworldly aliens.

Under cover of a cloud of black fog, the beetle tried to escape and very nearly succeeded. But to its great misfortune, its opponent was faster.

The red scolopendras, and that was the name of the new monsters, were already at its side. One of them jumped on the runaway fast as lightning. A second before the crusher got knocked out of the sky and fell into the black fog, I saw a scolopendra sink its flat head into the beetle's underbelly. The second creature didn't keep it waiting either and plunged after its comrade.

Mee and I exchanged puzzled gazes and understood one another without a word. We'd just been given a breather!

I turned my gaze to the extremely battered warband. Other than Farhas, there were four warriors still in formation, and it would be a big stretch to say they were in decent condition. Each of their bodies had a few deep wounds and bruises.

Ah, no... Not four. Five! Erg woke up and, snorting furiously, was trying to crawl out from under the stone slab that had him pinned to the ground. Two warriors heard him struggling and ran over to help.

Mee gave a jolt toward the wounded troll, but I stopped him.

"Take this," I said, extending a couple potions of satiety. "Drink them. And don't waste mana. We're going to need it soon."

The kid nodded and ran down. The harn and I

followed.

"What's happening over there?" Farhas asked when caught up to him.

"The crusher has been reborn," I answered, continuing to walk quickly toward the gap and adding over my shoulder: "And two level-fifty higher creatures have appeared from the portal and have just attacked the beetle."

The old man gave a perplexed cough.

"Where are you going?" he asked.

"I'm going to get a couple surprises ready for whoever wins that fight," I answered, making my way up the pile of stones.

Once outside the walls, I started throwing Blots over the path I figured the monsters would take. Bit by bit, the pile of stones and the internal courtyard after it turned into one huge trap. Exactly what we needed. I wasn't stingy with the spheres either. Now every little thing could determine the outcome of the battle.

When I'd finished with the blots, I ran over to Farhas who was making use of the break and spearheading the effort to get wounded trolls out from under the rocks.

"Here," I said as I ran, extending him a handful of Ticks and all the Fury scrolls. "Hand these out to your warriors."

My back already turned, I heard the elder chuckle in respect. He must have read the descriptions.

After that, he gave a few clipped orders:

"Dago, get the wounded into the tower! Everyone else take as many stones as they can carry up to the overlook platform!"

When all the preparations were complete, I went up and gazed into the distance. Based on the appendages periodically poking out of the black fog, the crusher wasn't going to give up too easily.

"Great," I whispered with just my lips and opened the map. "Hold out just a bit longer, big guy."

I gave the golem an order to return to the fort then checked his mana supply. Almost one percent remaining. Hopefully that would be enough for him to land a few blows.

The bronze giant overcame the pile of stones and stood in the center of the courtyard. Surrounded by Blots on all sides, he'd make a great lure for whichever creature won this battle. And I had almost no doubt that there would be only one winner.

Meanwhile the black fog gradually dispersed and, with it, my hope that the crusher could take down two level-fifty beasts. Although, based on the fact that the first scolopendra to attack was missing a few large chunks of its torso, the beetle was fighting valiantly. If not for its shattered underbelly shell and the slimy innards falling onto the ground through it, I definitely would have bet on it to win even still.

For the most part, the battle was already over. Both parts of the cloven scolopendra were still moving, but that was just death convulsions. They'd be over in a matter of minutes. Its counterpart, which had climbed up onto the crusher's back and was slowly stumbling and trying to stay on its feet, had begun the absorption process.

I didn't get bogged down guessing what might happen if we attacked the monster at that moment. First of all, we simply couldn't get there fast enough. And second, we didn't know how that might end for us.

Based on the trolls' stretched out faces, this was making a big impression on them. I just gulped with my dry throat. Just few minutes earlier, they'd watched a member of their tribe die.

Finally, the bright blue flame went out and we saw the reborn monster.

"The spirit has acquired a body," Farhas commented drily.

"Yep," I nodded. "And its weak for now."

"And hungry," Mee squeaked.

"A good opportunity to attack," I sighed. "But we're too far away."

"Then we should draw its attention," said Farhas and suddenly he started to roar ferociously: "Prepare for battle, brothers! This beast must die!"

The trolls, shaking their heavy clubs over their heads, responded to their ruler with a single unified roar. I think I also shouted something, as did Mee standing next to me while Gorgie imitated us with a fearsome growl.

That did the trick. The war cry drew the beast's attention. Its flat head turned in our direction and, a moment later, it was running toward us.

It reached the first blot in a matter of seconds. I was already mentally rubbing my hands together as I imagined the beast getting bogged down in the generous spread of traps. But the scolopendra surprised us...

Just three feet from the traps, it stopped to probe in front of itself with its long whiskers.

"It can sense them!" one of the trolls barked angrily.

"Keep screaming!" Farhas commanded. "We need to distract it from the traps!"

We gave another roar in unison. The beast reacted instantly — it dashed forward. My disappointment was immense when I saw its flexible segmented body smoothly bending itself around the Blots without losing speed and climbing up the pile of stones.

The monster's nimble movements drew a joint sigh of disappointment.

"Let's see how you like this!" I spat out angrily and activated lightning.

With a bright flash, electricity shot toward its armor in a jerky line. But nothing happened!

I lost the gift of speech for a moment, watching with wide-open eyes while the scolopendra just kept running our way as if nothing had happened, continuing to gracefully curve around the Blots.

This was the first time that foolproof spell hadn't worked! I was immediately reminded of something Master Chi said about defense against paralyzing magic.

Farhas gave a roar, tearing me from my stupor:

"Attack the fell beast!"

Large stones rained down on the scolopendra's head as it ran toward its prey. Or to be more accurate, that was what it looked like at first glance... The nimble creature, seemingly, was anticipating this twist of fate. It coiled up, froze for a moment and sharply turned forward, then back, then right and left... Only one stone hit its armor and it was a glancing blow. And for the record, by some utterly fantastic means, it also managed to dodge a ram, and Farhas' scourge and the stone spikes.

Something unbelievable was happening before my very eyes. After all, the scolopendra had just been weakened by rebirth. What would have happened if it was well rested?!

I must give the monster its due — this was the first time I'd fought such a high level creature. And for the first time, I truly understood that I could die at any second. That realization knocked the wind out of me. I think this is panic!

A moderately painful kick in the back brought me to my senses.

"Wake up!" Farhas barked at my face.

"Activate your warrior!"

With a burnt-out nod, I mechanically gave the command to "Attack."

The bronze titan, taking shelter behind its shield, burst from place. The creature reacted instantly to the lateral motion. Its long whiskers, vibrating at a very, very fine frequency, were clearly giving it a picture of its opponent. The trolls for the record, hoping the creature was distracted, were still throwing stones. But with its sharp and simultaneously lithe movements, the millipede was able to avoid taking any damage. It looked like some ravenous hypnotic dance.

When the golem got close, the throwing stopped. The warriors were afraid to accidentally hit our best fighter.

Waving the flanged mace, the golem made a long lunge. I was expecting the scolopendra to dash in for a counterattack, then the bronze giant would finally be able to hit our elusive opponent. But yet again, the beast managed to surprise us. It simply closed the gap and went left. And most impressively — it kept the golem between it and the trolls' line of attack the entire time.

The Bronze Gunnar made attempt after attempt to get near the monster, but nothing was working.

"How much mana does it have left?" Farhas asked grimly.

Looks like the old troll has realized, like me, what the crafty millipede was doing. It was trying to wear its opponent out.

That meant it was somehow able to sense magic supplies and how much they had in them. Add to that extreme agility and speed as well as resistance to paralyzing magic... I was perplexed and perturbed. I didn't want to imagine what would happen to us when the golem ran out of magic.

"This beast is clearly magical," Farhas said, intently watching the fight below. "If we can drain its supply, we'll rob it of its advantage!"

"Yeah," I nodded. "But you saw that — not a single Tick hit it. It avoided them easily, just like the normal rocks."

"Ugh!" the old man squeezed out between his teeth. "If we could only hit it properly one time! It's armor is weak."

Pointing at the scolopendra's side, Farhas added:

"Did you see what a deep scratch that rock left? And that was just a glancing blow."

"I'll distract it!"

Erg's voice made us shudder. The giant took a decisive step forward.

"It won't run away from me like it runs from your warrior," he continued. "I have many open wounds on my body. It will smell blood and certainly attack. And when it does, I'll try and activate your spheres and slow it down. That will give you time to finish off the vile beast."

Getting out ahead of the others' objections,

Erg raised a hand.

"No! I'm going alone! I will die with honor for my tribe!"

I glanced thoughtfully at Erg. He's right. The beast is hungry and he has lots of wounds on his body. And even though Mee's magic and my potions had healed many of them already, Erg would surely make a good lure.

"We don't want you to die, Erg," I shook my head.

"But..." the big fellow tried to object, but I interrupted him.

"I have one last trump card and you can play it properly."

Briefly laying out my scheme, I looked at the old man.

"It might work," he said laconically to the others. "Go start. Your shiny warrior's supply will run dry soon enough."

Erg, squeezing his club in his right hand and a handful of Ticks in his left, hurried down. I followed after him.

As soon as Erg opened the door, a notification appeared before my eyes:

— *Attention! Fort Stout's magic supply is empty!*

"The warrior has stopped moving!" I heard the trolls up above screaming.

"Get ready!" Farhas barked.

Erg, bending low, went out in front and roared loudly, challenging the crafty beast to a fight. I meanwhile, trying to keep to the shadows, slipped over to the wall. I waited for the door to set back in place and held it just barely open, leaving a crack two fingers wide. Through it, I had a great view of what was happening from the outside.

As we supposed, the smell of blood distracted the scolopendra from the frozen golem and it came running at the troll.

Erg gave another roar and, swinging his club, went out to meet the running monster. Seeing that its new opponent was of flesh and blood and not planning to run, the millipede quickened its pace. All that time it never once forgot about the traps.

"Stop," I said with my lips alone. "Move a bit to the right. Like that."

Of course, Erg couldn't hear me. But we had a plan and the warrior was following it to a "T."

The beast played the same trick as it did with the golem, using Erg to block the rock throwers. But that put it right where I wanted it. It was only a few yards from Erg when I began the activation.

— *Would you like to summon Snow Ghoul Spirit?*

After I agreed, the system drained the crystal of five hundred mana points. With a slight buzz on my bite mark, a familiar pale silhouette appeared at my side. Obeying my order, he dashed toward the running scolopendra.

Unthinkable! Sensing the threat, it sharply dove right. But fortunately for us, the ghoul was much faster! Slamming full speed into its fidgety muddy-brown body, it instantly took thirty-five percent of the beast's life force.

The unexpected attack disoriented the elusive insect for a few seconds, which the trolls took immediate advantage of. The stones they threw with Fury easily penetrated its thin armor, depriving the creature of its mobility. Meanwhile, a few Ticks hit their mark, draining the beast's magic supply in the blink of an eye.

Gorgie was already at my side. His whole body crouched to the ground, he was preparing to attack.

"Well? Wanna give it another shot?" I asked and activated lightning.

This time, to my relief, it all worked properly — the electricity paralyzed my opponent for twenty seconds.

As not to lose valuable time, the harn used Thorntail's Jump to get behind the beast and land a few lightning-fast blows.

Erg wasn't asleep at the wheel either. It was his club that smashed the monster's head in, finally bringing our fight to a close.

— *You have killed Red Scolopendra (50).*

— *Congratulations! You receive:*

— *Experience essence (10000).*

— *Diamond tablet of Intellect.*

— *Silver tablet (20).*

— *Monster Hunter Token (100).*

— *Attention! The Higher Powers smile upon you! You have replicated the legendary feat of Dalia the Magnificent! You defeated a creature more than 50 levels higher than you using a magic spirit!*

— *Congratulations! You receive:*

— *Experience essence (5000).*

— *Iridescent Tablet "Red Scolopendra" (1).*

CHAPTER 21

WHEN FARHAS WALKED UP to me, I was sitting on a rock, head down and eyes closed. I still couldn't believe we managed to take down the vile jittery beast. Beyond that, I was enjoying the calm. My headache had finally retreated.

"What do you feel?" the elder asked with a weary voice.

I raised my head and we met eyes.

"The portal has closed."

For the first time since we met, I saw an open smile on the old man's face. I still wouldn't call it kind. Although if you overlook the fangs and animalistic eyes — anything is possible...

It's a shame, but I have to disappoint him.

"We don't have much time."

"Why?" Farhas instantly went bleak.

"I can still sense it. It's amassing power. I think there's another outbreak coming."

"When?" Erg asked. He and the other soldiers had us surrounded, hanging on our every word.

I closed my eyes and listened to my feelings.

"Based on how I feel, we have a few hours. Although I could be wrong."

The trolls reacted with a joint sigh of disappointment.

I could have said the orcs had been desecrating the portal with blood sacrifices for so long they'd entirely destabilized it. But I decided to keep tactfully silent. After all, it was clear as day that it all happened with the tacit agreement of these very trolls or, to be more accurate, their chieftains.

The warriors are mad and afraid right now. Saying something like that might provoke a conflict and we have no need for that. I'll try a different path.

"I know a way to forestall the portal's opening," my words made the trolls shut their mouths.

Under their silent gazes, I took one of the ghostly crystals out of my backpack. Based on the way the trolls reacted, my guesses must have been right. They were also getting crystals and tokens for killing the armorbugs and crushers. But how to explain to them that without induction into the order and plenty of reputation, these objects would be absolutely useless to them?

Choosing my words carefully, I started:

"These crystals are the only thing that should

be sacrificed to the Tree of Spirits. They alone can mollify and calm it."

As I spoke, I walked up to a flat stone and started placing all my crystals on it. The higher the pile grew, the more the trolls' faces stretched out. And that wasn't the half of it! All told we had two hundred seventy large crystals.

"This is everything I have," I said. "And this is my contribution to keeping the peace in these lands. This is my sacrifice. Aid to you and your families."

"Are you certain you'll be able to win the Tree of Spirits' favor?" Farhas asked.

I saw and understood that the old man had long been willing to place his crystals on the pile and order the others to do the same. But seemingly, he wanted to get his tribesmen to make the sacrifice voluntarily.

"Absolutely," I nodded back.

"Then take mine as well!" Erg announced, taking a step forward and running a proud gaze over his tribesmen.

"And mine!"

"Mine too!"

The cries of the other soldiers rained down. The mountain of crystals grew by another thirty stones of various size. To be frank I was expecting more but, considering the rarity of this loot and the levels of the trolls, I figured a small amount was better than nothing.

"And mine," Farhas said calmly, placing a

large crystal on the pile. "But there's more..."

Everyone looked at him in incomprehension. Honestly, I quickly figured out what the old troll was driving at. He wants to gather all the dead trolls' crystals and give them to me as well. That might be a problem. The loot of fallen warriors belongs to their families. I wonder what he'll say to his warriors about that.

"Today is an important day!" he proclaimed. "We have prevailed! But we paid a high price for our victory! Our brothers died fighting for our families, for our tribe! So let's not deprive them of the honor of making a sacrifice of their own! Even if it is in death."

While the old troll continued his fiery speech, I looked to see how his subjects were reacting. Well, what could I say...? One glance at the attentively listening warriors made it clear — they were prepared at that very instant to follow him through fire and water. A wise and far-reaching move. I could learn a thing or two from this geezer. The backbone of a powerful tribe was being born before my very eyes. They had great things ahead of them. Now, Erg would hardly allow himself to treat Farhas with the kind of impertinence I saw on our first encounter. Doubtlessly, it was the battle that brought them together, but the proper words were only strengthening that bond.

While the trolls dug through the heaps of wreckage and took the bodies of their fallen tribesmen from under the stones, I took advantage of the short breather and decided to look through my loot.

The Great System awarded me a hundred tokens and ten large crystals for defeating the two crushers. Beyond that, Random generously granted me one small vial containing the spirit of an overgrown beetle.

Hm... No matter how much I wanted to solve the portal issue and get as far from this cursed location as possible, I'd have to stick around. It was gonna take a long time to recover from absorbing two spirits.

By the way, I'll still have fifteen of the vials I knocked out of the armorbugs. I hope someone will recognize their value in Orchus...

I was distracted by shrieks of joy with renewed vigor from the direction of the rubble. As it turned out, the young Dago, one of Farhas' assistants, had gotten a Gold Tablet of Intellect for killing the scolopendra, which he immediately activated without a second thought. And now his friends were sincerely delighted for him.

The newly-minted mage was smiling stupidly while the other trolls patted him amicably on the shoulder. Farhas even went so far as to give him a firm embrace. By the way, only then did I notice the physical resemblance between them — by all appearances they were relatives. Heh... And to imagine I used to think all trolls looked alike.

Seeing the other giants' delight I realized that, despite the loss of a large number of trolls, their tribe had become an order of magnitude stronger today. Sure Dago had merely unlocked Intellect and received a magic supply of fifty points, but that was just the beginning. Based on Farhas' expression of delight, he would have plenty of support.

By the way, speaking of Intellect. Today I managed to drum up something I'd never seen before.

— *Diamond tablet of Intellect.*
— *Level: 1.*
— *Category: Characteristic.*
— *Effect: + 5 to current progress in the Intellect characteristic.*
— *Weight: None. Takes no space.*

While reading the new tablet's description, I was for some reason reminded of Master Chi and his Hive. I wonder how many high-level monsters I'd have had to kill for him. Ten? Two? Or maybe a hundred? If so, based on the quality of the most recent loot, it was hard not to think his plan was genius. Chi really could have become one of the most powerful mages in our kingdom.

Every schoolkid knows that diamond tablets are the most valuable. Because they are the only way of getting more powerful at high levels. Well, with the obvious exception of iridescents, which most teachers considered legendary, if they mentioned them at all.

I opened my backpack and got out the nacreous sheet with a depiction of a small scolopendra on its backside and flowing with all colors of the rainbow. I gave a chuckle. I'd like to see my teachers' faces now.

— *Iridescent Tablet "Red Scolopendra."*
— *Effect:*
— *Unlocks 1 characteristic of your choice from Red Scolopendra.*

> — *Unlocks one skill or ability of your choice from Red Scolopendra.*

— *Unlocks 1 spell of your choice from Red Scolopendra.*
— *+10 to any characteristic/skill/profession/spell.*
— *Weight: None. Takes no space.*

After carefully studying the entire list, I breathed a sigh of disappointment. It wasn't enough that the majority of skills, characteristics and abilities were marked "anatomically incompatible." This giant millipede also didn't have a single spell to speak of.

Honestly, it did at least have one magical ability. And it was what was allowing the scolopendra to dodge all the Blots so masterfully, as well as to sense the golem's magic supply.

— ***Red Scolopendra's Sixth Sense.***
— *Level: 0 (0/20).*

— *Type: Active ability.*

— *Rarity: Epic.*

— *Description:*

— *Using magic, the Red Scolopendra is able to sense active/passive magical emanations, see the magic supply of an item/living creature/entity and determine the capacity and total quantity of mana in its supply.*

— *Requirements:*

— *Intellect — 15.*

— *Expends 160 mana points.*

— *Note:*

— *Duration: 5 minutes.*

— *Radius: 50 feet.*

Now I see how the beast was able to dodge all my traps. This ability multiplied by high Agility and Speed figures made it practically invulnerable. Honestly, the scolopendra had no real defenses to speak of. Its thin chitin armor excepted — that couldn't even save it from the trolls' stones. But it did have Regeneration, which I had been looking for, and there were no "anatomical" issues whatsoever.

— *Attention! You have unlocked the Regeneration characteristic!*

— *Present value: 10.*

The new characteristic got straight to work. I could sense the exhaustion gradually leaving my body as the last shreds of the headache retreated. I glanced at my seriously flagging energy and mana supplies. They were restoring noticeably faster. Great!

The fact I was feeling physically better logically also made for a better mood. The grim thoughts and uneasiness were gradually moving to the background — I wanted to act.

But what if?

— Attention! You have activated the magical ability Red Scolopendra's Sixth Sense!

I have to know how this thing works.

The ability worked approximately the same way as the maps of Stonetown and Fort Stout. However, those showed only the traps I was allowed to use based on my reputation with the order. I immediately realized that after activating the sixth sense and being pointed to two magical spots directly beneath the pedestal where the towering Bronze Gunnar recently stood.

The two light blue nearly gray little spots were so close to one another that they seemed like just one at first.

I slowly came nearer the huge slab as not to draw attention. I opened my map. I checked again. No, it definitely shows that one as a gray dot.

Maybe the issue is that I drained the fort's supply? And that's why I can't see anything?

Either that or, more plausibly, the weak

magical emanations coming from under the pedestal were not part of the tower's energy system. And that was why the map didn't recognize them.

I took a look around. No more surprises. Wait a second! Actually there was one more!

I had just over a minute left and decided to take a closer look at all our allies. Dago was first to catch my eye. He was helping Mee tend to the wounded. Exactly right. The young troll's weak little fifty-point magic supply was gradually accumulating mana.

I took a fleeting glance at the gremlin. The kid probably got some good loot. I saw the stones from his sling pelting the scolopendra's open wounds. He still hadn't said anything. And rightly so. No reason to draw attention. The trolls were still buzzing from the fight, but soon they'd all remember how our encounter began.

When I thought about the potential threat, my eyes found Gorgie all on their own. And I shouldn't have had any doubts — he's always on alert. Vigilant. Intelligent. What would I do without him?! Looking deceptively lazily, the cat was splayed out on some wall debris, having chosen his position carefully so all of Farhas' soldiers could see him.

By the way, speaking of Farhas — as I supposed, beyond the fact the old man was himself a mage, his staff had a magic supply of its own. In fact, it was quite large and quickly replenished itself. Surprising that the old mage was using spells so infrequently. I didn't want to believe that he was just tritely saving mana while his warriors died. Maybe it was all because of cooldown times? They really were powerful spells, so it would make sense if they required some waiting.

Obviously having sensed my stubborn gaze, the old troll turned but I averted my eyes and looked over at Erg. That little sneak! Oh yeah! Big Erg was what I meant when I mentioned surprises! His fifty-point mana supply clearly spoke to the fact that Dago wasn't the only one to become a mage today! For sooth, everything they say about the god Random is true!

Erg was resolutely clearing wreckage, trying to extract the bodies of his fallen tribesmen. I wondered why he didn't make an announcement about his trophy for all to hear like Dago. Will he do it later? I guess he'll keep it close to his chest until he gets stronger... I may have spoken too soon when I gave my estimation of the future of Farhas' tribe's. They still have internal upheaval and an attempted coup ahead of them. Apparently like Erg's impertinence toward the elder mage was somewhat more significant than a young warrior simply acting out.

I wondered what would happen if I told Farhas what I saw. I was sure he wouldn't be happy to have competition. He'd probably want to get rid of him. Not right away. The tribe had just lost half of its best warriors. Three of the survivors were seriously wounded too, so they wouldn't be back in formation any time soon. Not counting Farhas, the duty of defending the tribe would fall on the shoulders of just six warriors. But the old man was sure to want to get rid of a competitor nonetheless.

Although... Maybe I was blowing things out of proportion. Maybe Erg, as a more senior tribesman, had decided not to steal Dago's thunder.

I glanced at the big sullen fellow again and chuckled at my thoughts. No... Erg would never do that. Based on the way the troll was always running out in front, he wasn't the type to let someone else have the glory. He must have just been keeping it secret.

My ability's active time ran out as did the time to wait.

Farhas added another couple dozen crystals to the big pile and turned to me:

"Before we get started, I wanted to ask you a favor."

"Go ahead," I nodded.

"When we're done with the Tree, I'd like you to spend another few days here."

I got on guard. After all, I had a feeling we wouldn't be allowed to leave so easily.

"Why?" I asked coldly.

The old man nodded at two unconscious warriors Mee was keeping watch over.

"They've lost a lot of blood. Their bones have just started to heal. They need treatment and rest.

Without a healer, they will die."

Seeing that I wanted to object, the old man jumped out in front:

"I swear than neither I nor any members of my tribe will hurt you. When my warriors are back on their feet, we'll allow you to go. Beyond that, we'll show you the shortest way to the west and provide you with all the provisions you'll need for your travels."

Based on the way Mee shuddered in surprise and looked our way, he must have also received the oath text.

I considered it. To be frank, a breather was just what we needed. I had to absorb the spirits. Check for the source of the strange magical emanations beneath the pedestal. And just simply rest up before a long journey.

An oath is serious business. An oath is a guarantee. After carefully reading the text one more time, I got up and extended a hand.

"Agreed!"

Farhas responded to my handshake with an open smile.

CHAPTER 22

TWO HOURS LATER, we were at the portal. It was fairly easy to walk the wide clearing the otherworldly insects had cut through the forest. On the way, I checked the map. As it turns out, Gorgie's little outing before the attack had borne fruit after all. All the green traps had either been destroyed or deactivated. But then I leafed through all the victory notifications and did in fact find a few referring to the green traps and loot for their killing.

It was hard to recognize the area around the portal. At a distance, the trolls stopped fast with their mouths agape, afraid to come near the ugly semblance of a tree they very recently had proudly referred to as the Tree of Spirits.

It had grown noticeably over the last few days. It was eerier and viler. The black tar stuck to its trunk and branches was constantly pulsating, which made it look alive. The greasy black puddle around the tree had become wider by five paces at the very least.

With a heavy sigh, I met eyes with Gorgie.

"Well? What do you say?"

The harn growled in agreement and took the first step, by the same token showing me a safe route.

Although Mee tried to come with us, I left him with Farhas. I could not risk his life. And not only because he was the link that bound us to the trolls.

With every step, I could feel the portal more distinctly and manifestly. And the closer I came, the more I understood that we didn't have much time.

Surprisingly, I suddenly got the idea that I should activate Scolopendra's Sixth Sense and look at the portal. It took one hundred sixty mana points from my supply, then a gigantic coal-black spot appeared before my very eyes. Just looking at the new scene took my breath away.

The spot was pulsating measuredly, as if in time with a beating heart. It seemed to be breathing. A lump rose up my throat right away. It was a nastier sight than anything I'd ever seen before.

A slight nudge to my right leg pulled me out of the stupor. It was Gorgie reminding me why we came here with his scaled head.

"Thanks, buddy," I whispered with dry lips

and started taking out the crystals.

My new ability made it easier to see the black spot's reaction to having crystals thrown into it. It was shivering, quaking and constantly growing slightly smaller.

— Congratulations! Your reputation with the Order of Monster Hunters has been increased by 6250 points! Happy Hunting!
— Present value: 9530
— Removed:
— Large ghostly crystal (290).
— Medium ghostly crystal (10).
— Small ghostly crystal (30).
— From now on, you will receive a 70% discount on all items available in any of the order's arsenals!
— From now on, the brothers of our Order regard you as a Legend!
— Congratulations! You receive:
— Monster Hunter Token (1500).

"As I was expecting, I was not able to get the portal shut. It has gone untended for too long. The orcs have desecrated it too much with their blood sacrifices. The ghostly crystals we gathered are just delaying the inevitable."

I said all that when I got back to the trolls. This time I didn't neglect to mention the orcs — let them know whose fault this was.

"Will the sacrifices be enough for long?"

Farhas asked gloomily.

"It's hard to say, but a few months for certain."

When the warriors heard my response, they all exhaled in concert. Seeing my uncomprehending look, the old man explained:

"We were afraid we had just a few hours. But you pulled it off."

"Yes, but celebrating would be premature," I shook my head. "After all, it still will open one way or another, and then there will be another outbreak. Your tribe will come under attack again. The fort is in ruins and its supply is empty. Half of your warriors have perished. You cannot survive another attack of these beasts."

"We'll summon allied tribes!" Erg exclaimed hotly. "They will stand shoulder to shoulder with us!"

"The moment the elders of the other tribes find out what happened here, not a single one of them will allow their warriors to die in someone else's war," Farhas objected calmly. Based on the expressions on the others' faces, he'd just said what everyone was thinking.

But that didn't bother Erg. He proudly raised his chin and asked:

"Are you suggesting we tuck our tails between our legs and flee like cowards?"

The big fellow's words made the other trolls all frown, but Farhas was unflinching. Seemingly, he was actually happy not to have to give his rude compatriot another bop on the nose for flying off the handle.

"What's so shameful about fleeing?" he asked. "Simply to leave. Get some distance from this dangerous place. And in the end, find a new home. Where our children will have a future. The Stone Forest is great. Everyone knows that. But I understand you, Erg. You're young, strong and ambitious. Your heart pines for victory. You have no wife, no children. Your family died from the pestilence. You have nothing to lose other than your life."

Erg stood there scowling, his hefty fists clenched in anger. But the other trolls didn't give a crap. Farhas knew the right sore points to poke.

"I for one am scared to imagine such beasts attacking our settlement," the old troll continued, pointing toward the portal. "Children, women, the elderly... They'll all be torn to bits or assimilated for rebirth. Is that how you see the future of our tribe, Erg?"

Yet again I was convinced of the old troll's wisdom and cleverness. I must have been mistaken before. Farhas must have found out about the Intellect tablet somehow. He decided to try an alternative method. With Erg's help, he was showing everyone that the young upstart would never make a good chieftain. At the very least for the time being.

The big fellow had nowhere to hide. Sniffling angrily, he lowered his head and shut his mouth.

"How far do we have to go?" Dago asked.

"That portal was open a little over a day," I answered. "You saw how fast those creatures can be. The farther you get, the better. Beyond that, the portal will be left unguarded and who's to say how long it will be open for the next time? Or if it ever will close again..."

The last sentence I actually whispered. But everyone heard me. Just the way their faces turned bleak. What did they think was gonna happen? Without crystals, the portal would become unstable.

"If things really are how you say," Farhas began. "Then this land will soon be hell on earth. The beasts will just keep coming. First they'll conquer the whole forest and surrounding lands. Then they'll make their way onto the steppe. I don't feel sorry for the orcs, but will they be able to hold out for long?"

"We're actually lucky the beasts were brainless," I said. "They were working on instinct alone."

"What is that supposed to mean?" the old man asked in surprise.

"That intelligent otherworldly entities are bound to enter into our world as well. And I've seen what they can do. It won't take a hundred. Twenty creatures like that and we'd have died today."

"That means we have less time than I thought," the old troll said dismally.

* * *

— *Attention! You have absorbed Crusher spirit!*

— *Congratulations! Your reputation with the Order of Monster Hunters has been increased by 200 points! Happy Hunting!*

— *Present value: 9930.*

Regeneration, a potion of satiety, the improved Lair and a personal healer at my side — absorbing both of the spirits went smooth as butter. I had to take breaks between the rituals, but I had them both over with by evening.

In the end, I came away with two new marks on my body. The ghostly armorbug tried to slice through my wrist with its mandibles, while the crusher tried to pincer off a leg.

By the way, Mee also underwent a ritual and received an armorbug spirit. As for Gorgie, we weren't able to pull off the same trick. The Great System gave me a clear indication that the harn unfortunately lived by different laws.

As for the spirits themselves, I wouldn't say I was elated exactly, but I also wasn't too disappointed.

— ***Black Armorbug Spirit.***
— *Type: Magical spirit.*
— *Rarity: Rare.*
— *Effect:*

— *Attack.*

— *Description:*

— *Summons a spirit that deals 3000 points of damage.*

— *Summoning requires 400 mana points.*

— *Remember! You may only appeal to the power of the Black Armorbug 1 time every 5 days!*

When I opened the description of the crusher spirit, I was hoping deep down for wings. That would have been really nice! But alas, Random had different ideas.

— **Crusher Spirit.**

— *Type: Magical spirits.*

— *Rarity: Rare.*

— *Effect:*

— *Camouflage.*

— *Description:*

— *Summons a spirit that surrounds you with an opaque magical fog that disorients and confuses opponents.*

— *Summoning requires 200 mana points.*

— *Remember! You may only appeal to the power of the Crusher 1 time every 5 days!*

Hrm, so definitely not wings... But the low mana requirements were nice.

Farhas was keeping close watch over me. Watching me undergo the absorption ritual with two spirits had him pretty shaken up. I could understand that. Taming spirits was a very rare occurrence.

When I took out a third vial and extended it to Mee, his face was a sight to behold. Then, when the fourth came out for Gorgie, I thought Farhas was going to have a stroke.

So when it didn't work with the harn, the old troll rushed over to me. And before he even stopped walking, he asked:

"If you don't need that spirit, could I buy it or trade for it?"

Hm... And why not? Who ever said the trolls didn't have any stuff that might interest me?

"Do you have any items for my level?" I asked hopefully.

Alas, the old man shook his head "no."

"What about tablets?" I asked.

"They're too important to our tribe's development."

I understand — a strategic reserve.

"Maybe you have some mana crystals then?"

"No. But I do have this," Farhas said, taking a handful of hunter tokens out of his bag. "If this isn't enough, my warriors have more."

I have no idea how many tokens a vial like that might be worth. I think it all depends on exactly what the spirit inside it is. But still I want all their tokens. I suspect this isn't the last arsenal I'll come across.

"Do you understand that acquiring a spirit is a matter of great luck?" I asked. "The orcs wait years for it to happen."

"How much you want for it?"

"All the tokens you and your tribe have."

"That's fine," the old man nodded and walked in a quick pace to collect the "tribute" from his soldiers.

A few minutes later he brought me almost six hundred tokens and we made the exchange. Beyond that, he decided to give me back eleven Scrolls of Fury and nineteen Ticks — all the warriors had left after the battle.

"I understand that I gave you something I'd never have been able to use in the first place," the old troll said suddenly. "Beyond that, I only gave you back things you gave us yourself before the battle. So here..."

The old man slowly removed one of the amulets from his neck. It was a tusk. Based on the size, it was a troll tusk. Its whole surface was etched with fanciful scrawling that appeared nonsensical at first glance. I examined it.

"Friend of the Trolls" Amulet.

— *Type: Badge of honor.*

— *Rarity: Legendary.*

— *Description:*

— *The highest award for service to troll-kind.*

— *Recommendations:*

— *If you were given one of these, you must have performed a truly good deed, which the trolls appreciated highly.*

— *Nontransferable.*

— *Weight: None. Takes no space.*

Farhas solemnly hung the amulet around my neck.

"This is not some mere trinket," he explained. "The Stone Forest is the domain of the trolls. Outsiders have no place here. Now you are no longer an outsider."

CHAPTER 23

IT HAD BEEN TWO DAYS since we beat back the outbreak of otherworldly beasts. In that time, Mee got all the wounded on their feet, even pulling one of them back from the beyond. The potions of satiety were a big help.

While the gremlin upheld our end of the deal, I kept busy as well. Using my new ability, I walked around the surroundings of the whole fort. I walked past to the portal and altar again as well but, alas, I didn't discover anything new. There just had to be something valuable below the earth there, but my new ability was for magical emanations, so I couldn't see it.

For the record, in the middle of the day yesterday, I discovered that the sixth sense could detect things both on the ground and in the air. I don't know what it was that I saw, but its speed and the size of its magic supply made a grim impression. I suspect it was another of Master Chi's specimens that flew the Hive. I was glad it didn't notice me. The treetops were sufficient cover from the big old monster.

Farhas took my tale about the Hive very seriously. He spent a long time asking the details and levels of the beasts we encountered.

And the old man devoted extra attention to the vial of armorbug spirit. Hiding nothing, I told him everything in the description — damage, mana requirements, timeframes. Then I gave an instruction session on the absorption process. I even offered to safeguard the old troll with our spells and potions, but he refused. I didn't understand why at first, but later it reached me — he hadn't gotten the spirit for himself, but for young Dago. Although I may have been wrong. After all, the old man could have asked us to conduct the ritual for the boy, but he did not. That meant there might have been a few reasons. And if I considered it, the elder was right. Dago with his little supply wouldn't be able to summon a spirit anytime soon. Though honestly that was only if he didn't have any mana crystals. In any case, I didn't go wracking my brains with guesses — let the trolls carry out whatever scheme they had dreamt up...

Another odd thing that happened was that not even one of the giants wanted to loot the body of the defeated scolopendra. They did their best to avoid its corpse, not even so much as looking at it. And there was plenty there worth taking.

THE WASTES

I saw a notification after defeating the beast that I first dismissed. It said that Gorgie had discovered Legendary mandibles and ten Epic scolopendra barbs. They needed fifty skill points to butcher though, which was twenty points more than my gremlin pal had.

After a brief discussion, we came to the conclusion that leaving such loot behind would be a true crime. And so Mee invested all the silver tablets he earned into the butchery skill. I added five to that and we had exactly fifty points.

By the way, beyond the silvers, the gremlin also got a gold tablet of Intellect, which he tried to give to me. But I firmly refused to accept it. That tablet would be his personal capital one day. And in the future, if the kid wanted to leave me, he'd always have a starting point...

The remaining fifteen silvers I invested into the gremlin's health, which increased his life supply by one hundred fifty. Now I wouldn't have to fear for our healer quite so much.

Over the last two days, I didn't so much as approach the pedestal. I decided I'd look more into my discovery after Mee tended to the trolls. I didn't want to tempt Farhas again. Who could say what might have been down there? Any magic trump card would come in handy for the elder now — the tribe was on the verge of extinction. He could have done anything to guarantee the survival of his brethren. And the friendship amulet would be no help. He gave it, so he could take it away. But it would be over my dead body.

So when the trolls got on their way at the end of the second day, our desire to spend one more night in the tower caused no suspicions.

After tending to the giants Mee, draped head to toe in all kinds of gifted amulets, said:

"They asked me to stay with them."

"I never doubted they would."

"You aren't mad?" the gremlin asked in surprise.

"Why should that make me mad?" I asked back, surprised.

"But..."

"Listen, brother," I softly interrupted him. "You are free to do as your heart desires. You are a free gremlin. I will accept whatever you decide and support you."

"Thanks, Rick," Mee said seriously.

"What are you talking about? We're family!"

"And that's why I said no," the gremlin nodded toward the bushes where the trolls had disappeared a few minutes earlier. "I'd never be family to them, nor they to me. Despite their gratitude for saving their lives, I'm just someone with a useful gift which, by the way, you granted me. So your path is my path, too. No matter how hairy things get!"

In response, I just silently placed a hand on his shoulder. I won't lie — it was very nice to hear. And I was grateful to Mee for his loyalty.

After we accompanied the trolls and waited

another few hours just in case, we started excavating.

I'd already planned where Gorgie should dig and what direction, but the pedestal had a surprise in store for us. As it turned out, the heavy stone slab was fairly easy to just move aside with a clever mechanism.

And under the slab we found a hatch that led to an underground passage. The stone steps below, covered with a thick layer of dust, led us to a wide door

"Rick, look!" said Mee, pointing at a stone sign hanging above the door.

I brought the torch closer. The sign read:

"Here lies the last defender of Fort Stout — Err the Cold."

Hm... Err the Cold... Err the Cold... Somehow familiar.

Oh yeah! That's right! When I killed the Firepaw it said I had replicated his feat!

I activated the sixth sense and saw two magical spots just beyond the door.

I was not afraid of any traps even though the monster hunters were huge fans of them. In all our time here, I had fully studied the fort's whole power system. Thanks to the map and my new ability, I was able to tell exactly how the tower's main supply connected with the smaller supplies.

For the record, the smallest supply in the

intricate system was the golem's. My initial theory that it was a huge mana crystal proved false. It was actually much more complicated. In so many words, the golem itself was the supply. So all my barbaric ideas of busting the statue open to take the high-capacity crystal from its chest died then and there. All that remained was to applaud the unknown craftsman who created this marvel of magical design.

Overall, my guess about the burial vault we discovered was confirmed — the fort map had been made long before the celebrated hunter's interment. And that's why the burial chamber was not marked on it. Other than that, there was nothing blocking access to the body of the deceased.

I was curious about the words "last defender" and who in fact could have written them.

Considering it briefly, I reached for the considerable steel ring that served as the door's handle, and pulled it toward me. Both the ring and the door itself seemed sturdy and heavy at first glance but turned to dust in the blink of an eye.

We had to go up to the surface and wait a bit for the dust to settle.

A few minutes later, we went down again. As per tradition, Gorgie dove first into the mysterious opening. After investigating every corner of the burial vault, he gave his approval and we crossed the threshold into the tomb.

It was a fairly spacious square room with a

low ceiling and a carved-stone sarcophagus in the middle. Based on its modest dimensions, Err the Cold must have been approximately my height.

I activated the sixth sense again and saw weak magical emanations coming directly from the sarcophagus.

I checked for traps of all kinds again, then gave Gorgie a wave. The stone slab over the grave slowly moved aside under the force of his scaly paws. While watching the harn struggle, I listened to my feelings. I was not experiencing any pangs of conscience over the fact we were somehow defiling the grave of a great hero. After meeting the foxman's ghost, my opinions on the afterlife had changed dramatically. I imagine Err the Cold's spirit doesn't give a crap about what happens to his long decayed mortal shell. And if something that might help a young member of his order to survive were found next to it, I'd bet my hand that he would only be in favor of his despoliation.

When the slab fell to the ground, the three of us cautiously peeked inside. As expected, the body of the legendary hunter had long since turned to dust. As had all his clothing. Except for one item...

— *Ephemeral belt of the Twilight Mage.*
— *Type: Magical objects.*
— *Rarity: Legendary.*
— *Effect:*
— *+ 10 ephemeral inventory slots for crystals.*
— *Increases the effect of inserted crystals by*

20%.

— Note:

— After equipped, becomes part of wearer until death

Shaking with worry, I reached for the newly discovered item. The first thought that came to mind when I picked up the treasure was, "why didn't whoever buried Err take this item?" I did not want to believe the legendary hunter had been buried alive by his own comrades.

But the dark thoughts all ran for the hills when I finally realized what I was holding in my hands. Made of ten rectangles which were also crystal slots, at first glance the belt looked more like a large necklace.

Using my ability, I was able to recognize two sources of mana. As it turned out, two of the ten slots already had mana crystals in them. My heart aflutter, I dug deeper into the description...

— Large mana crystal:
— 21/1680 mana points.

— Large mana crystal:
— 17/1920 mana points.

Both crystals had just a little mana left. Those crumbs were what the Scolopendra's Sixth Sense was detecting.

I looked closer at the total capacity of both

crystals. I took the smaller one out of its slot. It changed to one thousand four hundred points. Got it. Correspondingly, the normal capacity of the second was one thousand six hundred. My heartbeat racing, I took out my eight-hundred-mana crystal and placed it in one of the belt's slots. The capacity instantly went up by one hundred sixty points.

I was distracted from contemplating the amazing discovery by the gremlin giving an admiring squeak:

"Four thousand five hundred!"

Smiling, I nodded.

"Adding my own supply to that, I'll have almost five thousand."

"Don't forget, you can also have another small crystal with five hundred whenever you want," Mee reminded me.

"True," I answered. But I quickly cooled his jets: "We will only be using your crystal if absolutely necessary. The last thing we need is for our healer to run out of mana."

I had to admit — Mee was right. The two crystals we had and the two we'd found, plus the bonus from the belt — our survival chances had just gone up significantly! What was I even saying! Now we had enough mana to activate an elemental crystal!

"Wait! Well of course! How didn't I think about that right away!"

Slapping myself on the forehead, I started

feverishly grasping for the elemental crystals. Out of the corner of my eye, I noticed a perplexed look on my friends' faces and hurriedly added:

"You're about to find out..."

When the fire-red crystal appeared in my hand, Mee exclaimed:

"If this actually works, the power of the spell confined in the crystal will go up several times!"

As I slowly lowered Heaven's Wrath into the belt slot, I think all three of us all stopped breathing.

"It worked!" Mee piped up first, having seen the elemental stone fit perfectly into one of the slots.

In the meantime, smiling happily, I read through the spell's improved figures.

Elemental Crystal "Heaven's Wrath."

— *Type: Magic confinement crystal.*

— *Rarity: Epic.*

— *Effect:*

— *Contains the spell Heaven's Wrath.*

— **Heaven's Wrath**

— *Description:*

— *One of the most powerful fire magic spells, created by Magister Pyrus.*

— *Type: Offensive/Area of Effect.*

— *Rarity: Epic.*

— *Magic School: Fire.*

— *Effect:*

— *Caster indicates a point and calls down a*

rain of lava upon it.
 — Requirements:
 — Intellect — 15.
 — Expends 5000 mana points.
 — Radius of effect: 200 feet.
 — Duration: 3 minutes, 36 seconds.
 — Note:
 — Must have reputation 2000 with the Monster Hunters to purchase.
 — Price: 500 tokens.
 — Crystal disappears after activation.
 — Weight: None. Takes no space.

I don't know how much the damage went up by but the radius of effect was up thirty-five feet. It also added an extra thirty-six seconds of spell duration. Some might call that a pittance. But if you consider that it was thirty-six additional seconds of lava raining down from the sky, it could end up thinning out the enemy ranks a good deal more.

I did the same with the other elementals and turned the belt over in my hands.

— Attention! Would you like to use item: Ephemeral belt of the Twilight Mage?

After I gave my agreement, the belt dissolved into thin air as the backpack had before, and I saw a familiar message.

— *Tab created: Ephemeral Belt of the Twilight Mage.*

I glanced at my supply.

— *Mana supply: 710/4770*

My Wisdom instantly detected the higher capacity and started filling it. Overcome, I closed my eyes tight in pleasure. When the supply filled up, I could stop worrying about the constant lack of mana.

Early morning the next day we got underway. Yesterday Farhas gave us a detailed explanation of what paths to take west. He described every prominent landmark in painstaking detail, be it an unusual tree, rock or clearing. He warned me about the other troll tribes and explained how to behave when meeting them and what to say when doing so.

Once we reached the edge of the forest, I turned and cast a final gaze at the collapsed walls of Fort Stout, which had sheltered us and given us protection.

I understood that I would never be coming back here. And that didn't bother me one bit. Very soon this area would basically be hell on earth. We'd only delayed the inevitable. The portal is not stable and the situation will only get worse. I hope Farhas has the strength and authority to convince his tribe to leave these lands.

THE WASTES

Waving goodbye to the golem, who was frozen in an awkward pose, I turned and walked under the shade of the trees after Gorgie and Mee.

CHAPTER 24

I T'S THE MIDDLE of day five since we left the hunters' fort. I must note that Farhas did not lead us astray. The trail was exactly how he described. All the landmarks and natural markers fit his descriptions to a "T." Except one — in our five days underway, we hadn't encountered a single other troll!

On the one hand, the conspicuous lack of the forest's native inhabitants put me on guard. But on the other, it made me happy to some degree. After all, any encounter would waste precious time. The orcish horde would soon be thronging over the whole borderland, and avoiding their wolf scouts would be problematic.

"What do you think — why haven't we seen a single troll?" I asked Mee, who was walking next to me.

"I overheard Dago talking to Farhas," the

gremlin answered. "The geezer said all the tribes probably knew about our battle with the spirits."

"I see," I nodded. "Decided to get out of here."

"Cowards," Mee said angrily. "After all, they could have come to our aid!"

"I don't think it's a matter of cowardice."

"Then what is it? Were they not afraid?"

"Of course they were afraid. But that doesn't mean they deserve to be called cowards."

Mee furrowed his brow comically and said:

"I don't understand at all. You have me all confused."

I smiled.

"Alright, let's try to figure it out. Answer this question for me. When we fought the beasts, were you afraid?"

"Yes," Mee nodded. "Especially when you told us they were coming."

"I was scared too," I added. "I'm sure that Farhas, Dago and the other trolls, even big old Erg all felt the same way... But we didn't flee. We all stayed to fight. Yes we were afraid, but does that make us cowards?"

"I guess not," Mee answered thoughtfully.

"What about the neighboring tribes?" I continued. "Their leaders have a mandate and, to be precise, their task is to safeguard the women and children of their tribe. Do you understand now?"

"Yes," Mee answered darkly. "But I don't accept it. If we lost that battle, it isn't hard to guess who they'd come after next..."

"I'm in complete agreement with you there. The trolls live in small communities. Here the law of the land is every troll for themselves."

"They need a chieftain! A king!" Mee exclaimed.

"Hm... King of the trolls..." I muttered thoughtfully. "You might be right. But I don't think that would make things any better."

"Why?" the gremlin asked, sincerely surprised. "Is it really bad to have everyone unified under one ruler?"

"Well, at first it might be good, in case of war for example... But what would happen when the troubles recede?"

"Peace?"

"You sure?" I chuckled. "As a rule, kings surround themselves with the strongest and most influential of their kind, and they grow accustomed to power very quickly. With time, they turn into leeches that their whole people must feed. At the very least, that's what always happens in the western human lands. I have to imagine it wouldn't go any differently for the trolls."

"Yeah, that's exactly what happens with the orcs too," Mee said perplexedly. "The chiefs and shamans live better than the rest..."

"And their right to power is maintained by the wolf riders," I added and the gremlin nodded slowly.

"That's what I'm saying — I don't think it

would make things better. But who knows? maybe the quiet tribal life is just the thing us humans need. Where every person is a member of just one clan. After all, a clan is a family..."

"Family is good!" Mee nodded again. "Families stick together through thick and thin!"

Our talk was interrupted by Gorgie growling. The harn warned that we were going to start up a hill soon.

Farhas called this promontory Giant's Brow. The old troll said that, according to ancient legend, it was originally the skull of a titan that turned to stone over the centuries. The earth had nearly swallowed it up. On the surface, the only part still visible was the wide forehead, which was gradually becoming overgrown with stonetrees.

By the way, if you compare the tales of the orcs and the trolls about the battle between light and dark titans, you might come to the conclusion that such a battle really had taken place. Although, if I started believing every fairy tale I'd heard in my short life I'd end up with a highly implausible version of world history. Like the one that said our world was created by the Ancients and that they came here like the spirits from otherworldly portals but merely in pursuit of fun. Pure nonsense...

When we got on top of the hill, those grim thoughts receded to the background. They were squeezed out by feelings of delight while contemplating the view from high up.

Slowly surveying the area around the hill, I gave a puzzled snort. The top really did look like a forehead. Wide, rectangular and with a slight bulge.

To my right, the Stone Forest stretched all the way to the horizon. And the distant trees were drastically different than the ones that grew on the border with the steppe. They were much taller and older. Farhas' tribe would have plenty of room to hide.

To the left, the hilltop gave a good view of the edge of the steppe. The harn, who could see the farthest, told me that something strange was happening on the border with the forest at the foot of the hill.

After conferring for a bit, we decided it was worth finding out what was happening down there. Beyond that, our journey was going to take us along the edge of the forest from here.

Mee rode off on the harn's back to scout with a clear order to keep a low profile. Honestly, at first I was planning to send Gorgie alone. But Mee argued that he could tell me better what they saw and in greater detail, which convinced me to let him join the recon squad. And recognizing that his reasoning made sense, my heart groaning, I agreed.

My friends were back after an hour, which I spent in uneasy anticipation.

Then from the distance I noticed the gremlin looked dismal.

"Orcs," he said darkly, jumping off the harn's back.

"They spot you?" I asked.

"No," the gremlin shook his head.

"Then why are you pale as a ghost?"

The kid took a heavy sigh and lowered his head.

"They're drivers," he answered sadly.

"Like shepherds you mean?"

Mee raised his head and, clenching his teeth angrily, answered:

"Yes, but instead of sheep, they drive slaves."

Unexpectedly, the gremlin's anger transferred to me as well. Obviously, that reaction to slave drivers was in my blood now and something was telling me there was no ridding myself of that hate.

"Are there many orcs?"

"Eight."

"Riders, shamans?"

The kid shook his head no.

"Slaves?"

"Almost twenty. Four of them are renegades."

"You mean the ones that voluntarily help the orcs?"

"Not quite, but basically."

"I see," I said, stroking my chin. "We just have to find out why they're here. What are they doing?"

"With the renegades as overseers, the men are cutting down trees while the women and children gather kindling," Mee answered and added: "The people are very afraid."

"Well, I bet," I nodded. "They're probably seeing forest trolls behind every tree. By the way, what if..."

Thinking for a second, I didn't notice how the gremlin was looking at me right away. His mouth spread into a predatory smirk.

"What are you talking about?" I asked in surprise.

Mee, still smiling, replied:

"Hehe... It's just that every time you talk like that, we wind up with even more esses and tablets. You must have decided not to just pass them by."

"I hope neither of you are opposed?" I chuckled and in my turn looked my friends in the eyes.

As I expected, the response was a pair of predatory grins.

"What do you think, why do they need so many trees?" I asked Mee in a whisper when we'd come closer to the forest edge and were lying behind the wide trunk of an old, fallen tree.

The risk of us being discovered was minimal — the people really were afraid of the Stone Forest. The women and several children were always trying to keep a few yards from the forest edge.

And for the record, the orcs weren't particularly brave either. They were all around a behemoth fire and, other than occasionally peering into the darkness of the glade with fear, doing their own thing.

"They're preparing a camp for their tribe," Mee said. "A big camp. This place will be packed to the gills soon."

"Hm... That explains a lot," I whispered thoughtfully.

"What scheme have you come up with now?" Mee asked.

"I want to give these people the right to choose. Based on their appearance and condition, they won't last long at this rate."

"Agreed. The orcs don't give a damn about them. Look at those men over there. You see them?"

"With the burn scars?"

"Yes," Mee nodded. "They give those marks to runaways. The only reason they weren't killed is because they can still provide esses and tablets. Based on how thin they are, they haven't been fed in a while. They also have almost no warm clothing. They'll die soon."

"The orcs have strange logic. Why kill people who they could be exploiting?"

"It's a punishment. A lesson to the others," Mee replied. "The slaves cannot be allowed think their lives are valuable to the orcs. Yes, they benefit the orcs, but that is no reason to let them go breaking the laws of the tribe unpunished."

"Hm... I guess that makes sense. What about

the women and children?"

"Those are their families. The orcs allow their slaves to cohabitate and have children."

"The more slaves, the more they can exploit," I hissed angrily through my teeth.

"True," Mee responded sadly.

Before getting started, we decided to observe for a bit. And the longer I watched, the angrier I became.

The men all have exhaustion on their faces. They must be giving their food to the women and children. And they're scarcely doing any better. They're all wearing ragged clothing. Not people, these are skeletons.

The skinny renegades look like fatted hogs compared to them. And their clothing is more or less wearable. Even a fool can understand — they must be stealing it from the other poor bastards.

The people range in level from ten to three. The tallest guy is carrying an axe. By the way, that is the only axe between them. The four traitors are armed with sticks they periodically put to use doling out canings. At times like these, it was hard for me not to fly off the handle. But I was trying to keep myself in hand. Everything had to be done quickly and cleanly. Otherwise the captives might die.

Watching the orcs snickering and munching, I quietly turned to the gremlin:

"Hey buddy, could you remind me of the radius of your dome of invisibility?"

"Ten feet," Mee answered quickly. "Duration — ten minutes."

"Ten minutes?" I chuckled predatorily. "That might as well be a whole eternity..."

Taking another look around, I asked Gorgie:

"Are you sure there's no one keeping watch?"

In response, the harn just snorted condescendingly and impatiently tapped his scaled tail on the ground.

"Nice," I nodded and turned to Mee: "When you're ready, activate the spell."

Before a second was up, the system informed me that we were covered by a Dome of Invisibility. Trying to take our steps at the same time, we fairly quickly came out from beneath the trees and cautiously headed toward the firepit.

The late shaman's spell worked impeccably. Nobody noticed us. If there were anyone among the orcs with high sense scores, we'd hardly have been able to freely walk through their whole camp. But what kind of idiot would send serious warriors to guard half-dead slaves? And deep behind their own back lines? The highest-level driver was twelve.

When I was less than thirty feet from the vilely snickering orcs, I activated a Ram. Because they were sitting very close to one another, the spell hit all eight of them. The Dome of Invisibility disappeared. Gorgie and Mee, not wasting time, ran out to gather their blood harvest. I then turned around and looked at the renegades.

Our attack was so unexpected and fast that

they froze like stone statues, their mouths open in surprise. But the man with the axe, who by the way had the most burns on his face, got straight to action.

His heavy tomahawk came down full force on the head of the nearest overseer, and it burst into red scraps of flesh like an overripe watermelon.

The henchman's death promptly sobered up the other three but, much to my surprise, they didn't run at the lumberjack. Instead they scattered. But the people they'd been beating with sticks just a few moments earlier didn't let them get far. Seemingly, this was the first time I'd seen a group of people united in rage and fury. The renegades' comeuppance was short and sweet. They got stabbed, beaten then torn to pieces. Everyone took part in the slaughter — men, women and children. A few seconds later it was all over.

After dismissing the victory notifications and waiting for my friends to join me, I headed toward the former slaves.

As expected, they regrouped fairly quickly. The women and children walked behind the men, but not because they were hiding. Each woman and child had a stone in their hand.

The "lumberjack" was standing front and center. The six other men of varying level and age were standing side-by-side with sticks and knife-shaped sharpened bones in their hands. All their faces looked somber, determined and fateful. They must have understood that our trio had easily taken out their overseers, and we could do the same to them just as easily.

Eight paces away, we stopped.

"Was that all the orcs in the camp, or are there more?!" I shouted, looking the lumberjack right in the eyes.

"That's all of 'em!" he shouted back in a rasping voice. "The rest of the clan won't be here for three or four days!"

"That means you have time to eat and prepare for the journey!"

The "lumberjack" shook his head fatefully and lowered his axe:

"It's no use, good sir mage! The wolf riders will catch up to us quickly. We'll be doomed no matter what. But don't get the wrong idea. We're grateful to you for the rescue and aid! And anyway, it's better to die free!"

"Well, I don't know about you, but us three are not planning to die," I chuckled and took a step forward.

"The Clan of the Yellow Snake is one of the strongest clans on the steppe!" the man proclaimed, dumbfounded. "Six shamans, a few hundred wolf riders. Do you really think you can defeat a whole clan?!"

I chuckled again and asked:

"Do we look like idiots? We'll keep making west through the Stone Forest."

When we mentioned the forest, the people shuddered and started exchanging glances. Seeing their discouraged faces, I guffawed:

"Looks like you do doubt my mental health after all!"

We stopped a few steps away.

"You're misunderstanding us, good sir mage," the eldest of the men started. "I mean, the Stone Forest belongs to the trolls."

"We have been in the forest for over a week and, as you can see, we're still alive," I contested, spreading my arms.

The people exchanged sullen glances and started discussing quietly. But we considered the conversation over and headed toward the nearest trees without saying goodbye. The gremlin had been collecting the most valuable items off the orcs' bodies as we agreed. We'd already decided to leave the weapons, clothes and food for the people.

When we were only a few yards from the trees, they shouted out to me:

"Good sir mage! Good sir mage!"

We turned around. It was the lumberjack. Breathing heavily, he was leaning his elbows on the handle of his axe. The others were awaiting the result of their leader's negotiations.

"Good sir mage, I beg you. Please don't be mad! We heard you're heading west."

"Yes," I answered calmly. "To human lands."

The man cast a fearful gaze behind me.

"And will you really go through the Stone Forest?"

"Yep," I nodded.

Even an idiot could tell what he wanted — to have his whole band come with us. But the forest of the trolls has them very afraid. And now this guy is trying to figure out our secret. But I'm not going to get his hopes up with any promises or guarantees.

I think the guy knew that and said:

"Good sir mage, we understand that we are a burden, but we have no one else to turn to. Is there even the slightest chance that you would agree to lead us and our families west?"

This guy has a way with words. He clearly knows the right way to butter up mages and nobility.

"In other words, you want to come with me?" I clarified.

"Yes, good sir mage!" the man nodded, and his chestnut eyes lit up with hope.

I cartoonishly considered it for a moment, then said:

"Okay then, let it be. But I have one condition. For the duration of our journey, all my orders must be carried out unquestioningly."

"Of course, good sir mage!" the man called out happily and turned back to his people.

When he waved his hands, the people reacted with shouts of joy.

"Look over the bodies of the orcs," I said when the man turned back to me. "We left you all their weapons, clothes and food."

"Yes, we know," he nodded. "That is one of the

reasons we asked you for help. You didn't merely rescue us; you also didn't leave us empty handed."

To say I was embarrassed would be to say nothing at all. It took effort to keep my composure. In response, I just gave a brief nod and said:

"Take everything you might need for the journey and follow me."

The man opened his mouth, but I got out in front of him:

"I know you're all very tired and hungry, but it isn't safe to stay here. When we get into the forest, I promise we'll make camp and then you can eat and sleep."

The "lumberjack" nodded and hurried back to his people.

Standing on the forest's edge and watching the former slaves picking through the loot, I weighed all the pros and cons of what I'd just done.

As if he heard my thoughts, Mee, who was standing at my side, said:

"I wouldn't have been able to abandon them either."

CHAPTER 25

WALKING THROUGH THE FOREST, from time to time I caught intrigued and puzzled looks being cast at me and my friends. And of course, special attention was paid to the harn. The people were plainly afraid of him. And I understood why. They'd seen the big huge armored kitty tear eight orcs to shreds in the blink of an eye. And just the sight of him could make anyone hiccup.

Their reaction to the gremlin, though, was surprising. They looked on Mee more with scorn than fear. Curious. I wonder why. Gremlin slaves must occupy a particular position in orcish tribal societies. Either that or, more likely, they all figured Mee was simply my slave.

We decided to set up camp for the night on the opposite side of a hill in a little forest glade. It gave us good cover from the icy winds, and would protect us against unwanted attention from the steppe dwellers.

The men were able to start a fire fairly quickly because the women had gathered plenty of kindling. When everything was ready, the people seemed to just collapse around the fire. But they were in no rush to sleep. They were all waiting for the food to be ready first.

As far as I understood, the orcs had a successful hunt a few hours before we showed up. They'd caught a large deer and had already sat down to eat, but their plans were ruined by our sudden arrival.

And that deer was being butchered just now by three men while the women carried the meat over to the fire.

The gremlin and I were sitting on our own a few yards away from the fire on an old fallen log waiting for the harn to return from his hunt. We could have gotten by with potions, but my body was begging for regular food. And so, when our noses picked up the pleasant aroma of meat roasting over coals a few minutes later, our stomachs gave simultaneous groans of hunger.

When the first portion of meat was ready, one of the older women walked up to us. Gaunt as all her friends in misfortune, but sturdy. She was the only woman still on her feet. And her level eight said a lot. Although if I considered it, the orcs were probably not letting her progress as normal.

She was holding a little wooden bowl in her hands filled to the brim with aromatic pieces of roast venison. The fire in the background made the steam coming off the meat especially visible.

Out of the corner of my eye, I noticed that no one had started eating. I wonder why. They must have been waiting for my permission. That was probably it. And to look at the meat it was obvious that I'd been given all the best pieces. These people were treating me like a nobleman.

"Apologies, good sir mage," she said quietly, her gaze downcast. "We had to overcook the meat a bit..."

At first I couldn't tell what she was talking about, but then I glanced at the level of the dish and it hit me.

"You have nothing to apologize for," I nodded, accepting the bowl of hot treats. "Thank you for taking care of us so well."

When the woman heard the word "us," she cast a scornful gaze in Mee's direction. I could see her teeth clenching on her sharp temples. I wonder what is causing this distaste.

Mee by the way immediately grew embarrassed and lowered his big-eared head. I then, as if I didn't notice her unhidden antipathy for the gremlin, calmly said:

"Honorable Master Mee, I invite you to partake of the fare this kind woman has so graciously prepared."

The gremlin slowly raised his head and looked me in the eyes uncomprehendingly. Seeing me wink at him, he finally got himself together and reached for the first piece of meat.

A-ha... It was hard not to smile when I saw the woman's face. Her mouth agape and eyes bulging, she was staring at Mee as if she was seeing him for the first time.

"What is the matter, your grace?" I asked, hiding a smile. "Are you feeling unwell? If that's the case, is it anything our honorable healer might be able to help with?"

As I said the last phrase, I nodded toward the gremlin who was eating the hot piece of venison measuredly and in a dignified manner.

The woman made a pitiful sight. She looked like a fish out of water. Her eyes went even wider, her jaw hung down, her brain was clearly struggling to give any kind of adequate response. Seemingly, in the end, she failed to find one. This gremlin was a mage and a healer to boot — the poor lady's whole worldview had been blown to bits today.

Finally, the lady found her footing, gave an awkward bow without saying a word and walked a brisk pace back toward her people. They were waiting for her at the fire. Her delay must have put everyone a bit on guard.

Hrm... and when she started telling her people what she'd just heard in a muted voice, they looked excited. After every word she said, the people would glance over our way, and more accurately Mee's way. And all that attention had him very embarrassed.

I then was watching the proceedings with a satisfied smirk. To be frank, that was about the kind of reaction I was expecting out of the humans. No matter how strict their society may have been, healers certainly occupied a separate and highly respected niche in it. Not even just that. When I gave the gremlin the iridescent, I understood that it would serve for him as a pass into my world.

The people gradually settled down. For the next hour they were busy cooking and eating venison. And they clearly didn't have enough meat.

That was enough time for me to figure out who the goddess Fate had bound us together with. There was a total of sixteen of the runaway human slaves. Seven men, five women and four children. After a bit of observation, I was able to easily pick out four couples. One of them still had no children but, based on the woman's clearly rotund belly, that was a very temporary state of affairs.

The lady who brought us meat had no partner, but that didn't stop her being in charge of all women and running their little daycare. For the record, the group leader, the one who cut down the first renegade was also single.

Due to the humans' pitiful physical condition, it was hard for me to tell their age. Off the top of my head the oldest one was forty, and the youngest thirty or twenty-five.

The kiddos were easier. They were all about the same age — seven or eight. Although I could have been wrong.

Despite the levels, the fact that their characteristics were lagging behind jumped out at me. Old man Burdoc jumped to mind all on his own. In his day, the orcs had squeezed him for all they could get...

The kids were not particularly active. Evidence of their deathly exhaustion. Beyond that, I heard the youngest girl giving a strong violent cough, so she must have been seriously ill. She was lying in her mother's arms, seemingly unconscious.

I took a fleeting glance at the gremlin. Mee had spotted her too. I could sense that he was waiting for the go-ahead to run off and help her. But alas, no matter how badly I wanted to, her parents or the group's elders had to take the first step. In other words, we couldn't force our magic on them. The people might have had a hostile reaction to that. Their fear of unfamiliar sorcery was incredibly great. It was somehow easier with the trolls in that regard... Although, we fought shoulder to shoulder — that was totally different.

Hm... Before an hour had gone by, my remark about the fact we had a healer among us hit fertile soil. A whole procession came in our direction. All seven of the men and women were carrying the ill girl in their arms.

Stopping a few steps away, they bowed in unison which put me even more beside myself.

"Good sir mages!" the lumberjack addressed us in a respectful tone. "Maya told us what you discussed..."

"We haven't offended her, I trust?" I asked.

"Come now!" the man waved his hands. "Nothing of the sort! You brought her joy!"

"How so?"

"She told us that there is a healer among you."

"That is true," I said and nodded toward the gremlin: "Master Mee."

As if on command, they all turned where I pointed and gave another deep bow, embarrassing my familiar even more.

Hmm... Where were their scornful gazes now?

"Master Mee!" the group leader proclaimed. "Little Rita is very ill. I'm afraid she won't survive until morning. She wasn't even able to eat normally. She needs your help. But alas, we have no way to pay you. The only thing we can do is swear a debtor's oath for however much money you like."

Mee glanced at me, puzzled.

Yes, brother, get used to it. This is how people treat healers. But as for oaths, we don't need them. Who knows what nonsense might come into the heads of these desperate people if they suddenly wanted to get out of the oath?

Coughing loudly, I drew their attention.

"In other words, if you're asking for help, you trust our magic? I want you to understand us. We don't want problems with the authorities when we reach the western lands. Who can guarantee that you won't go shouting about some gremlin subjecting you to sorcery?"

While we discussed, the other members of their group appeared behind the men's backs.

When I finished talking, I slowly ran a gaze over everyone and stopped on the lumberjack. The people didn't have to think for long. One after the other, oaths rained down on us agreeing to our use of magic. Two of the kids also shouted out promises, to which their fathers just nodded in agreement.

Reading over the text of every oath again, I glanced at Mee and said, pulling out a few bulbs of potion of satiety:

"Here, this should be enough. Try and get them on their feet as fast as you can. We cannot afford to stay here long."

It's been three days since we met the former slaves. Thanks to Mee's efforts, my potions and the Lair I set up for the night, the humans had made a marked improvement. We managed to save little Rita. She'd been able to walk at her mother's side for some time already.

As for our relations with the humans, they'd been coming together fairly strangely. Despite all our efforts to help them, the humans still treated us with apprehension and mistrust. And yet it wouldn't have been very apparent from an outside perspective.

In theory, I could understand their thoughts. The initial shock of the battle and escape had passed — the people had probably started asking questions because they suddenly had plenty of time on their hands.

A kid mage, a gremlin healer and a strange beast travelling at their leisure through the Stone Forest in the heart of the Wastes. There's a ton of questions to be asked there. So although we were moving as a group, we still weren't a unified cohort. More like temporary allies. Although if I truly considered it, these people were a burden to us. And we were helping them purely out of the goodness of our hearts.

Despite the fact that our movement speed had obviously fallen, I had to give the people their due — they were carrying out all my orders unquestioningly. Clearly the slave's habit of obeying and the fervent desire to survive were both playing their part.

But alas, Tom the "lumberjack" did not engage. My attempts to get the man to talk all failed. I was only able to get the basics out of him. They'd been captured, enslaved, and now escaped. Nothing more.

To sum it up, they were all subjects of the Steel King. They were taken captive during an orcish raid. They'd tried to flee many times, but never succeeded. Overall, they didn't have anything new or unusual to tell me.

The only peculiarity that stood out was that Tom was clearly not the same as the others. And to be fully accurate, he was the opposite of them. All the other people in his group could be summed up in one word — peasants. And they'd been taken captive young. But as for Tom, if he really was a "Tom" at all, he had certain distinguishing mannerisms. Seemingly he was the only one who knew how to hold a scimitar for example. And he was also quite deft with an orcish bow. He also had a large number of burn scars on his body both old and fresh, which only added to the overall picture. It was clear that Fate had brought us together with a very obstinate man that loved his freedom dearly. Honestly, based on the fact he was level ten, he must have been taken captive many years ago, while still a child. And now he was probably more than thirty years old.

Despite all the distance in our communication, I saw sincere gratitude in the peoples' eyes. After all, for the last three days, Gorgie had been providing us meat without fail, all the while keeping a watchful eye on the surrounding countryside.

Honestly nearer evening today, while we were setting up camp for the night, the harn came back without prey and with some unpleasant news. We'd finally drawn the attention of the locals. Our camp was gradually being surrounded by trolls.

"Tom!" I shouted. "Gather your people in the

center of the clearing! Ready your weapons, but don't use them without my command!"

"What's happening?!" the man asked in agitation, never forgetting to urge on and push the others. I must give the people their due. Even though they were afraid, they were acting in an organized fashion.

In response, he got a predatory howl of many voices that seemed to come from every direction.

It scared me just to look at the people. Grimaces of fear and horror on their faces.

Another roar came, this time closer. The trolls understood that we wouldn't be running anywhere.

"We're being surrounded!" I shouted to the men. "Prepare yourselves! Attack only on my command!"

Out of the corner of my eye, I looked over our pitiful warband. Erg would only need to swing his club a few times to take down our whole flimsy formation. Trying to at least somewhat raise the peoples' fighting spirit, I shot my right hand over my head and it was instantly enshrouded in magical lilac smoke.

Hm... I guess that did the trick. The people suddenly remembered they had a mage with them.

Gorgie and Mee stood at my sides. The scales on the back of the harn's neck stood on end. The beast, already baring his teeth at our unseen opponents, was nervously flicking his own sides with his flexible tail.

After a few minutes of tense anticipation,

gigantic silhouettes started appearing from the darkness of the forest. One of the women squeaked pitifully, while little Rita started crying in fear. Her mother immediately covered her mouth.

Quickly looking around, I counted seven of the giants, but Gorgie warned me that there were another six somewhere in the darkness. The trolls were slightly lower-level than Farhas' warriors. The highest among them was fifteen. For the record, that titan appeared to be their leader. Compared to Erg, I'd even call him a bit feeble if that kind of designation could ever apply to forest trolls. Not quite as considerable or broad-shouldered as Erg, but the tight muscles on his arms, chest and stomach bore witness to a high physical strength.

But as for his face and especially eyes, I'd never seen such an intelligent look even in Farhas' best warrior. Seemingly this troll had not neglected Mind when spending his tablets. I don't even know if that's good for us or bad.

For now, the titans were not attacking, just taking position. I hurried to start negotiations the way Farhas had taught me.

"Peace be upon you, masters of the Forest!" I shouted in the language of the trolls.

The giants, not expecting such a turn of events, froze in place and exchanged puzzled glances. And to be accurate, all the trolls gazes turned to their leader.

"Outsider, do you know our language and our laws?" he asked, tilting his large forehead to the side.

"I speak your language, but I do not know much of your laws so I beg forgiveness if we have broken any of them!"

"You are outsiders and have come to our land! That in itself is a violation of our laws!" Sure the troll was accusing us of a crime, but there was no menacing in his voice, just intrigue. "Tell me, outsider. Is there any reason for us not to kill you?"

I led my gaze over all the trolls and stopped on their big-foreheaded leader. After that I slowly raised my right hand, showing them the amulet Farhas had gifted me. Mee did the same. But in his hand was a whole bunch of medallions and amulets.

"The trolls that gave us these artifacts said that we are no longer outsiders in this forest!" I announced solemnly.

A graveyard silence hung over the clearing. This must have been the first time such a thing had happened in these parts. What puzzled looks they wore.

The troll ringleader, slowly and without any sharp movements, took a few steps forward and stopped six feet away from me. As he walked, I got ready to activate lightning just in case.

Finally, the titan broke the silence and, smiling openly, asked:

"So you're the ones that helped fend off the attack of the spirits at Black Fang?"

CHAPTER 26

"YES, IT WAS A GLORIOUS BATTLE," I answered very melodramatically. "The heroes that laid down their lives to save the Forest will forever remain in our memories!"

The troll ran a gaze over his warriors and nodded:

"Your words warm our hearts, shaman! I am Narg and I affirm the word of our brothers from the tribe of Farhas!"

After he said that, he raised his big huge right hand over his head and gave a loud roar. The other trolls joined his war cry, including the ones hiding in the forest.

It took me a lot of effort to hold back the sigh of relief. The humans then, not understanding a word of the growling speech of the forest giants pressed up closer to one another. I'm sure our conversation didn't look peaceful from their perspective.

"Are these the slaves you took from the orcs whose bones are now being picked clean by scavengers at the foot of the Giant's Brow?" Narg asked, nodding at the crowd of people.

"Yes," I answered calmly. "Now they belong to me."

I didn't want to tell them the people were free. Who's to say how the trolls might react to that? After all, the former slaves don't have friendship amulets of their own. But if they were travelling as my supposed property, there shouldn't have been any problems.

Narg winced as if he'd just eaten a sour plum.

"I don't understand what need you have for these half-dead little folk, but I know for certain that their former masters have sworn to avenge the deaths of their tribesmen."

Seeming me tense up, the troll hurried to reassure me.

"We did not allow them to enter our Forest. They have sent many riders to intercept you at Dry Gully."

Then I really winced. The dried-out former riverbed formed something of a natural boundary between the western lands and the Wastes. There was no other way but to go across.

"But that's only half the trouble," Narg continued. "They ride with Sarkhaat."

When Mee heard the last sentence, he squeaked in fear. His ears drooped and the fur on his back stood on end.

Seeing me have no reaction, the troll decided to introduce some clarity:

"Sarkhaat is the Great Shaman of the Horde. One of the Five Elect. Top advisor to the Supreme Chieftain of the orcs. Level fifty-seven."

I frowned in incomprehension. I was totally lost.

"Does this Sarkhaat also thirst for revenge? And is that not a bit too much honor for eight slave drivers?"

"The old man doesn't give a crap about the drivers," Narg waved it off. Then with a predatory squint, he added: "He is hunting the people who killed his grandson, who left for the Tree of Spirits many days ago."

Mee hiccuped in fear, which gave us away lock stock and barrel.

The troll, smiling, tilted his big old head to the side and asked:

"How did the grandson of the most powerful shaman on the steppe wrong you? Actually, you don't have to answer. I know perfectly well how orcs treat someone when they feel superior."

After saying that, Narg revealed an ugly scar on his left forearm.

"You know," I said. "I will answer nevertheless. On that day, the apprentice shaman and his riders fell upon us. Two of our companions died in the ensuing battle, but we defeated them in the end. And with the Great System as my witness, the advantage was not on our side. But if some great shaman has taken it in his mind to avenge the death of his grandson that just means I have one more enemy."

"Hm... I'll be honest," Narg chuckled darkly. "I'd rather have a hundred enemies than one like Sarkhaat."

"Well, where'd you get the idea you are not his enemy yet?" I asked. "And in fact, you could already be a sworn enemy of all orcish shamans as a whole."

My question struck the troll.

"We have no quarrel with the orcs," Narg replied. "Yes, sometimes we have our squabbles, but we are not enemies. We're more like uneasy neighbors."

"Hm..." I kneaded my chin. "What are you gonna say when you find out the orcs are at fault for the desecrating of the Tree of Spirits?"

"What are you talking about?" Narg asked gloomily.

"The shamans were blinded by greed. Out of a desire to subjugate the most powerful spirits, they made blood sacrifices to the Tree for decades, and that defiled it. And that is what caused the recent onslaught. We were only able to mollify the Tree temporarily with the correct kind of sacrifice. But there is sure to be another outbreak. And another after that, and another... And only the gods can say what kind of beasts will come to ravage your Forest. This time the passage into the world of the spirits was open for one day, but who can guarantee that it will close at all next time?"

"The things you're saying are unbelievable!" Narg exclaimed, dumbfounded.

"Don't believe me? Ask Farhas," I answered calmly. But then as if in passing, I added: "Although that will not be too easy. The elder is probably very far from here by now, deep in the Stone Forest. He's leading his tribe away from the Tree of Spirits."

While Narg furrowed his heavy brow in thought, his soldiers exchanged perplexed glances.

"By the way," I said. "I almost forgot. Before you attack us, the grandson of the great shaman sacrificed Farhas' daughter to the tree and almost killed his grandson. We found the boy half-dead next to the altar. My brother here healed him before it was too late. But you know... I think you're right. Whether the orcs are your enemies or 'uneasy neighbors' is no longer up to me."

After a heavy silence, Narg hit me with a harsh gaze:

"Today I have heard lots of new and unbelievable things. I must communicate all this to our elders. Farewell!"

After he said that, Narg turned and started in a quick pace toward the forest. The other trolls followed their leader without delay.

I don't know why, but I suddenly shouted out to him:

"Narg!"

The troll turned.

"You have very little time!" I shouted.

The troll nodded gratefully and, before hiding amongst the trees, answered:

"Same to you, friend!"

There were two paths leading to Dry Gulley — over the steppe or through the Stone Forest. The latter was significantly shorter. Based on what Farhas told us, taking the forest paths had saved us approximately twelve days. Just under two weeks. But that's only on foot. Our pursuers were riding wargs, which made the calculations totally different and unfortunately, not in our favor.

In other words, if we had any chance of avoiding an encounter with the orcs it was, to put it lightly, a long shot. But still there was hope.

It's been five days since our run-in with the trolls. That same evening, I told the people about my conversation with Narg, not forgetting to mention who exactly was after us, which put them into shock. Beyond that, I was also forced to come clean about whose soul the great shaman of the orcs was really seeking.

When I suggested we split up, saying the shaman wanted me not them, they almost all refused. Tom said they were already doomed so there was no reason to take their hope of returning home away from them, no matter how modest it may have been.

After Tom, Maya said her fill. She expressed a readiness to walk as long as it took, regardless of how tired they got or how difficult the path became. Just to get back home. Overall, the people were unexpectedly in support of my plan of travelling at an accelerated pace, stopping as little as possible and for six hours at most only to sleep at night. The exact amount of time my Lair would stay active.

My and Mee's spells plus the potions of satiety helped us keep up quite a respectable tempo. The people were having a tough go of it, but they weren't complaining. The time they'd spent in slavery had taught them not to whine. And the little ray of hope that soon they'd be free only pushed them on. Beyond that, the whole way there they were trying to earn as many tablets and esses as possible by any available means. After all, now nobody would be taking them away.

By the way, speaking of loot. The first few days were hardest of all on the kiddos. At first they were trying to walk side-by-side with the adults, but they quickly grew tired and the men had to carry them. But then, at one of our pitstops, Mee convinced the parents to let their little ones take turns riding on Gorgie's back. That way, the kids were able to level Riding a couple points in just a few days. And that also brought up their Strength, Agility and Endurance.

THE WASTES

The harn treated the young riders patronizingly. Only little Rita was able to find the key to his heart. Well, to be more accurate, to his stomach. She quickly realized his name was Gorgie because of his voracious eating habits and was constantly trying to find tasty treats to give to her new friend.

In the end, we travelled quickly enough that our cohort reached the western edge of the Stone Forest by day eight.

"Do you sense anything?" I asked Gorgie, who was lying next to me.

The harn gave a negative sniff, but it was clear something was bothering him.

We hid behind the trunk of a tree on the forest's edge and spent almost an hour examining the dry bed of the one-time steppe river known as Dry Gulley.

All around is peace and quiet. It's like everything living on the steppe has died out. No orcs to be seen. On the other side of the riverbed looms a dark western forest just like the kind I knew back home. My heart wants to run forward to freedom, but the harn's anxiety is transferring onto me. Were we too late? Did the riders manage to get ahead of us? And now were they hidden by the great shaman's magic and waiting for us to flitter out like a flock of careless little birds right into their waiting hands?

In any case, we couldn't just wait around. A few days from now, there'd be so many orcish yurts here you couldn't swing a cat.

"We need to move, brother," I said quietly, patting Gorgie on his firm side. "Ugh, too bad the Sixth Sense has only a fifteen-foot range. If it was two hundred paces... No wizard would be able to hide from us."

"Hrn," Gorgie agreed.

I gave a signal to the people hiding behind the distant trees and nodded to Mee.

A few days ago, we tossed all the silvers that dropped from the orcs into his characteristics. At first we wanted to improve Dome, but in the end we invested forty tablets into Intellect. That brought his mana supply up to five hundred twenty points.

In essence, the plan was simple. While Gorgie, the men, women and I distracted the potential enemy, Mee would lead the children to safety on the other side under his Dome. He supposedly had enough mana for forty minutes of invisibility.

He gave me the five-hundred-point mana crystals and, thanks to the Ephemeral Belt of the Twilight Mage, my overall supply went up to five thousand three hundred seventy mana points.

We wished each other luck and quickly walked out from the shelter of the stonetrees.

Mee's group meanwhile was running over to the opposite edge of Dry Gulley. The spell worked amazingly. The only thing that gave away the invisible children's presence was their footprints on the snow.

THE WASTES

Once we reached the bottom of the dry riverbed, many breathed a sigh of relief. Now nobody would notice us for a while. At that very moment, the guttural cry of a war horn reached our ears. A regiment of ants instantly started marching up my spine. I think the hair on the back of my head started moving, too.

One lone thought was clanging around in my head like an alarm bell: "We didn't make it!"

The harn sensed my fear and gave a menacing growl of encouragement. The women all started sobbing all at once. But I had to give them their due — there were no hysterics. They just kept running, keeping pace with the men. Brandishing the drivers' short spears, the women were going to make their lives come at a high cost.

When the roar of the horn came again, Tom stopped stock still and looked at me. His dry lips, cracking in the cold air, spread into a timid smile.

"It's not orcs!" he rasped.

Gorgie, standing on the top of the right bank of the hollow, snarled down to confirm.

"That is the horn of our lord's retinue!" Tom called out gleefully, no longer holding back.

The people supported him with a joint shriek of elation. And I suddenly realized that I was also smiling happily. Were our days of roaming at an end? Had we finally made it to civilization?

Quickly making our way up onto the opposite bank of the dry riverbed, we froze for an instant and peered into the distance.

Tom was right. It was the retinue of the Steel King. A crimson banner with a gray crown in the center was attached to the saddle of one of the soldiers, serving as clear evidence.

I counted twenty-four lightly armed riders. Seemingly, we had the good fortune to be spotted by a border patrol company.

While my companions, waving their arms in glee, shouted to the warriors riding quickly our way, I looked where the children's tracks were going. Mee, keeping the Dome up and not slowing down, was still leading the kids to the forest. I mentally praised him. Unlike the others, the gremlin was cold-bloodedly sticking to the plan, not losing his head.

Strange as it may have been, my familiar's actions sobered me up instantly. My joy was replaced by a sense of tension. Yes, that was the retinue of the Steel King. And what of it? Who could guarantee that wouldn't take us for spies of the steppe dwellers and cut as all down where we stood? Tensions on the border ran extremely high. I'd bet every poor sap in the kingdom's capital knew about the coming orcish horde.

For a few moments, I could easily make out bleak looks on the warriors' bearded faces. They were all over level twenty — these guys were no joke.

Light equipment. Lots of bows. I didn't see any mages — I wasn't even sure whether to be happy or sad about that. On the one hand, Mee and the kids had made it undetected. But on the other, if the orcs did show up, one more mage certainly couldn't hurt...

My companions, seeing that the approaching riders didn't share their delight, fell silent and all bunched up behind my back.

I wondered how that looked from an outside perspective. Twelve adult men and women hiding behind an unprepossessing skinny little boy. Furtively, I'd recalled Gorgie with the amulet a few minutes back. No reason to play on the authorities' nerves.

I overheard some of the parents figure it out and celebrate for their kids. For the record, over the last eight days, Mee's authority among these people had shot up sky high and was only continuing to rise.

"Lower your weapons, but do not throw them to the ground," I started calmly. My voice sounded confident and quiet, but it was loud enough for all to hear.

"Do not display aggression, but be ready to defend yourselves. We don't know what these people have in mind. And, more importantly, we don't know what kind of orders they have about people like us."

I had to give my companions their due. They had been carrying out my orders unquestioningly for the whole duration of our journey together. And now as well, they obeyed me without asking any questions.

The riders seemingly noticed our drastic mood shift. Just the way they started exchanging comprehending glances.

A matter of seconds later, our group was encircled. More than ten spear and arrow tips were pointed at us.

"Who goes there?!" the strict booming voice of the mounted company commander made several of the women shiver.

Gray hair, a few scars on a wide face, a nose that pointed slightly to the left, level twenty-three — I could tell right away the man had been an active participant in all kinds of local conflicts. And he had the company to match — cutthroats just like him. Despite the menacing tone, I didn't see even a hint of hostility in the commander's brown nearly black eyes. By the looks of things, he could tell who he was dealing with from afar.

"We have fled orcish captivity, Captain sir!" Tom answered for the rest, taking a step forward.

"What clan?" the captain asked.

"Clan of the Yellow Snake," Tom answered back right away.

They gray-hair briefly exchanged gazes with the lean rider.

As for me, I took an immediate disliking to his big-nosed narrow face. There was something rat-like in his appearance. And he had a greasy little goatee, teary closely-set little eyes and a nasty mouth with thin lips and yellow teeth that jut outward, making him look even more rodent-like.

Despite his level sixteen and combat equipment, he most likely did not have such rich war experience. I took him for an agent of his Majesty's secret chancery. I couldn't have been far off. Honestly, I didn't know what he was doing out here on the front lines. Father loved to say that this kind of guy always tried to keep as close to big cities as possible.

By the way, going off the grim and disgusted gazes the soldiers were casting at the rat man, I was not the only one who felt that way.

"You've made it rather far from their main encampment." the big-nosed man's voice rasped like an ungreased door hinge. "More than two weeks on the steppe and you didn't get caught? Very strange and suspicious..."

I had to admit, setting the man's appearance aside, he was asking very right-minded questions.

"We didn't go over the steppe," Tom answered boldly and turned his head my way.

The man's answer instantly caught the attention of the rat-face and all the others as well. Although the riders' faces could have been characterized as measuredly intrigued until that point, afterward we were being drilled into by warily predatory gazes from all directions.

"Hm... Curious," the scrawny man rasped. "So how were you able to reach the border then? Not by the sky I assume."

I heard menacing and mistrust in his repugnant voice.

I could see Tom looking embarrassed and could feel the gazes of all my companions focusing on the back of my head.

I suspected I'd have to answer some uncomfortable questions, but I didn't think it would be so soon. I won't hide it — I was hoping I'd be able to quietly lead these people to the border and just as quietly bid them adieu. But alas, the gods willed otherwise....

Alright, time to come to Tom's aid. I'll be twisting and squirming my way out as always...

Now I saw only one way out of the situation. Pretending to be a pitiful child that fled from orcish captivity wasn't gonna work this time. I'd exposed myself fully. I'd have to play the role of a mage. Although why play? After all, I was in fact a mage, even if no one knew me and I was not very powerful...

"My companion is right," I started, doing my best to make my voice as calm as possible. "Travelling across the steppe in times like these would be equivalent to suicide. And that's why we made our journey through the Stone Forest."

When I saw their jaws drop and bearded mugs stretch out, it took me some effort to hold back an acrid smirk. Obviously none of them were expecting to hear something like this.

The rat-man was first to come to his senses. His face warped into an evil grimace.

"How dare you lie in the presence of a special agent of the secret chancery and the captain of the

Gray Martens?!"

That turned this into a curious scene. First of all, my companions were obviously deflated by the words "secret chancery" and "Gray Martens." All clear with the chancery, but as for his company name, I felt like an ignorant buffoon. I had never heard a single thing about them.

And second, which played into my hand, the ratface made an error but hadn't noticed. He said his own title before the captain's, which made him sound superior to him. But the commander of the Martens and all his warriors were clearly not going to just let that go. Based on the angry and indignant looks on their faces, it was clear that the "special agent" would have to answer for his words later. At a more appropriate time for reprisals. Nevertheless, the secret chancery is not to be trifled with, even if you're thrice the respected commander of the most distinguished military company in the kingdom.

But I was going to play on his error. I needed to try and get myself on the war dogs' good side.

Tilting my head to the side and summoning all the self-control I could conjure, I tried to make my voice sound as cold as possible and addressed the chancery agent ingratiatingly:

"I hope 'special agents' are taught good manners and, when they recognize their mistakes, are capable of begging forgiveness? If not, I'm afraid I'll have to fill the gap in your training myself. Before you say anything else, let me warn you — the two defensive amulets around your neck will be precious little help!"

The longer I spoke, the more dark-lilac haze balled up around my right hand. Beyond that, I was ready to unleash the Ysh spirit at any second. I knew I was on thin ice and it was crunching loudly with every step, but seeing the puzzled and satisfied looks on the faces of the riders all around us was only egging me on.

Demonstrating my membership in the magical estate had a positive effect for the umpteenth time. The secret chancery agent or "pig" in common parlance instantly dropped all his haughtiness and gave a short involuntary bow.

"Good sir mage," he hissed through his teeth. "I pray you won't harbor malice for a modest servant of his majesty such as I. I am only carrying out his will to the best of my abilities. Might I be allowed to know who I have the honor of speaking with?"

I held a pause for appearances and then, with false begrudging, let the lilac smoke disperse.

"My name will mean nothing to you," I answered evasively. "But you must all know that I harbor no ill will toward his Majesty, may the gods extend his reign! I swear it!"

While the riders read the text of my oath with relief, I continued:

"These poor people really are former slaves who I managed to liberate. Their only wish is to quickly return home to their families, who I presume have long thought them dead and buried."

"And the weaponry in their hands, it once belonged to their drivers I assume?" the captain asked, putting on a clever smile.

Chuckling back, I shrugged:

"Exactly right, Captain sir. Those orcs are dead now, so they didn't need them anymore."

I heard several of the soldiers laugh, so I figured my joke was to all their taste. Other than the secret chancery agent's, naturally. Thinking I couldn't see him clearly, the rat-man basically impaled me with his vile searching gaze. If he could have performed sorcery, I'm sure he'd have turned me to ash then and there. Okay then... There's one more enemy for my list. I've been picking them up suspiciously quickly...

But as my mom always used to say, "there's always a silver lining." They'd all stopped aiming their weapons at us. The tense atmosphere had grown less charged. Some of the riders jumped off their horses and started offering to help the women, who were weeping for joy. The men meanwhile, smiling happily, embraced the warriors and thanked them for the rescue.

It happened somehow all on its own, but I was quickly swept aside. As if an invisible line had been drawn between me and the people. I suddenly felt like a third wheel.

Hm... More exclusion. A strange feeling... I used to be treated like an outcast, cripple and freak. Some pitied me, some were disgusted to be in my presence, and others meanwhile openly mocked me. But now I was being excluded because of fear. They were plainly wary of me, and some of them were simply afraid.

And that wasn't to say I was happy at the lack of attention. More the opposite. I'd be glad to celebrate with the others but, alas, mages had earned a certain reputation over the centuries.

While they all embraced, I'd already started thinking about how and when I could find a good opportunity to slip away from the border guards and their watchful eyes. And I wouldn't mind no longer having these people as my responsibility. All that remained was to find Mee, return the children to their parents, wish the soldiers luck and get moving toward Orchus. My thoughts were already far from here, in my homeland. But at that very moment, I heard a howl that froze the blood in my veins. I could never have confused that sound with anything else...

Shaking in worry, I turned. There were a few dozen wolf riders rushing our direction from the open steppe. One orc was riding a coal-black warg that especially stood out. It wasn't hard to guess which one was after my soul...

CHAPTER 27

THE SUDDEN COMING of the band of steppe warriors caused a stir among the people. To be more accurate, my companions panicked, and the soldiers reacted the way military men should — rushed but well-coordinated. The captain was giving out orders in short choppy phrases. The riders, grabbing some by the collar and simply giving a hand to others, were pulling the people up onto the backs of their horses. I was shown somewhat more respect. A young bowman, lightly bending down, gave me a hand:

"Good sir mage, hurry!"

My fingers latched onto his forearm, and I was on his horse's back in the blink of an eye.

"Hold on tight!" he shouted and hurriedly struck his heels into his steed's sides.

The horses, slowly but surely gaining speed, were carrying us to the edge of the forest to the

417

west.

For the record, the special agent's bay horse was racing far ahead of the pack. The valiant secret chancery man ran for the hills at the first sign of danger without waiting for anyone or offering any help. All the while he was squealing hysterically that we had brought an army of orcs behind us and that he would not fail to include that in his report to leadership.

But the rat man never even made it to the forest...

As it turned out, Gorgie's senses were dead on — the orcs really had set a trap. A short hunchbacked figure draped in a long-skirted black cape and wearing a hood over his head appeared on the edge of the familiar western forest as if parting the century-old pines with his hands. And a moment later, orcs on warg-back started to appear around him as if from thin air.

The great shaman played us like a fiddle. Like an experienced angler, he set a net and waited calmly for it to fill up with stupid little fish. And being a naive idiot, I had already started to think we'd gotten ahead of the orcs... I'd even started dreaming about returning to my hometown once free of the abominable debtor's oath.

I quickly looked where the wolf riders had come from and breathed a sigh of relief. Mee had led the children to a different place. Hopefully the shaman hadn't figured out our little trick and the gremlin had successfully found shelter among the trees.

Meanwhile, the "pig" was still out in front and, when he saw the orcs appearing from out of nowhere, tried to get his horse to turn back. But it was running full-speed, and he was clearly not the most experienced rider. So the poor animal bucked, not able to take the abuse. Once rid of its ill-fated rider, the steed ran to the right, away from the terrifying wargs.

And the pig didn't even have time to get up off the ground. Orcish bows shot him full of arrows immediately. From a distance, the man's body looked like a pincushion.

I'm ashamed to admit it, but I was relieved. That busybody spook was just paying too close attention to me. It was both suspicious and bothersome. I was sure he had already composed a full-length novel reporting me to his superiors.

To be honest though, in the catastrophic situation we found ourselves in, we didn't give a crap about any reports. We had a matter of minutes left to live...

But the Captain of the Gray Martens had his own opinion about that.

"Northeast!" he roared boomingly and, setting an example for his soldiers, veered his steed to the right.

I didn't understand what was happening at first but, when I looked closer, my lips spread into a timid smile. It seemed we had a crumb of hope after all.

The trap had been set perfectly, but the orcs made a small mistake. The wolf riders that appeared on our right flank were slightly behind the others. And suddenly there was a gap in the ring closing in around us, which the experienced captain immediately took advantage of.

The horses, furiously driven on by their riders, were racing full tilt. I took a quick glance and saw mischievous smiles on the soldiers' concentrated faces. Were we really gonna get out?

Seeing that their lively prey was slipping through their fingers, the wargs and their riders howled in disappointment. The orcs whose mistake allowed us to escape were blustering especially hard. Their taut bowstrings, thrumming nonstop, rained down dozens of arrows in our direction. The black dots flew up into the sky like a swarm of enraged wasps, blotting out the sun for a moment. But nothing came of it. They realized what was happening too late. The arrows fell far behind us. I was afraid to imagine what the shaman might do to the screw-ups if we did actually get away...

By the way, where was the shaman?

I turned and looked where the warlock should have been. As it happened, the orcs blocking our path to the steppe were crossing the dry riverbed to link up with the troops accompanying the shaman.

The fastest and most lightweight riders were trying to get around and flank us to shore up the only gap. From a bird's eye view, the orcs' formation must have looked most of all like a horseshoe.

I finally found the shaman. And what I saw, to put it lightly, was not to my liking. Let me be more accurate. The dark figure hovering atop a ghostly ashen-gray cloud had me hiccupping in fear. When I looked closer, I realized it was not a cloud at all but some kind of semi-transparent creature...

Seemingly, my guesses were correct — the sacrifice experiments at the Tree of Spirits had borne fruit. This shaman had lured a higher creature to the portal and absorbed its spirit. And I had no doubt that the beast the orcish warlock was riding atop was indeed a higher creature. When I recognized that, my heart started beating twice as fast. And when I saw that the shaman had started gradually gaining speed it dawned on me — there was no avoiding a chase.

I didn't need the gift of clairvoyance to guess what this outraged mage would do to us if he caught us. Narg said the orcs had sworn to get revenge. Probably, anyone not dead after this battle would be tortured to death. At some point, Mee had told me about the orcs' refined sense of cruelty. The stories still made a chill run over my skin.

I also knew what mages of that level were capable of. The memories of Master Chi's fight with his former colleagues left me with a firm impression.

In the meantime, the shaman was inexorably catching up to us. Everyone had noticed, both the victoriously roaring orcs and the people. I saw the frightened faces of the women and the sullen countenances of the warriors. I also saw Tom, sitting behind the captain, shout something strained into the commander's ear. When they both turned simultaneously in my direction and I saw their eyes, it was clear what Tom was screaming about.

I can't say what happened after that surprised or disappointed me. As a matter of fact, a new part of me had been forged over the last few months of constant danger and it was already subconsciously prepared for just such a turn of events. But there was a tiny little piece of boy Rick, hidden in some deep secret corner of my soul that felt a sense of grievance. But it was instantly squeezed out by a flurry of strong emotions — fear at first, then rage and fury.

"Micky!" the captain roared, causing the bowman I was sitting behind to shudder. "You're lagging behind! Drop the excess weight!"

The warrior quickly turned his head toward his commander and gave a barely perceptible nod. Then a moment later, I was thrown off the horse like a bag of turnips.

Thankfully, I activated Muckwalker's Aura quickly enough to absorb the impact of landing on the ground. Other than that, the fall was also alleviated by the previous night's snowfall.

I took a few somersaults and froze for a second, coming to my senses. Then I spat out a mouthful of snow in disgust and started standing up.

I didn't look toward the people that abandoned me. They no longer existed as far as I was concerned. Instead I glanced toward the waves of orcs. The nearest riders were no more than six hundred feet away. I quickly checked the figures of my Aura. After hitting the ground, I had a bit more than one thousand points of defense left.

My magic supply was almost full. Wisdom had already started replenishing the mana I used on the spell.

Seemingly, this was the very moment to use one of the elemental crystals. I was left to decide which one precisely. Fire, earth or ice?

I had thought over the spells contained in the crystals many times. What was their destructive power? Where and how best to use them?

In the end, I concluded that an earthquake would be the most effective in the mountains or near a large concentration of buildings. The fire wall and ice storm then were best for open space. So I crossed out Earth Tremor right off the bat. Although maybe I was wrong to do so. It's always hard to make the right decision when you don't know exactly what you're dealing with...

No matter how badly I wanted to see lava rain fall down from the sky onto the orcs' heads, I ended up choosing the Ice Storm. First off, that spell would last longer. And second, I was hoping that it would bring a full whiteout and temporarily disorient my opponents.

All these thoughts flickered by in my head in the space of a second. Hurriedly taking a bottle of potion of satiety from my backpack, I got ready to activate the crystal.

— *Would you like to unleash the spell "Ice Storm?"*
— *Attention! Performing this action requires:*
— *5000 mana points.*

Another couple dozen paces and the orcs would have stomped me down like a flea.

"Yes, I would!" I rasped with my dry throat.

— *Select activation point.*

— *Warning! The element you are summoning knows no mercy! Either take care to provide adequate defense or try to keep away from the epicenter of the storm.*
— *Warning! Spell damage radius: 165 feet.*

While reading the system notifications, I felt a chill run over my skin.

Setting the activation point right on the dark-robe-clad figure, I unleashed the spell from the crystal. Then, not delaying another second, I rushed toward the forest.

As I ran, I took a gulp from the bulb and gave a contented grunt. Wisdom, having received a little boost, started refilling my mana.

Before I made it five steps, I heard a sound that turned the blood in my veins to ice. I whipped around. What I saw struck me with its large scale, dangerous beauty and primordial cruelty. It forced me to stop and stand in place with my mouth open in astonishment.

A silver wall flowing with thousands of sparks appeared right where the orcs had been standing a few seconds earlier. Upon closer inspection, I realized that the wall appeared to flow because it was made up of hundreds of long spindly whirlwinds. And in their turn they were chaotically darting from side to side and humming with an eardrum-bursting buzz...

The effect of the doubtlessly high-level spell gave rise to a feeling of my own insignificance. If that was just a fraction of the spell originally interred in the crystal, I was afraid to even imagine the kind of force Ava the Great, the Ice Storm's creator, could bring about directly. I consoled myself with the hope that I still could meet mages of that level one day.

Not even twenty seconds later, I got my first victory notifications:

— **_You have killed Orc Rider (20)._**

— _Congratulations! You receive:_
— _Experience essence (4000)._
— _Silver tablet (10)._

— **You have killed Steppe Warg (18).**

— *Congratulations! You receive:*
— *Experience essence (3600).*
— *Silver tablet (10).*

— **You have killed Steppe Warg (18).**

— *Congratulations! You receive:*
— *Experience essence (3600).*
— *Silver tablet (10).*

....

And a few seconds later, so many notifications rained down on me it was like I was seeing colors...

The abundance of flickering text just about made me miss the most important part — the ice storm was moving. I couldn't be sure if it was because of the wind or something else, but it had been in motion all along. The element I'd awoken with ancient magic was racing fairly quickly my way.

Not delaying for a second and no longer looking around, I started running toward the forest again. I took a fleeting glance at the timer. The spell was going to stay active for another minute and a half.

Meanwhile, the fearsome din behind me was growing louder and louder. And I was running slower and slower. My energy supply was noticeably sagging. Red circles appeared before my eyes and a sickly rasp tore itself from my throat with every step. By all appearances, I was about to be swallowed up by the monster I'd summoned. It would be hard to imagine a stupider way to die.

While losing consciousness, I felt for the summoning amulet and activated it. The last thing I thought before the darkness swallowed me up was that Gorgie and Mee would survive...!

CHAPTER 28

I BURST TO CONSCIOUSNESS all at once, as if swimming up out of a deep whirlpool. Darkness all around. I listen closely. The scratching of trees swaying in the breeze is unmistakable. So some magical means allowed me to crawl to the western forest.

But if I'm in the forest, why am I so warm? Patting myself down head to toe, I realize I'm lying on soft furs and covered with a thick comforter. Curious. Where am I?

I was still coming to, but vague guesses were already starting to faintly glimmer in my mind. At that very moment, the darkness around me stopped being complete. Right before my eyes appeared a triangle of light which I finally recognized as a slightly opened tent flap. Someone carefully threw back both flaps and let in a refreshing icy breeze, smoke from a bonfire and a small shred of the night sky.

When I saw the outlines of a pair of wide ears, I smiled with relief.

"Rick?"

"Hey there, brother," I rasped back.

"Praise the gods you woke up!" Mee exclaimed joyfully and jumped into the tent.

We embraced firmly, then the gremlin struck flint to steel a few times and lit some kindling. The inside of the tent lit up with a timid little tongue of flame and Mee extended me a wooden bowl filled with something that smelled tasty.

"Here's something to help clear your throat..."

"Where is Gorgie and why am I still alive?" I quickly asked.

"He's doing fine. He's the one that dragged you to safety."

I sighed with relief and took the first gulp. Had we really made it out of another close call?

"After we brought the children to their parents and came back here, the harn went out to hunt," Mee continued. "I'm sure he's already sensed that you're awake. He'll probably be here soon."

"Are you saying you found the people?" I asked in surprise. To be frank, I was not expecting the timid gremlin to be such a self-starter.

Mee had his own interpretation of my reaction.

"Yeah, it wasn't exactly a big deal... Their camp was blowing smoke over the whole area. Gorgie sniffed them out right away."

"Hold up... So how did the captain and his

warriors react to you?"

"They didn't," Mee answered. "They didn't see us. We showed the children the way and they walked the last hundred yards to the camp on their own. I wasn't feeling bold enough to join the people. I saw what they did to you."

"Very wise decision," I praised the gremlin.

"Why did they do that?" he asked angrily.

"Tom was considerate enough to tell the captain who the shaman was after. And you know what came next..."

The gremlin clenched his teeth hard and hissed:

"Ingrates."

"But living ingrates..." I chuckled.

"And all thanks to you again!" Mee exclaimed with admiration.

"And you, brother... By the way, did the Dome work properly?"

"Yes," Mee nodded. "It's a miracle we avoided the trap. We were walking along the forest's edge. The gods must have intervened in our favor. After that we watched you meet the human company. It was hard for me to hold those little ragamuffins back when they saw their parents hugging the warriors."

"I see..."

"But when the orcs showed up, they stopped trying to run."

After Mee said that, he gave a happy chuckle.

"What's that about?" I asked in surprise.

"The children thought you jumped off the horse on your own to defend the others..." the gremlin's mouth spread into a wide smile.

"Uh huh," I laughed back. "A hero..."

"Feel free to believe this or not — but you'll forever remain a hero in their memory," Mee said seriously. Then he added:

"A dead one..."

"What are you talking about?"

"I told them you died."

I nodded understandingly.

"So the captain wouldn't send his cutthroats out for our souls?"

"Yes," the gremlin answered. "Let them think you're dead."

Smart. Mee is a clever boy. He interpreted the situation properly. I told him so right away, not forgetting to praise him as well, which made him very embarrassed.

After a bit of silence, the gremlin said:

"I saw you awaken the element."

"A ghastly spectacle," I said quietly. "I get a shiver when I think back on it."

"Was that one of those stones?" Mee asked.

"Yeah," I nodded. "Good thing you convinced me to take your crystal. Otherwise I wouldn't have had enough mana to activate the spell. Or more accurately, to unleash it."

"It is highly powerful and fearsome magic," Mee whispered and the fur on his back stood on end. "Even the great Sarkhaat wasn't brave enough to stand up against it."

"What are you trying to say?" I asked, dumbfounded. "Did he not die?"

"Of course not," the gremlin shook his head. "A few seconds after the spell's activation, he dissolved into thin air, leaving his whole band to be torn to shreds by the element. Honestly, most of the orcs also fled for the steppe when they saw it. All told, the storm only took down a couple dozen wolf riders. Gorgie and I combed the scene after, too, hoping to pick up some loot. But it's terrifying magic — there wasn't a single trace of the orcs left."

I scratched the back of my head in perplexity. And I didn't care about the loot. I had slightly more important questions on my mind. Why had the warlock just given up? It wasn't like he just figured he was outgunned by little old me, right?

Actually, that sounded plausible! In fact, it all came together. Following the trail of his grandson's killer, he probably saw the Tree of Spirits and the wide swath the otherworldly beasts cut through the forest along with the monster hunter fort... It followed then that the shaman came prepared to fight an experienced and powerful mage. Otherwise why drag so many riders along with him? But by the looks of things, the Ice Storm spooked even him and he concluded I was the more powerful mage.

All that time, I was sitting and smiling stupidly. I was imagining the look on the shaman's face when he found out just who he was up against. I suspected the orcs had spies among the subjects of the Steel King — humans were not hard to corrupt with money. Mee, without even realizing it, had done a great thing by starting the rumor of my demise.

There was a lot I still wanted to ask the gremlin, but our conversation was interrupted. Gorgie was back and he looked delighted...

Mee turned out to be right. Looking over the system messages, I counted sixty-four victories. And for accuracy's sake, the Ice Storm had swallowed up thirty-two wolf riders along with their wargs. The number of silver tablets I got in that battle boggled the imagination.

At that moment, I had seven hundred thirty Silvers in my backpack. I even had to rub my eyes and glance into my backpack again.

But that wasn't all. The Great System decided to generously reward me for the "display of gallantry."

— *Attention! The Higher Powers have taken note of your accomplishment! Fighting alone, you defeated 60 creatures more than 10 levels higher than you in one battle!*
— *Congratulations! You receive:*
— *Experience essence (20000).*
— *Silver tablet (30).*

— *Attention! The Higher Powers have taken note of your accomplishment! Fighting alone, you defeated 60 creatures more than 15 levels higher than you in one battle!*

— *Congratulations! You receive:*

— *Experience essence (30000).*

— *Silver tablet (40).*

— *Attention! The Higher Powers have taken note of your accomplishment! Fighting alone, you defeated 30 creatures more than 20 levels higher than you in one battle!*

— *Congratulations! You receive:*

— *Experience essence (15000).*

— *Silver tablet (20).*

— *Attention! The Higher Powers smile upon you! You have replicated the legendary feat of Ava the Great! Fighting alone and using just one spell, you defeated 60 creatures more than 15 levels higher than you in one battle!*

— *Congratulations! You receive:*

— *Experience essence (100000).*

— *Magic bracelet of Ava the Great (1).*

I bit my lip and took the magical artifact from my backpack. My heartbeat racing, the first thing I did was glance at its level. Finding no limitations in its description, I sighed with relief. I wanted to shout loudly and jump for joy. But Mee was sleeping next to me, so I set the mad dances aside for tomorrow.

Somehow taking control of my gushing emotions, I finally started looking over the artifact. The bracelet looked like an icicle bent into a wide ring and had no fastener. Probably, like my little ring, it had some way of adapting to its owner's wrist. I couldn't be sure exactly what material the unknown craftsman used, but it bore a near perfect resemblance to ice. Based on the name of the spell and style of bracelet, I assumed Ava the Great belonged to the magical school of Ice.

I admired the ancient item until I had my fill then delved into its description.

Magic bracelet of Ava the Great.
— *Type: Personal magical artifact.*
— *Rarity: Legendary.*
— *Intellect +30.*
— *Wisdom +30.*
— *Special effect:*
— *Raises level of all the wearer's spells/magical abilities by 5.*
— *Note:*
— *Weight: None. Takes no space.*

I put the ice ring on my quavering arm and looked at my characteristics. In an instant, all my spells and magical abilities shot up by five levels! Feverishly reading their descriptions one after the next, I gradually started to realize just how significantly my abilities had grown...

Finally tearing myself from the reading, I gave a weary yawn and looked at my friends dozing peacefully next to me. My mouth spread into a satisfied smirk. You two are gonna get a lot stronger tomorrow...

We were standing on top of a hill covered with old crooked pines, the very edge of the western forest. At the foot of the hill below, the plains began. After yesterday's snowfall, they looked like a huge tabletop covered with a festive pure white tablecloth.

It took us just over two weeks to cross the western forest. Honestly, a few of those days were spent on my friends incorporating all the tablets. The process took a while, but it was worth it.

I brought Gorgie up to level eleven. Almost all his characteristics were at their maximum. Visually the harn was twice as big. The scales on his body had grown tougher and larger as well.

After the cat hit level eleven, I noticed a sharp spike of bone slowly sprout from the tip of his tail. There wasn't a word in the beast's characteristics about his new weapon yet, but I was willing to bet something would reveal itself at the next level.

Yesterday the harn scratched his front paws on the trunk of a pine. A few seconds later, the poor tree fell to the ground with a plaintive cracking. And Gorgie's face looked so surprised that the gremlin and I couldn't hold back and started laughing loudly.

Mee had also grown both in level and physically. Now he was level seven. Other than the vitally important characteristics, we'd paid special attention to his spells while spending tablets. For example, Wave of Healing now replenished fifty percent of its target's life while the level three invisibility spell's duration had gone up to twenty-five minutes.

Tearing my gaze from the plains, I turned. Beyond the forest, in the borderlands, the Great Horde was amassing. We even saw its first "wave" rolling in. Now it looked like a seething sea of disorder, growing wider and wider with every new incoming wave.

Seeing the army of thousands of orcs struck my imagination. I do not envy the Steel King. The ruler of the west will probably lose a couple of baronies this year. Although, if I considered what the spells of high-level mages could do — the orcs' expectations could end up being dashed.

On that day, we saw lots of slaves of many races. There were people, gremlins, gnomes, trolls... In fact, it looked like there were more of them than the orcs. It was scary to imagine how many tablets all these unfortunate souls surrendered to their tormentors every day. At that time I was thinking that, if they all banded together, they might be able to escape. But I immediately remembered the disgust and disdain in the eyes of the liberated humans when they first saw Mee... No, they were not exactly primed for unity.

I looked back to the peaceful valley and breathed a heavy sigh. We had to go faster. The Great Horde would be here soon.

"I don't know about you, but I never want to meet another orc for the rest of my life," I said and added with a chuckle: "Although, looking at you two, I have to admit that every encounter we've had with them so far has been to our benefit."

When I mentioned the orcs, Gorgie snorted scornfully and trotted forward. But Mee didn't seem to be listening. Based on the grim look on his face, the gremlin was not in the mood for jokes.

"The world of humans scares me, Rick," he suddenly whispered.

Placing a hand on his shoulder, I said:

"Yes brother. It scares me no less. But over the last few months, I've realized something. With all of us together, I'm not so afraid."

Mee looked me in the eyes and said seriously:

"Thanks to you, Rick, I'm no longer a slave! Let's go. Now it's your turn to get free!"

END OF BOOK TWO

Want to be the first to know about our latest LitRPG, sci fi and fantasy titles from your favorite authors?

Subscribe to our **New Releases** newsletter:
http://eepurl.com/b7niIL

Thank you for reading *Underdog!*
If you like what you've read, check out other LitRPG novels
published by Magic Dome Books:

**Interworld Network LitRPG Series
by Dmitry Bilik:**
The Time Master
Avatar of Light

**Reality Benders LitRPG series
by Michael Atamanov:**
Countdown
External Threat
Game Changer
Web of Worlds
A Jump into the Unknown

**The Dark Herbalist LitRPG series
by Michael Atamanov:**
Video Game Plotline Tester
Stay on the Wing
A Trap for the Potentate
Finding a Body

Perimeter Defense LitRPG series by Michael Atamanov:
Sector Eight
Beyond Death
New Contract
A Game with No Rules

Level Up LitRPG series by Dan Sugralinov:
Re-Start
Hero
The Final Trial
Level Up: The Knockout (with Max Lagno)
Level Up. The Knockout: Update (with Max Lagno)

Disgardium LitRPG series by Dan Sugralinov:
Class-A Threat
Apostle of the Sleeping Gods
The Destroying Plague

Adam Online LitRPG Leries by Max Lagno:
Absolute Zero
City of Freedom

**The Way of the Shaman LitRPG series
by Vasily Mahanenko:**
*Survival Quest
The Kartoss Gambit
The Secret of the Dark Forest
The Phantom Castle
The Karmadont Chess Set
Shaman's Revenge
Clans War*

Dark Paladin LitRPG series by Vasily Mahanenko:
*The Beginning
The Quest
Restart*

Galactogon LitRPG series by Vasily Mahanenko:
*Start the Game!
In Search of the Uldans
A Check for a Billion*

Invasion LitRPG Series by Vasily Mahanenko:
A Second Chance

**World of the Changed LitRPG Series by Vasily
Mahanenko:**
No Mistakes

**The Bard from Barliona LitRPG series
by Eugenia Dmitrieva and Vasily Mahanenko:**
*The Renegades
A Song of Shadow*

The Neuro LitRPG series by Andrei Livadny:
*The Crystal Sphere
The Curse of Rion Castle
The Reapers*

Phantom Server LitRPG series by Andrei Livadny:
*Edge of Reality
The Outlaw
Black Sun*

Citadel World series by Kir Lukovkin:
*The URANUS Code
The Secret of Atlantis*

The Game Master series by A. Bobl and A. Levitsky:
The Lag

You're in Game!
(LitRPG Stories from Bestselling Authors)
You're in Game-2!
(More LitRPG stories set in your favorite worlds)

Moskau by G. Zotov
(a dystopian thriller)

El Diablo by G.Zotov
(a supernatural thriller)

More books and series are coming out soon!

In order to have new books of the series translated faster, we need your help and support! Please consider leaving a review or spread the word by recommending *Underdog* to your friends and posting the link on social media. The more people buy the book, the sooner we'll be able to make new translations available.

Thank you!

Till next time!